Sergio Olguín was born in Buenos Aires in 1967. His first work of fiction, *Lanús*, was published in 2002. It was followed by a number of successful novels, including *Oscura monótona sangre* (*Dark Monotonous Blood*), which won the Tusquets Prize in 2009. His books have been translated into English, German, French and Italian. *The Best Enemy* is the fourth in the crime thriller series featuring journalist Verónica Rosenthal, following on from the success of *There Are No Happy Loves*, *The Foreign Girls* and *The Fragility of Bodies*. Sergio Olguín is also a scriptwriter and has been the editor of a number of cultural publications.

CW00551636

THE BEST ENEMY

Sergio Olguín

Translated by Miranda France

BITTER LEMON PRESS
LONDON

BITTER LEMON PRESS

First published in the United Kingdom in 2025 by
Bitter Lemon Press, 47 Wilmington Square, London WC1X OET
www.bitterlemonpress.com

First published in Spanish as *La Mejor Enemiga* by Alfaguara
(Penguin Random House Grupo Editorial Argentina), 2021

Bitter Lemon Press gratefully acknowledges the financial
assistance of the Arts Council of England

Work published within the framework of "Sur" Translation Support Program
of the Ministry of Foreign Affairs and Worship of the Argentine Republic
Obra editada en el marco del Programa "Sur" de Apoyo a las Traducciones
del Ministerio de Relaciones Exteriores y Culto de la República Argentina

© Sergio Olguín, 2021

This edition published by arrangement with VF Agencia Literaria

English translation © Miranda France, 2025

A CIP record for this book is available from the British Library

PB ISBN 978–1–916725–096
eBook USC ISBN 978–1–916725–102
eBook ROW ISBN 978–1–916725–119

Typeset by Tetragon, London
Printed and bound by the CPI Group (UK) Ltd, Croydon, CRO 4YY

Supported using public funding by
ARTS COUNCIL
ENGLAND
LOTTERY FUNDED

To Carolina Salvini, Paola Lucantis and Amalia Sanz

Contents

Is it more foolish and childish to assume there is a conspiracy, or that there is not?

CHINA MIÉVILLE, *The City & The City*

…all the way upstairs he kept thinking what a shame it was that none of the newspapers had any guts any more. He wished he'd been living back in the days of Dana and Greely, when a newspaper was a newspaper and called a sonofabitch a sonofabitch, and let the devil take the hindmost. It must have been swell to have been a reporter on one of those old papers.

HORACE MCCOY, *No Pockets in a Shroud*

What was it to love someone, what was love exactly, and why did it end or not end? Those were the real questions, and who could answer them?

PATRICIA HIGHSMITH, *The Price of Salt*, or *Carol*

The dead mature;
with them, my heart

SALVATORE QUASIMODO,
Metamorphoses in the Urn of the Saint

Prologue

THE DEAD MATURE

I

In the duty-free shop of the Parisian airport of Charles de Gaulle, Peter Khoury bought M&M's in a range of packages, along with some miniature Mars bars, a bag of Kinder Bueno and two more of Toblerone. He wasn't a lover of sweets (he'd bought some tins of Planters peanuts and Blue Diamond almonds for himself), but he reckoned it wouldn't be a bad idea to stock up for the children he was going to be treating in the next few years – not that the chocolates would last long. Like any good paediatric doctor – recently graduated, with honours, from Imperial College London – he knew the promise of a treat helped sweeten the consultation. Some children would arrive crying and leave happily clutching a Mars bar. Sweets like these had extra appeal because they weren't usually available to the children he would be treating at Al-Shifa Hospital on the Gaza Strip.

At the age of twenty-six, Peter Khoury had decided to make a change in his life. The kind of change that marks you forever. In his family there had always been talk of returning to Palestine. His four grandparents and father had left Haifa when the Israeli troops entered the city in 1948. They'd had no choice but to go, with only the clothes on their backs. They had locked up their houses and taken the keys with them, in hopes of returning one day. Peter's father was a baby when they arrived in England. His mother, like Peter, had been born in London. And yet all of them (including his siblings, aunts, uncles and cousins) had grown up with a nostalgia for the country lost after the Nakba.

While still a student, Peter had taken a course in emergency medicine at the University Hospital of North Norway. The course was led by Mads Gilbert, a renowned doctor known also for his activism; he regularly travelled to Gaza to give medical training. Gilbert was a very good teacher and Peter an outstanding student. Not surprisingly, an affection sprang up between them. At the end of one class, Gilbert asked him: "Khoury, your family are Maronite Christians from Lebanon, right? I'm guessing from your surname."

"We're orthodox Christians from Palestine. On my mother's and father's sides."

"From which cities?"

"Haifa, both sides."

Gilbert nodded. "Let's go for a beer sometime, Khoury, and I'll tell you about my own experience in Palestine. I think you'll be interested."

Peter was interested, of course, in whatever the Norwegian had to tell him, for example about the challenge of treating so many people with insufficient staff, supplies or medication. Or the fear that a person cured of pneumonia one day might die the next in a bombing. Gilbert knew Khoury was specializing in paediatrics.

"We really need paediatricians in Al-Shifa."

"When the time's right…"

Peter thought it would be years before that time came. He finished the course, returned to London, got his degree and began specialist training at Great Ormond Street Hospital for Children.

He planned to take a break in the summer: a trip through the Netherlands, Germany, northern Italy and France. Forty days alone with his backpack. As he was preparing for the trip he received a text from Mads Gilbert, his old Norwegian teacher. It wasn't a private message but one that had obviously been sent to lots of people. It read: *On behalf of Doctor Mads Gilbert in Gaza, thanks for all your support. Two hours ago the central fruit and vegetable market in the city of Gaza was bombed. 80 wounded, 20 dead. All of them were brought here to Al-Shifa. It's hell! We're deep in death, in blood and amputations. Lots of children. Pregnant mothers. I've never experienced anything so horrible. Even now we can hear the tanks. TELL people, pass it on, shout it out. Whatever it takes. Do something! Do more!*

Peter decided that he must go to Palestine, the land his father had imagined, the one his grandparents yearned for. He thought of abandoning his trip and setting off for Gaza straight away, but his parents and grandparents persuaded him to do his European tour first. He wouldn't have much time later on, and this would be a good way to bid farewell to his youth before entering the adult world once and for all.

After Europe, Peter would go straight to Palestine without returning to London. His grandparents gave him the keys to their houses in Haifa, although he wouldn't be going to that city, which was now part of Israel.

"Many Palestinians have a key, but I have two. I'm a millionaire," he told his paternal grandfather.

"We Palestinians are millionaires every time we dream."

There was a lot of turbulence on the flight from Paris to Tel Aviv, so much that Peter Khoury found himself praying, something he hadn't done since he was twelve. He hated turbulence; it terrified him. The last few minutes of the flight, over Israeli territory, were reassuringly smooth, not that Peter ever felt reassured on a plane. When they finally touched down in Tel Aviv, he offered up thanks to the three versions of God he knew.

He had enjoyed his trip through continental Europe, visiting museums, bars and parks. He had met people from far-flung places and in every city he visited he had fallen in love and then tried to fall quickly out of it again. Those German, French and Italian girls had conquered his heart, but his soul was in the Middle East, in Palestine.

Now, in Ben Gurion airport, the events of a few weeks ago seemed distant, as though they had happened to a Peter who no longer existed, or who existed in another dimension, one in which he was still drinking beer, smoking weed and kissing blondes and brunettes who spoke a hesitant English.

His grandparents' keys were in the backpack that had gone in the hold. As a precaution he had put some old keys with no value next to the other two on his key ring. Just as well, because at Customs the agents had decided to open his bag. The key ring caught their eye. "They're for a cottage I have outside London," Peter explained with an easy smile, one he had practised in the mirror.

The Immigration guy looked at him and saw a British man loaded down with duty-free, doubtless hoping to have some fun with Israeli girls. Peter carefully repacked the shirts and jeans and put the keys in his jacket. From then onwards he wanted to feel them close to his body.

There were no problems at passport control. A tourist arriving from London didn't attract much attention. Peter was asked where he planned to stay and for how long. He had deliberately booked a return ticket for ten days later, one he had no intention of using. He lied about his lodgings and length of stay, as he had been advised to do.

Outside the controlled area, he found himself in a hubbub of travellers reunited with their families, taxi drivers touting for work and tourists who already seemed lost. Peter looked around him, but it was Mads Gilbert who spotted him first and came bounding over to give his friend a warm embrace. He looked a little older, but preserved that youthful spirit Peter associated with Nordic men. Gilbert offered to carry his backpack. Peter handed over some of the duty-free bags instead. They walked towards the parking lot.

They must have looked like two Europeans without a care in the world. Gilbert asked him about the Champions League games and complained bitterly because there had been power outages the last few days and he had missed the round of sixteen away games. Despite being Norwegian (or maybe because of it, since Norwegian teams never went far in the Champions League), he supported Manchester United, whereas Peter was an Arsenal fan. Man U had drawn away to Milan, and Arsenal had won, at home, against Rome. Peter told Gilbert he had watched that match in a Roman bar, surrounded by the local *tifosi* as they hurled insults at their rivals. "When van Persie scored I clutched my head so as to look distraught, but inside I was shouting 'gooooaaal!' I was weeping tears of joy."

They arrived at Gilbert's Hyundai Tucson. The car, which must have been at least five years old, was dusty and covered in scratches. They got in and drove out of Ben Gurion airport.

15

"The drive's about an hour, not including Israeli police checkpoints. We shouldn't have any problems getting through the controls with our papers. Although you never know…"

In fact the journey took them nearly three hours. At every roadblock they were asked the same questions. Peter wasn't a British tourist visiting the country's natural attractions any more but a doctor heading for Gaza. There were no objections to his journey, though, just a lot of questions and wasted time.

And so they entered Gaza. The panorama of a desert with buildings in the distance was gradually replaced, first by one in which rubble from destroyed houses lined both sides of the road: a city both bombed and flattened by Israeli bulldozers. Then, like a miracle, out of the ruins emerged a teeming cityscape of precarious buildings mixed in with modern pizzerias, electronics and phone shops, even a school surrounded by walls painted with Palestinian flags and drawings of children's faces. People moved calmly along the sidewalks and drifted into the streets, to the fury of drivers leaning on their horns.

"I wanted to show you around Jabalia before I take you to your apartment," said Gilbert.

Peter had never been anywhere like this. In some ways it reminded him of the favelas in Rio de Janeiro, which he had visited a few years ago. What he particularly noticed wasn't the sheer number of people and precarious structures, but the bombed buildings, half destroyed yet still serving as homes.

"The refugee camp at Jabalia is one of the largest in Gaza," Gilbert explained. "It's overcrowded and there's a lack of habitable rooms, gas cylinders, electricity and drinking water. Yet these people never stop trying to live with dignity. Oh, and we've got several hospitals."

Peter looked around him in astonishment: the place was much poorer than what he had imagined, or seen in photos, back in London.

"I'll take you to your apartment, it's not far from Al-Shifa. Spend today resting, because tomorrow you're going to start a new life."

"I've already started," ventured Peter.

III

Every day of the next five years Peter was busy saving lives, mostly of the children who came to Al-Shifa Hospital. A resident doctor in any part of the world can expect to come across every kind of sickness, disease and scenario, but in Gaza all these factors were multiplied by a hundred. It would be rare, in a hospital in Berlin or Buenos Aires, to see twenty children arrive on the same day with bullet wounds, or with the beginnings of asphyxia (because the Egyptian security forces attacked children who entered the tunnels), or collapsed lungs (because the Israeli navy shot at fishing boats). Gaza was overpopulated with children, and so everywhere they were victims. And that was without taking into account all the everyday, run-of-the-mill cases of malnutrition, chronic respiratory problems, endemic illnesses and deformities of the arms or legs.

There were operations that had to be postponed because Israel cut off the electricity supply; blood and plasma ruined for the same reason; poisoning caused by contaminated water; shortages of vaccines or of dental prostheses, knee and hip replacements. The outlook was bleak for a society essentially made up of children, adolescents and young people.

For the first few years Peter – dubbed "the English doctor" – worked alongside other professionals from around the world. A Brazilian surgeon, a Syrian epidemiologist, French orthopaedic surgeons, Israeli ophthalmologists, a South Korean dermatologist and many other clinicians from Médecins du Monde, Médecins Sans Frontières and Medical Aid for Palestinians. Some arrived in Gaza and couldn't cope with the pressure. They would leave after a month, two months, six months. Others, either more courageous or more stubborn, lasted a year, maybe two. They were carrying out a vital mission in a country that urgently needed doctors. Afterwards they would return to their countries, write papers, give lectures. The clinicians came and went, but the English doctor stayed on in his small apartment, with a balcony from which he could watch Gaza in real time.

As time went on, the newly arrived doctors didn't even know he was English because he spoke quite good Arabic (thanks to his grandparents and the family custom of keeping the language of the elders alive). Mothers would no longer say *My son was treated by an English doctor*. They asked for Doctor Khoury and assumed he was Libyan or Palestinian. And he was pleased by that confusion, because in five years he had grown a thicker skin, he had learned not to cry when a child died in his arms of blood loss; he had comforted mothers (the fathers rarely put in an appearance); he had made home visits, taking food and medication; he had even risked his life crossing the border through the tunnels that led to Egypt, in search of supplies for the hospital (and stocking up on sweets while he had the chance).

Life in Gaza was as close to miraculous as an atheist could credit. The blockade inflicted a form of collective torture rarely seen before. The Israeli armed forces achieved levels of refinement or barbarity for which it would be hard to find comparison.

The Israeli troops rolled in, demolishing the homes of suicide bombers (as punishment for the whole family), destroying flour mills and water sources, avenging the death of one of their own soldiers by killing dozens of civilians, older people, women and children. The death count was recorded everywhere, in newspapers and magazines, on websites and Wikipedia. For Peter those numbers were the bitter bread that fed his love for his family's people.

It was only logical that he would fall in love with a woman from Gaza. Azima was a widow with two children, a surprisingly small family for a Palestinian woman. Peter had been a doctor to both her children – Nahid, a little girl of two who had been born after her father's death, and Omar, a ten-year-old boy whom Peter called Messi because the first time he came to the hospital he was wearing a number ten Barcelona shirt. There was nothing seriously wrong with Omar at that appointment; he had bronchiolitis and was a little run-down. Peter made sure the girl got the right vaccines for her age and asked Azima to come back a week later for a check-up.

He wasn't surprised to see Omar on the beach a couple of days later, playing soccer with some other boys his age. He was even wearing the same shirt. Peter liked seeing soccer played, so he stood to one side and watched these boys who dreamed of one day playing for Barcelona, or Juventus, and for Palestine. Omar scored a goal. When the game had finished the boy recognized him and came over.

"Doctor, Doctor, did you see the goal I scored?"

"It was very good, Messi, congratulations."

The other boys also wandered over and Omar told them proudly: "He's my doctor, aren't you, Doctor?"

One of the boys, pretending to be worried, asked: "Is it serious? Will he die?"

Everyone laughed, Peter included.

At the next appointment, Azima brought lemons and garlic. They chatted about his encounter with Omar on the beach. She told him that she was a widow and lived with her mother and another sister, also a widow.

Azima returned several times more on different pretexts, usually at Peter's instigation. On one occasion she came without her children and in the company of a young woman she introduced as her cousin. Her name was Iman; she was twenty-two years old and studied nursing. Azima wanted to know if Peter could help her, and he suggested she come once a week to the hospital. They had no budget, but she would learn a lot helping in the emergency department. Iman was happy, even though Al-Shifa Hospital was a long way from her home in Rafah.

Peter, so quick when it came to solving problems in the hospital, took a long time to find the courage to ask Azima out on a date. And when he did, the young widow said no. Peter was disconcerted, even embarrassed. But then Azima invited him to eat at her house instead, in the Shati encampment, close to the hospital.

Despite all the years he had spent living in Gaza, Peter didn't have a clear idea of what to expect. He realized this wasn't going to be a romantic lunch for two; presumably at least the children would be with them, and most likely Azima's mother, and perhaps the sister, with her own children. He was right to consider these possibilities, and yet he still fell short: there were also two brothers and an uncle – because a man couldn't visit women alone at home – and Azima's cousin Iman with one of her sisters.

There were also about ten children who would run in, cram food into their mouths, and run out again. The women were cheerful and good hostesses, but the men seemed more uncomfortable, as though they had been obliged to take part in the meal against their wishes. Peter had a knack for putting people at ease, so it wasn't hard for him to win round the men of the family.

They ate a delicious *maqluba*, made with incredibly tender

lamb, pine nuts and almonds. The saffron rice was infused with cinnamon. There were also cucumbers dipped in yogurt with mint and garlic, hummus, and the inevitable stuffed vine leaves. They finished the feast with sweets made from figs and honey. Later there was coffee and a hookah. Peter didn't partake (he had never got the hang of this apparatus), but he was surprised to see both Azima's mother and sister smoking, even though Hamas had forbidden women to use a hookah. Political prohibitions seemed to be ineffective, at least in this house.

The five women came outside to see him off and kept waving until he turned a corner and was out of sight. Peter had enjoyed the occasion, but he didn't know what to make of it. He had been so careful, during his visit, not to keep staring at Azima, who seemed to him sweet and intelligent, and more and more beautiful. If only he could have had even two minutes alone with her, at least when they said goodbye. Had this been her way of showing him she wanted him only as a friend of the family? His doubts were dispelled when, minutes later, he got a text message from her: *You're a wonderful man. Inshallah we can see each other soon. Would you like to walk on the beach tomorrow evening?*

Of course he would.

Peter was on duty that night, but he swapped his shift with an American woman, also a paediatrician. Azima and he met late, walked on the beach beneath the moon and stars, talked a lot. Peter told her about his grandparents, about how they had left Haifa during the Nakba, about his life in London, how happy he was living in Gaza. She told him she had never left Gaza, and that was why she liked the sea at night, when you couldn't see the Israeli patrol boats, because she could imagine a world out there that she might visit one day.

They kissed and held each other. Peter quickly told her that he would be willing to marry her.

Azima had a beautiful laugh. "All in good time," she said.

IV

Where might Azima and Peter first have slept together? In some corner of that almost empty beach? In his apartment, which was in a building mostly occupied by foreign doctors and therefore more tolerant than the Muslim neighbourhoods and settlements? Would they have married? Would they have had children? Four or five, like a typical Gazan couple? Would he have obtained a passport for Azima so she and her children could leave Gaza and visit his family in London? Would they have lived happily ever after, like in fairy tales?

Would Iman, injured by Israeli missiles at the door to her house, have finished her nursing studies? Or would the deaths of her mother and two siblings in that same attack have meant she attended the Rafah Community Centre for Mental Health only as a patient?

Omar runs with the ball along the beach, dribbles past one opponent and another, gets kicked. There's an argument, shouting, then they resume the game. They're exhausted. They throw themselves down on the sand. They make filthy remarks about the girls in their neighbourhood. They laugh raucously. They walk towards the jetty. Some of them get in the sea, the others look for cigarette butts in the sand. Omar goes off alone because he's spotted something shining a few yards from where they are. He thinks it may be an emerald or a ruby. He could sell the precious stone, become a millionaire, buy his mother a house. But when he gets there he sees it's only a piece of broken glass from a bottle. Omar is a believer, so he asks Allah what kind of gift this is. And the heavens seem to answer him, because right then there's an explosion. He's paralysed by terror. The thunder – because that's what it seems like – strikes the beach where his friends were playing. It takes a second, less than a second. When he can, he turns towards the place where his friends were. And there are people there screaming, moaning, imploring God, clawing at their faces. Omar can't recognize the bodies, but they are his friends. His best friend, Ismail Baker, nine years old, is dead. Ismail was with his cousins: Aed, ten years old, dead; Zacarya, ten years old, dead; Mohamed, eleven years old, dead.

Would Omar ever play for the Palestine team?

When the bombardment of the hospital began, would Peter have thought of his parents, growing old alone in their house in Islington, or of that girl he had met in Amsterdam five years ago, or of Azima holding him? Would he have thought he didn't want to die, not that day?

And the skilful pilots of the F-16 planes that bombed, with surgical precision, the houses, mosques, universities and hospitals of the inhabitants of Gaza on those days in 2014? Would they later have nightmares, fears, moments of doubt?

And that person who gave the order to attack Al-Shifa Hospital, who ordered missiles to be shot at the children on the beach, what did he do after seeing his orders carried out, what did he eat, where did he travel, whom did he love?

1   *Three Escapes*

I

The first time Verónica Rosenthal ran away from home she was five years old. This was no spontaneous flit but one that had required careful planning. She took the backpack she'd got as a birthday present and put into it everything she was going to need: underwear, socks, a magic wand with lights and sound effects, two small teddy bears (the big ones wouldn't fit in), a Suchard cookie – which later became half a cookie, then one and a half when she managed to filch another – a toothbrush, her mother's tweezers, a scrunchie, a fine-toothed comb for nits, and a packet of La Yapa sweets, left over from the birthday party of one of her nursery friends.

Verónica had a good reason for leaving home: she didn't want her mother to treat her the way she treated Dani. Because, for their mother, Leticia was the perfect daughter: pretty, industrious, respectful. Whereas Daniela was a disaster: a messy, lippy dimwit. Verónica knew that when her mother's gaze fell on her (up until now she had been ignored, or treated like one of the teddy bears), she'd realize Verónica was just like Daniela. For that matter, she *wanted* to be Daniela. That's why she decided to go and live with her maternal grandparents.

They would surely be thrilled to have her, since every time they visited Bubbe made strudel, with lots of Chantilly cream. And Zayde took her for rides on the merry-go-round and promised that when she was older Verónica could go with him to watch a game at his beloved soccer club: Atlanta.

For more than a month she had been stealing around twenty cents a day from Ramira, the woman who cleaned for them and looked after the girls when their mother was fed up. Now Verónica had amassed a fortune in coins and planned to spend it on a taxi to her grandparents' house.

One morning, when she hadn't gone to nursery because of chickenpox, Verónica saw her chance. She felt fine; her face, back and legs were still itchy, but she wasn't allowed to scratch them because that would leave scars. Her sisters had already left for school, her mother must have been at the hairdresser, and Ramira was at the supermarket. Verónica found the spare key that was kept in the kitchen, shouldered her backpack and let herself out of the house. It was a beautiful sunny day.

Not wanting to be caught, or to run into her mother, she walked along Calle Posadas as far as Avenida Callao. She crossed the avenue – carefully watching the traffic lights – and began looking for a taxi with its red Free light illuminated. There were loads of taxis, so she picked one with a nice-looking driver, an older man with a white beard who could easily have been Santa Claus moonlighting as a cabbie to make enough money for Christmas presents.

When the taxi stopped, she got in, settled into her seat the way she had seen her mother do, then, trying to imitate her voice when they were out together, said: "To my grand-parents' house."

The taxi driver didn't know where her grandparents lived, and neither did she (her description of a house with big trees at the front didn't help). So the man got out and went to fetch a police officer, who was standing at the corner. Verónica wanted to cry. They were going to take her to prison for stealing the coins and her mother's tweezers, and for scratching her legs with no thought for the scars. In fact the officer simply asked where she lived. Verónica, unable to speak, pointed towards Calle Posadas. Then the police officer asked her to show him which house was hers. And she was so stupid, or frightened of going to prison, that she obeyed. He took her to the front door, rang the bell, and Ramira loomed up in the doorway, looking enormous. She hugged and squeezed the child, and wept, and thanked the officer, and then, as soon as the door was closed, spanked Verónica so hard that thirty years later it still hurt.

II

Caniggia first and foremost, then the others: Maradona, Goyco, Ruggeri, Olarticoechea, Burruchaga and even Basualdo. These were Verónica's first idols. She was ten, the World Cup was taking place in Italy and, for the second time, she wanted to go and live with her maternal grandparents.

Her Grandmother Esther's cooking – she made the best knishes in the world, an unforgettable gefilte fish with chrain, incredibly delicious *varenikes* and a sublime strudel – would have been reason enough for anyone to want to spend their days in the house on Padilla and Malabia, but Verónica had another motive: she wanted to be a boy. It was obvious to her that boys had a better life than girls. They got dirty, had fights, played soccer and hung around in the street until dark. And even though she never told anyone about her desire to be male, especially not her sisters, who were both so feminine (because by then Daniela had given in and started imitating Leticia in everything), Verónica discovered that her Grandfather Elías understood. That was why he talked to her about soccer, took her to watch games at Atlanta (her grandfather had been a director of the club in the 1960s, the glory days) and let her go to Parque Centenario to kick a ball around with the boys from the block. It was like a secret pact between them, because her grandmother (and her mother) thought she was going to play with Lucía, a neighbour one year older than Verónica. In reality both girls went to play soccer with Martín, Gonzalo, Hernán, Flavio and El Chino against boys from other blocks.

Gonzalo and Hernán, twelve at the time, were the eldest in the gang; Flavio was the youngest, at nine. El Chino, Lucía and Martín – who were twins – were eleven. When they took on another team, Lucía didn't play, but Verónica did. If they were playing among themselves, Lucía joined in too. On the way home they would buy a litre of Coca-Cola at the news-agent. They would be dirty and sweaty, but nobody wiped the mouth of the bottle before taking a swig. What Verónica liked best was that the boys treated her like one of them; they never mocked her for being a girl, or treated her any differently: they burped, swore and cleared their nostrils with a farmer's sneeze. Nobody used her full name; they called her Vero, perhaps because it sounded more masculine.

She used to see El Chino and Hernán at the Atlanta ground. They would go with a brother or an older friend and she went with her grandfather. According to family lore, Grandfather Elías first went to games with Grandmother Esther, until motherhood kept her at home. Then his son Ariel accompanied him, until Ariel got older and preferred to spend Saturday afternoons with his friends, rehearsing in a rock band. Elías's last companion was the youngest daughter of his oldest daughter – Verónica.

Whenever she stayed over at the house in Villa Crespo, Verónica slept in the room that once belonged to her Uncle Ariel, who had married her Aunt Lisa years ago. She loved that room full of posters and photos. There were the lucha libre wrestlers from *Titanes en el ring*; the 1973 Atlanta squad; a promotional poster for Pink Floyd's *The Wall*; a picture of the crowd in the Plaza de Mayo on 10 December 1983, the day democracy was restored; Maradona and the Hand of God. Verónica had decided this would be her room now and didn't plan to change a thing, although perhaps she would add a photo of Caniggia celebrating his goal against Brazil with Maradona.

On the day Argentina was to play Yugoslavia, her grandfather came early to pick Verónica up from home. Although she didn't want to say anything to anyone, she was feeling terrible. She had vomited and was shivering. She had secretly taken four children's aspirin (not for the first time; she liked their fruity flavour) and, as she and her grandfather got into the taxi, managed to hide her sickness pretty well. Verónica watched the game alongside her grandparents, her Uncle Ariel and Aunt Lisa and their baby. She cheered the penalties saved by Goycochea. At lunch she barely ate, and her grandmother, realizing she wasn't well, put her to bed in Ariel's old room. Verónica begged Bubbe not to tell her parents. She told her grandmother she wanted to stay and live with them, and go to a school in Villa Crespo, and visit her parents on Sundays. Her grandmother stroked her brow and said yes to everything. That day and night Verónica had extraordinary dreams; she was very cold, then sweated buckets (her grandmother made sure she stayed covered), and her head hurt. By morning she felt better. Her grandmother made her a milky coffee and, since she no longer had a temperature, allowed her to eat a croissant. As she was getting ready to watch the day's games, the doorbell rang. Her parents had come for lunch with Daniela and Leticia. When the time came to return to their apartment in Recoleta, Verónica tried to stay back, clinging to her grandmother, but Esther averted her gaze. Besides, her mother was showing Verónica the palm of her hand in a menacing way.

As they left she saw Lucía and Martín, coming out of the house next door, off to play in the park. The twins eyed Verónica with pity. She couldn't have felt worse if the police had come to take her away.

All the same, Verónica was back the next week, and the one after, and the one after that. She continued to play soccer with the other children while knowing this couldn't last much longer, that at some point she would grow up and wouldn't be able to play with them any more. Verónica didn't want to be a girl.

Despite the atheism inculcated by her family, she begged God not to let her body acquire a feminine form.

"Dear God, don't let me get boobs, please, don't let me get boobs."

And that bastard God answered her prayers.

III

Verónica knew better than anyone that she had escapist tendencies. She could list them, classify them, analyse them. What she couldn't do was avoid them. If the problem had been limited to running away from home, everything would have been simpler, but over the years Verónica had managed to evolve so many subtle forms of escape that she could have filled her hours talking over them in therapy – if she hadn't been someone who disbelieved in religions and psycho-analysis alike.

Every time she took (or didn't take) a step in life, Verónica considered whether she might be running away from something. This process had become so byzantine that she sometimes wondered if she was running away from running away, that is, staying put out of cowardice. Was her life with Fede good, or was she simply running away from running away? Although an expert in self-interrogation, Verónica rarely came up with an answer. For that she had Paula, or any of her other friends, all of them ready with a prognosis much cheaper than one you'd get from a Lacanian psychoanalyst and much less boring than a priest's or a rabbi's.

The question wasn't to do with Federico so much as with Verónica herself (she could honestly have told him "It's not you, it's me"). But what did she really want? As Verónica approached her thirty-fifth birthday, she felt that certain desires and aspirations were reaching their sell-by date. Should she rethink her life? Look for a better-paid job, become an editor, get married, have children, take tango lessons, improve relations with her sisters, write a book, have cosmetic surgery? If she thought about her life from the perspective of her twenty-five-year-old self, things hadn't gone so badly. She had everything she'd dreamed of back then: her own apartment, a staff job on a magazine, fairly regular sex and a guy she both loved and liked. Apart from Atlanta's promotion, eternally postponed, everything else she wanted had been achieved.

Because she loved Federico. Of that there was no doubt – or was there? She did sometimes wonder if they had got back together too soon, if it might have been better to reconcile in their forties, when life had calmed down a bit (if it ever did). She was at the stage where many couples decide to have a baby and channel their impatience into child-rearing. Should she do the same? It wasn't that she wanted to play the field with other people or that she was dissatisfied with all Fede gave her. What she missed was that feeling of excitement at the beginning of a relationship, of falling in love, of discovering it was possible to share with another person a desire, a quest, an obsession. Perhaps having a baby would offer that: the chance to start a new story, to feel different, unexpected emotions.

She had been thinking about motherhood for some weeks now, but fearing rather than wanting it. There had been a few days when she had forgotten to take her contraceptive pill and they had decided to use condoms that month as a precaution. So it was just their luck that one should go and break. They must have been really going at it, because when Federico went to take off the condom, he discovered it was torn, and semen was spilling out. Fede wasn't exactly a sexual superhero, though. The semen couldn't have gone all that far, and there was no reason to fear it had fertilized one of her inattentive eggs.

Perhaps it was through some combination of false assurance and prejudice that Verónica neglected to take the morning-after pill, and the one for the day after that, and the one that works even at seventy-two hours. She was on a deadline, she had lots of stuff to sort out and, above all, she didn't believe it was possible to get pregnant on the contents of a broken condom.

So Verónica forgot all about it for a few days, although anxiety lingered at the corner of her mind. As soon as emergency contraceptives were no longer an option, she began to feel pregnancy symptoms: morning sickness, tiredness; she was even convinced her ankles had swollen up. Her breasts were the same as always, and she didn't know whether to feel relieved or disappointed about that. When her period was late she started to panic. What more proof did she need?

Leaving the newsroom of *Nuestro Tiempo* after an exhausting day of editing copy, Verónica dropped into the pharmacy and bought a pregnancy test. As she walked home, Pili called to ask if she wanted to go out drinking and she said no, to the surprise of her Spanish friend.

"You've turned into a boring old housewife, running home to make a stew for your husband."

Verónica told her to fuck off, hung up, then carried on swearing for a few seconds, something she did often but which that night seemed like another symptom of unusual irritability.

Arriving at Federico's apartment, she found him in the kitchen trying to follow a recipe for boeuf bourguignon on YouTube. Since they had started living together Federico had been making a big effort to learn to cook, and he liked surprising her with elaborate dishes. Verónica did her bit by mixing the drinks while he cooked. Unless it was one of those days when she was in a bad mood or stressed about some article she was writing, Verónica thought that having a man to cook for her was worth more than good sex, good conversation or anything else a partner might have to offer. That night she wasn't inclined to be easily impressed (although the sauce certainly smelled good); she gave him a kiss and went to the bathroom.

She'd heard somewhere that it was better to do a pregnancy test in the morning, when the urine is more concentrated. Her anxiety about doing the test properly conflicted with her desire to have a peaceful night. The best thing would be to get up in the morning, urinate on the goddamn plastic, find out if she was or wasn't, and get on with the day. A carefree dinner, an episode of *The Walking Dead*, a more or less respectable fuck, a bit of time reading *Aspects of Love* – the David Garnett novel she was currently gripped by – then sweet sleep. Wait until tomorrow to deal with the formalities of her uterine situation.

But who was she kidding. Better to get it over and done with.

Verónica went into the bathroom, threw the clothes from her bottom half into a corner, carelessly tore into the packet, read the instructions without understanding them (she never understood instructions, especially when she was nervous), pulled off the protective cover, positioned the reactive strip under the stream of piss for a few seconds, and put it on the side of the bath. Then she waited, sitting on the lavatory.

One minute, two, three. And two possible options.

A pink line: *I'm an idiot, inventing things to worry about.* Two pink lines: *I'm an idiot, inventing things to worry about.*

The instructions said to wait three to five minutes.

Minute four. OK. Time to check the result.

She held the test in her hands and looked at it. Two pink lines. Or rather two lines that were very pale pink, as though inhibited by the way Verónica was staring at them. Two little lines that showed she was pregnant, that inside her was an embryo fertilized by a sperm she couldn't help imagining with Federico's face and doggedness and an ovum needier than she was when drunk.

Now she would have to come out of the bathroom with the test in her hand, smelling of piss (not a big deal) and tell him, "Darling, I'm pregnant."

They would hug and cry and laugh together, like in the movies, or as she imagined her sisters, so reliably fertile, would have done.

That cursed fecundity of the Rosenthal women.

Verónica put on her underwear, left the test on the basin and looked at her reflection in the mirror. She saw herself as old, flabby, her eyes bulging a little – not surprisingly – and she was tempted to cry, but the image in the mirror forbade it. She would keep her head held high.

There were urgent decisions to be made. She thought rationally and came to some calming conclusions: the next step was to throw away the pregnancy test. Better to avoid a scene.

2   *Nuestro Tiempo*

I

In 1985, Patricia Beltrán was a journalist in her twenties trying
to get a staff position in some newsroom while she freelanced
for various publications in Buenos Aires. Like nearly all
freelance journalists, she wrote on whatever subject she was
commissioned to cover: politics, interviews with intellectuals
or celebrities, culture, lifestyle, social issues, commentary. The
only subjects not on her radar were crime and sports, which
were usually left to specialists who didn't look kindly on any
trespassing by other journalists.

Her friend Carlos Arroyo worked on the morning edition
of the daily newspaper *La Razón*. So, whenever she was delivering a piece to their Arts or Society pages, she would take
the opportunity to visit him on the International News desk.
He had an easy smile and cheeks that would redden at the
slightest thing, hidden behind a bushy moustache that called
to mind a Genoese immigrant or a Soviet bureaucrat. It was
Arroyo who, knowing about her work situation, recommended
Patricia speak to a friend of his who was an editor at *Siete Días*.

"Call Homero Alsina Thevenet and mention my name.
He's Uruguayan like me, but older and grouchier."

He wrote down the magazine's telephone number and gave
it to her. Then he started reminiscing about his homeland and
the time a TV skit made fun of HAT (that was how Homero

Alsina Thevenet signed off his famous movie reviews). The conversation turned to novelist Juan Carlos Onetti and his wives. Arroyo relayed these anecdotes with the delight of someone who knows he is passing on juicy gossip. Patricia left the *La Razón* newsroom feeling happy and with a hunch that she was going to get more work.

And so it proved. Old Homero, as bad-tempered and demanding as he was, soon offered her a job as journalist on the Society pages at *Siete Días*. This proved a fruitful time for Patricia, who wrote important pieces on the crises in children's homes and in psychiatric hospitals, and on the first cases of trigger-happy officers in the Buenos Aires police force. She still wrote about politics sometimes, but gave up Entertainment for good. And with no regrets.

Meanwhile, Alsina Thevenet left *Siete Días* to join the founding team of *Página/12*. As his replacement, the Civita brothers, owners of the magazine and of the publishing house Editorial Abril, brought in Andrés Goicochea, a promising young journalist, who had been linked to pro-government media and came from the Télam agency.

Goicochea was only a few years older than Patricia. He was tall, skinny and loose-limbed, with unruly blonde hair that soon began to recede. A chain-smoker, his voice was firm but somewhat loud, emphasizing his authority. He was clear about what he wanted, and opaque about what he desired. Patricia and he hit it off immediately: she had an easy way with complicated subjects, while he knew how to sniff out a story, something Patricia had always admired.

Good editors make their presence felt from day one: in the way they treat their team, what they're looking for in a section, how they organize the work, whom they ask for what, how they protect their writers from the neuroses and nonsense of the bosses. Andrés Goicochea was one of the good ones. He had a natural talent that showed even in small gestures: the way he hovered near the journalists as they typed, or smoked as he thought up the best headline for an article.

They were both single, both lived for their work (although Andrés's was more complicated because it involved meeting politicians and other powerful people). So it wasn't surprising that one night, after a long press day, they had gone for drinks and ended up in his apartment. They slept together that night and on a couple of other occasions. There wasn't enough spark for them to fall in love, though, or make something more serious of the relationship. Not long afterwards, Patricia met Raúl, an architect who became her first husband and the father of her older son.

The liaison with Andrés was forgotten, although neither of them brought what had happened in private into the newsroom. It was something Patricia was grateful to him for, and doubtless the feeling was reciprocated.

Andrés Goicochea didn't last much longer at *Siete Días*. Fontevecchia took him to Perfil, where he worked his way through many of the company's publications, before landing as a managing editor at *Noticias*. Patricia also left the magazine at the end of 1988 to join a new venture: *Sur*, a left-wing daily backed by the Communist Party. It was an experience as heady, and timely, as joining a tsarist newspaper in 1916.

II

The world of journalism is big enough not to bump into a colleague in the newsroom yet small enough for paths to cross in other professional and social activities. Although Patricia and Andrés didn't work together again for many years, they saw each other at events, openings and colleagues' birthdays. They would greet each other fondly, exchange a few words, then find they had nothing more to say to one another. Each would return to their own friendship group. Although she didn't make a point of following his life and career, Patricia tended to know what her old friend and brief lover was doing. Andrés got married and divorced twice (just like her) and crested the waves of various different news publications, partly on his own merits as a journalist, partly thanks to his contacts in high places, whether political, business or institutional.

When Andrés joined the management of *Nuestro Tiempo*, he called Patricia and offered her a position as editor. The magazine was part of a small editorial group, Grupo Esparta, with ambitions to expand (it already owned two FM radio stations, a news portal, a trade magazine for doctors funded by a private laboratory, shares in some provincial newspapers and a media training company). Patricia had no hesitation in leaving a similar job at a weekly magazine owned by Publirevistas, and that was how, two decades on, she and Andrés began working together again.

The years had changed them. Patricia was no longer that redoubtable journalist who would do anything to get a story, but a lucid editor, albeit cynical when it came to talking about her work. As for Andrés, he was no longer the hot young thing obsessed with being the best. He had become urbane, suavely attentive to the powerful and influential people who visited or took him out to lunch, and an impatient, mistrustful boss. He didn't want to put out the best magazine; it was enough just to put out a magazine that satisfied advertisers and the lobbyists *du jour*. With every passing year he took fewer risks. He knew that if he lost the job of editor, he'd be unlikely to find another one like it. On every birthday he said the same thing to Patricia: "I'm getting older and more expensive." And no business wants old, expensive employees. But a journalist, however tamed and timorous they become once in a position of power, occasionally fulfils the fable of the scorpion, plunging a deadly sting into the mendacious and corrupt forces of society. Every now and then, *Nuestro Tiempo* dared to strike at the jugular of a powerful man who had stepped over the line. And most of the time that venom was delivered from the Society section, where Patricia and some of her writers served to remind Goicochea why he had become a journalist in the first place.

Or at least that was how Patricia Beltrán liked to think of Andrés Goicochea. That he hadn't given in despite his cowering, his capitulations to the powers that be and his fear of losing the small but solid fortune he had amassed in the last two decades.

The first years at *Nuestro Tiempo* went well. In journalism that means there were arguments, a lot of back and forth, veiled censorship, yet despite everything it was possible to work and to publish worthwhile copy, including articles that influenced society in different ways. The salaries may not have been spectacular, but they were always paid on time and at the end of the year everyone was given a box of Christmas goodies. Freelancers were paid late and little, as at all other publications. Then everything started to go wrong. First came the half bonus paid in two instalments, then salary arrears, elimination of per diems, voluntary redundancies with significantly reduced severance pay, freelance work curtailed, non-existent pay rises. The logical consequence of all this was union meetings, stoppages lasting hours and work that got held up because everyone was more focussed on what was happening inside the office than in the world outside it.

As things came to a head, the bosses of Grupo Esparta (Sergio Mayer and Aníbal Monteverde, fifty–fifty partners) announced two big changes: the arrival of a third partner, Ariel Gómez Pardo, who bought seventy per cent of Monteverde's shares; and the replacement of the editor. Goicochea was going to leave, and Julio Tantanian, a journalist famous for having a cable programme nobody watched – but who regularly appeared on bizarre TV round-ups and gossip shows (his wife had once been a burlesque performer) – was taking his place.

There were many rumours about what happened in the highest echelons of power, and perhaps not all were true. Mayer and Monteverde were at loggerheads, barely speaking to each other. Apparently it was Mayer himself who had approached Gómez Pardo, an obscure gambling entrepreneur who owned casinos in several provinces, among other lucrative ventures. Now Grupo Esparta had three partners, Monteverde was frozen out of the decision-making and Gómez Pardo left all decisions to Mayer. At the same time, Mayer had other enterprises that were much more successful than the newspaper group. In fact, the magazines, the web portal and the radio stations were shock troops he used when he needed to put the pressure on.

Goicochea's exit was not traumatic. He wasn't a journalist his colleagues on the newsroom front line would have fought for. And now he had no political support outside the magazine either. Meanwhile, the media-friendly Tantanian arrived with a good chunk of advertising money for health insurance schemes from his trade union buddies, who would generously buy ads in return for being kept out of the news.

For Goicochea, the redundancy equated to early retirement. Old and expensive, he would no longer find a job in a different newsroom. But he had enough money to get by and could doubtless secure some consultancy work, or get his fix by teaching journalism in some university or other.

He left the newsroom one afternoon, bidding his colleagues a fond farewell. In an attempt to show there were no hard feelings, Human Resources laid on a leaving party with soft drinks and a finger buffet. Goicochea's only condition was that Tantanian not be present on his last day. He had no desire to cross paths with that loathsome individual he considered more of a clown than a journalist. The petulant gesture carried weight all the same: he was going out on a high, honouring his profession while dismissing an arriviste.

III

Things gradually improved at the magazine. Once again staff got paid on time, expenses were available for certain stories and Human Resources pompously announced that, although the Christmas boxes weren't coming back, supermarket discount vouchers would be handed out. The journalists' mood also improved now that they could concentrate on reporting and writing their articles. The demands for pay rises continued, but people no longer feared that the magazine's days were numbered.

Meanwhile, Patricia was told that although she couldn't hire the new writer she had requested, she was allowed to bring in freelancers. That meant she could give work to Rodolfo Corso and María Magdalena Cortez. She had first met Rodolfo Corso several newsrooms back and had faith in his ability to get to the heart of a story. María Magdalena had done some investigative journalism with Verónica Rosenthal, and Patricia had been impressed by her good writing and willingness to engage with contentious issues, qualities that were evident in every piece she submitted. The addition of these two to her regular writers made for a good team.

Once things began to settle down, Patricia and Andrés met for lunch far away from the office at Prosciutto, in Congreso. The last images Patricia had of Andrés at the magazine were of a man overcome by reality: anxious, distracted, irascible. He looked much better now. He had regained his old composure, put on a little weight and let his beard grow. Although nearly sixty, he was an attractive guy.

They caught up on each other's personal news: Andrés talked about his children and his new girlfriend, a lawyer and a court clerk who was nearly twenty years younger. She was more like a semi-girlfriend, he said, because she was still married and hadn't yet separated. "I have to be discreet until she leaves her husband," he added, with a wink.

Then Andrés tore into the owners of *Nuestro Tiempo*, mocking the new editor (he had it on good authority that the man secretly liked dressing up in the feather boas his wife used to wear in revues). He spoke with contempt about journalists who took money from the state and used it to advance their own careers (he could have done the same and had chosen not to). He told Patricia he was considering an offer to edit a newspaper in Salta, but that for now he was concentrating on other work.

"I'm carrying out an investigation," he announced while the waiter served them coffee. "Like in the old days."

"Fantastic. About what?"

"About the same thing as usual: the links between the powers that be and the criminal world. There's a bit of everything in there: influence-peddling, international espionage, links with the Argentine state and complicit media."

"Sounds great. If you don't have anywhere lined up to run it, I'll take it. We don't pay much, though."

"I get the feeling that showgirl they've employed as editor won't bite. But let me see what I come up with. The information I have already is pure gold."

They said goodbye, promising to reprise this lunch between old comrades at least every four weeks. Then, of course, they didn't speak again for months. Every so often Patricia remembered about the investigation Andrés was doing and which she hadn't seen published anywhere. Perhaps it hadn't come to anything after all.

Late in October, on a cold and dreary afternoon of intermittent rain and strong wind, Patricia received a call from an unknown number. It was Andrés. He needed to speak to her urgently. That same afternoon. Not in a bar. He had to show her some very sensitive material, share some details from his investigation and ask her advice about what to do with it.

"Shall I come to your apartment?" she asked.

"I've moved out for a while. I'm staying at a house in Haedo. Note down the address. And obviously don't tell anyone you're coming to meet me."

He sounded uneasy rather than merely anxious, and much more serious than usual. Patricia wished she could speak to someone about what was going on. She thought of Verónica Rosenthal, who was in the newsroom, but remembered Andrés had asked for maximum discretion, so instead went back home to pick up the car and set off towards Haedo. She didn't like driving in the rain, but there was no other way to get to Greater Buenos Aires.

The GPS guided her through an area she didn't know. She took the western access freeway, came off at a street called Dolores Prats and followed the signs until she reached a neighbourhood of nice middle-class houses. According to the GPS her destination was ahead on the left-hand side and Patricia found a place to park a few yards before it.

There was no let-up in the rain, and the inadequate street lighting meant she couldn't see much in the dark. She stayed in the car for a minute, not because she was having second thoughts about meeting Andrés, but to get her thoughts in order.

As Patricia was preparing to get out of the car, she saw a man approach the front door – not Andrés, but perhaps someone else who was living there with him (after all, this wasn't his usual home), or a friend. The man appeared to force the door and entered the house. Patricia got out of the car and followed him with a sense of foreboding.

Her fears were confirmed as she reached the door: the man hadn't let himself in with a key – the lock was broken. She heard barking coming from inside the house, then a dull noise and a dog whimpering. Patricia didn't have to think too hard to realize the man had just shot an animal.

Not knowing what to do, she retreated to the car and, hands shaking, tried to dial 911. An operator answered and Patricia told her a criminal had broken into a house and gave her the address. The woman said a patrol car was on its way. It was bound to come late, though, too late. Patricia needed to act now if she wanted to save Andrés. The only option she could see was to get into the car, drive it towards the house's garage and slam it once, twice, three times into the door. The noisy banging set off her car alarm, and Patricia saw lights coming on in some of the houses opposite. She got out of the car and went towards the house. The front garden was sodden. From there she could see there were lights on inside, but she couldn't see or hear anything more. She walked forward. Between the sound of her feet squelching in the mud and the noise of the rain, Patricia thought she heard again the sound of a gun with a silencer. Her heart was pounding fit to burst, she could hardly breathe and her legs were heavy, as in a dream, but she continued walking towards the front door.

Everything that happened next took less than a second: Patricia stepped onto the ceramic tiles in the hallway and her leather-soled shoes slipped. And saved her life, because she started falling in the same instant someone shot at her. Lying on the floor, she felt a sharp pain and then a burning sensation in her left armpit. Her clothes were wet, not only from the rain but from her own blood. She saw the feet of a man moving towards her and knew he was going to kill her, but just then came the noise of people shouting from the front door. The feet pivoted and their owner disappeared through a back window. Patricia made a great effort to look up. In the distance, lying limp on the ground, was Andrés.

Her fear had gone, but Patricia felt weak, like when her blood pressure was low. She tried to stand up, clambering onto her knees with a great effort. There was no strength in her left arm, but she managed to crawl towards Andrés. Perhaps he was only wounded like her, and unconscious.

Reaching his side, she saw that he had been shot in the head and chest. Dark blood covered much of his body. Patrica called to him, shook him. To no avail. She started crying; the burning sensation in her arm had gone now and she realized that in a few seconds she was going to faint. With her last remaining strength, she embraced Andrés. She heard voices behind her, then everything went blank, soft and painless.

3   *How to Stop Smoking*

When she woke up, the pregnancy test was still there, its two pink lines seeming to mock her. Not wanting Federico to find it discarded in the bathroom trash, Verónica had put it in a drawer of her nightstand, planning to dispose of it later. Fede had gone to the office and, as on every other morning, Verónica was alone in that apartment that no longer seemed alien to her, especially now Fede had allowed Chicha – the little dog she had brought back from northern Argentina a few years ago – to move in too. That was a loving gesture that deserved acknowledgement. He had never liked having animals in the house even before he knew what havoc the following months were going to bring: the playful destruction of socks, the pissing everywhere, the night-time walks intended to prevent the dachshund pissing or shitting on the bedroom carpet (but which she sometimes did anyway). Federico had the patience of a saint, but Verónica feared that one day (or more likely one night, when she was out drinking with friends and Fede took Chicha for a walk through the streets of Caballito), her dog would mysteriously get lost or turn up dead, a victim of poisoning.

It had been Federico who suggested she move in. The gradual transfer of her stuff to his place (toothbrush, items of clothing, various lotions, books) and the micro-modifications

Verónica made (changing his Colgate toothpaste to Desensyl, gifting him the Jim Beam she liked, swapping his Melitta for a Volturno coffee pot) reached a tipping point when Fede said she should just bring over everything she needed to live with him. And so she moved in the rest of her clothes, creams, some books, a big box full of papers, her laptop, a couple of large cushions, some sheets and towels she particularly liked, a collection of Turkish spices a friend had brought back and which Federico would surely know how to use, a Jack Vettriano print and, last but not least, Chicha. She didn't put her apartment on Airbnb, despite her sisters' urging (so keen were they to see her cross the Rubicon between courtship and cohabitation), but instead left it ready in case she wanted to be alone there sometimes. Perhaps she would have done well to follow Daniela and Leticia's advice, though, because the apartment soon became an alibi and hideaway for her friends, whether single, separated or negotiating marital crises. She hadn't spent another night in Villa Crespo, although every so often she went over there to do a bit of maintenance and catch up with Marcelo, the doorman, whom she missed a little.

Verónica got up and made a coffee, put on the radio to listen to the news, weather forecast and traffic update, then lit a cigarette. As she took a drag, a rush of nausea turned her stomach over. Feeling stupid, she put out the cigarette: how could she have all the symptoms of pregnancy when she was only just pregnant? Surely she wasn't so obvious. Verónica lit another cigarette and set about smoking the whole thing. Drag after drag. But she hadn't even smoked half when the nausea turned into an irrepressible urge to vomit. She ran to the bathroom and threw up a yellowish-brown liquid.

This might not be a bad time to give up smoking, pregnant or not. It would improve her lung capacity, her teeth would look whiter, her clothes would stop reeking of smoke and her breath of stale tobacco. Thinking how much better her life could be, Verónica made this her immediate goal. She would think about everything else in time, with a calm head. These were still early days, after all, and anxiety was a bad counsellor. She put on jeans, a nice black T-shirt, a little cotton jacket, lilac-coloured, and a raincoat on top because the radio predicted squalls around midday and thunderstorms in the evening. "I am my own storm," she murmured, and it struck her as a grandiloquent and pretentious phrase. She planned to use it at the first opportunity.

II

Verónica arrived early at the newsroom. As was usual on Thursdays, the day on which the new edition of the magazine hadn't yet come out and the one after it was beginning to take shape, the journalists sloped in late, or invented some meeting with sources whose existence was hard to confirm. Anything to avoid going to the newsroom. Verónica liked Thursdays because she still had six days ahead to finish whatever she was working on. That week she hadn't yet been assigned anything, though, nor had she started looking for material for a new article. The day before, she had finished writing that week's cover story, on the disbanding of a gang that kidnapped pets from wealthy owners, demanded a ransom, then killed the animals anyway. Evidently no weightier story had been found for the front pages, so her original four-page spread had grown to eight, with text boxes, opinion columns and lots of photos. One of those most staunchly pushing this story for the cover had been Verónica herself; the mere thought of someone kidnapping and murdering Chicha struck her as abhorrent. Patricia had her doubts, but after a couple of meetings with the magazine's bosses, she was resigned to running with photos of puppies and cats massacred by this gang, whose leader was a vet. The headline OUR PETS CAN FINALLY BREATHE EASY: DR DEATH'S GANG HAS FALLEN would not go down in the annals of journalism.

There was nobody else in the newsroom, apart from a couple of kids on the Sports desk, the Politics intern and an editor. None of the designers were there either (some had the day off, given that there were rarely any articles to lay out that day), nor any photographers or subeditors. Only the admin team, who inhabited a parallel world to the journalists, was fully represented. The Human Resources assistant walked past and announced that all salaries had been paid (cue applause from the boys at Sports, but more for the assistant's miniskirt than the payment). Verónica checked on her computer, and yes: there was her money. She used it to pay off her credit card and the service charge on her apartment in Villa Crespo.

While Verónica was catching up on foreign news sites, María Magdalena appeared. She had come in to the office to cash in some late payments. "Now they've paid me, I can afford to invite you for coffee," she said.

Verónica accepted and they went to a bar on Avenida Álvarez Thomas.

María Magdalena had once been a nun and had always been a journalist. One of the really good ones, the kind who take a whole day to confirm a fact that will only appear once in an article. The kind who consult more than one source, who don't get swayed by platitudes or preconceived ideas; the kind who value facts over opinion and an honest opinion over vested interests (her own or the company's). Moreover, she wanted to be known by both forenames and not simply "María". Vero and she had become friends, and there was never a month when they didn't have lunch together at Rondinella, or a whisky at the end of the day in some bar round Boedo or Caballito, near their respective homes. Verónica found it amusing that the ex-nun drank as much as or more than her. Drinking seemed to be the closest María Magdalena ever came to sinning. She had never, as far as anyone knew, had a partner or any kind of love interest.

At that time of day, and with thunderclouds gathering, coffee seemed like a better idea. Lately, María Magdalena had become a journalist specializing in all kinds of trafficking. She had brought to public attention the clandestine sweatshops along the River Riachuelo in Lanús and exposed a commissioner from the Partido de la Costa who had been prostituting teenage girls brought from Corrientes and Misiones.

"Now I'm rather lost. I'm not sure what to do next," María Magdalena told Verónica as she stirred her coffee. "I was thinking of suggesting something lighter to Patricia, maybe a piece on the taxi mafia."

"You think that's light?"

"Or I could pitch something on the wedding planner mafia."

"She'd definitely go for that."

It crossed Verónica's mind then to tell María Magdalena about her pregnancy, ask her advice, but she feared some colleague from the newsroom might interrupt them, and this wasn't a conversation to cut short one day and pick up the next. Perhaps at some later date, when they went for lunch or, even better, after a few whiskies. Whisky, though? Was she planning to drink alcohol?

It was late when she got back to the newsroom. The rain was falling harder and Verónica couldn't decide whether to wait in the office until it let up or go out and hail a taxi, to get home quicker. In either case, she was in plenty of time to meet Paula at Lupita, a Mexican bar and restaurant that had opened recently on Pedro Goyena. It suited both of them better than a club like Martataka; besides, Vero needed to talk to her alone.

There was hardly anyone left in the newsroom now, apart from Patricia. They didn't talk about the edition about to hit the streets. It was already old news for them, off their radar. Nor did they talk about the next one. Verónica thought her boss seemed agitated, as though distracted. That was unusual for Patricia, and Verónica guessed some personal problem must be the reason. She asked if anything was wrong, but Patricia said she was fine. Verónica watched her go. She would try again the next day if her editor's mood hadn't improved.

III

She arrived early at Lupita, a small place strung with green and red lights, containing a few tables and a bar. One wall was plastered with old liquor advertisements and on the other was an abstract painting in cool colours. Looking back and forth between them, you could imagine yourself either in an Irish pub or a bar with avant-garde pretensions. Only the quiet background music suggested a Mexican theme. Verónica assumed it was corridos or some other music typical of that northern nation.

A not insignificant detail: there were no other customers apart from her; all the tables were empty. The waitress, leaning on the bar with a bored expression, observed Verónica settling into her seat with no particular interest. She waited a few minutes before coming over with a menu, swinging her hips as though on a catwalk. Verónica looked at the list of wines and spirits. She wavered for a few seconds before saying decisively: "A sparkling water, please."

Verónica thought she detected a flicker of contempt from the waitress, but she wasn't interested in playing power games. Her priority was to organize her thoughts so she could clearly express them to Paula. It would be best to have a relaxed dinner first, she thought, and then share her news.

Paula arrived a few minutes later, phone in hand and with a certain breathlessness, as though trying to shake off a horde of admirers. She put down her purse and a bag of books and placed her phone on the table, then removed her soaking jacket and finally collapsed in the chair with an air of exhaustion.

"I've had a horrendous day. I need a drink, and fast. What are you having?" Her eyes fell on Verónica's glass of water and she stopped short, looking from the glass to her friend's face. "Are you pregnant?" she asked, voice shaking.

Verónica opened her eyes wide, like someone accused of stealing lingerie in a shopping mall, then swung her arms like a boxing referee declaring a knockout, blew out her cheeks like an angry boar, opened her mouth as though to speak her last words and found she had no breath. Finally she murmured: "Yes." She took a long drink of water.

Paula waited for her to finish, then grabbed the glass and had a drink herself. "And you're happy?" she asked.

"Whatever happiness is."

"Don't be an idiot. I'm asking you if it was intentional, if you were trying – if both of you wanted this."

"OK, how about a little less of the aggression?"

"…"

"I'm feeling sensitive and like I might start crying in front of everyone."

"…"

"…"

"There's literally no one here, Vero."

"In front of the waitress, then."

Paula put her head in her hands and seemed ready to pull out hanks of her hair, when the waitress approached, with her weary step.

"I'd like a glass of red wine," said Paula.

"Which one?"

"I don't know, have fun picking one for me," Paula said, and waved her away before returning her attention to Verónica. "How could you have accidentally got pregnant?"

"It's a long and tangled tale. I wasn't taking the pill, a condom broke, I didn't take the morning-after pill, and here we are."

"Oh Vero, I can't believe it. What do you think you'll do?"

Verónica took a deep breath, waiting for the waitress to deposit a glass of wine in front of Paula and for Paula to take a slug of it. "I don't know."

"Have you spoken to Fede?"

"He doesn't know anything yet."

"Aren't you going to tell him?"

"I don't know."

Paula cast around her, as though seeking inspiration or patience. She looked like a police officer interrogating a difficult witness.

"I can believe you're scared or confused, but not that you don't know," Paula said, looking Verónica straight in the eye. You know when you're waiting for a blind date in a bar? Every time someone comes in you're wondering if it's him, but when the right person walks in you know straight away that it's your date. You might not have known whether you wanted to have a child before you got pregnant. Now there can't be any doubt. If you say you don't know, it's because you don't want to have it."

"What would you do?"

"I've had one already, darling."

"I know, genius. I mean what would you do in my shoes?"

"Wait – it's not irrelevant that I've already had one. I got pregnant at the age you lot were tearing up half the city."

"Slight exaggeration."

"But now I see so many of our friends and acquaintances desperately worried about their biological clocks and about finding a guy to share the medical bills, I'm happy to have gone through the rigmarole when I did. My boy's growing up, he's turning out nicely, and I can get on with life without worrying too much about having a stable relationship."

"We're not talking about you, though."

"True, apologies. If I were you, in my thirties with a guy capable of busting a condom while he's fucking, both of you with good jobs, with your own apartments, with up-to-date medical insurance, with sisters who also have kids, if I were you... I wouldn't have it."

"Why wouldn't you?"

"Because you don't want to be a mother, Vero. You want to be an aunt, taking your nieces and nephews out, buying nice presents for your friends when they get pregnant. Look, no special sensibility is required to be a mother. If you continued with this pregnancy I think you'd be a good mother, a proper one. But why would you do it? To please your family, to strengthen your relationship with Federico?"

"It doesn't need strengthening."

Paula said nothing but shot her a sceptical look.

"You can be a real cow, you know that, right?" Verónica said.

"I'm only telling you what you would tell yourself if you put emotions to one side. Do what you want, but in your place I'd have an abortion."

The waitress came over with a notepad. "Would you like to order some food?"

55

"We still haven't decided," said Verónica.

"I don't suppose you have babies in blankets?"

"See what a bitch you are?"

IV

They ate some bland quesadillas and tacos that came too spicy, even though they had ordered them with the chilli on the side. It became clear why there was no one else in the bar apart from them. Although the chat continued over dinner, the real conversation had been over for a while and now the women were exchanging words only to keep the phatic function of language alive, as Jakobson would say (this was one of the few things Verónica remembered from her social communication studies).

Neither of them felt like ordering dessert, and the espresso machine wasn't working. It seemed that the restaurant, which had only been open for a month, was already in decline. They asked for the bill.

Each would have gone her way then if Verónica hadn't received a call.

"Rodolfo Corso, just what I need."

Verónica answered in the same tone of voice, somewhere between sarcastic and irritated, that she habitually used when taking a call from Corso, even though this particular colleague had saved her skin more than once. But the tone didn't last long. What Corso told her stopped Verónica dead. Paula's face mirrored her friend's concern. When the call was over, Verónica repeated what Corso had told her, not yet believing it.

"Goicochea's been murdered. Patricia was with him, and she's been injured."

Paula began asking questions Verónica couldn't answer. She'd had no news of Goicochea since he left the magazine, although she did know, office politics aside, that he and Patricia got on well. They had worked in several newsrooms together, and that always generates a certain camaraderie. She'd had no idea Patricia still saw him, much less why she was with him when he was murdered, nor how any of this had happened. She knew only that Patricia had been taken to the hospital in Posadas.

"I have to go and see her."

"I'll take you. I've got the car."

Verónica thought of calling Federico, but he was out having dinner with friends and she didn't want to interrupt his only outing of the month. On the way to the hospital, Verónica contacted various colleagues from work to let them know about Patricia, and about Goicochea's murder. Everyone was dismayed.

As they were about to arrive, Verónica looked on some news websites but could find nothing about the incident.

The hospital parking lot was all but empty. Once inside the building, they were sent from pillar to post trying to find out where Patricia was. There wasn't much information available to visitors at that time of day. In the emergency department they walked down long corridors and could see the waiting room packed with desperate people. Finally they got to the inpatient area, where they found Rodolfo Corso, Atilio, Patricia's current husband, and Ernesto, her oldest child. They seemed relaxed, and that reassured Verónica, who had been feeling close to collapse.

"She was shot in the left armpit," said Corso. "They've operated to take out the bullet and she's fine, despite losing a lot of blood. Luckily the ambulance came quickly."

"Can I see her?"

"She's still in intensive care, but they said they're going to move her onto the ward. If she's better tomorrow, they'll take her to a more central hospital."

"What happened?"

"We still don't really know," said Atilio. "Looks like some kind of break-in."

"Vero, will you join me outside for a cigarette?" said Corso, who didn't smoke.

The two of them went outside, leaving the others to wait for Patricia to be brought out of intensive care or for a doctor to emerge with an update.

"Sweetheart, not to alarm you, but I don't think this was a break-in," Rodolfo said once they were alone.

"What do you mean?"

"I've known Patricia and Andrés for years. This meeting at a house in Haedo wasn't some friendly get-together. It must have been to do with something Andrés was caught up in."

"What makes you think that? Did you know they were going to be meeting?"

"No, far from it. When Atilio told me that Patricia had been shot and Andrés had been killed, I ran out straight away, not here but to the place where it happened. The police were still there, securing the scene. As a seasoned crime reporter, let me give you a heads-up, as they say these days: get hold of the police right after something happens, and they tell you everything. Later, they all get their story straight and parrot whatever the bosses have told them to say. So as soon as I arrived I went up to a police officer who looked bored and was obviously annoyed because the forensics still hadn't arrived – apparently they'd been held up by a suicide in Ciudadela. I showed him some big notes that might come in handy for the police welfare fund. The guy told me they'd found Andrés's body in the living room and Patricia unconscious next to him. And get this: Patricia's car was jammed into the garage next to the house. A neighbour, who had seen everything, told the police that Patricia drove her car into the garage door several times, setting off the car alarm. So it seems she went into the house at that point."

"She might have arrived just after some thief broke into Andrés's place."

"You think Patricia would have crashed her car first and then gone into the house if she thought this was a standard burglary? She would have called the police and stayed outside waiting for them. If she acted so impetuously it was because she believed, correctly, that Andrés's life was in danger. She didn't do all that to prevent a robbery, but to prevent him being murdered."

"But why would anyone kill Andrés, a retired journalist?"

"That I don't know. I asked the cop if anything had been stolen. At first glance, nothing seemed to be missing. I said that in that case Andrés's computer must still be somewhere in the house. Our man in blue had a good think – miraculous to observe – and a few seconds later said no, they hadn't come across any computers. Whatever Andrés was investigating, the details must have been on his computer."

"But – Andrés investigate? I mean, when he edited *Nuestro Tiempo* he couldn't even write a column."

"Never write off a journalist. Much less a wounded journalist, as Andrés was after he got fired."

They agreed that there wasn't much point waiting in the corridor for Patricia to be brought out, since she was bound still to be sleeping off the effects of the anaesthetic. Corso went home, promising to return the next day during visiting hours to talk to Patricia. Verónica and Paula stayed a few minutes longer to support Ernesto while Atilio was busy signing papers at the reception desk, then they too left.

Now it was no longer raining, the wind had cleared the sky and a few stars were visible. It was beginning to feel hot, or perhaps there was too much humidity. They walked through the deserted parking lot listening to the sound of their own footsteps on the asphalt. Verónica took a few seconds to WhatsApp Federico: *I've been with Pau at Posadas Hospital, trying to see Patricia. She got injured in "unclear circumstances". Coming home in Pau's car.*

"Remind me next time that heels aren't the best footwear for an early-morning dash to the hospital," Paula complained. "My feet are killing me."

They got into the car and, as Paula pulled out of her spot and looked for the exit, Verónica fiddled with the radio, searching for a news bulletin that might mention Goicochea and Patricia. Neither of them saw the black Fiat Siena coming towards them with its lights off until it smashed into Paula's door. Instantly the airbags inflated. The combined shock of the crash and the airbag slowed Verónica's reactions. Amid the confusion she saw some men get out of the Fiat, but she didn't register that a person had opened the back passenger door on her side in order to hit her with a hard object. She felt the heavy blow, then lost consciousness.

She could hear a phone ringing in the distance – hers – but couldn't wake up. Verónica made an enormous effort to open her eyes. The phone was still ringing. Finally she regained consciousness. She was still sitting in the car, with a thousand hammers battering her head.

But Paula had gone.

4   *A Day in the Life*

I

Man is a creature of habit, Federico Córdova told himself as he parked his Renault Sandero Stepway 1.6 Privilege in his bay, one of five the Rosenthal practice had in this building. A couple of years ago, Federico would never have imagined having his own car, or living with Verónica, or going back to work for Aarón, his girlfriend's father. All those changes had occurred within the space of a surprising few months. Sometimes he looked in the mirror (while in the bathroom, or the elevator, or his car) and couldn't recognize himself: it was as if his life had been given to an actor who was playing him and greatly improving his existence.

He had always wanted to live with Verónica; and leaving the firm had been the result of exceptional circumstances. He hadn't been happy away from Vero and his work at Rosenthal and Associates. He had liked his job as a prosecutor, but missed the challenge that came with working for Aarón. Defending was harder, more ambiguous and more necessary than prosecuting.

And now he had everything he wanted, he felt as though his life were happening to someone else. He briefly regretted leaving Dr Cohen, the psychologist who had treated him for several months and refused ever to discharge him. It hadn't been easy ending the treatment. Dr Cohen tried to dissuade him with clichés ("All that glistens isn't gold"; "No love is ever perfect"), but Federico stood firm. They parted on bad terms and, as he left the building, he saw Dr Cohen leaning out of the consulting room's third-floor balcony and shouting: "You'll be back, mark my words!"

"Your problem is that you go round and round in circles, like a carousel. Face forward, brother, or the game will catch you up and have you for breakfast," advised one of his friends, mixing his metaphors with a nice footballing analogy.

And even if he sometimes felt like a fraud inside his elephant-grey suit, Federico had grown accustomed to the daily happiness of life with a woman he loved, work he could pursue in the way he wanted and a car that allowed him to avoid public transport most of the time.

Since he hadn't had breakfast (he didn't like to eat it alone, and Verónica never got up early enough to have it with him, clearly marking the limits of her love for him), he popped into the kitchen at work and helped himself to a double cortado and two croissants. He took his breakfast into his office, where Nina, one of the assistants, passed him a list of appointments for that day. The most important of these was already occupying his mind: a meeting with Aarón Rosenthal and the other partners in half an hour.

Four decades after leaving the office of Lanusse and Associates to start his own law practice, Aarón Rosenthal now owned sixty per cent of the company. The other forty was divided among six lawyers who had won his confidence through their successes in lawsuits and negotiations. They had also been selected because they specialized in areas of law in which Rosenthal was not himself proficient but at which the firm nonetheless excelled. From the start, Verónica's father had focussed in advising state agencies and financial institutions. That didn't mean he left the more complicated cases in other areas to his partners. He gave his opinion on all cases, and was generally right. He was an old fox who could sniff out the chickens (and also the danger) from afar.

Federico had a ten per cent stake, the same as Mario Iñíguez, a specialist in constitutional law, who had joined the practice soon after Aarón started it. He was almost the same age as Aarón and had witnessed the growth of the firm, something that could – as with any witness – be helpful or not, depending on the context and the circumstances.

The other four partners had five per cent each. There was Marcelo Paz García, who specialized in procedural law; and Lucas Broderson, a brilliant Harvard-educated commercial lawyer who for eight years had worked at one of the big firms in New York, until he was fired following an accusation of sexual harassment from a female colleague. It was Iñíguez – who knew Lucas's father, also a lawyer – who had pushed for Broderson to be hired, and there was no doubting his ability. He quickly became indispensable, and Rosenthal rewarded him with his stake. Another minority partner was Antonio Rivadavia – great-great-grandson of the politician who in 1824 had put Argentina into debt for the first time ever. His work in the area of international, public and private law had brought in major multinationals as clients. And lastly came Diana Veglio, the only woman in the top tier at Rosenthal and Associates. Diana was their no-nonsense specialist in family law and worked for Rosenthal via an independent subsidiary, a freedom only justified by the significant turnover and contacts she generated.

When people asked after Federico's own specialism, he sometimes said it was the Law of Rosenthal Impatience. Having joined the firm when he was not much over twenty and been quickly taken under the wing of that old fox Aarón, he knew how to adjust to whatever his boss needed. That was how he learned to deal with the legal questions that kept Rosenthal awake at night, first as a clerk, then as a lawyer who had graduated *cum laude*, and finally as a partner. Federico was the only one to earn his stake shortly before his thirtieth birthday. Not even the year and a half Federico had spent away from the firm, trying his luck in the National Prosecutor's Office, had made Aarón doubt his decision to make him a partner or give up the fantasy that his star lawyer would also one day become his son-in-law. Since his return, Federico had completely regained Rosenthal's trust; he was the joker Rosenthal played in every tricky court case.

The men, dressed formally in shades of grey, and Diana in a variation on the Chanel suit, her jacket a darker blue than her skirt, waited in the meeting room for Aarón Rosenthal to arrive and deliver his habitual, though mercifully short, homily. He was a practical man, mindful that his partners were past the age for seminars.

Aarón sat at the head of the English-style mahogany table and spoke briefly about the current political situation, the possibility of winning a contract to represent a state body against a former contractor, before turning to the most complex case currently on the firm's books: that of businessman Sergio Mayer.

"We should ask your daughter to help out with this one," said Diana Veglio, wryly. Mayer was a successful entrepreneur in various sectors, but his name had become particularly associated with his media group, and *Nuestro Tiempo* was one of his magazines. Even though he wasn't the only owner of Grupo Esparta, he was the major shareholder and its driving force. He also had other business interests: property, security, and even a port concession on the Paraná River.

"I don't think she can help us much in a real estate case," said Rosenthal in his usual dry tone.

Antonio Rivadavia read his notes and took the floor. "The Mayer case isn't easy because we have three cross-claims: the environmental NGO Cuidar opposes the construction of a riverfront building complex in the area near Tigre. The land falls into two municipalities, and neither wants to grant construction permits. And to top it all off, there's also a divorce in progress, which could be complicated if the courts have to make an exact audit of Mayer's properties."

"Let's hope we can persuade his widow not to go down the legal route and —" Diana began, then stopped when she saw that the others were all laughing.

"You said 'widow'."

"Widow? Sorry, I meant ex-wife. Let's hope she drops the suit and takes a big payoff instead."

"Given the complexity of this case, I'm going to ask you two" – Rosenthal gestured to Rivadavia and Veglio – "to funnel everything through Federico. And Federico, if you have any other cases pending, delegate them. Keep me in the loop. Today I'm having lunch with Mayer, so Diana and Antonio, prepare a brief for 12.30."

Aarón closed the meeting and everyone went back to their offices, apart from Federico, who tended to hang back for a brief chat. Those few minutes alone with Aarón signalled Federico's status in the firm to the other lawyers, although the conversation usually turned on family matters: Aarón's daughters, the grandchildren, the odd family gathering. Federico felt that the Rosenthal sisters didn't pay enough attention to their father. It was the ultimate irony: a man admired by judges, politicians and lawyers of every stripe was treated like a slightly gaga grandfather at home. Only Federico took the time to listen to him, perhaps because he moved in both the worlds Aarón inhabited.

"I'm thinking of bringing forward the inheritance," said

Aarón as he reached into his jacket for a cigarette, which he would light only once he got back to his office, since that was the one room in the office set up for smoking.

"Do you want to pass some property on to the girls?"

"Anything I can, the firm included."

"Are you planning to retire then?"

Aarón shook his head and looked longingly at the cigarette. "I'd like to have everything as neat and tidy as possible. Not that I want you to start working on that, I'd rather you concentrate on Mayer. But keep it in mind for when we're less busy."

"Whenever you want. It's not complicated."

"How is Vero? I haven't seen her for weeks."

"That sounds like your daughter all right, she's a workaholic."

"A chip off the old block."

"She's fine though, happy with how things are going at the magazine."

"Daniela's invited us all to dinner."

"Yes, I think we're going."

Aarón slapped his shoulder and the men went back to their respective offices.

Federico stood at the large window, watching a small boat navigating the River Plate. He thought it might be nice to take a vacation with Verónica, to go somewhere together, far from work and obligations.

Someone came into the office, interrupting these thoughts. He didn't need to turn round to know who it was; her perfume gave Diana Veglio away.

"Have you got a minute? I thought we could talk about Mayer and Roxana Soldati, the wife."

Federico gestured to her to sit down, but Dr Veglio preferred to prop her backside on the edge of his desk. She was tall, generously proportioned and had a way with sexy little suits.

"Do you know why Al Capone was imprisoned for tax evasion? Because he never had to go to a divorce court," said Diana. "Wives are the worst karma for a criminal."

"Mayer isn't a criminal, as far as we know."

"There's no fortune in Argentina that isn't stained with blood. Are you still going out with the boss's daughter?"

Federico went over to the desk, passing next to Diana, who swivelled her body towards him. He sat down opposite her.

"Let's say I am. Do you think Mayer's future ex-wife is a threat?"

"We women are so fucked up. Just imagine if Virginia Rosenthal gets angry with you and runs off to tell her daddy. You'll be an office boy again before you know it."

Federico smiled to himself. Diana could misname his partner or throw out all the barbs she liked. It was her way of showing him affection after all these years. "What are you thinking of offering Roxana Mayer?" he asked.

"Property, money, shares, jewellery, and a lot more besides. A fortune, in other words, but I fear nothing will be enough."

"She'll only push her luck so far."

"You should get that girl of yours pregnant – not that she's a girl any more. That will guarantee her father keeps you close."

"We need at least another two lawyers to work with you and Rivadavia," said Federico, ignoring the jibe.

Diana nodded without saying anything. She knew that when Federico gave instructions, he expected them to be followed. That was harder for her than for the other lawyers. Even if most of the other partners had known Federico since he first joined the firm, when he wore suits that were too big and was forever eating schnitzel sandwiches in the kitchen, she was the only one who had slept with him.

It had been a brief relationship. Federico was on the rebound after being wounded one too many times by Verónica, and for some reason ended up confiding in his colleague. Diana was twelve years older than him and much more experienced. The first time they went out, she took him to a bar to talk, then straight back to her place. Federico discovered a world he had thought only existed in porn films, as fascinating at the start as it was troubling. Diana used him like a sex doll, one of several in her life, which didn't bother him because he wasn't looking for a girlfriend. And while her sadomasochistic games had helped banish painful memories of Vero, in time he got bored with them. He no longer wanted to try out the new set of handcuffs Diana asked him to put on her, or to cast a wary eye over the collection of vibrators she was keen to show off. Four months after their first night together, now half a stone lighter and much more sexually knowledgeable, Fede stopped seeing Diana. That didn't prevent them from being good work colleagues, and both continued to thrive at Rosenthal and Associates. He thrived more than her, though, and Diana likely thought that this was unfair, that she had been passed over because he held the trump card: Aarón's youngest daughter. If she did in fact believe that, Diana had never used it as a way to get back at him at work. She limited herself to sarcastic jokes.

"Rivadavia will definitely want to do his own thing, with Pousá. I'd like you to team up with Ángeles," said Federico.

"With Legally Blonde?"

"Don't call her that. She's very good with family stuff, and she's also started doing corporate litigation. She complements us nicely."

"What if Aarón finds out you're eyeing up the pretty little lawyer... and disinherits you?"

"Let's not talk about Aarón's inheritance. Come on, get to work with Ángeles and show her everything you know. About the law, I mean."

Diana uncrossed her legs and stood up. She seemed about to walk over to him, but instead she tapped her files on the edge of the desk and, smiling, left the room.

II

Federico had another meeting with Aarón after the lunch with Mayer. Later he met Rivadavia, Diana and the two junior lawyers: Mauro Pousá and Ángeles Basualdo. First Federico briefed them on his conversation with the client, then he asked them to focus on the Fundación Cuidar suit. The team spent a couple of hours exchanging ideas and information. Pousá and Basualdo were young but talented; when building arguments they knew how to be creative (something unusual among lawyers) and cunning (a common trait among lawyers but one few know how to channel). The meeting ended abruptly because Federico remembered he had to be in San Cristóbal before seven o'clock.

He had arranged to meet his friend Pablo to play a game of five-a-side at Cochabamba and Pichincha. Luckily he had his gear in the car, so he arrived with time in hand to get changed. He hardly knew his teammates, although some of them had probably been at Pablo's birthday party. They were all high school teachers, like his friend, who taught philosophy. Another player had dropped out and Federico had accepted the invitation to take his place.

As he strapped up his feet and put on his shorts Federico felt a sense of anticipation unique to the locker room – those pre-game minutes of male camaraderie, when the guys are getting ready to go out onto the field. They never talked much while they changed; some might apply pain-relieving liniment to their legs or flex their toes, stiffened by hours of sitting down. They barely exchanged glances with the other team's players, who always seemed to have better strapping, better gear and better shoes.

"Will you play at the back?" asked – or rather ordered – one of his teammates, a guy with a goatee, as they left the locker room.

"Sure, no problem," said Federico, who considered himself a box-to-box player in five-a-side. He started warming up while watching a group of women playing handball on a neighbouring court.

"That blonde is really sexy," said Pablo beside him, stretching his legs, pointing to the goalkeeper.

It was true that she was hot. A tall blonde reminiscent of Elle Macpherson in the nineties. The woman looked in their direction and Pablo blew her a kiss, which she ignored.

"She's playing hard to get."

"Or perhaps she really is. Maybe your receding hairline doesn't do it for her."

"Oof, OK, Tiny Tears."

That was a low blow. Federico had been known as Tiny Tears for the first few years of high school. After he was about ten, he'd only got called that when someone was looking for a fight. But Federico still dreaded the nickname. Luckily, they were then urged to get on the field so the game could start.

Truth be told, Federico was weak on the ball, giving it away easily, struggling to find the right pass. The guys on the other team were good and got stuck in. A couple of times he dawdled too long and lost the ball. His own teammates called him "bro" because they couldn't remember his name (thank God they hadn't heard the allusion to Tiny Tears). When they were 4–2 down, Federico scored a goal, and that was the highlight of his ill-starred afternoon. A few seconds later, he was cleaned out by a dirty tackle and saw red. Smarting from the blow, he got to his feet and chest-butted the guy who had kicked him. A scrap ensued that was quickly broken up by the other players from both teams. When he had cooled down, Federico noticed that his knee was sore and a bit swollen. It hurt to walk. He played the rest of the game standing in the middle of the field so as not to leave his team a player down. Nobody thanked him for this altruistic gesture.

Pablo fetched him some ice from the club cafe. Then they said goodbye to the others and headed to the San Antonio pizzeria on Boedo and Garay, where the rest of the Dámaso Centeno gang – the group of high school friends Federico still met regularly – were waiting for them. The other four had already ordered beer and empanadas. Federico and Pablo got more empanadas and beers for the two of them, plus two pizzas, one with ham and red pepper and the other a *fugazzeta*, and four slices of *fainá* flatbread.

They skimmed over the matters of the day with a kind of indifference, something not unusual for a group of friends who could easily spend a whole night debating the existence of extraterrestrial civilizations but seemingly had little time for local politics. Perhaps there was an unspoken agreement to avoid treading on each other's toes. They were more interested in establishing exactly what had happened in the game Federico and Pablo had played. The blonde handball goalkeeper was also the object of some absurd speculation.

Before the cheese and desserts arrived, Federico said his knee was really hurting and that he'd better go home and ice it. Some of the gang were sympathetic, others made fun of him.

He limped from the pizzeria to his car. Once he reached it, far from the gaze of his friends, Federico dropped the pretence. His leg might be slightly inflamed and painful, but not enough to justify limping. He felt a little bad, not so much for lying to his friends but because leaving meant missing out on the chat.

It took him nearly half an hour to reach the building on Cabrera and Thames. The apartment he shared with Verónica was only fifteen minutes from the pizzeria. If he had gone home, he wouldn't have found her there: she was out having dinner with Paula. Was he trying to avoid the empty apartment, then? Was that it? No. If that had been the reason he would have stayed out with his friends, who were likely going to hang out for another hour.

Before getting out of the car he examined himself in the rear-view mirror, pulling his lips back to check his teeth. Pizza so often left a residue of oregano. Ideally, he'd have brushed his teeth in the pizzeria, but that would have made his friends suspicious. Who cleans their teeth before going home? He popped a mint into his mouth and stepped out into the perfidious night.

At that time of night nobody was going in or out of the building. He rang the apartment bell. It was answered almost immediately.

"It's me," said Federico.

"Who's 'me'?"

"Come on," he said impatiently.

She seemed to find it amusing to repeat this performance every time he buzzed the entryphone.

Ángeles came down dressed in leggings and a long T-shirt, very different to how she looked at work. "I like dressing up as a lawyer when I'm at work and as a middle-class girl when I'm at home," she had once told him. Then she had taken a sip of her cocktail and added: "Would you like to see me dressed up as a homebody?"

Ángeles smiled at him from the other side of the glass. She obviously enjoyed seeing his discomfort as he waited. Then she opened the door and gave him a quick kiss on the mouth. Federico walked past her towards the elevator. She stroked his back, down to the top of his ass. They went up to the apartment.

III

Ángeles Basualdo had come to Rosenthal and Associates the same way as most of their lawyers: recommended by one of the partners. Antonio Rivadavia had taught her in the department of International Public Law and been dazzled by his student. Not only was she brilliant and young (only twenty-two at that stage), but she had a strong, determined character. Rivadavia closely followed her progress through the last stages of her degree and, once she had passed the final module, arranged a meeting to offer her a place at the firm. Ángeles wanted to study abroad; she had applied for a master's degree at Harvard. Rivadavia persuaded her to put off graduate school until later and first gain experience in the real world, learning on the job with Aarón Rosenthal's team. For any law student at the Universidad de Buenos Aires, joining the Rosenthal firm meant joining the big leagues. She said yes and decided to put off her master's in the US for two years.

Federico hadn't paid her much attention at the start, on one occasion even taking her for a secretary. He wasn't one of those men with a built-in radar for women who were single, or even available. Since he was very young he had been prone to falling in love, but he didn't always notice when attractive women were orbiting him who might be interested in hooking up. It was likely that Ángeles would soon find out he was practically Rosenthal's son-in-law and would not want to gamble her career on a lawyer who was important but not that important; attractive, but only up to a point. As she would one day say to him, he was hardly Mark Ruffalo.

The scene was set for nothing to happen between them: Ángeles would have her two years' experience in the firm and go on to Harvard; Federico would stay on quietly at the office, for all the world a loyal man and a devoted partner.

But that didn't happen.

Federico quickly noticed that Ángeles was a more lucid and discerning lawyer than most of the lower-ranking lawyers in the practice. So, every time he needed someone to work with, he turned to her. Rosenthal himself commented to Federico that the girl had a bright future. "So long as she doesn't fall in love with some idiot and ruin her career," he added with a sigh. Neither then nor later did it occur to Federico that Aarón might be talking about him. Aarón didn't go in for subtexts.

On more than one occasion, after some court case or other, Federico and Ángeles had gone for lunch together at a nearby fast-food place. Over hamburgers and fries, Ángeles told him about her family, who were from Junín, her ophthalmologist father, her teacher mother, the difficulties and pressure that came with having a sister who lived in Switzerland, leaving her as the only child at home with her parents. She also told him about an ex-boyfriend in the police force who used to remove his gun when he visited her place and leave it on top of the fridge. Federico was more circumspect, speaking little or not at all about his life with Verónica, although he told her at such length about the chaos caused by Chicha that every time they went out to lunch, the first thing Ángeles did was jokily ask after "the little bitch".

It was only much later that Federico registered the ambiguity in that question. She could have been referring to Verónica, not the dog.

Federico wasn't altogether sure how his desire to get involved with Ángeles first began. One day the idea wasn't in his head, and the next it had begun slowly but steadily to eat away at his brain, like a worm burrowing through earth. To make things worse, his relationship with Verónica was in a strange place. Not in crisis as such, but he was finding it hard to live with her. Or rather he was finding her absence more difficult than her presence: she nearly always came home late, she might work all weekend and then get bored on a Wednesday because there was nothing urgent to do; sometimes she went hours without speaking and at other times she would talk non-stop all night. It was true she had always been like that, since the first day of their relationship, but they hadn't been living together before, or trying to follow a routine.

He could hear Dr Cohen's voice saying to him: "Save those arguments for when your concubine catches you with your lover – but don't lie to me. The desire for infidelity comes before the feeling of absence. It's not that Señorita Verónica isn't offering you the full package, it's that you *want* to see an incompleteness so you can go hunting the other bird. And don't make me repeat the word 'incompleteness' any time soon."

Federico could imagine fucking Ángeles, but he couldn't contemplate taking a lover. Perhaps he should confine himself then to the realm of fantasy, dream of kissing her breasts after savagely ripping off that white blouse; imagine this scenario while he was fucking Verónica. That was as far as he would let himself go.

However, one cold winter night, when the frost seemed about to turn into sleet, something unusual in Buenos Aires, Federico became an unfaithful man. It was – how could he ever forget? – Ángeles's twenty-seventh birthday. She had decided to hold a small party in her apartment, just six colleagues. Nobody else. Federico wondered if she didn't have enough friends or close family to fill out a bigger party. Months later, he still wasn't clear on that aspect of Ángeles's life. He knew there were parents in Junín and a sister in Switzerland, friends from university and the odd one from school, but the truth was that she lived for work, including when it came to parties. By that logic, it made sense that she might also satisfy her sexual needs there.

At the party, Federico hadn't been able to help looking at her every time she got up to go to the kitchen for drinks. Ángeles was dressed informally, in tight jeans and an oversized pullover. A few times their eyes met and they held each other's gaze a little too long.

Her work colleagues, Federico included, gave Ángeles a leather bag with a compartment for her laptop. The conversation wasn't sparkling – they couldn't help talking shop – and the pizzas and empanadas Ángeles had ordered weren't particularly good. At one o'clock in the morning, the six guests had all decided to leave at once. Ángeles accompanied them to the door, shivering in the cold air. She said goodbye to everyone and gave Federico a kiss on the cheek which he felt lasted half a second longer than was usual.

He had also been shivering as he walked towards the car. His mind was a volcano of feelings, of burning desires; at the same time he was walking quickly so as not to die of cold. His phone buzzed. It was a message from Ángeles: *You forgot your scarf. Come back and get it.*

Federico had spun round, knowing he was about to fuck Ángeles.

IV

Two months had now passed since Federico and Ángeles had embarked on their risky affair. If word got out there would be a scandal in the firm, with unequal consequences: Ángeles would certainly be fired, and he would be banished to the office next to the lavatory – the one nobody wanted and which served as a storeroom – at least for a while, until Aarón needed him for some important case and he could row his way back to a place of privilege. Aarón wouldn't be swayed by the betrayal of his daughter – although everyone else would, because it was more salacious – but by the lack of professionalism. He detested sentimentality, romantic dalliances and anything that could detract from work performance.

It wasn't in either party's interests for the affair to be discovered, so from the day after that first fuck, Federico and Ángeles began to put much more distance between themselves at work than they had before. They no longer went for lunch together, and tried not to share cases or made sure another lawyer would be involved too. They became cool enough towards one another to worry that this approach might itself seem suspicious: before long someone would doubtless conclude that Federico had propositioned Ángeles and been rebuffed, and that was the reason for their estrangement. At the same time, Federico didn't want to lose her as a colleague, because he knew her worth and needed her expertise. So they went back to being seen together again, not much, just now and then. Professional smiles and an easy rapport. Ángeles invented a boyfriend so everyone would think that was the cause of her happiness. And they always met at her apartment. Any other kind of outing – dinners, movies, concerts – was verboten. They couldn't afford any false moves.

Federico spread out in the comfortable armchair in Ángeles's living room while she went to the kitchen for a beer. His phone buzzed; it was a message from Verónica: *I've been with Pau at Posadas Hospital, trying to see Patricia. She got injured in "unclear circumstances". Coming home in Pau's car.*

He didn't give this much attention.

"Do you like my sporty girl look?" Ángeles asked as she passed him a little bottle of Corona.

"Very much."

"I'm thinking of taking a pole-dancing course. I want to do a striptease for you like in the movies. First I'd do a show on the pole, taking my clothes off, then I'd dance for you."

Ángeles removed her T-shirt, sneakers and leggings. Now she was in underwear and socks, which, it turned out, were also sports ones.

"Do you think I'd make a good stripper?" She turned around and pressed her hands high against the wall, sticking out her ass.

"I think you're gorgeous."

Ángeles turned around with a laugh, seeming surprised at herself. Her long blonde hair was tousled from her improvised moves. Perhaps the soundtrack to a B-movie was playing in her head, one of those ones where the girl gets naked and a few frames later either winds up murdered or kills her partner. Hopefully neither scenario applied here.

She walked towards Federico, who was now eager to kiss her, to run his hands over her, but she seemed to want to remain in control, acting out the scene as if it belonged to that imaginary B-movie in her head. She kneeled in front of him, spread his legs and unzipped his trousers, looking into his eyes. And then Federico's phone rang. Not a message this time but a call, and from the ringtone he knew it was Verónica. He didn't even think about answering. Ángeles was already sucking his cock with a tenderness and dedication he always found moving. He couldn't wait any longer, pulling her up to him as they kissed and he yanked off her bra to reach for her breasts. Forgetting the pain of his bruised leg, he lifted her as she straddled him, and carried her to the bed. That she was petite made a difficult task easier with so much furniture in the way. He threw her onto the bed. Ángeles smiled. Federico loved the way she treated every instant of sex as though it were a game. His phone rang again, once more with a call from Verónica. He didn't answer. Whatever she wanted to tell him could wait until the next day. He pulled off Ángeles's underwear and began to lick her legs, then her stomach, slowly approaching his target. Ángeles began to moan. The phone rang for a third time. Verónica might have many faults, but she would never call three times unless it was an emergency. He stopped licking and looked up at Ángeles, who was watching him seriously, with no trace of her earlier laughter.

"I'm sorry, but I have to answer."

Federico walked over to his phone naked. He must look ridiculous trying to talk on the phone with an erection, but he made an effort to speak normally. On the other end, Verónica sounded desperate.

"Fede, I need you to come and get me. I'm in the parking lot at Posadas. Some really weird things are happening. Please, come."

His erection was already subsiding. Just as well; it would make it easier to get dressed and leave quickly. "I'm sorry, I have to go," he said, without looking at Ángeles. It wasn't the time for explanations.

5　*A Frantic Search*

I

Verónica's nose was bleeding, her head was pounding and the phone kept ringing. It took her a couple of minutes to work out what had happened: somebody had hit her on the back of the head to knock her out; Paula wasn't in the car; and the Posadas Hospital parking lot was still as desolate as it had been when they got into the vehicle. She picked up her bag and took out the screeching phone. On the screen it said *unknown number.*

"I hope you're feeling well."

A man's voice, warm, friendly and unfamiliar. Verónica wiped away the blood running over her mouth and chin.

"Who are you? Where's Paula?"

"Don't worry. Paula's fine. She's with us. Nothing bad will happen to her. We just need your help."

"My help? What are you talking about? Where have you taken her?"

"I'll explain. We've taken your friend as a guarantee that you'll do something for us. Think of it as you doing us a favour, and in return we look after your friend for a few hours."

"I don't understand what you're talking about." Verónica felt like crying but held the tears back. She wouldn't give the men that satisfaction.

"It's simple: we need something and believe you can get it in record time. Listen to me. Goicochea had a tablet. He took it everywhere, but it seems that yesterday he left it in the care of his ex-wife. Do you know her?"

"Elisa?"

"No, that's Malena's mother."

"Viviana?"

"Bingo."

Verónica had met Viviana once and Malena a few times when she was a teenager and came to visit her father in the newsroom at *Nuestro Tiempo*.

"But I have no way of contacting Viviana. I don't even know where she lives."

"We can give you the address. But that's not the problem. It seems your ex-boss left the tablet with her, and Viviana decided to hide somewhere. She isn't where she usually lives. So knowing your brilliance at solving problems, we'd like you to find her, get the tablet and bring it to us. In return, we'll give you back your friend. And we're pushed for time. You know what it's like to work against the clock. We need it by midday today."

"You're out of your mind. I can't find this woman."

"Come on, Verónica. Don't put your friend in danger. You go, you find Viviana and you bring back the tablet. Then you and your friend go off for lunch as if nothing had happened. The worst part of all this is the damage to the car, but Paula told us she has insurance, so don't worry about that."

It terrified her to hear him name Paula.

"Don't do anything to her, please."

"I promise we'll treat her like a queen. Just get hold of the tablet and it's all over."

Before ending the call the man added:

"I don't need to remind you that calling the police will put your friend's life in danger. If you need help call Federico, but no police or any other agency. You've got that clear, right?"

II

Verónica got out of the car and her body seemed to splinter into a million pieces. This was a totally new and unbearable pain. She steadied herself against the car, took a deep breath through her mouth and tried to calm herself. Her shirt was covered in blood, but her nose was no longer bleeding. She looked around her, guessing that the guys holding Paula might be watching her from somewhere close by, but there was nothing to be seen in the dark, empty night. Only a few cars on the western highway.

Going over to the driver's side, she got back into the car. The key was in the ignition and she tried to start the car, but the engine didn't respond. Verónica kept trying in vain, swearing and smacking the steering wheel.

She had less than eight hours to find Viviana. Before asking Federico to help, as the kidnapper had suggested, Verónica called Rodolfo Corso and told him what had happened. If anyone could find Viviana, he could.

"If she's hiding it's because Goicochea warned her that her life was in danger," said Rodolfo. "And if this lot haven't found her, it's because she's very well hidden."

"Any idea how we track her down?"

"As far as I know, she worked at the Foreign Ministry. She was taken on in a temporary role after the Alianza came to power. I'd start there. I have some contacts in the foreign service who work in the Palacio San Martín. They'll get quite a surprise, though, me calling them in the middle of the night."

"This is life or death, Rodo."

"Do you need me to come and get you?"

"No, I'll ask Fede to come."

"Perfect. Give me a few hours, then we'll meet in a bar somewhere. I'll call you."

Verónica felt better after speaking to Rodolfo. Something unnerved her, though: Corso's tone. The guy could crack a joke in the most bizarre circumstances, but after she'd told him what had happened that night, he had sounded uncharacteristically grave. As if he'd realized what was happening wasn't simply serious. It also had the potential to get much worse.

She called Federico. When he didn't answer, she kept trying. He might be asleep, but he was a light sleeper; he usually heard his phone. On the third try, Federico answered with a voice she couldn't place, nor did she want to, given the circumstances.

"Fede, I need you to come and get me. I'm in the parking lot at Posadas. Some really weird things are happening. Please, come."

Verónica ended the call and stayed inside the car. At least there she was more shielded from any potential surveillants. It crossed her mind to go back into the hospital and tell Patricia's husband what had happened, but that would be pointless: Pato was no longer in danger. These men were only interested in the tablet, and Verónica had to focus on getting it for them.

Twenty-five minutes after her call to Federico, Verónica saw his car come into the lot and waved to him. Once more, the valiant prince was coming to rescue his damsel.

III

Federico's apartment looked ghostly to her in these circumstances. Everything seemed unreal now she knew her friend was being held by criminals who had already killed Goicochea and wouldn't hesitate to eliminate anyone else who got in their way. How could she sit and have a cup of coffee while Paula was at the mercy of those thugs? Federico had put on the coffee and was looking for rubbing alcohol and cotton wool. Chicha, as if aware of the ordeal Verónica had endured, cuddled up to her protectively. Fede cleaned her bloodied nose, put an ice pack on the back of her neck and gave her two extra-strong ibuprofen. But should she be sitting there while Corso did all the legwork?

Without a thought for the late hour, and without any explanations, she started calling colleagues from *Nuestro Tiempo* who had worked alongside Goicochea for years and might know his ex-wife. Manzini, from Economy, remembered that Viviana had relations in Tandil. Iriarte, a retired proofreader, had once known Viviana's brother, who had a shop selling electric fans in Vicente López. Nobody else knew her. The only one to scold Verónica was Álex Vilna, the current managing editor.

"You're ringing me in the middle of the night to ask if I can remember anything about Goicochea's ex-wife?"

"Yes."

"You get crazier by the day. If you need to speak to her, wait for Goicochea's wake. I'm sure you'll see her there."

"I need to find her right away. It's urgent."

And the bastard hung up on her. Verónica swore to herself that when all this was over she'd make him pay for that.

While she made calls, Federico was also chasing leads. His sources, as always, were in the court system.

"So far, the only thing I have to go on is her work résumé. Viviana Smith first worked at UNESCO, then moved to the Inter-American Development Bank in Panama and ended up at the Ministry of Foreign Affairs, first as an employee paid by the IDB itself and then on a temporary contract. She's always worked in the field of human development. Sorry, this isn't all that helpful."

"It is helpful, as a way of understanding her better. If we find her, I'm going to have to persuade her to give me the tablet. Viviana Smith. She sounds like an English spy."

Federico was limping a bit, thanks to his dogged efforts on the soccer field, and he looked tired. Verónica told him to go and sleep for a while but he laughed off the suggestion, then picked up his laptop and continued with the search.

Dawn was breaking when Verónica received a surprise phone call: María Magdalena Cortez.

"Rodolfo told me to let you know: I think we've found Viviana."

Why hadn't she thought to ask for María Magdalena's help with the search? Once again, Rodolfo Corso had showed himself to be more clear-thinking when push came to shove. Mind you, he hadn't had to deal with a blow to the head and the kidnapping of his best friend.

"Rodolfo passed on some information about a couple I used to know when I worked at *Vida Cristiana*, Pablo and Elvira. They're graphic designers who did some work for the magazine in the nineties. They also happened to be good friends with Goicochea and Viviana – in fact, both couples separated around the same time. Viviana and Elvira remained close friends. I called Elvira and she sounded very anxious. Anyway, long story short, after a lot of talking, I managed to wheedle out of her that two weeks ago she lent Viviana an apartment in Villa Urquiza. I've got the address. I can go with you, if you like."

"Yes, yes, let's go together."

Verónica arranged to meet María Magdalena in half an hour. Federico wanted to go too, saying she wasn't fit to drive, but Verónica swore that her head didn't hurt any more, nor any other part of her body.

"You're more of a wreck with all your soccer injuries than I am. I'll call you and keep you in the loop."

IV

They left the car on Calle Miller, a few yards from the entrance to the apartment block, which was a grey building that had been put up in the last few years and was unlikely to feature in any history of Argentine architecture. By now dawn had broken. Soon the neighbourhood caretakers would appear, sweeping the sidewalks while keeping an eye on the residents' movements. María Magdalena and Verónica went to the entryphone. They rang several times, then waited a few minutes before trying again. It was useless. Nobody answered the call.

"It doesn't look like she's there," said María Magdalena.

"What if we try to get into the apartment?"

"I think we should go back to the car and plan our next move. If we stay here much longer, the doorman will come out and start asking questions."

So they got back into the car, feeling frustrated. Verónica called Corso to bring him up to speed and see if he had any news. Corso was surprised there had been no answer at the apartment and wondered if Viviana might be in a deep sleep. Verónica had to point out that they had buzzed the entryphone a few times. She asked if he could think of a plan B, but Corso had nothing to offer. He was still on the phone when María Magdalena said: "That's Pablo."

Verónica quickly ended the call and squinted through the glass, but she couldn't see clearly, which often happened when she took off her glasses. María Magdalena got out of the car and Verónica followed.

The man had come out of the building with a bag in his hand and was walking away from them. María Magdalena quickened her pace and called after him: "Pablo." But he seemed not to hear her. María Magdalena shouted louder: "Pablo."

Forced to acknowledge her, the man turned back with a worried expression, looking all around.

"María Magdalena, what a surprise. What brings you to these parts?"

"We've come to see Viviana."

Pablo looked as if he didn't know who she was talking about. Verónica pointed at the bag he was carrying. "I'm guessing Viviana's asked you to take her some clothes. She must be pretty frightened if she left the apartment with nothing and isn't planning to come back here."

"I... don't know what you're referring to."

"Pablo," María Magdalena said, "we know about everything that's happening. They've murdered Goicochea, and Viviana must be terrified. This is Verónica Rosenthal, one of Goicochea's colleagues from *Nuestro Tiempo*. She needs to see Viviana urgently."

The man seemed highly agitated. Clearly he was uneasy talking in the street but didn't dare run away. After a few seconds he admitted that he knew where Viviana was. María and Verónica pressed him to take them to her, and finally Pablo was persuaded. María Magdalena would go with him and Verónica would follow in the car.

"Believe me, this is better for everyone," María Magdalena said in an attempt to calm him, casually adding: "I didn't know you had stayed in touch with Elvira after the divorce."

"I only see Elvira because of the children," Pablo said, curtly.

María Magdalena made a quick mental recalculation, coming up with a timeline of divorces and new relationships.

As Pablo explained his new arrangement with Viviana, Verónica reflected that at least María Magdalena's comment had succeeded in making him forget his fear for a few seconds.

V

Verónica was weaving through traffic on the south-east access highway, focussed on not losing sight of Pablo's car. She didn't know the southern part of Greater Buenos Aires all that well and regretted telling María Magdalena to go in Pablo's car with her following while simultaneously trying to talk by phone to Rodolfo Corso, who was marvelling at Viviana's stringent security measures.

"As well as having the tablet, she must know why they killed Goicochea."

"All I want right now is for them to free Paula. I couldn't care less about the investigation."

"There'll be time to find out more once they've let your friend go."

Pablo took the Quilmes exit, leading them through the whole social spectrum of that area before they arrived at an upper-middle-class neighbourhood with private security guards on the street corners. It made sense that Viviana would feel safer somewhere like this. They parked in front of a house with a garden and high fences, similar to the other buildings on the block: homes that had been built in the sixties for a middle class on the rise until the short-lived bonanza ended; now all that remained of that promising past were these solid, proud buildings. Easy to see out of and hard to get into: not bad for a safe house, thought Verónica.

María Magdalena told her that Pablo had called Viviana from the car. With difficulty he had persuaded her to let them visit. Now it was their turn to be persuasive and get her to hand over the tablet.

Pablo rang the bell three times then opened the door with his own key. They entered a large room, with squashy sofas and a smell of hardwood. The perfect space to spend a rainy weekend watching movies. Viviana appeared from the kitchen. She was carrying a flask and a *mate* set. Her relaxed demeanour seemed at odds with the ring of security around her.

They greeted one another affectionately, Goicochea in all their minds. It was as if they were at his wake. For a few seconds nobody spoke as Viviana poured out the first *mate* and sipped it through the metal *bombilla*. Then she poured another and passed it to María Magdalena. Only then did she say: "I don't think I can help you."

Verónica repeated what Pablo had already told Viviana on the phone: that the gravity of the situation left no room for any negotiations with her ex-husband's killers. If she had the tablet those men wanted, there was no option but to hand it over. Viviana listened carefully, like someone who already knows the details but graciously allows someone else to repeat them. Pablo had also drunk some *mate*, and now Viviana was refilling the gourd for Verónica as she finished laying out the facts.

"I've got the tablet those people are looking for, but it won't be any use to them," Viviana said.

"That doesn't matter to us."

"It matters to me because those people, as well as being dangerous, are intelligent. Why do they want a tablet that's encrypted, whose content probably can't be copied or even photographed, when they know the content anyway?"

Verónica realized she had absolutely no idea about anything to do with the tablet. She neither knew what was on it nor for whom it was so important.

"But Goicochea did know how to access the information on that tablet."

"Because he had the right passwords."

"They could have them too, or believe they can decipher them."

Viviana got up and went to another part of the house. Verónica put the *mate* gourd down on a side table and the three of them waited in silence until she returned. In her hand she held a tablet only a little bigger than a phone. She passed it to Verónica. "Those people aren't only after this," she said.

"But what can be on it to make them kill Goicochea, kidnap my friend and be so desperate to get their hands on it?"

"What the whole world wants: information. What kind of information, I can't tell you. It's already been the cause of so much misery. I don't want there to be more. Take it. I hope it's enough to make them leave your friend alone."

Verónica and María Magdalena left the house with a sour taste in their mouths. It was clear that complying with the criminals' demands was not going to put an end to this story. Viviana had seemed sure of her misgivings. Something else was going on that Verónica couldn't grasp. They could only get a fuller picture by ascertaining the content of the device. She checked the time: it was 10 a.m. She had two hours to get the tablet to the criminals. She picked up her phone and called La Sombra.

"Hi, Sombra. I have in my possession a tablet that doesn't belong to me and whose contents, so I'm told, are impossible to copy."

"Have you tried?"

"No, I'm in the car and I have to hand it over to some fucking bastards who've kidnapped my friend."

"Vero, one day call me because you need me to copy Office or because a program keeps crashing."

"Do you think you could clone it or something? You'd need to do it right now."

"Where can we meet?"

"I'll come by your place in half an hour."

María Magdalena was holding the tablet. She hadn't tried switching it on but kept looking at it as though hoping to intuit its secrets. Verónica drove in silence back into the city.

"Shouldn't we just hand it over without trying to copy the content?" María Magdalena asked.

"That was what I thought to start with, but now I think it would be better for us to know where we stand. Otherwise we're groping in the dark, which is more dangerous."

They messaged La Sombra a few blocks before his house. When they arrived, he was already waiting at the door, knapsack on his shoulder. He climbed into the back seat and took a laptop out of the bag. María Magdalena passed him the tablet and he studied it for a few seconds, then turned it on and connected it to the computer. Verónica watched him out of the corner of her eye as she drove on with no particular destination. It seemed safer to drive than to stop somewhere. Although she couldn't see what her favourite hacker was doing, she pictured him as a master pianist playing his signature piece. There was a kind of magic in that work that elevated hacking to one of the fine arts. But great artists could also fail.

"Can't you see what's on the tablet?" Verónica asked, a wave of frustration washing over her.

"Give me a few minutes."

Verónica continued to drive in circles, as though operating a merry-go-round. María Magdalena phoned Corso a couple of times, and Federico too. Neither had any news for her. Verónica glanced at her phone, waiting for the kidnappers to call.

"How strange," said La Sombra, still at work on the tablet. "You told me it had a complicated security system."

Verónica glanced at him in the rear-view mirror. "That's what I was told."

"It doesn't seem complicated at all. If anything I'd say the encryption codes are quite basic. I mean, I'm already in."

"Then copy all the files, please."

"That's going to be difficult. There aren't any files."

Verónica slammed on the brakes in the middle of the avenue. The car behind only avoided hitting her because it had been keeping a sensible distance. Its driver honked and swore at her all the same as he passed their car, but Verónica was in no mood to respond.

"That can't be. There must be something. Whatever they're looking for, it must be there."

"There's nothing. I'm checking and there aren't even any deleted files. It's clean, as though they formatted the disk then encrypted it."

María Magdalena was the first to say what all three were thinking: "Viviana's given you a different tablet. This isn't the one they're looking for."

Verónica felt a bolt of terror, a fear that surged up from her stomach to her brain, blinding her. There was only one thought in her mind: *they're going to kill Paula*. She couldn't hold back her tears; she knew that, if she tried to speak, the words wouldn't come.

Then the phone rang. The criminals were calling again, this time from Paula's phone.

"Please don't do anything to her," Verónica managed to gasp. "I'll get the tablet for you."

But when she expected to hear the killer's voice, instead she heard crying. The tears of her friend Paula. The bastards had put her on the line so Verónica could hear her suffer.

"Paula?"

"It's me, Vero. Please come quickly."

She was speaking through tears, barely articulating the words. Her voice sounded thick, as though she were sleepy. Verónica was alarmed.

"Are you all right?"

"Yes, yes. They've left me here. I'm standing by the Puente La Noria, on the Provincia side."

"I don't understand," Verónica said to La Sombra and María Magdalena, who returned quizzical looks. María Magdalena took the phone out of her hand.

"Paula, it's me, María Magdalena. Are you on your own? Have the men gone? Listen, can you see any bars nearby? No, of course not, why would there be. A bus stop? OK, get to one of them, somewhere with people around. We'll pick you up in twenty minutes. Keep calm. If you're worried about anything, call us. We're on our way."

She ended the call and turned to Verónica.

"When I asked if there was a bar nearby, she swore at me and said she wasn't in Palermo. So at least she hasn't lost her sense of humour. Take a left down José María Moreno."

The nightmare was beginning to lift; all she had to do now was find Paula. But the bad dream wouldn't go away. Had Viviana really tricked them by providing a tablet with no data on it? Did the criminals know there was nothing on the device? Why go to all that trouble with a kidnapping charade? Why release Paula without a word about the tablet?

Verónica was driving faster than the speed limit, running the odd red light. María Magdalena had to ask her to calm down or let her drive. If only it were possible, Verónica would have teleported herself to the Puente La Noria, to where her friend was.

"These guys know there was nothing on the tablet," La Sombra said. "These guys already have all the information they need."

"Goicochea's laptop," María Magdalena murmured. "It must all be on that. They had what they needed all along. But then what the hell were they looking for?"

Verónica drove through an amber light, honking at a car to let her pass. She touched her forehead, sensing a fever coming on. That febrile state allowed her to see clearly what was happening. "The fucking bastards," she said, almost shouting. "They've used us, María Magdalena. They never wanted the tablet – they wanted to get to Viviana. They knew we could find her and they couldn't. The tablet was only ever an excuse. Call Pablo right away and warn him they're in danger. They need to get out of the house immediately."

María Magdalena dialled Pablo's number. "He's not answering," she said, voice shaking.

"I want to die," Verónica wailed, and felt that she was jumping straight from one nightmare to another, without ever waking up.

6   *The Gospel According to Verónica*

Here begins the Gospel of Verónica Rosenthal, journalist and daughter of Aarón and Miriam.

An early influence can be as nourishing to the soul as a well-roasted rib of beef is to the stomach. In both cases the experience is unforgettable. Something like this happened to Verónica in early infancy when she came across *A Child's Story of Jesus*, a full-colour illustrated volume on the life of Christ that combined the three synoptic Gospels with minimal theological rigour.

Verónica was five and had just started at the Escuela Argentina Modelo, a school that both her sisters Daniela and Leticia were already attending, with notable academic success. The same was expected of the youngest Rosenthal, and Verónica didn't disappoint. She was the best student in the year, perhaps because she had learned to read at four years old and liked looking through her older sisters' schoolbooks. It didn't take much more than that to stand out.

She had a little classmate who had fallen in love with her – whatever the concept of love might mean to a six-year-old. Verónica certainly didn't have much idea what it meant, and if anything found it a nuisance that the boy (what was he called? This kid had left their school the year after she joined, and she had forgotten his name) followed her everywhere at break time. She tried to get rid of him, a life skill she would hone in years to come.

At any rate, this little friend (Gabriel? Gustavo?) used to bring her presents: sweets, pencils, a notebook and, at the height of his affection, a book: *A Child's Story of Jesus,* published by Ediciones Paulinas, illustrations by Sister Ángeles (she always read this to mean that the drawings had been done by one of the angel's sisters, a baby with wings). Verónica accepted the gifts, but that didn't mean she was interested in the boy, who eventually ran out of ideas to win her attention. Although later he worked it out: stop paying her attention and focus on another, more friendly girl. The boy asked for his presents back and Verónica returned some of them and kept others, including the book.

As one accustomed to reading stories about travelling turtles, little lantern sellers and adorable dogs, this gospel for children was a revelation. She read and reread, until she knew them by heart, the simple sentences that told of such extraordinary events: the birth of Jesus, surrounded by animals; the visit of the Three Wise Men; Jesus's friendship with birds (one of the less rigorous episodes in this version, but Verónica would never know that); his struggle in the desert with the Devil (one of her favourite parts); the miracles through which he healed the sick and multiplied loaves of bread; his condemnation; his death on the Cross, and the final resurrection. Verónica suffered, rejoiced, wept and laughed for joy when Jesus rose from the dead.

It was lucky that nobody in those days asked her what she wanted to be when she grew up, because she would have answered without hesitation: Jesus. The idea of wandering the world preaching and performing miracles seemed so much better than wanting to be an astronaut, a teacher or a doctor.

If she hadn't grown up in a family of atheists, with little interest in ancient customs, perhaps Verónica would have spotted the contradiction between her own Judaism and her desire to be the leader of Christianity. Although she might have been quickly reassured to remember that Jesus was a Jew, like her, her parents and sisters.

She wouldn't have been the first Jew to convert to Christianity, nor the first child of atheists fervently to embrace religion. But something happened that made Verónica rethink her theological aspirations.

At the end of that same year, for some reason her parents signed her up for Zumerland, a Jewish summer camp, so that she could have fun, play sports, learn to swim and make friends, as her sisters were already doing. For both Daniela and Leticia, the presence of their seven-year-old sister was more of a nuisance than anything else, even though Verónica never cried or went running to her older sisters when she got thrown into the pool off the diving board.

Leticia and Daniela could get on with the semi-wild life the summer camp allowed without their little sister bothering them. But Verónica quickly came to detest the place. From then on and for the rest of her days, she would not make even the slightest attempt to lead a healthy or sporty life or to be in touch with nature. She would never go camping or hiking (although she did take a backpack on her first trip to Europe) and would never know the joy of singing folk songs around a campfire. And never, ever, did she regret what she did that summer in Zumerland, or the abrupt curtailing of a life filled with nature.

It wasn't that she hated physical activity or sports. What she hated above all else was the institutional aspect of camp life: now everyone has tea, now everyone runs and jumps, now everyone dives into the pool, now everyone is happy or sad because they won't see each other until next Monday.

That insistence on order, those emotions prefabricated by the camp counsellors, the submission of her peers – all these struck Verónica as detestable. And she made her resistance clear to the staff and the other children: she ran away from her group, wouldn't jump in the pool (but then went and jumped in with other groups), didn't learn the songs, refused to look happy like everyone else. Looking back at that time, Verónica couldn't help thinking that to the counsellors she must have been the closest thing possible to a demonic being: little sister to Linda Blair rather than to the charming Rosenthal sisters.

She couldn't remember how or under what circumstances she began to tell her friends at camp that she was a Christian. In a community of Jewish children like Zumerland, where the majority might not be very devout but were certainly conscious of their roots, that declaration sounded extraordinary; she might as well have claimed to be a Martian or from Vietnam.

Word quickly spread among the children. Some were intrigued, others mocked her, but all of them were interested, asking if Verónica was Christian (or Catholic, which came to the same thing). And she said that she was. She used the opportunity to talk to them about Jesus and his love for humanity, with a passion that would have moved the Venerable Bede or Cura Brochero, the "Gaucho priest", to tears.

Verónica may have detested the regimented life at Zumerland, but she enjoyed having become the centre of attention and started attending camp with much more enthusiasm. However, her friends' curiosity about the life and passion of the Nazarene was never going to last long, and gradually they lost interest in Verónica, seeing her simply as an exotic being who had misunderstood the virtues of the Jewish religion.

She wasn't going to give up so easily. What she needed was to soup up her Christian stories. Verónica's brainwave was to tell the other children she could perform miracles.

At the age of six or seven nothing seems impossible. Most of the children believed her and, if some did express doubts, they were prepared to lay these to one side if she could demonstrate her powers. Verónica accepted the challenge.

I I

The first miracle was an ingenious imitation of the one performed by Jesus at the wedding at Cana. Just as the son of Mary converted water into wine, so the daughter of Miriam turned a bottle of Sprite into chocolate milk. She poured out some of the lemonade and added mud to the bottle. Then she put on the lid and shook the bottle well, so the damp soil mixed with the liquid. The group of children gathered around her waited expectantly. Verónica passed the bottle to one of them: when he opened it, thanks to all the shaking, the contents exploded over the boy's face and clothes and the shock made him throw the bottle on the ground. Consequently, few children were able to taste the miraculous liquid. Some agreed that it tasted like chocolate milk, and others, the usual unbelievers, said it tasted like sweetened mud.

Three children refused to believe that a miracle had taken place: a blonde boy with green eyes, a dark-skinned boy with unruly hair, and a girl with brown curls and freckles, called Carolina.

The second miracle was the multiplication of bread and fish. Verónica asked her camp mates to place something they loved in her lunchbox. One boy put in a soccer card from the 1986 World Cup; a girl put in a strawberry Aventura cookie. Verónica told the other children that the next day they would see that the card and the cookie had been multiplied. She had to steal money from her mother and ask Ramira to take her to the kiosk. There she bought two packets of cards and one of Aventura cookies. She opened both packets and added the contents to her lunchbox. The next day Verónica opened her lunchbox in front of an enthralled audience. Someone objected that the original Aventura cookies had been strawberry-flavoured and now they were chocolate. Verónica laughed off the sceptics (there were only two: the dishevelled, dark-skinned boy and freckly Carolina), and those who could now consider themselves her followers did the same. Religions have been born out of less.

The third miracle was not instigated by Verónica but requested by one of her followers. Verónica was asked to cure one of the boys (coincidentally the green-eyed blond, one of the early doubters), who wasn't feeling well. He was coughing and seemed to have a fever. She walked towards the boy, touched his head, murmured a prayer (invented on the spot, since she didn't know any) and blew on his eyes. "There, you're cured," she told him encouragingly.

To be fair, the boy did make an effort to seem well although, seconds after one of the camp counsellors came looking for him (because his parents had arrived to take him home), he collapsed. Since the other children had seen how the boy had made an effort to seem well, and not witnessed the subsequent collapse, they judged the miracle to be authentic. All of them apart from one: Carolina.

Verónica knew that in this girl, only a little younger than herself, she had a fearsome adversary. She would have to pull out all the stops to convince this sceptic. That was when she decided to perform her most spectacular miracle yet.

The *Child's Story of Jesus* wasn't altogether rigorous, either in historical terms (Christianity has always been vague about the details) or even when it came to the most accepted gospels. One of the miracles it related described how Jesus, as a boy, found a dove that couldn't fly, held it in his hands and threw it up towards the heavens. The dove swooped across the sky of Galilee, before the astonished eyes of some children watching below. Neither Matthew, Luke nor Mark describes miracles in Jesus's childhood, and these are only found in one of the Gospels that is wrongly considered apocryphal.

As on previous days, Verónica was surrounded by the other children from her group. First, she made a gesture of benediction. Then she turned to Carolina, the unbeliever, who was giving her a funny look (it would take years for Verónica to identify this expression as scepticism), and said: "If I want, I can make you fly."

There was a collective murmur of surprise, admiration and expectation such as Jesus may never have experienced during the three years of His ministry. Carolina, disconcerted, took some time to react. Finally she managed to say: "I don't believe you."

"Believe. Do you want to fly? I can make you fly."

"Make *me*, make *me!*" cried some of the acolytes, but neither Verónica nor Carolina paid them any attention. This was a duel between the two of them.

"OK, go on then," said Freckle Face.

They walked towards some trees in the garden. The children accompanied them in silence, as though conscious of experiencing an epic event in their short lives. They reached an old poplar tree that was throwing generous shade.

"Climb up," Verónica instructed Carolina.

The tree's lowest branches began some distance above the children's heads. They had to form a human pyramid to raise the little girl high enough. If Verónica's messianic ambitions had been more modest, she might have been pleased enough by that human structure of children standing on one another's shoulders. It was a pretty good miracle for a group that had never before come together in such a formation. But Verónica wasn't in the mood to settle for less. Carolina climbed on her fellows' shoulders and reached the lowest branch.

"Higher," Verónica ordered.

With difficulty, the girl climbed from one branch to another until she reached a considerable height. The children all looked up at Carolina and the cloud-filled sky. Verónica, standing at the centre of a circle of children, was overseeing everything. She raised her arms towards the sky, proclaimed another false prayer in an invented language (telling her classmates it was Aramaic) and stared at Carolina.

"Jump."

The girl didn't understand. "What do you mean, jump?"

"Jump as though you were jumping into a pool, and flap your arms like a bird."

Carolina hesitated, but Verónica fixed her with those feverish eyes and with such authority that the little girl wanted to believe her. She launched herself into the void, flapping her arms like a dove. But she was a girl, not a dove.

The fall was quick. If Verónica hadn't got out of the way, Carolina would have landed on top of her and crushed her. That lucky escape was in itself miraculous, but nobody else seemed to see it that way. Carolina hit the ground hard, and painfully. She screamed, but only briefly, because once on the ground she lay motionless, as though dead. That was when the other children began to scream and cry. Tentatively, Verónica approached Carolina, who was bleeding from the mouth. She didn't even dare pretend to resuscitate her, like Lazarus.

IV

Verónica's short career as a messiah ended that afternoon, with Carolina's fractured ribs, three lost milk teeth and a broken arm. Plus a lot of frightened children who wanted never to return to Zumerland, for fear of running into Verónica.

The camp directors spoke to her parents. Aarón and Miriam also had to meet Carolina's parents. Guiltily, and with great embarrassment, they begged forgiveness on their daughter's behalf. They took charge of all the hospital expenses and threw in a couple of Barbies the little girl wanted. At camp, the consensus was that it would be difficult to allow Verónica back into the group. The children were badly shaken, including the ones who hadn't witnessed Carolina's fall, because the tale had spread quickly through camp. They fervently recommended that Aarón and Miriam send their youngest daughter to a child psychologist.

For days the couple debated what to do with Verónica. At times they were persuaded that this had been a childish prank that got out of hand. Like the time Daniela and Leticia cut Verónica's hair when she was two years old. At other times they were alarmed by this mystical delusion about being Christian. Because it was one thing to come from an atheist family and another to renege on Judaism at the age of six or seven. Something was wrong with the girl. They briefly considered consulting a cousin who was a rabbi, then decided against it.

While Aarón would hear no talk of child psychologists, Miriam was more willing to believe that might be the solution, and a mother's opinion counts for double. They had already asked for an appointment with Dr Cohen (by a remarkable coincidence, her son would many years later become Federico's therapist) when Grandma Esther, Miriam's mother, appeared on the scene. And a bubbe's opinion is worth double a mother's.

"What the child needs is peace, good food and the love of her grandparents."

And that was how Verónica stopped going to summer camp (to the delight of her sisters and of many of the other children and their parents) and started spending her afternoons with her grandparents, Esther and Elías. The *Child's Story of Jesus* was thrown in the trash. Soon she would forget the stories she had read, retaining only a vague memory of the drawings and of Jesus's fight with the Devil. But before abandoning her brief flirtation with Christianity, Verónica couldn't help thinking that a miracle must have occurred for her to have been taken out of that dreadful place and brought to the closest thing to Paradise she could imagine: her maternal grandparents' house.

7   *The Stele of the Vultures*

I

Not much time passed, an hour at most, between Verónica and Paula's reunion on the Puente La Noria and the discovery of Viviana's body, with two fatal bullet wounds, in the house at Quilmes. The fact that her partner Pablo wasn't with her suggested that he had been able to escape. Viviana's murder had been the work of a professional: clean, quick and effective, with no collateral damage and not a trace left behind.

Paula was unharmed, despite the trauma of having been kept captive for eight hours. As they drove towards the bridge, Verónica had spotted her from some distance away, standing next to a tree, gazing into the distance. A few yards before reaching her, Verónica hit the brakes and rushed out to hug her friend. The two women wept together for a good while, to the surprise of passers-by, who had no idea what they were witnessing. La Sombra and María Magdalena also got out of the car and watched the scene.

When she managed to stop crying, Verónica asked for forgiveness. She felt responsible for what had happened to her friend. Paula swore at her a bit, but when she saw how badly Verónica was taking it, she changed her tone and explained that, although physically terrified, she had been treated with respect.

"I thought they were going to kill me. In the movies, when kidnappers let you see their faces it's because they're going to kill you."

"Oh, Paula, I'm so sorry."

"It wasn't your fault. If anything, it's my fault for having you as a friend."

Verónica looked set to start crying again. Paula smiled at her.

"It could have been worse – the kidnapper looked like Maluma."

Reconstructing events later on, Paula clarified that there had been at least two men, but only one who communicated with her (the one who looked like Colombian rapper Maluma) and that he had constantly tried to reassure her. Paula hadn't even known her life depended on the location of a tablet.

Verónica wanted to take her back to Federico's apartment, but Paula said no, because her ex would be bringing their son over soon and she wanted to be at home waiting for him. "I'll have a bath, drink a beer and put on a Fabi Cantilo LP. That's all I need. Maybe I'll order a pizza too."

Once everyone had agreed that this was a safe option, Verónica took Paula home, where, as they were saying goodbye, her friend reminded her of the other worry.

"Decide quickly what you're going to do. You've still got time, but the sooner you make a decision the better."

"I've got other problems right now."

"Don't pretend this isn't happening. Oh, and talk to Fede."

News of Viviana's death had reached them thanks, as ever, to the efforts of Rodolfo Corso.

Verónica felt lost, like a punch-drunk boxer staring into the corner of the ring, unsure how to defend herself, let alone go on the attack. But at least María Magdalena was in her corner.

"Let La Sombra take the tablet away and analyse it while we meet up with Rodo and decide what to do next."

"I should go to the newsroom."

"Meeting first, then you can go there."

Vero agreed; she trusted María Magdalena completely. Meanwhile, her brain was trying to make connections between the two deaths, Paula's kidnapping, the tablet, the investigation Goicochea had been carrying out and the evident sophistication of the murderers. Everything seemed so opaque. She needed to find a way in, to start bringing transparency.

11

Federico showered and, once Verónica had confirmed Paula was OK, put on a suit and set off for the office. He hadn't slept all night. The previous day, when he had met Rosenthal and the other lawyers to talk about how they should handle Mayer, seemed like ages ago. He needed to get back into his normal work routine, not let himself be dragged off course by Verónica and her problems.

First thing that morning he had called the office to let them know he had a few appointments and so might not be coming into work, something that wasn't unusual, especially if no meeting was scheduled with Aarón. And he had spent the rest of the morning looking into Viviana Smith and trying to work out who might have kidnapped Paula, without managing to get any further than what they already knew. He had also taken care of more practical matters, like sending a tow truck to Posadas Hospital to pick up Paula's car and take it to be repaired by a mechanic he knew and trusted. Her insurance would probably cover a large part of the cost, but he could hardly get Verónica to ask the kidnappers for the insurance details Paula must have had on her. Verónica would pay for the repairs out of her savings. Or he would. Their respective finances were delicately poised between separate and joint. That wasn't something he worried about, so long as Verónica didn't decide to bring down a plane or buy a missile to take out one of her enemies (neither scenario struck him as entirely impossible). But he could cover the cost of the car with his salary, bonus and earnings from Rosenthal and Associates.

There were also some WhatsApp messages on his phone from Ángeles. Those messages with emojis that he found hard to decipher once there were more than three or four. Humanity had taken centuries to evolve beyond the pictographic stage of writing, only for new generations to ditch the clarity of the Latin alphabet in favour of a little squinty face and some renditions of fire that were open to interpretation. He didn't answer any of those messages and simply deleted them, as he tended to do with any personal WhatsApps from Ángeles. She must have registered his silence, because after ten o'clock that morning she had sent only messages referring to the visit she and Diana Veglio would shortly be paying to Mayer's ex-wife.

Federico was about to leave for the office when he got a call from a law clerk he knew, a young guy like himself with whom he had a friendly arrangement built on the exchange of inside information and small judicial favours. His father was a retired career diplomat, and for that reason Federico had written to him asking about Viviana Smith.

"I spoke to my dad," the man said. "He knows the woman. Came across her when he was the ambassador in Panama. Sometime around 1995, 1996 or thereabouts. She wasn't yet working for the Ministry of Foreign Affairs but for an international organization, he doesn't remember which. She asked to meet him because she wanted to blow the whistle on some Argentine officials who were using Panama as a stopover between money-laundering trips."

"Panama was already a tax haven."

"Could be, I don't know. What my father said was that there were fewer controls. You didn't have to open an account and make a bank transfer like nowadays, the money changed hands in suitcases. According to her allegation, the money went from Panama to Europe or the United States."

"So what happened?"

"I'll tell you my dad's version. I trust that it's the truth, but I wouldn't put my hand in the fire. According to him, there was a low-profile investigation, the officials were removed without any media hoopla, and he carried on as before. Viviana left Panama sometime after that, and he lost track of her."

"Could there still be people around who took umbrage at Viviana's allegations?"

"I don't think so. From what I could find out, those officials were transferred to other public roles. They were small fry. Nobody came out of it badly damaged."

Federico thanked him for this information, and they agreed to have lunch the following week at the Palacio de la Papa Frita.

The story his friend had told him wasn't all that useful, except to confirm that Viviana was a woman who liked to probe and call out wrongdoing. On that occasion her whistle-blowing had no serious consequences. This time, though, she had got mixed up with serious criminals and paid for it with her life. Federico thought of calling Verónica to fill her in, then he saw he had a message from Ángeles.

We've just come out of the meeting with the ex. More questions than answers. She struck me as quite sinister. She's not going to make things easy for us.

First answer Ángeles's WhatsApp, then call Verónica. Be careful to avoid mix-ups, be as discreet as possible. The stress of having, on one side, a lover who was sweet and attentive to everything that happened to him and, on the other, a partner who was distracted when it came to personal stuff but extremely quick to pick up on signs that something was wrong, was making him old before his time.

III

María Magdalena, Rodolfo and Verónica met in Barcelona Asturias, an old-school bar on Avenida Córdoba, close to the *Nuestro Tiempo* offices. Over beer and some ham and cheese sandwiches, they looked at the material they had gathered so far.

"There are two related questions or mysteries we need to resolve," said Verónica. "On one hand, what Goicochea was investigating and what he had discovered. On the other, who murdered him and Viviana."

The waiter brought over another bottle of beer, ordered by Rodolfo, who picked up where Verónica had left off.

"I'd add a third question, one I'd venture to say might be the most troubling at this point: are they thinking of killing more people? We thought Goicochea was the target, but then they went and killed Viviana too. Will there be a third death?"

María Magdalena brushed crumbs off her hands before speaking. "What strikes me is that, although they are willing to kill, they have also let people live. Patricia first, then Paula and finally Pablo."

"Three names beginning with *P*," said Rodolfo, pouring out the second bottle of beer.

"That's a line of enquiry we should quickly drop," said Verónica, while texting Paula to ask if she was all right.

"They're clearly professional assassins," said Rodolfo. "They have a plan, and they execute it. They're not a bunch of desperate lunatics. In fact, I'd say they show remarkable sangfroid."

Verónica laid out what they knew about the first two murders. It was enough material for a preliminary piece, which could be published in the next edition of *Nuestro Tiempo*. All three were stricken by sadness: they were planning this work with no input from their editor. Patricia should have been the one calling the shots and handing out assignments.

"Just as well Patricia isn't here," said Rodolfo, "or she'd be pushing us to look into all the recent attacks on journalists in Argentina. Let's do things our way until the boss gets back and whips us into line."

Verónica left the others having coffee and walked over to *Nuestro Tiempo*, hoping to arrive in time for the editors' meeting. She may no longer have been an assistant editor – she'd given up that role long ago – but figured she could sit in, given the notable absence of her boss.

An air of tension and grief hung heavy in the newsroom. Barely had she set foot in the office when the administrative staff and journalists, all desperate for news of Patricia and knowing how close Verónica was to her, started peppering her with questions. She tried to reassure everyone by saying Patricia was well and out of danger, but she didn't go into details. She wanted to get to the meeting, which had already begun.

As she walked towards the glass-walled meeting room affectionately known as the fishbowl, Verónica gestured to be allowed in and Álex Vilna, the managing editor, nodded. Tantanian wasn't there. Even on a day like this, their editor-in-chief saw no reason to drop by the office. He must be making shady deals over in Palermo Hollywood.

The deputy editors, on the other hand, were there, along with all the section editors, various subeditors, the assistant editor from Society, Eugenia Pérez, who was heading up the section in Patricia's absence, the Art and Photography directors. An unusually well-attended editorial meeting.

"Speak of the devil… come on in, Verónica," said Vilna, leading the discussion. "As you can imagine, everyone's feeling distraught about the death of Andrés and the attack on Patricia. We're fielding calls from all over the media, and there's a great appetite to know what we're going to run with."

"I have an overview of the events I can share," said Verónica, perching on a side table for lack of a chair.

"Good, good. Before we get to that, I just mentioned you to Carlos, who wants to ask you something."

The art director nodded and said, "Do you happen to have a photo of Patricia?"

Verónica was taken aback, not understanding the question.

"Yes, a photo," the art director added tautologically. "To put in the magazine. All the ones we have are poor quality. Have you got any of your own?"

"I… don't tend to take photos."

"What about Andrés?" Vilna asked. "We've got some of him, but we're going to need more."

"No… I'm afraid I don't."

"There are some of Goicochea from last year that were taken for an article in a Rosario newspaper," offered the head of Photography.

"Ones we have to pay for?" asked Vilna.

"Well… the photographer might like to get paid."

"Forget it then."

"Listen, Álex," Verónica interrupted, "I want to write about what happened."

"Yes, I already thought of you. We're going to devote the cover to Andrés. How ironic to think he must have planned cover stories in this very office without ever imagining he was going to be one himself."

"I think that's a good idea," said Verónica.

"The current headline is 'Farewell to the Maestro'. We're giving him eight pages. The main piece will be about his career, we'll put in a few sidebars, some opinion pieces. Even Mayer has asked to write a column. Eugenia, get someone to record him, write the column and send it to him for sign-off."

The assistant editor at Society made a note of this instruction.

"I imagine there'll be a piece about the circumstances of his death," said Verónica. "I'd like to write that."

"I thought you could write something about Patricia."

"Yes, of course, I can do that too. After all, the murder and the attack on Patricia are connected."

"I'd prefer you to try a different tack. I'd like an intimate piece on what it's like to work with Patricia, throwing in some personal details about her family life, her children. Something colourful, witty, to compensate for the sadness of the first pages."

Verónica looked around her colleagues, seeking allies to challenge the stupidity of the managing editor, but nobody met her eye.

"If you want the truth, that sounds like bullshit. Who's going to write about the actual attack?"

"Eugenia, are you doing that, or are you commissioning someone else?"

"No, I'm doing it. I've already spoken to the head of the operation, one Superintendent Giménez. He gave me figures for the number of armed crimes in the West Zone. Robbery, breaking and entering – it's hair-raising."

Verónica turned to look at the woman who was now her direct boss. "Listen, Euge, this thing with Goicochea wasn't an attempted robbery. People went there to murder him. He was chasing a story and it got him killed. They stole the computer with the details of his investigation on it."

"I love a good conspiracy theory," said Vilna, "but we're about journalism. Hard facts, not fever dreams. If the head of operations says this was a robbery followed by a murder, that's what we're going with."

Verónica straightened up and placed her hands on the shoulders of one of the assistant editors, as though to focus better on Vilna. The assistant editor didn't dare move, or make any gesture.

"Are you fucking kidding me? I've been working on this all day with Corso and María Magdalena."

"Uff, those pals of yours Patricia brought in."

"I don't know if you're aware that Goicochea's ex-wife, Viviana, has also been found dead? We have proof that the two deaths are linked."

"We're well aware of the dangers that come with living in Greater Buenos Aires. That's the line we're taking. If you don't like it, you can write that piece on the Tinder app for famous people."

"Listen, you little piece of shit —" began Verónica, squeezing her colleague's shoulders with all her might.

"Stop, Verónica," said Paco Gutiérrez, the Politics editor. "Let's step outside for a moment."

"Yes, off you go. This is a meeting for section heads," said Vilna, his face reddening.

Verónica went outside with Gutiérrez, the oldest journalist on the magazine, a calm and honest man. If not for him, Verónica would have launched herself on Vilna and ripped out his tongue with the tip of a Uniball.

"Verónica, calm down, this won't get you anywhere."

"But the guy's full of shit."

"He's a guard dog, growling to protect his owners. Or do you think he was the one who came up with the idea of framing Andrés's death as just another violent crime? It was an order that came from the top."

"Paco, Andrés was killed by a mafia. I don't know which, but I have no doubt they killed him because of what he was investigating."

"You won't get Vilna to change what he already has planned."

Right then the woman from reception came to tell Verónica she was wanted in Human Resources.

Gutiérrez added one more observation: "It's a small comfort to know that my friend Andrés wasn't killed by a petty thief but because he took risks as a journalist."

Verónica walked over to the office of Vidal, head of Human Resources.

"Looks like you're in trouble," Vidal said as soon as he saw her. "Álex says you went too far and wants you suspended for three days."

"How many days off do I have left?"

Her response threw Vidal. He looked up this information on his computer. "You've got five in total this year."

"OK, I'll take them all after the suspension ends."

"That has to be authorized and signed off by your boss."

"My boss is in hospital. Send her the papers and I'm sure she'll sign them, don't worry about that. If I call you a slimy toad, will you add on a few more days of suspension? If I go back to the fishbowl and punch that son of a bitch Vilna, could you sort me a whole week without pay?"

Vidal looked at her without smiling. "Just go, before you make things worse."

Verónica made to leave but, before walking out of the office, she yelled back towards the fishbowl: "You monkey's ball sack, you bunch of turds! Cowards!" She smashed through the door, stepped straight into the elevator, which seemed to be waiting for her, and burst into tears as it descended. Now she was furious with herself for crying, on top of everything else. She wouldn't usually react like this. It was her fucking mixed-up hormones that had made her cry when what she actually wanted to do was smash Vilna's stupid head against the glass wall of the fishbowl.

IV

For more than two hours, five lawyers were gathered in Federico's office poring over the various cases in which their client Sergio Mayer was involved. Antonio Rivadavia started by explaining the details of the real estate case. The construction of a luxury gated community on land with protected flora and fauna had been halted owing to complaints from an ecological association, Cuidar. This was no minor green group, nor a little band of indignant ecologists, but an NGO with international heft that had already won several disputes in other Latin American countries and in Spain. Not even Greenpeace could claim such resounding victories. The Argentine branch of Cuidar relied on the support of businesspeople who wanted to demonstrate their green credentials – so long as that didn't interfere with their work – as well as prominent celebrities, artists and professionals.

According to Rivadavia, Cuidar had so far managed to prevent building permits being granted. But part of the land on which construction was planned lay outside the environmental protection area, so Rivadavia proposed dividing the project in two: advancing in the zone where there were no

116

legal problems, to strike an early blow against Cuidar. That would have a large and favourable media impact. At the same time they should exert pressure to redesignate the site for business purposes. The biggest difficulty was that the land extended across two municipalities. They could start with the one where the local legislature would be more amenable and open to making the necessary changes. Then they could move on to the other municipality, which was in principle less inclined to make the same changes, for fear of a backlash from local residents. In order to win them over they needed an initial victory in the courts and to show that the changes approved in the first municipality had not had serious collateral consequences.

Federico listened carefully to Rivadavia's presentation. The situation didn't seem so bad, nothing that couldn't be resolved with a little time, a little guile and a lot of money. The Rosenthal team had enough of all three to carry the day for Sergio Mayer.

The divorce suit, on the other hand, looked more complicated. The proposal put forward by Diana Veglio and Ángeles hadn't gone down well with Roxana Mayer, the ex-wife.

"As agreed, we made her an offer far in excess of fifty per cent of Mayer's declared assets," Diana explained. "That includes not only property but also foreign bank accounts, shares in various companies and trusts, as well as cars, a yacht and a monthly annuity in dollars for her."

"Surely she can't ask for more than that," said Federico, pressing the point of his pen too hard against the paper on which he was making notes.

"Roxana Mayer wants a fifty-one per cent stake in the security firm Tuentur. That percentage would obviously give her control of the company, of which she is currently vice-president."

"Tuentur makes that much profit?"

"It makes a lot," said Diana, "but not as much as other Mayer companies."

"And what does Mayer say about this counter-demand?"

"He says no, it's not up for discussion."

"Clearly," added Ángeles, "that business has an important symbolic value for both of them. They started it together twelve years ago, not long after they first became a couple."

"It looks like there are no other Mayer assets Roxana would be happy to take instead."

"None."

"What about threatening that, if the divorce goes to court, she'll very likely get much less than what we're offering now?"

"I told her that, but she laughed. She knows Mayer doesn't want things to go that far. But," said Diana, stretching out this last word, "there is one way we can keep the negotiation open. I'll let Ángeles explain, because she deserves all the credit for this."

Ángeles blushed, then smiled to demonstrate that she could handle the situation.

"We were sitting in the living room of her house, and there were various books on a coffee table. One caught my eye because it had no writing on the cover, just a picture. I said, absent-mindedly, '*The Stele of the Eannatum Vultures*', while she was serving us a second cup of tea." Ángeles, her blush deepening, explained: "I'm good at remembering weird names," then continued her story. "Roxana looked at me, surprised."

"As did I," said Diana. "I thought she was distracting Roxana instead of focussing on the matter at hand."

"Roxana asked me how I knew the image. I told her that I had always been interested in Sumerian culture, especially in its spiritual dimension."

"Who knew we had a theologian in our midst!" exclaimed Rivadavia, with a little irony but more admiration.

"To be clear, I don't know anything about Mesopotamian cultures, but my older sister, who lives in Switzerland, is into all kinds of spiritual matters, meditation, yoga et cetera. For a few years she's been involved with a group called Orígenes – I don't know if you know it?"

"Isn't it a pension fund?"

"No, Orígenes is a community that reveres the Mesopotamian gods. It's the oldest known ancient religion, its roots go back to prehistoric times. Orígenes developed a system of meditation that to me doesn't seem all that different from all the others, but they claim it is. Last vacation I was at my sister's house in Switzerland and read several books on the subject. That's how I recognized the reproduction of that bas-relief from Lagash. I decided to lie to Roxana and tell her I was an admirer of the Sumerians."

"Well played," said Federico.

"So Roxana invited me to go round some time and talk about the Mesopotamian gods, and she also said she could take me to meditation group meetings. Of course, I said yes."

"Is it a cult?"

"From what I know, I'd say they have a cult mentality, but their behaviour is more like what you'd find in a meditation school. They aren't dangerous."

"Ángeles, if you have to fall into a cult to get that woman to sign the papers, don't think twice. Afterwards we'll kidnap you back and deprogramme you."

The meeting ended on a cheerful note. Diana was first to leave, and the others went to their offices. Ángeles left a little piece of rolled-up paper for Federico that called to mind the Dead Sea scrolls, perhaps because he was still thinking of their last conversation. He waited until he was alone to open it. The note said simply: *Finish what you started. I'll wait for you in the apartment after work. 7 p.m.*

Federico tore the note into tiny pieces. Once the letters were no longer legible, he threw the pieces into the waste-paper basket.

V

Verónica stormed out into the street, not sure where she was heading. She had gone more than a day without sleeping and felt not only physically but mentally exhausted, as though her brain had decided to stop thinking. She got into her car, which had been parked outside a supermarket, and drove to the apartment. The priority was to sleep, even if only for a few hours.

Before setting off, she called Atilio, Patricia's husband, who reported that her boss was better and would within hours be transferred to Sanatorio Mitre, in central Buenos Aires. Verónica should definitely be able to visit her there the next day.

At the first red light Verónica sent a voice message to the WhatsApp group she shared with Rodolfo and María Magdalena, telling them about everything that had happened in the newsroom. Surprised and tearful emojis from Rodolfo, a furious GIF from María Magdalena. She had come to expect such things.

Verónica got home, played with Chicha for a bit, drank a glass of cold water and got into the shower. For nearly half an hour she stood under the water, until she felt her fingers wrinkling and her body begging for a change of position. Then she wrapped herself in a big towel and jumped onto the bed. She breathed in the scent of the sheets and bedspread and immediately fell asleep. It was like falling into a black, silent well, from which she only emerged once she began to feel cold. Wrapping herself up in a damp towel hadn't been a good idea – better to get into bed. Far off, she could hear the continuous croaking of a frog: it was her phone, which she'd left in her bag. Who was sending so many messages? Despite her exhaustion, Verónica went to get the phone, intending to get back into bed as soon as possible and to cover herself with the sheet and bedspread. The messages were from her friends' WhatsApp group.

Pili, her Spanish friend, was proposing a drink at Martataka after work. Vale and Marian accepted immediately and gave various reasons why they urgently needed a drink, from shitty bosses and infuriating partners to filling time before the cinema. It occurred to Verónica that she had unimpeachable reasons to go for a drink with her friends, including pregnancy, death and guilt over her part in the kidnapping of Paula. She didn't just need a drink but a whole Uco Valley winery; all the Jim Beam warehouses in Tennessee; a Scottish archipelago to herself. But she couldn't contemplate going out with friends while Paula was still trying to absorb what had happened to her the night before. Better to stay at home and sleep as much as she could.

A few seconds later a message from Paula popped up in the chat: *I need a beer transfusion. What time shall we meet?*

Which meant that Verónica could add underneath: *I'm in. See you there.*

And that exchange set off a chain of emojis, which she hated and never sent, except to Federico, who hated them even more than her – one of those happy coincidences Verónica had at some point confused with divine confirmation that they were made for each other. So every now and then she sent Fede a horrible little smiley face, an ugly fist with its thumb pointing up or that stupid image of a girl shrugging.

Federico: she hadn't seen him since going out that morning in search of the tablet. A feeling similar to grief, but not quite grief, settled in her chest. She wanted to see him, to be with him, to spend time together without worries or problems. She decided to come home early tonight and stay in with him. She sent him a quick message outlining her plans for the next few hours, to which he responded with a terse *OK*. He must be up to his eyeballs at Rosenthal and Associates, but he could at least try to muster a cheerful reply. So, by way of revenge, she sent him a thumbs-up emoji.

Her friends were already at Martataka when Verónica arrived. The music, as usual, was turned up higher than she would have liked, but luckily they were playing a Virus song, and that immediately raised her spirits; it was exactly what she needed on a night out with the girls. Not many of the tables were occupied, so there wasn't much of a nightclub vibe yet. As she gave each of her friends a kiss on the cheek, Valeria was telling them all how her mother-in-law kept interfering in her life.

Before even sitting down, Verónica chided Valeria: "You're feeding a stereotype about mothers-in-law. I thought we had got past that stage in history."

"Hello, twenty-first century," said Marian, in support.

"Well, wait until Federico's mother starts going through your underwear."

"Is that what Gonza's mother does?"

"No, it's only an example."

Verónica and Paula greeted one another as though they had not just lived through a night of terror. Although they hadn't explicitly agreed on this strategy, neither was inclined to tell the others about what had happened. Better stick to less tragic subjects, like evil mothers-in-law and oedipal boyfriends.

The waitress came over to take the new arrivals' orders. Marian asked for a glass of red wine.

"Bring the bottle," Verónica instructed the waitress. She could sense Paula's quizzical gaze. "Yes, I do plan to drink all the alcohol in the world. Is that a problem?"

"Far from it. I'm all in favour of you getting drunk."

"Paulita, it would be strange for Vero not to leave a bar like a well-soaked sponge," said Pili, sipping her mojito.

They had also requested a sharing board, not Martataka's strong point, so they weren't expecting much from the salamis, cheeses and fries, which were notable less for their quality than their paucity. Somewhere along the line Vero must have lost the conversational thread, because when she started paying attention again, Pili was describing how a choreographer had sent her a video of himself jerking off. There were exclamations of disgust, disbelief and surprise.

"But aren't all choreographers gay?" Marian asked.

"A few are bisexual," Valeria noted, seriously.

"This one is heterosexual. Complete with wife and two kiddies."

"How come he sent you the video?"

Verónica drank deeply from her glass. It was her first encounter with alcohol since learning she was pregnant. She needed this.

"You didn't send him one of you, did you?"

"Paulita, if I had sent him a video of me I'd have said, *Girls, I'm swapping nudes with a fucking amazing choreographer*, because the guy *is* a great choreographer. No, I didn't send him anything. He told me I turned him on. Perhaps I did say something a bit suggestive. I was so bored, you know how I hate waiting at the dentist."

"That dentist's a pervert too."

"That's irrelevant. The guy, out of the blue, sends me a video of him fiddling with his dick, first tediously slow, then faster."

"Horrible, horrible."

"While making some really strange, not at all sexy noises. Ugh, none of it was sexy, not the place, not the body, not anything."

"The guy's depraved. You have to report him."

"And did you write anything back?"

"Immediately. I wrote: *Next time try sticking your dick up your own ass, you prick.* And then I blocked him."

"And that's how it ended?"

"Everything ends in this world, darling. Or were you asking if he came? Yes, but I've seen better climaxes, in real life and on video."

Verónica watched Paula, who seemed to be taking Pili's story seriously as she sipped her drink. She wouldn't be surprised if her friend was acting that way to show that she was fine, that the kidnapping was a bad memory with no after-effects. She was probably overcompensating, and perhaps that night she would have nightmares, but at least some kind of healing had begun with this gathering of friends. It was as if this nonsensical conversation were a continuation of the one they had started in that horrible Mexican restaurant, and none of the intervening events had ever happened. Verónica also noticed the pressure in her chest diminishing. Her body was still on high alert, awake to what she needed to fix in her personal life and find out in her professional life. That was stressful, although the wine coursing through her body worked like an instant massage.

VI

The secret with potatoes was to boil them first (after peeling and slicing them) and then fry them in butter, so they were crunchy on the outside and very tasty. The perfect accompaniment to the fillet with Roquefort he was making for dinner. Federico had managed to get some nice sole from his trusted fish seller. They were already closing and pulling down the shutter when he arrived, so he'd had to beg to be served and, since they recognized him, they had relented. He had asked for the sole and a handful of prawns, which he could fry up in garlic one of these nights, like his mother used to. Unfortunately he hadn't been able to find any authentic Roquefort in the supermarket. The Argentine versions tasted of nothing, and the two French brands were out of stock. Luckily, he found a Danish blue cheese that reminded him of the Argentine one he used to have as a child; it had that strong, spicy taste he loved.

Verónica also liked Roquefort and any pungent cheese, like Camembert or Reblochon. Federico knew no other woman capable of eating Reblochon like a piece of Quartirolo, and that robust love of cheese, so similar to his own, was one of her many charms.

Federico had had to do this shopping at the last minute. When Verónica texted in the afternoon to say she would be home in time for dinner (which for her was always after ten), he had decided to cook something. They could have ordered takeout, or picked up a rotisserie chicken on the way home, but that night Federico wanted to cook, if for no other reason than to prove to himself that the affair with Ángeles hadn't affected his routine with Verónica. If he had gone straight from work to the apartment, he would definitely have cooked, which meant that now he had to do it. It was a stupid and irrational way of trying to manage the guilt that came with infidelity.

He had gone to Ángeles' house knowing he couldn't stay too long; he wanted to get home before Verónica, to be waiting for her with food in the oven, an open bottle of wine and a board of sliced cheese and salami.

This time, Ángeles had been in her office clothes. Since she had left work some time before him, if she hadn't changed it must be because she wanted to create a kind of continuity between the workplace and fucking. As though they were doing it on her desk, or in one of the bathroom stalls.

That, at least, would have been Dr Cohen's interpretation. His old therapist was still messing with Federico's head. He should try harder to forget him.

The apartment looked the same as it had the night before, except that the bed was made. Ángeles was a tidy person, someone who even straightened out the bath mat.

"Do you want a beer?"

Federico accepted while making quick calculations in his head: how long it would take them to fuck, to cuddle, to chat for a while and then move swiftly on to goodbyes without her suspecting that he was in a rush to get to the supermarket before it closed. He was unused to the world of infidelity, and it surprised Federico how much more careful he was to shield Ángeles from suspicions about his evident married life with Verónica than he was to make sure Verónica didn't think he was seeing someone else. If someone had woken him in the middle of the night and asked him whom he was deceiving with whom, his instinct would have been to say: "Ángeles, with Verónica."

Ángeles also appeared to be in a rush, although clearly not for the same reasons as him. After a few glugs of beer in the kitchen, she walked over to him and began stroking his face.

"Last night I wanted to kill you, but when I saw you at the office, doing battle with Rivadavia, I felt very protective. I wanted to gobble you up right there."

"That would have been a surprising sight for everyone else."

"I didn't tell you that Diana hinted that you two had slept together."

"It wasn't long after I joined the firm, when she was still working with Aarón. We had a couple of encounters."

Ángeles had lowered his fly and put her hand inside his boxers, but she removed it when he confirmed this history with Diana. "So you fucked her and yet you carry on working with her?" she said, somewhere between surprised and annoyed.

"She's the best at her thing. Do we have to talk about work?"

Federico realized he would have to seize the initiative before Ángeles started an argument that might extend the duration of this tryst longer than he had allowed for. He started kissing her neck and stroking her breast beneath the badly buttoned shirt.

"The best at her thing," Ángeles repeated. "And what might that thing be? Blow jobs, or what?"

"She's the best at tackling the patrimonial violence men visit on their wives."

He kissed her lengthily, hoping that when their mouths parted she wouldn't return to the same theme. While kissing he redoubled his fondling. Ángeles didn't press her point. Her hand went back to his crotch and she started to caress him while seeming to think about something else. Was she going to continue the argument or... No – she lowered his trousers and kneeled down. Federico stroked her head while silently thanking God.

Afterwards, they went to bed. He was naked, while she was still dressed. Ángeles took off her skirt, revealing a white thong she didn't remove, even when he penetrated her. After a while her shirt and bra came off. The next day, Federico thought, she was sure to wear similar clothes to work, so he would remember them fucking.

Now, in spite of everything, he was on schedule. Browning the potatoes while drinking a glass of wine as he waited for Verónica seemed to him the best possible plan.

Vero arrived a few minutes after ten. As she opened the door and Chicha rushed to greet her, he poured her a glass of wine.

"It smells amazing. You're an angel, Fede," she said as she went towards him and kissed him lengthily, pressing herself against his body. Federico ran through a mental checklist to see if he had done everything right: showering, changing his clothes, eliminating any trace of his encounter with Ángeles.

Verónica was drunk. Not very drunk, not off her head drunk. At times she loosened up and laughed; then she would grow tense and a dark shadow would come over her face. She went from seeming carefree, telling him about the chat in Martataka, to remembering what had happened two nights ago – the deaths, the kidnappings.

"I have to find out what happened, why they killed Goicochea and Viviana. Are there any other possible victims? Might they kill someone else? Who could be behind this, Fede?"

"Whoever it is, you'll find them. But you must take care of yourself."

Verónica remained deep in her thoughts. "They've decided to ignore everything at the magazine, to treat Goicochea's death as though it were another robbery gone wrong. And they're not going to publish anything on Viviana. A woman who was in the middle of an important investigation, and those jerks at the magazine look the other way. They'll never be brave enough to publish anything that might put them in a compromising position."

Fede served up the fish and potatoes, opened a second bottle of wine and began to feel a little tipsy himself. Verónica, looking at him closely, reached over and removed a long blonde hair from his shirt. How had that hair ended up there if he had changed his shirt, washed, scrubbed everything clean? Because there was no doubt the hair belonged to Ángeles.

"And this?" Verónica asked, in a tone of irony.

"Looks like a hair, probably from the girl at the fish shop, or the woman who lives on the fifth floor and came up in the elevator with me."

Verónica studied him carefully, like a police officer poised to carry out a breathalyser test on someone who's left a party. "Not from some other girl?"

"Not as far as I know."

"Just as well, because if you had a lover I would find myself obliged to kill her."

Federico looked serious. Verónica burst out laughing.

"To kill her with my indifference. I wouldn't even waste my breath on a woman who makes do with my leftovers."

"What a strange image."

They ended up in bed, Verónica naked on top of him, fucking him hard, biting him, leaving marks he hoped would disappear by the next time he got together with Ángeles, not that he thought of her at times like this. Verónica fucking left no room for anyone else, not even in the imagination.

By the end they were exhausted, him more than her. Federico stared at the ceiling, thinking that he was going to need a few days off to recuperate from so much sexual activity.

Verónica leaned on him, looking closely at him while she rested her elbow on his ribs. "There's something I have to tell you. I'm late this month, I did a test and I'm pregnant. I've decided I'm not going to have it. It's not the right time."

Then she laid her head on his chest and he stroked her back for a long time.

8   *Bohemia*

I

The divide between Verónica's social and emotional upbringing and that of Daniela and Leticia occurred when the youngest sister stopped going to Zumerland in order to spend
summer days with her maternal grandparents. Esther and
Elías were both happy to have their youngest granddaughter
at home. Now their children were married, there were empty
rooms in the house, and many empty hours each day. They
would have been delighted to look after their older grand-
daughters too, but the girls already had a social life at camp
that they wouldn't have given up for the world. Verónica,
on the other hand, had always dreamed of going to live in
her grandparents' house and regarded the daily trip to Villa
Crespo as the best thing that had ever happened to her.

Grandmother Esther had problems with her hip and
didn't go out much, not even for shopping, so this task fell
to Grandfather Elías. Verónica accompanied him on his
rounds of the store, the vegetable market and the butcher.
Sometimes they would drop into a haberdashery to get something for Bubbe, or they would walk a few blocks to the hard-
ware shop, where Zayde liked to buy strange items he would
later use to fix things in the house. They also visited the odd
kiosk, where her grandfather would buy Verónica a chocolate
Milkybar, or Billiken fruit gumdrops, or they would go to

Parque Centenario so she could play on the merry-go-round. And every so often they would go right across town (that's what it seemed like to her, but it was less than ten blocks) to Avenida Córdoba, to have an ice cream at Scannapieco. Gradually the streets of Villa Crespo grew familiar to Verónica, much more so even than those of Recoleta, where she lived but didn't walk around much, except when her mother took them to have tea at La Biela.

Verónica loved watching her grandparents make things. Elías would paint the window frames or change the rubber washers in the taps. Esther darned socks and put patches on the girls' clothes (Verónica was fascinated by the speed of her sewing, and the use of a thimble struck her as high-tech gadgetry), but above all, Bubbe cooked. Her kitchen was the place where she seemed most comfortable and happy. And, for all the fascination the little girl felt watching her grandmother mixing flours, lighting ovens and burners, preparing home-made mayonnaise (something Verónica couldn't watch, for fear she would cut herself), she never learned to cook, nor could she remember, years later, the recipe for gefilte fish or strudel. Her sister Daniela, on the other hand, who had barely ever seen Esther cook, successfully recreated their bubbe's recipes.

The end of the vacation brought an inevitable return to the school routine. That meant no more daily visits to her grandparents' house. Verónica was heartsick with sadness and, more importantly, her grandmother also suffered very much as a result of the separation. So Verónica's parents made a new plan: she could spend the weekends at her grandparents' house. They would take her over there on Saturdays, a little before noon; the next day the rest of the family would go to have lunch at Villa Crespo, bringing Verónica back just in time to get her homework done. Both grandmother and granddaughter were quickly cured, and the first Saturday of this new arrangement there were celebrations, with cake and other treats.

As time went on, Verónica not only learned to recognize the neighbourhood's streets, avenues, squares and shops, but its residents too. Older neighbours, her grandparents' age, would call out "Hello, Verónica" from the other side of the road, to which she always responded with a smile and frenzied waving. There were also other children on the block. It wasn't until the second year of spending weekends at her grandparents' house that Verónica started going out on the sidewalk and mixing with them. Around the same time her grandfather decided to take her to see Atlanta play. These were two experiences that would leave their mark and still resonate with her many years later.

II

Between the ages of eight and eleven, Verónica belonged to a gang of children in Villa Crespo. At the Escuela Argentina Modelo, she had a group of friends she saw at birthday parties and on the odd group excursion, classmates who were her age and whose families were similar to hers. The children from Villa Crespo, on the other hand, were completely different, especially in the freedoms they enjoyed. Friendships at school were contained and even controlled by the perimeter walls, while the Villa Crespo gang roamed all over the neighbourhood, far from the adults' eyes. Verónica had more female than male friends at school, but at her grandparents' it was the other way around: the gang on her block comprised five boys and only two girls.

Verónica couldn't say for sure when she first crossed the threshold of her grandparents' house and started joining in the street games with her neighbours. It certainly wasn't the first year, when her grandparents always kept her indoors and Verónica only went out to accompany Elías on his shopping rounds. It must have started with visits between herself and Lucía, a girl almost the same age as her, who lived three houses away and had a twin brother, Martín. One day Vero's grandmother must have suggested to Lucía's mother that she send the girl over to have a glass of milk with her granddaughter. Lucía would have arrived with one of her dolls, for reassurance, and would have been surprised to discover that Verónica didn't have any. Vero didn't like playing with dolls, despite having a few Barbies at home, some of them inherited from her sisters. She knew it was important for girls to play with dolls, and so she concealed her lack of interest and pretended to be the teacher or the mother, but she never played with the dolls on her own.

It was easy to be friends with Lucía. She was kind, cheerful and went along with everything Verónica proposed, like that time they went up to the roof terrace and covered the ground with little plates of ham and cups of milk, hoping to attract some neighbourhood cat and turn it into a pet. No cat appeared during the two hours they spent sitting under the water tank, but the long wait, that passage of time with nothing to do, cemented the friendship between the two girls.

Later, it would be Verónica who went to have tea at Lucía's, and there she would meet Martín, who looked nothing like his sister (which confused Verónica, who thought twins were always identical) but shared many of the same gestures and characteristics. Even so, Martín paid the girls no attention to begin with, nor they him. He played in the street with the other children, whom Verónica didn't yet know. When she went out shopping with her grandfather and saw Martín with the other children, she said hello and he would answer.

Doubtless he followed up by telling the others she was his sister's friend, by way of an apology.

At some point, either Lucía's mother or Vero's grandmother decided it was fine for the girls to be outside unsupervised, and they would play at teachers, or skipping games, or read from a children's storybook, or from some volume of *Choose Your Own Adventure*, never mixing with the boys who ran past because they were playing hide-and-seek, or ran past because they were playing tag, or ran past because they were playing ball. They were forever running past the girls, who looked on indignantly, tutting, "What brutes."

And yet at some point the girls joined the boys. Perhaps the rapprochement started in Lucía's house, when Martín agreed to play them at foosball on the table they had in the garage, so breaking the implicit pact by which girls and boys played separately. Then they began to play together on the sidewalk. The three of them might have been playing tag outside the door one afternoon and another boy might have asked to join them, or perhaps they were playing statues. Or the boys might have been playing dodgeball, throwing balls at each other while Verónica and Lucía made mocking comments or laughed at them, which would surely have hurt their masculine pride and prompted a challenge to see if they could play any better; and the girls must have entered the game that way. Because after that they often played dodgeball and were great at swerving balls or landing hits, as required. And since they didn't cry when they were hit but laughed it off like the boys, it was logical that they came to be accepted as equals. That must have been how the group of children came together.

There were six and sometimes seven of them. When Vero was eight, Lucía and Martín were nine. El Chino would have been the same age as the twins. They called him Chino because he had little eyes, although he was blonde with freckles, and sometimes he also got called Freckles, especially when someone was annoyed with him. He lived opposite Vero's grandparents. Hernán was the eldest, already ten, and was the son of the caretakers at the building on the corner. Very skinny and permanently dishevelled, he wanted to be an astronaut and would spend summer nights up on the roof, looking through his telescope. Once Hernán invited the others to share this night sky with him and the children saw everything they could imagine: stars, planets, human and extraterrestrial spacecraft; even aliens who didn't need flying saucers to fly over Earth.

Flavio was the youngest, just seven, but he was large for his age, so he seemed older than Verónica. He liked annoying Hernán, who every so often would give him a slap; on one occasion Flavio went crying to his mother, which caused a minor crisis among the friends because their parents banned them from playing together. But soon the adults got tired of watching over them and both boys returned to the gang without grudges or complaints.

There was another boy of ten, Gonzalo, but he lived three blocks away. He sometimes came to play with them because he was at school with Hernán. Gonzalo excelled at everything: he was good at soccer and telling jokes and knew the weirdest things about diverse topics, like dolphins, the living dead, and how to climb Aconcagua without falling.

It was the girls who joined in the boys' games, never the other way round. But they didn't mind leaving their dolls and books behind. It was more fun to run and joke around, or simply stroll round the block with the others. The boys accepted them without protest, except when it came to play- ing soccer, the one refuge of an emerging manhood their fathers were carefully cultivating. Girls didn't play soccer. They stayed away from the spontaneous sidewalk games and penalty shoot-outs for more than a year. Verónica realized that she needed to practise, and so for Children's Day she asked her parents for a ball. When her parents presented her with an inflatable pink beach ball adorned with the faces of Snow White and Cinderella, Verónica was inconsolable, crying so much that finally Aarón went out in desperation to get what she really wanted: a size five leather soccer ball. If her parents ever expressed any anxiety about this new passion, Verónica was none the wiser. She took the ball to her grandparents' house and practised there, on the roof terrace, alone or with Lucía.

III

Their friendship grew by virtue of small gestures and big achievements. Like the time Verónica learned to ride a bicycle thanks to El Chino, who had lent her his. She didn't know how to ride without training wheels, so El Chino offered to teach her. She got on the bike and he held her up, gripping the seat as he ran alongside, telling her to keep going straight. Then, without Verónica noticing, he let go and she kept riding. When she heard El Chino's voice in the distance, she realized what had happened and fell off, giving herself a painful whack. But the next time she could ride without a hitch. The bicycle she had at home in Recoleta was too small for her, so she asked her parents to give her a bigger one for her birthday and let her take it to her grandparents' house. It was still a month until her birthday but, once again, Aarón decided this early present could be justified, provided that Verónica never took her new bike into the street. Since none of the children was allowed to ride their bikes in the road, this seemed like a promise his daughter could easily keep.

One of the discoveries Verónica made in her Villa Crespo gang was earth. It wasn't like the greyish soil at summer camp, perfumed by nature, but more like the dirty dust that settles on abandoned things, the black substance exuded by greasy old tools or bicycle wheels, the mud they fell in, into which they stuck their hands, looking for bugs to feed to a spider they had adopted as a pet and that had its web in an abandoned house around the corner. There wasn't a day Verónica didn't end up covered in dirt, and her grandmother would make her bathe with lots of soap, asking her please not to let her parents see her like that, or they wouldn't let her stay over any more.

Verónica thought of Gonzalo as the boy who came from far away, because he lived three blocks from her. She didn't realize that the one who came from somewhere else was her. The others didn't ask her, and she never spoke much about her life in Recoleta except to mention her sisters sometimes, or the famous cemetery (Gonzalo wanted her to tell him what it was like, and she invented something because she had never been). They accepted without question that she arrived on Saturdays and left on Sunday afternoons. It was better in the summer and winter breaks because then she could stay longer and spend more time with the other children. Any of their birthdays that fell on weekdays during school term time were celebrated on Saturdays, so Verónica could be there too.

As they grew older, the constraints on the children loosened; they began to cross roads, one of them might have money to buy something at the kiosk: sweets, fizzy drinks, a bag of salted pretzels. Every step further from home had to be negotiated with their parents or, in Verónica's case, grandparents.

"Señora, please can Verónica come to the ice-cream shop on Corrientes?"

"Isn't that a bit far?"

"No, it's only six blocks. We go all the time."

"Your mother lets you go?"

"Yes, she just tells us to be careful crossing the roads."

"All right, but only cross when there's a green light. And don't talk to strangers."

And off they would go on a new adventure, trying to keep their promises, although they were forever having to scold Flavio, who wanted to cross on a red light or steal fruit from the market.

In time, the friendship between Verónica and Lucía lost its singularity and merged into their bond with the boys. They weren't greater friends with each other than they were with Hernán or Flavio. They no longer went to each other's homes as much and, if Vero did go to Lucía's, it was natural for Martín to join them too. The definitions of male and female had blurred.

Verónica was nine years old when they started going to Parque Centenario to play soccer, taking El Chino's leather ball. They played among themselves, sometimes arranging games with other boys who would be surprised to see girls playing, but Vero and Lucía left no quarter for mockery. Lucía was fast, had good ball control and read the game well. Verónica was not as good technically, but when let loose she could leave marks on the opponents' legs. She was a fearsome defender and hard to read on the attack. Verónica liked to think those games of soccer had shaped her behaviour in later life.

Occasionally a game would get scrappy and everyone would end up getting walloped, spat on or even running away before things got any worse. A couple of times, other people in the park threatened to call the police and the children had to run for it. They would stop only once they reached somewhere safe, that is, the blocks around their own houses, where the neighbours knew their names. Sometimes they bought a fizzy drink, competing to see who burped the best (Verónica and Lucía refused to take part in these contests, keeping a lofty distance). They all drank from the same bottle and whoever got the last slurp would be reminded that they were drinking everyone else's spit, but that didn't stop them wanting to share it.

One baking hot Saturday afternoon, at siesta time, when the other children had not yet come out to play, El Chino suggested he and Vero go to buy a bottle of Coke at a kiosk that was four blocks away and less expensive. Vero had a better idea: she would fetch a returnable lemonade bottle her grandmother had and make it even cheaper. El Chino waited for her, and two minutes later Verónica appeared with the bottle in her hand. They trudged along the sidewalk that was in shade, their silence interrupted only by the singing of cicadas and El Chino's snotty sniffing, the consequence of a heavy cold. As they turned a corner, they saw on the opposite sidewalk a group of kids a little older than them, who had surrounded a boy. Looking closer, they saw that the boy in the middle was Hernán. None of the other kids, who must have been about twelve years old, were known to them. Vero and El Chino crossed the road.

"Hey, Hernán, what's up?"

"Ooh, is that your boyfriend?" said one of the boys.

"His boyfriend's turned up, ha ha," repeated another one, trying to be witty.

The five antagonists had been hitting Hernán, whose face was red from the slaps, his hair dishevelled, his eyes full of tears.

El Chino stepped forward and into the boys' midst. "Leave him alone."

"Ooh, the boyfriend wants some too."

One of the boys shoved El Chino, who tried to throw a punch but stumbled, hitting the air.

"Nice try, asshole."

El Chino had fallen onto the ground and one of them was kicking him. So focussed was the group on him that they had forgotten about Verónica, perhaps thinking a girl posed no threat. The first boy to get hit by the bottle she was holding surely regretted such a presumption. The boy screamed as though he'd been stabbed, startling everyone, including El Chino, who was now back on his feet, and Hernán.

Verónica was wielding the bottle like a machete. The boys, having learned their lesson, moved away from her, while Hernán and El Chino went to her side. Now the two groups faced one another. Once their shock had passed, the others realized that there were more of them, that they could easily disarm the girl and launch a group attack, and so they pressed forward. That was when Verónica threw the bottle at a boy's head. Her target had quick reflexes and ducked, sending it smashing against the bars on a nearby window, where it exploded in such a way that a shard of glass flew out and cut one of the boys on the face. Blood ran down his cheek. Inside the house two or three dogs started barking. They heard someone opening the door and a man came out, at which point everyone ran off and, luckily for Verónica and her friends, the others ran in the opposite direction.

Hernán, El Chino and Vero only stopped running once they reached the kiosk. They were exhausted but exhilarated, laughingly oblivious to all the dangers they had narrowly avoided, including the possibility of killing a boy, had the bottle hit him.

"Who were those guys?"

"No idea," said Hernán. "I think they must have mixed me up with someone else. They're not from the barrio."

"If my grandmother finds out I broke her bottle, she'll kill me."

"Let's buy a disposable litre and a half."

They drank the Coke on the way home and never ran into the other gang again, not that afternoon or ever. That adventure aside, there was something else that united El Chino, Hernán and Vero and that they didn't share with the other kids in the group: they were all Atlanta supporters.

IV

Verónica had only vague memories of the first time she went to the Atlanta ground. The visit was long anticipated, because Grandfather Elías had been talking to her about the club for ages. He was a fanatical supporter who would leave the table before the end of a family lunch to go and watch his team; he'd be gone for a few hours and would then reappear, sometimes happy, sometimes – more often – dejected. Verónica, longing to share in that emotional roller coaster, begged him to let her go, and he promised he would take her along when she was a little older. And one day he delivered on his promise.

Perhaps the reason she had so few memories of that first game was because it had been a resounding defeat, 3–0 against Nueva Chicago. What Verónica remembered most was the terror she had felt climbing the steps of the stands. It gave her vertigo to be so high up, and she was terrified of falling between the boards into the unknown abyss that lay hidden beneath. There were loads of fans that day, or so it seemed to her. On many occasions after that she would find herself in crowded stands, but she never again felt as suffocated as she had that day. Nor did she understand why she had to stand up during the game and could only sit down at half-time. One thing she liked was that they kept shouting "Storky" at one of the players, and she had recently seen a photo of a stork at school. She thought she would be able to pick him out from among the eleven players, but none of them looked like a stork. It was also the first time she ever saw (or rather heard about, because she had no memory of seeing him on the field) Pepe Castro, who became her idol for a few years, so much so that when she was twenty Verónica used to say if she ever had a son she would call him Pepecastro – or, to be precise, Pepecastro Rosenthal, because she was sure she would be a single mother.

Going to the local stadium with her grandfather became a fortnightly routine at best. She had to miss the rare weekday matches, because she couldn't persuade anyone to take her over to Villa Crespo (on those days Verónica would listen to the game on the radio, picturing her grandfather in the stands). What most struck her about those outings was the sight of her grandfather swearing, getting angry, yelling, shouting encouragement, protesting, pleading. He seemed so different to the mild-mannered man who took her shopping. In time she would take on every one of her grandfather's mannerisms, right down to the sweaty palms at the end of a game. That hand he gave her when they walked back home together.

Verónica's grandmother liked her going to games with Elías. Before they set off she would tell her to take care of him. Doubtless she thought his passion for the club could push her husband into a heart attack and that if he went with his granddaughter, his behaviour would be more civilized, lowering the cardiac risk. Verónica never disabused her of this miscalculation.

In the stand, Verónica was reunited with two friends from the block: El Chino and Hernán. Oddly, they barely spoke to each other and behaved almost like strangers when they ran into each other en route to the stadium or in the stands. Hernán went with his older brothers, two surly teenagers. Not to be outdone by them, he also behaved like a little prick, refusing even to say hello to her when those two lummoxes were around.

With El Chino it was even stranger, because then the one behaving oddly was her grandfather. El Chino went to the club with his father, a polite man who always greeted Verónica when he saw her in the street. Her grandfather couldn't stand him, though, and it was clear El Chino's father felt the same, because when they were at the club he pretended not to see him. Her grandfather, on the other hand, would assert his presence by staring daggers at him; or at least that was how it seemed to her.

Verónica was never able, during those years, to delve into the reason for this behaviour. What little she did learn was thanks to an observation by her grandmother. She managed to wheedle out of Bubbe that El Chino's grandfather, who was dead by then, and her grandfather had been on the board of Atlanta in the 1960s. They had fallen out over ideological differences. Her grandfather would always be a Communist, no matter what. How an argument over Communism could have affected the running of Atlanta enough to bring them to blows, and why her grandfather transferred his anger onto El Chino's father, were questions to which Verónica had no answer.

When Verónica was around eleven, the pupils were set an essay on the theme "I am..." They had to replace the ellipsis with their own idea and develop it. Verónica wrote *I am a Bohemian*, and over three pages (much more than the teacher had asked for) explained her love for Atlanta, her joy in their triumphs, the pain of their defeats, the fear of relegation and the hope of promotion to the First Division that never came, the unforgettable goals and spectacular tackles by heroes whose names she would always remember. She also wrote about her grandfather; how he had arrived in Argentina and become a supporter of Atlanta, even rising to be one of the club's directors. She told how her grandfather took her by the hand to the stadium every time their team played at home.

The teacher congratulated her in front of the whole class and awarded her a ten. That was the first time Verónica realized that telling stories was what she liked best. Not invented stories, though, but true ones.

V

The spring of the year Verónica turned twelve marked the beginning of the end. There was a premonition that their world was collapsing when Lucía got her period. It was the first thing her friend told her when they saw each other that Saturday, on their own, away from the boys. That attempt to forge a complicity between the two of them, excluding the boys from their gang, like when they were eight or nine, seemed out of place to Verónica. She tried to play down the revelation and change the subject, but Lucía would speak of nothing else, so there was no choice but to listen to her. That afternoon, Lucía didn't want to go out and meet up with the boys because she wasn't feeling well. Verónica thought of telling them why her friend wasn't joining them, then decided against this. It was Lucía's brother Martín who broke the news to the group. "She's menstruating," he said, and all the boys looked disgusted.

Not much happened in the following weeks, except that Lucía seemed a little distant from the group in general, and from Vero in particular, as though she had taken a step ahead of them all. But one day she came back, with more confidences. She took Verónica up to her building's roof terrace and, full of emotion, announced that she was in love with Hernán.

"But... how? You can't be."

Yes she could. Lucía's face went dreamy as she told stupid anecdotes about them both that confirmed they were made for one another. Verónica, in a state of shock, was putting her patience to the test.

"And yesterday afternoon he kissed me."

The situation was much worse than Verónica could have suspected. The two lovebirds had gone on their own to Parque Centenario and there Hernán had kissed Lucía on the mouth. Then he'd given her another kiss on the way home, but she hadn't let him give her a third in case a neighbour saw them.

It wasn't long (thanks again to Martín?) before the others found out about the romance between Lucía and Hernán. To start with nobody expressed an opinion, either in favour or against, but everyone found it unacceptable that Lucía and Hernán should go with them to the park only to end up kissing under a tree while Martín, El Chino, Flavio, Gonzalo and Verónica kicked a ball around. Nobody said anything to them, but the bad feeling was evident, and Lucía and Hernán started to go their own way.

Could the gang survive the loss of two of its members? They did their best, pretending nothing had changed and keeping faith, clinging to their friendship like survivors of a shipwreck clinging to a plank out in the middle of the ocean.

The second blow was as strange and sudden as all misfortunes. One day Verónica arrived at her grandparents' place to discover that El Chino and his family had moved house. From one day to the next. Martín and Flavio had seen El Chino's family loading boxes and furniture into a van. El Chino had said they had to leave, that they couldn't stay in the neighbourhood. He gave no further explanation, no telephone number or address. Nothing.

That hit Verónica hard. El Chino was her best friend, even if she had never admitted this to herself because everyone was equal in the gang and loved each other the same. But now he had gone she realized she loved him, a lot. Verónica cried over her friend for a few days. She asked her grandfather if he could find anything out, but he simply shrugged, saying, "I like them better at a distance."

It was summer by the time the third blow came, and that was the hardest and most tragic. This was a blow that would change Verónica's life for ever and bring her face to face with death for the first time. Her grandmother, Esther, suffered a stroke, spent two weeks in hospital and died. Verónica felt as though she were shattering into a thousand pieces inside. She couldn't comprehend that her grandmother would no longer be in her life. There were days of inconsolable pain.

Verónica suffered on account of what she had lost, but also as a witness to her grandfather's despair. Esther had been his companion for nearly fifty years, and now he was left alone. The sight of him weeping inconsolably was for many years (until her mother died and she saw her father cry) the most heartbreaking experience she had ever had to endure.

Her mother's younger brother, Ariel, took her grandfather to spend a few days at his home in Villa Urquiza, a beautiful house with a garden and lots of space. But what had been intended as a short stay, until he felt better, became permanent. Her grandfather no longer wanted to live in Villa Crespo, which held so many memories of his wife. Ariel generously suggested he stay with them. His wife agreed to this, as did Vero's mother. And that's what happened.

That was the end of Verónica's life in Villa Crespo, her afternoons with the other children, her adventures in the barrio. One day she went with her mother to fetch some things her grandfather needed from the house and took the opportunity to see her friends, asking them if there was any news of El Chino, but none of them knew anything. There was a general atmosphere of sadness among them, even with Flavio, who had always been the most light-hearted member of the gang. Vero said goodbye, promising she would come back, that she would learn to take the bus and go to see them. But when she did start travelling on her own, it wasn't the same going back to the block when her grandparents were no longer in the house, now occupied by strangers. So she didn't return to the barrio. She never saw her childhood friends again.

Her grandfather didn't want to lose the bond he shared with his favourite granddaughter. Nor his bond with Atlanta. So, a few months after the tragedy, Elías suggested he and Verónica return to the stadium. They wouldn't go to all the home games, just once a month. From then onwards, her grandfather would pick her up and they would go to the ground together on the number 93 bus then come back afterwards to have café con leche and a toasted sandwich in the Iberia bar on Honorio Pueyrredón and Juan B. Justo. Her grandfather would stay over at the apartment in Recoleta, have Sunday lunch with the family, then she and her mother would take him back in the car to Ariel's house.

This new routine lasted for a long time, until Verónica was twenty and her grandfather died. She was travelling at the time, on her first trip to Europe. Her mother called on the brand-new phone she had bought especially in case of emergencies. Verónica came back home on the first flight she could find. After that she regularly returned to the Atlanta ground. She went alone. Or rather holding the hand of her grandfather's ghost, which still felt warm, firm and protective.

9   *A Delicate Truth*

I

It wasn't the first time Verónica had attended Dr Laura Rivarola's clinic. The previous time had been while she was investigating the criminal activities of Rivarola's ex-husband, a doctor who trafficked newborn babies, and on that occasion, ironically, the doctor had thought Verónica wanted to have an abortion. Now that she *was* there for that reason, Rivarola would think her visit was connected to some investigation. Verónica would have to tell her, calmly, that she was there for personal reasons.

Verónica studied the faces of the other people in the waiting room. All were women and, save for the odd mother accompanying her daughter, all of childbearing age. She tried to work out who was there for birth control and who had come for the same reason as her.

It had been the right decision not to let Federico come with her, although, when she explained the situation, he had become defensive. It was clear he was making an effort to be supportive: if she wanted to have the baby, he would rejoice like any happy father-to-be; if she decided on an abortion, he would be beside her all the way. In either scenario, he had her back. That moved Verónica, making her feel safer and surer about the decision she had made.

"I want you to know that, if I do have a child one day, you'll be the father."

"We've got plenty of time for that."

"Of course. I just don't feel ready now. I've got so many things to do."

"You have to choose your priorities. Whatever you decide, I'll be in your corner."

It was so reassuring to have Federico as a partner. Or maybe not. It would probably be easier to terminate a pregnancy if your partner was a jerk. If two people loved each other, were good together, why not have the baby? Verónica asked herself this every morning before getting up and every night before going to sleep. The answer was always the same: because she didn't feel like dedicating her life to a child. Nor did she like the thought of a being growing inside her body. There was nothing beautiful about it. The idea of a little boy or girl playing with her and Federico (as they played with her sisters' children sometimes) was delightful. But to go through a pregnancy, a birth, the postpartum period, the care of a baby, of a child who wouldn't walk or talk for well over a year, seemed like a horror show to her. Perhaps sometime in the future. Not now. She was a hundred per cent sure about that.

The doctor called her in, giving her the same frosty welcome as the last time they had met. That didn't bother Verónica; for her, bad vibes were consistent with being a good professional.

"I always thought something like this would bring you back one day. You're pregnant, right?"

How Verónica hated it when someone strayed from the script she had imagined for them.

"Yes. I've done a test and it was positive."

"Right, first things first. I'm going to do an ultrasound scan. Please lie down on the bed and roll up your top."

Verónica did as she was told.

"Undo your trousers."

Dr Rivarola sat beside her, put some cold gel on her abdomen and started to move the scanner. "Yes, you're pregnant," she said after a few seconds, and passed Verónica some paper towels to wipe off the gel. "All done. You can put your clothes back on."

There was no miracle, then. The doctor made notes: about the date of her last period, any previous abortions, any allergies. She weighed her. She asked if Verónica had thought this through, if she had a partner and what his opinion was.

"Not that I think his opinion is particularly important, but I like to know if a woman is supported or on her own."

"He supports me completely. He wanted to come today."

"He can come with you next time. I'll do a check-up in a few days. Another scan, just to be sure."

Once the doctor had a full picture of Verónica's situation, she started explaining what was going to happen next.

"Time's on our side, but it's always better to do things as soon as possible. As I'm sure you know, we can do this with misoprostol pills or surgically. I'm rather traditional and tend to use the latter. It's more invasive, but it allows me to keep everything under control. We carry out the procedure in a consulting room, not this one but one equipped for any contingency. I have an anaesthetist and a nurse working with me, two excellent professionals, and there are never any complications. You arrive with your partner, he waits for a while looking at old magazines, and in less than an hour you're on your way home. Does that sound OK?"

"Yes, I trust your opinion."

"Very well, the fee is one thousand dollars. You can pay it in pesos, of course. And it needs to be cash, for obvious reasons."

"Can I leave you a deposit today?"

"That won't be necessary. Just let me check my diary. Is Thursday the twentieth at 2 p.m. for the check-up all right, and then Monday the twenty-fourth at 11 a.m.?"

II

Verónica emerged from the appointment feeling a little dizzy. She should have asked the doctor if it was normal to experience so many pregnancy symptoms. The suffocating heat of recent days didn't help. When would this spring mini-heatwave end? She bought a bottle of ice-cold water and toyed with the idea of pouring it over her head to cool down, but resisted the temptation. What most surprised her was that she had no desire to smoke. For a week she hadn't even touched the packet of cigarettes she had in her bag. Even the smell of cigarette smoke made her nauseous.

She needed to hurry if she was going to make visiting time at Sanatorio Mitre and get in to see Patricia, but she didn't have the energy to take a bus, so instead hailed a taxi and collapsed in the back seat. Verónica prayed the taxi driver would be silent, and for once her prayers were answered. She used the time to WhatsApp Fede with the appointments the doctor had given her. His answer was brief: *Perfect. It's in the diary.* Well, what had she expected? That he'd start sending emojis and GIFs? She decided to call Paula.

"I've been to the doctor."

"OK – and?"

"Everything's fine. She gave me a date for the termination."

"Why didn't she give you pills?"

"I don't know, she said this was better. Do you think she's wrong?"

"No, just asking. Are you all right?"

"Apart from dying of heat, I'm very well. I spoke to Fede about it and he was amazing."

"That boy's worth his weight in gold."

"Then his value must have increased notably in the last few months."

"Don't be mean. You're hardly the same as you were a year ago either."

"What a cow. I'm going to hang up on you and play Candy Crush."

"You're not someone who plays Candy Crush, though."

Verónica ended the call just as a text message came in from Patricia: *Come at 14.30 today with Rodo and María Magdalena. I'll chuck out the family then and we can get down to work. We'll only have an hour, so let's not waste any time on emotional scenes.* Patricia was clearly beginning to feel her old self.

Since it was still early, and the taxi was going at a snail's pace down Avenida Corrientes, Verónica decided to get out when they reached Pueyrredón and walk the rest of the way. She was hungry and had an inconvenient craving for prosciutto and butter on pumpernickel. She looked out for a bar and went into the first one she came across.

"I can't do you pumpernickel," said the bar attendant. "We've got rolls, flatbreads, baguettes."

"A roll. But don't forget the butter. And a Coca-Cola."

"Light?"

"Did I say light?"

Verónica gave the attendant – who couldn't have been more than twenty – a meaningful look. He responded with an indecipherable gesture and walked away. Verónica regretted her rudeness. "Never answer a question with another question," her mother used to say when she was a girl and, although she had never understood why, every time she did this she had the sensation of doing something bad.

She arrived at the hospital ten minutes before the appointed time and found María Magdalena and Rodolfo already waiting there. He was smoking a filterless cigarette, which was how he liked them. Verónica greeted them both, trying to avoid the tobacco smoke. Rodolfo seemed agitated.

"I can't stand hospitals – the smell, the patients wandering in the corridors, visiting times, the relatives who stay all night, looking for water to make *mate*."

"You mean you can't handle your fear of death."

At two thirty they went upstairs, running into Atilio, who seemed to be keeping a calm head. He was firm with them all the same.

"Patricia is still convalescing. She shouldn't really be seeing you, because I'm sure you've come to talk about work. Try to avoid anything contentious."

The three of them agreed, to reassure him, and went into the patient's room. There were two beds, but the other, luckily for Patricia and any potential occupant, was empty. Patricia's bed was in its highest position, so she was almost sitting up, with the sheets at full stretch. Doubtless she had been readying herself for their visit moments before they arrived. For all that she wanted to impose her usual presence, she seemed weak to Verónica.

"You should take some days to rest, Pato."

"I've survived being shot, I think I can survive you lot pitching bad articles. I've had a lot of practice, after all."

They arranged themselves around her and she pulled a bed table over her knees on which to balance a notebook and pen.

"Have they given you morphine?" Rodolfo asked.

"Yesterday they did. I'm on some less strong opiates today. Perhaps you'll find me nicer than usual."

"Don't underestimate yourself," said Verónica.

"What's going on at *Nuestro Tiempo*? I spoke to our editor today, the mysterious Tantanian, and also that numbskull Vilna and, although they tried to paint a rosy picture, it sounded utterly grim."

"They're working on the hypothesis that you and Andrés were the victims of a robbery."

"Which is partly true, because they stole Goicochea's laptop," conceded Rodolfo.

"What a bunch of idiots," said María Magdalena.

"No, they're worse than that," said Patricia. "They want to undermine Andrés, who was in the middle of an investigation. Perhaps we expect too much of these people. They run a media company, there's no reason why they should also know about journalism. Vero, what happened with Viviana?"

Verónica gave her boss a potted version of events. Somehow Patricia had heard about Viviana's death, but she didn't know her journalists had met Goicochea's ex shortly before she was killed. Verónica also relayed all that had happened in the newsroom meeting and how she had come to be suspended.

"I suspect they won't dare suspend or throw me out while I'm still in bed, but bearing in mind the things I said to them today, I wouldn't put it past them."

Rodolfo poured her a glass of water and Patricia gratefully drank from it. She was tired and still had twenty minutes of acting like an editor ahead of her.

"It's obvious that, as long as I'm not at work, we'll struggle to get our findings published. Then again, by the time we're in a position to reveal everything that's happened I should be back in the newsroom anyway, so let's proceed as though we were in the fishbowl."

"We need to identify the most useful sources and witnesses," said Rodolfo, "and I think it's worth starting with the closest and arguably the best informed. That's you, in other words, dear Patricia Beltrán, alias the Belter."

"You're right. I've spent quite a lot of this time in bed going over the conversations I had with Andrés over the last year. There weren't many of them, unfortunately."

She drank more water. It was clear that mentioning Goicochea made her emotional and affected her focus on the job at hand. Perhaps she would have liked to say something about how much she had loved him, how close they had been, about the bonds that had formed during decades of sharing an office. But Patricia wasn't going to cry, at least not in front of her writers.

"I had lunch with Andrés three months ago. He told me he was investigating something, but he didn't go into detail and I didn't probe all that much. I thought he was tight-lipped because he hadn't got very far yet. But it seems he just wanted to keep me away from what he was doing. Seeing what happened to Viviana, his precautions were wise."

Patricia explained that Goicochea had been investigating links between secret agents, secret services and businesspeople.

"Secret agents and secret services sounds redundant, no?" ventured María Magdalena.

"Unless he meant the secret services of other countries."

"Could the CIA be involved in this?" Verónica asked.

"That wouldn't be unusual, but I find it hard to believe the CIA would set up an operation to kill someone in a country with no geopolitical influence," replied María Magdalena.

"There's something else that struck me at the time. When I said, half joking, that if he finished the article he should give it to me to publish in *Nuestro Tiempo*, he replied that the magazine wouldn't want to run it."

"When a journalist leaves a media job, it's quite common for them to be blacklisted to a degree."

"But it's not to a degree, it's an outright ban."

"Even if Andrés left on bad terms with the magazine's owners," said Patricia, "they came to an arrangement and publicly all seemed well. They signed an agreement on the supposed voluntary redundancy, they didn't have to fire him, there was no employment lawsuit. And Andrés was a prestigious journalist. If he came to me with a scoop, I'd run it with his name on the cover."

"Unless the article touches on vested interests. Advisors, friends, accomplices?"

"I think it could be something like that. But I still don't understand their malice towards him. Because if he was about to expose your friends and didn't get that far, at least say he died working as a journalist. I think it may be better to keep this team outside *Nuestro Tiempo* if we want to find out anything."

"They won't want to publish us either," said Verónica.

"We'll see about that. What do you two have?"

"We're concentrating on Viviana for now," said María Magdalena. "Since 1993 she's been employed by international organizations or on Foreign Ministry projects. In fact, as of 2004, she's worked solely for the Foreign Ministry, under an agreement with the Food and Agriculture Organization. If you speak to people who knew her, everyone describes her as a difficult person. Not so much in her dealings, but because she was always looking for the fifth leg on a cat."

"She could have made a good journalist then," said Patricia, shifting in the bed and suppressing a moan of pain.

Verónica and Rodolfo exchanged glances, as though to say *The drugs have made her optimistic about journalism.*

"There are formal complaints by her against colleagues, diplomats, civil servants," said Rodolfo. "None of them high-profile people. It was as if she was more concerned with rooting out bad apples than overturning the whole cart."

"She didn't have to act like a prosecutor, though. That wasn't her job."

"Yes, of course. It wasn't meant as a criticism. At any rate, there are so many cases that it would be difficult to establish if any are linked to the deaths."

"To simplify the search," Patricia suggested, "focus on the cases that seem closed but which could still have some social or economic importance. That should narrow things down quite a bit."

"I was thinking about what you said regarding links with *Nuestro Tiempo*. Wouldn't it be worth checking the owners' interests?" Rodolfo asked.

"They have multiple companies across many sectors, but it might not be a bad idea to see if there's anything unusual in the mix. And if you do find any irregularity, we can save it for a future article," Patricia said with a wink. Nothing entertained her as much as annoying the magazine's owners. It perked her up as much as the opioids.

"There's one detail we're not considering," said Verónica. "Viviana retired a year ago. She no longer worked for any organization. If she still had material from the time she was working, why hadn't she done something with it herself?"

"In other words, Andrés and Viviana were two pensioners who became dangerous people for spies, the secret services and a long et cetera. If they hadn't wound up dead, they'd be setting a wonderful example for the third age."

"Neither of them was technically old," said Rodolfo.

"There's something that worries me," said Verónica, "and that's whether someone else's life is in danger."

"As I said before, Andrés was very careful about that. He didn't even tell me what the investigation was about."

"I was thinking of his elder daughter."

"Malena? Me too. In theory she shouldn't be compromised. She's Andrés's daughter from his first marriage. What does she do?"

"She studies political science at the Universidad de Buenos Aires," said Rodolfo.

"Try to contact her. OK everyone, if you need me, give me a call. Luckily they haven't confiscated my phone."

Rodo gave her a kiss and almost a hug. Patricia looked a little disconcerted, and was unable to speak. The gesture had obviously undone her.

III

At the hospital door they agreed on the next steps: Verónica would look into how far whatever Goicochea was investigating had touched on the interests of *Nuestro Tiempo*'s owners. María Magdalena was to study the cases of corruption and abuse Viviana had called out during the years in question, and Rodolfo was planning to contact people in the Foreign Ministry who had worked with Viviana.

"I've got something to tell you," Rodolfo said with a guilty expression. "I already know Malena Goicochea."

"Know her how?"

"We've got history… a sexual one, if you want me to be explicit."

"A sexual history with that girl? She's a child, you pervert!"

"She isn't. She's over twenty, and this was last year."

"All the same, aren't you a bit of an old goat for a girl like that?"

"As if you haven't had dalliances with old goats yourself."

"Never with anyone as goatish as you."

"Rodo, let's not get sidelined," said María Magdalena. "You know her, so what exactly do you know about her? And can you find her?"

"I'll tell you briefly because I'm saving the longer version for my *Memoir of a Casanova*. Last year she contacted me – her own father gave her my number – because she had to do some university project that included interviewing journalists. We met, enjoyed some repartee, exchanged highbrow thoughts on literature, philosophical notes for a Cioranesque, nihilistic ethics of life, and the gods did the rest: Bacchus, Aphrodite, Eros."

"You're missing Hermes, the god of miscreants," put in María Magdalena. "But let's stick to what's important. Malena has a very good relationship with Viviana. She wasn't her mother, but they had a strong bond. Viviana even got Malena an internship at the Foreign Ministry."

"She works at the Foreign Ministry?"

"Not any more. She had a six-month internship. But to return to your previous question, if anyone is in danger, I think the answer is yes: Malena is in danger."

"Can you contact her? We should organize some kind of protection for her."

"I'll get on to it," said Rodolfo.

Verónica had a few free hours and was relatively close to the courts at Tribunales. She wanted information on the owners of *Nuestro Tiempo*. Perhaps it wasn't the strongest lead to follow, but, as Patricia said, she might find something for a future article.

The magazine belonged to a multimedia group whose original owners were Sergio Mayer and Aníbal Monteverde, but when Goicochea was fired they had added a third partner, Ariel Gómez Pardo. Unlike Monteverde, the other two had not started out in the media world but came from different business sectors. Mayer, from real estate and security, and from renting a dock that processed imports; Gómez Pardo, oil, casinos, bingo halls and, before that, taxi fleets. Monteverde had land now and exported cereals. Taken together, the three of them must have represented about ten different kinds of crime in Argentine society.

Verónica could ask Federico to get hold of information on these people, but she didn't want to bother him. She knew a brilliant commercial court clerk, someone who was possibly too honest and direct ever to become a judge herself. This woman's name was all but banned in the magazine, precisely because from her humble position she had pushed several cases against Monteverde a couple of years ago. However, she had also been a reliable source of information for Verónica and other journalists.

"Hello, Alicia... It's Verónica Rosenthal... How are you? Are you still at the Palace of Justice? I need some information on the antics of a group of gentlemen. Who happen to be owners of *Nuestro Tiempo*. Mayer, Monteverde and Gómez Pardo... Yes, exactly... the Three Wise Men."

Dr Alicia Karlic suggested meeting up the following afternoon, in a bar called Usía.

"Which one's that? I can't place it."

"I'm surprised you don't know it, as someone who belongs to the legal family. These days it's called Establecimiento General del Café. A horrible name, don't you think? Usía was better. It's on Tucumán. I'll see you there at four."

Verónica would have preferred to meet later, somewhere more fun and with alcohol thrown in, but she wasn't bold enough to make a counter-offer. She and Alicia weren't friends, but they got on very well, and this could have been an opportunity to get to know one another on a more personal level.

She decided to drop by her apartment in Villa Crespo to pick up the bill for services and check that all was well. The apartment looked the same as ever, as though it had been suspended in time the day she left it to go and live with Federico. It reminded her of those houses that had survived for centuries under the lava of Vesuvius. Lifting the blind in the living room to let in daylight, Verónica felt some nostalgia for her single life. If she wanted, she could reprise it then and there; only Chicha and her computer were missing. There was even a bottle of Jim Beam under the table that had survived the visits of various friends. She poured herself a glass and sat back in the armchair, thinking of Goicochea and Viviana. A journalist and his informant. That could be her and Federico in twenty or thirty years. Where would they be by then? Would they still be together, or would each have gone their own way? Would they be dead? She wondered how Goicochea must have felt when he met up with his ex again and she passed him the information he needed for his story. And what about her? There must have been a time in their lives when every time they met they'd wanted to tear each other's clothes off, when they had liked making plans together, imagining the future as a shared path. You don't think about all the shit that will happen, just as you don't think about the inevitability of death. Then twenty, thirty years later, having loved or lusted or obsessed over other people along the way, you meet up with your ex again. Would the old desire still be there or would there be nothing left, only those unreliable phenomena that are memories? Verónica hated memories, not because she had no good ones, but because the bad ones were stronger, stirring an anguish she couldn't always acknowledge. Loved ones who had died, moments that could never be repeated. She thought of Lucio. How many years had passed since she had sat in that same armchair thinking she was facing the most important moment of her romantic life? Five, six? And if he hadn't died (if he hadn't died in her arms on that terrible night), he might be able to come now and tell her about some corruption case at the railway company. What would she feel if he reappeared in her life after so many years? Nothing, perhaps? Could life be such a bitch? Could you really feel nothing for someone who had once made your heart explode? What would she feel for Federico in twenty or thirty years? At least Lucio's death had succeeded in freezing her feelings in the instant prior to their final separation. Those feelings would always remain true to themselves, without being corrupted, like the mummified bodies in Pompeii, surprised in their sleep by the lava of death. It's so easy for the lava of death to catch you dreaming.

And that's what happened. Verónica fell deeply asleep in the armchair. She woke up bothered by moonlight shining through the uncovered window. Her mouth was dry and she needed to piss. She felt hung-over, despite having drunk only one glass of Jim Beam. She went to the bathroom, washed the glass and picked out a book from the shelves, *Two Lives and a Dream*, by Marguerite Yourcenar, then she left the apartment.

IV

That same night and the following morning, Verónica received several calls from Rodolfo Corso, who was worried because he hadn't been able to contact Malena Goicochea.

"She's not at home, nor in any of the places she usually goes to. I tracked down a friend of hers I know a little, and she said that a few days ago Malena told her she was going to be uncontactable for a time. She also told me Malena had been working at a consultancy that does political polling. I called them and they said the same thing: she asked for time off the day after her father's death and a few hours before Viviana was murdered."

"She acted with impressive speed."

"If you think about it, so did Viviana."

"Viviana had been hiding since before they killed Goicochea."

"What if, by searching for Malena, we get her killed?"

Verónica considered this. Corso was right. "Let's forget Malena. We'll get what we need through other channels. Today I'm meeting Alicia Karlic."

"The court clerk. I think I met her once at a birthday party of Federico's. Speaking of your husband, why haven't you asked him for the information? He could definitely get hold of it."

"What's it to you?"

"Federico Córdova is one of my favourite sources. Always so elegant, so sober in his suit. And he's the only source who'll pay for coffee. You don't see that any more."

When she arrived at the bar once known as Usía, Dr Karlic was already waiting, drinking tea and looking a little nervous. Seeing her like that, Verónica asked, "Are you OK?"

"Yes, I just forgot to have a cigarette before coming in here. I haven't smoked for three hours. Do you smoke?"

"Yes, no – well, I'm trying to give it up."

"Good for you. Wait a second and I'll be back."

Verónica took this chance to order a coffee and look at her messages. María Magdalena was on a roll with her investigations into Viviana. Rodolfo was in touch with people from the Foreign Ministry. Patricia agreed that they should leave Malena be. Alicia Karlic came back to the table.

"That's much better. So you're investigating your bosses. Are you thinking of blackmailing them for a pay rise?"

"Even physical violence wouldn't achieve that. The truth is that I'm groping in the dark. It's not that I have anything against them, I'm just trying to find out if I ought to. Sorry, that sounds weird. I haven't gone crazy. Or perhaps I have, but not because of this. I'm investigating some irregularities connected to the death of a journalist."

"Goicochea?"

"Exactly."

"I saw it on TV. They were trying to mug him, poor guy."

"This doesn't have the hallmark of your average robbery. What's strange is that there's no appetite at the magazine for finding out what he was investigating when he was murdered. And I think, we think – because I'm working on this with some colleagues – that he may have been looking into something connected with the business dealings of *Nuestro Tiempo*'s owners."

"Now I understand. Look, if I were to bring you all the files circulating round the various courts connected to these three, we'd need a truck to transport them. Monteverde's accused of slavery in his cereal businesses, cattle rustling, tax evasion, money laundering, illegal exports via shell companies. Gómez Pardo, money laundering through his bingo halls, pimping, various threats, an allegation of sexual harassment by his ex-secretary, fraudulent imports, embezzlement in three companies that filed for bankruptcy. Moving on to Mayer, money laundering, yet more dubious exports, falsification of papers to award himself public land in Patagonia, constructions of gated communities that violate the building regulations of various localities, diversion of funds from his foundation, bribery, evasion of bidding processes by his security company. All three share a penchant for money laundering and illegal contributions to political campaigns."

"Any traffic infractions?"

"Well, since each one of them owns a fleet of vehicles of every shape and size, I'm guessing there must be a few unpaid speeding tickets in there."

"They don't come much worse."

"Not worse, but there are many who are equally bad. These men aren't unique, and that's part of the secret of their impunity. There are a lot of other powerful men like them. And judges are sensitive souls who don't like getting involved in cases that involve powerful people."

"I don't know where to start."

"Well, now that you tell me this has something to do with the death of Goicochea, I have an idea where you can start." She sipped some tea, paused dramatically and smiled. "Don't bother with any of the cases I've just mentioned."

"I'm not sure I understand."

"All the crimes I've just listed, even if they are worthy of a chapter in the Old Testament, or a new Code of Hammurabi, can be managed if the perpetrators are found guilty. Nobody will suffer particularly – they might lose some money, but it's a pittance compared to what they gain. Nor would they lose symbolic capital. In Argentina nobody shows you the door because you're a cattle rustler, a slaver, a pimp or a money launderer. These three are businessmen, not politicians. Even if they did get involved in politics, voters would likely view their criminal mindset as essential to doing business in such a difficult country. How can one not be a pimp or a slaver when the taxes are so high? What I'm trying to tell you is that none of these three men, together or separately, would have a journalist killed over the kind of allegations I've told you about."

"So it must be something really serious. Like, I don't know, they're involved in a paedophile ring."

"Could be. But even in a case like that, these people use a lot of intermediaries and proxies. The long arm of justice never reaches them. It's the little people who go down."

"OK, I'll rule out the traffic offences then."

"Good call."

They both fell silent. Verónica was trying to digest what the lawyer had told her.

Alicia had more to say: "While I was looking through the files, I found something I hesitate to ask you about."

"If you could stomach the files, feel free to bring up whatever you want."

"You did know Rosenthal and Associates are representing Sergio Mayer, right? No, you didn't know. I can tell by the face you're pulling."

"Me, pull faces?"

"Sometimes. Just now you looked like a combination of Munch's *The Scream* and the emoji of a surprised cat."

V

They had made a plan: to go out to dinner, chat, drink, eat great food. To forget, as far as possible, that in a few days she would have the abortion. Verónica knew that she was in the hands of a really good professional, that the sanitary conditions were excellent and that Federico would be waiting for her outside. Much better than the time she'd had to have a wisdom tooth out and the doctor had shaky hands, and nobody went with her. But it was still a shitty ordeal to have to go through.

What must have been going through Federico's pretty little head? What does a guy think about at times like this, Verónica wondered. Had he fantasized about fatherhood? About her growing belly and breasts, about running out to buy her ice cream at dawn, or appearing with some awful plush toy she would think delightful because it came from him, the father of her child? Well, none of that was going to happen. If Federico regretted it, he hadn't let it show. Perhaps he was happy not to be a father, to carry on with life as usual, with nothing to tie them down or interfere with the routine they had built together.

Either way, Federico had made a gesture that moved her. He had invited her to dinner at Los Bohemios, the restaurant at Atlanta's stadium. They had never been there together (she'd had lunch there a few times, but not dinner) and this seemed like the best plan in the world to her.

They arrived early, a little after nine, but the restaurant was already nearly full. The acoustics weren't the best, but that didn't bother Verónica. Those walls decorated with every one of the Atlanta shirts made up for anything and everything. While Federico headed for one of the few available tables, she went over, as she always did, to look at the framed shirts. She recognized the number seven Bichi Paredes shirt from the end of the nineties, with the Banco Patricios sponsorship, which she had worn as a teenager and still owned.

After a while she joined Federico at the table. He had already ordered water, ice and a bottle of Luigi Bosca (which the menu called "Vosca", in a marvellous example of their indifference to more expensive wines).

"I've left you the seat facing the wall with the shirts."

"Thanks Fede, for that and for bringing me here. This is my private Disneyland."

They ordered calamari to start and then gnocchi with mushroom sauce for her and for him braised pork shoulder with a demi-glace and honey, served with Greek *fava*. Federico was very taken with the gourmet description of this dish.

When they had finished the calamari and were waiting for the main dishes, Federico broached the subject preoccupying them both.

"So, Monday, at eleven."

"That's right."

"If we leave at ten we'll get there in plenty of time."

"We can leave at ten thirty. They're not going to cancel if we arrive ten minutes late. We should get there in half an hour."

"Do we need to take anything?"

"Nothing, apart from cash."

"I'll go to the bank tomorrow."

"Would you rather I went?"

"No. I'll get it out of the safe-deposit box. We'll pay in dollars and avoid quibbling over the amount in pesos."

"I don't think we'd end up arguing about that with a doctor."

"Doctor and also health entrepreneur, if I can call her that."

"She's what's available."

"Of course. I don't dispute that. And if it were twice the price we could, and would, still pay it."

The waitress arrived with their main courses. They both stared at their dishes.

"Are you OK, Fede?"

"I'm fine, honestly. It was meant to be a wry comment. I'm reassured to know you trust the doctor."

Verónica took his hand and smiled at him. Then she tore open a sachet of Parmesan and sprinkled it all over the gnocchi, repeating the action with a second sachet.

"I swear they bring less cheese every time."

They finished eating and, although there was only a little wine left, opted not to order more, just water and two coffees. Neither wanted a dessert either.

"Hey, Fede, why didn't you tell me Rosenthal are working with Sergio Mayer?"

"We don't tend to talk about the cases we handle at work. There are a lot of them."

"But Mayer is one of the owners of *Nuestro Tiempo*. I'd almost say he is *the* owner."

"This case isn't connected in any way to the magazine. I doubt you'd be interested in Mayer's travails in the world of real estate, or the twists and turns of his messy divorce."

"You're right about that."

"Did he call you?"

"No, I found out because the magazine is being very odd about the way they're handling the deaths of Goicochea and his ex-wife. There's something strange going on."

"And that was enough for you to conclude that he had them killed. Nice work."

"No. But I want to know what Mayer, Monteverde and Gómez Pardo are playing at. That's all. So far I haven't discovered much, apart from all the various criminal tricks they use and that you'll already know about."

"My lips are sealed."

Back at the apartment they went to bed, exchanged kisses and fell asleep.

Early the next morning, something woke Verónica. Federico was having a nightmare. Before she could try to waken him, he seemed to calm down and rolled onto his side. She stroked his hair. It was a relief not to be the one having nightmares this time.

VI

On Friday at eleven, Verónica, María Magdalena and Rodolfo met at Celta, a bar close to Congress that was equally handy – which is to say not at all handy – for all three of them.

"I have important news that may put us on the path to truth and justice, if we know how to navigate it," said Rodolfo. "But first I'd like to know how Patricia is doing."

"I've just spoken to Atilio and he told me Patricia is making a good recovery, and that if she keeps on like this they may discharge her on Monday, so long as she rests," Verónica said.

"She won't be out jogging any time soon," said Rodolfo.

"We could get together on Monday afternoon at her house," María Magdalena suggested.

"I don't know if I can. I have a medical appointment," said Verónica.

"Everything all right?"

"I'm getting an abortion."

"Ugh, I'm sorry to hear that," said María Magdalena.

"Do you know who the father is?" asked Rodolfo.

"Shut up, moron."

"But how are you in yourself?" asked María Magdalena.

"I'm fine, relaxed – well, anxious and tetchy, but sure of what I'm doing."

"That's the main thing."

"Without wanting to put my foot in it again, if you need anything, someone to go with you or whatever —"

"See how you can be a good human being when you put your mind to it, Rodo? I'm going with Fede, the man who planted this little seed, bastard that he is."

"Let's leave our meeting until Tuesday," said María Magdalena.

"Or we can get together later on Monday. Don't postpone it on my account. If all goes well, there's nothing to stop us meeting."

"We can always make up a bed for you next to Pato's."

"That's enough, Rodo, be nice."

"Well, let's see if the news I have will lift your spirits."

"I don't need my spirits lifting."

"Listen up, everyone. I think I mentioned before that I have some contacts in the Foreign Ministry. I didn't want to pursue the Malena line of enquiry, so I concentrated entirely on Viviana. Turns out she's worked with some people in the area of international cooperation. She seems not to have had any friends, but she did have good contacts. Since she wasn't a diplomat, she was one of those employees who are kept away from decision-making and who are not exactly frowned on by the diplomats but more like invisible. Until they're needed or called upon for some reason. An old acquaintance told me Viviana worked on a programme promoting business links with Greece, Israel and Turkey. She did it in tandem with another contractor. They told me he was in his office, so I went to see him. There's really nothing glamorous about those further reaches of the Ministry; the staff are basically civil servants who speak several languages, that's all. Anyway, I went to his office and there he was, sitting at his laptop and staring at it in deep concentration, as though he were saving the world from global catastrophe. When he got up to greet me, after I had made some extravagant gestures to catch his attention, I saw that he was about six foot one, light brown hair cut very short, nape cleanly shaven, a white shirt so tight it seemed about to burst, not because of a beer gut, God forbid, but thanks to some powerful muscles, a set of pecs that looked harder than the San Martín monument in the square outside. He smelled of cologne. I mean, let's get this straight: it's the end of the day and the guy smells of imported perfume. And he was remarkably welcoming. As soon as I started telling him I was trying to speak to people who knew Viviana, he said: 'How about we continue this chat over a drink?' You'll notice I haven't yet told you his name."

"And that's significant?"

"Very much so, I think, especially for one of you. Anyway, we went to a bar in town. We had a few beers and I told him I was doing a journalistic investigation. He asked me for which publication. I'll reproduce for you our exchange:

"'For the magazine *Nuestro Tiempo*.'

"'I know the one. It's very good. Verónica Rosenthal works there.'

"'That's right. In fact, I'm working on this investigation with her.'

"Apologies for ignoring you, María Magdalena. On with the story:

"'Seriously? I don't believe you,' he said, and burst out laughing. Once he had recovered from his own fit of laughter, he ordered another round of beers. I wasn't going to say no."

Rodolfo was approaching the climax of his story, savouring each line before arriving at the surprise finale he doubtless wanted to spring on them.

"I asked if he knew you and he said: 'Do I *know* her? I don't think many people know her as well as I do.' Inside I was thinking that if he had been your boyfriend or lover, he was very misguided. He should get in line with all the other people who think they know you. Anyway, get this, the guy only goes and says: 'Now that I know Vero's involved, I only want to speak to her. I'm sorry, not to sideline you, but this is my chance to see her again, and I don't want to miss it. Tell her I'll be waiting for her tomorrow' – in other words, today – 'at six in my office.' So he wants to see you on your own."

"But who is he, what's he called?" Verónica almost shrieked; she was getting bored of Rodolfo's mysterious little game.

"Steel yourself. He's called Eitan Boniek."

Corso was silent, waiting for Verónica's reaction, but no reaction came.

"Eitan Boniek," Rodolfo repeated.

"I don't know anybody by that name."

"You're kidding me."

"I swear I'm not."

"Let's google him," said María Magdalena, ever practical.

Their search threw up no Eitan Boniek matching, either in appearance or activity, the one described by Rodolfo, who now seemed disconcerted, which was rare for him.

"I reckon he's a psychopath who reads all your articles and thinks he knows everything about you," said María Magdalena.

"Then I should meet him somewhere public and safe, which the San Martín building is."

"He's in the building opposite, but it's equally safe."

"Give me the details and I'll go and see him."

And that's what Verónica did. At the appointed time, she went to the Foreign Ministry and announced to the reception-ist – who didn't deny the man's existence – that she had come to see Eitan Boniek. Perhaps María Magdalena was right and the Beefy Diplomat (as her friends would call him) was simply someone with an unhealthy fixation on her. She would have to be firm with him, and crystal clear that, whatever his game was, it could not continue.

She reached his office and knocked on the door. A man's voice said, "Come in."

Verónica opened the door and saw Eitan Boniek, who must indeed be about six foot one, and yes: his white shirt seemed ready to burst open under the pressure of those muscles.

"Hello, Vero. Such a long time since we last saw each other," said Eitan, smiling shyly.

But that idiot Rodolfo had been wrong about one thing: the man's hair wasn't brown, but blonde. And he had also failed to mention an important detail: he had a lot of freckles over his cheeks. Verónica felt an ocean rush through her. With a happiness rare in her, and with an urge to shout and jump for joy (when had she last felt like jumping?), she cried: "Chino, it's you! My beloved Chino!"

10   *The Others*

Not even his secretary knew where he was going, and that was rare, but it was worth making an exception for this appointment. Mabel tended to get very worried, more so even than his daughters, and Aarón had no desire to give her explanations and answers that he wasn't yet prepared to put into words.

After seeing the results of his last tests, the neurologist had referred him to an oncologist with a clinic in Belgrano. Aarón took a taxi that went quickly down Avenida Libertador, but not quickly enough to stop his mind racing. If he had learned anything in fifty years as a lawyer it was that you should always anticipate the next step but never in the expectation of bad news. Keep busy and don't worry. And yet he was already imagining reams of misfortune written all over the tests Dr Raimundi had ordered.

He hadn't wanted to read them himself; he wasn't a doctor. He despised people who thought they could become lawyers because they had once skimmed an article about law on the internet, that school for prize ignoramuses. And he had no desire to put himself on the other side of the desk, interpreting the results of blood and urine tests, CT scans and MRIs.

Dr Gálvez's secretary asked him to take a seat. There was no other patient waiting, just the one currently being seen. Aarón Rosenthal tried to overhear what was being said in the consulting room, but the voices sounded distorted from where he was sitting; he could hear a man talking but couldn't make out a single sentence. Fifteen minutes later the consulting room door opened and the doctor saw out a woman accompanied by someone who must be her son. The woman was perhaps ten years older than Aarón, but she looked fine. Then again, he looked fine too.

The doctor asked Aarón to come through. He was at least sixty, bald, skinny, and wearing thick glasses. He studied Aarón's notes and the test results. Then he looked up and confirmed what the neurologist had already said, in part. He employed the same kind of words and manner that Aarón did when wearing his lawyer hat.

"I'd like to get a second opinion," said Aarón when the doctor had finished speaking.

"I think that's a good idea. I don't know if you have someone in mind, but I can recommend some medical centres abroad you could send the results to. If they request additional tests, Dr Raimundi or I can arrange those."

"Thank you. I'll mention it to Raimundi, if you don't mind."

"Of course not. How about we discuss treatment options?" the oncologist asked.

"Absolutely."

"As Dr Raimundi has already explained, the tumour is operable. So an operation would be the first step. Argentina has some really good surgeons."

Aarón shifted in his seat. He had already discussed this with the neurologist and decided to have an operation abroad.

"There's an Argentine surgeon working in a clinic in New York," Aarón said. "I'd like him to do the operation. He carries out the whole procedure with the patient awake. I want to avoid general anaesthesia."

"And Dr Raimundi agrees?"

"He's the one who suggested it."

"Very well. What symptoms have you had so far?"

"Bad headaches, temporary loss of vision – that was brief, but dangerous, because I was driving. I hit the brakes and the car behind went into me. Nothing too serious, but I've stopped driving altogether now. I feel physically exhausted. I don't know if that's related to the tumour."

"You're low on iron, which could be another reason."

"I'm taking a supplement."

"Good. Well, after surgery, which is the major risk, all those symptoms will largely disappear. At that point we'll begin radiotherapy and chemotherapy to prevent metastases in other parts of the body."

"With that treatment, how much longer can I expect to live?"

"Medicine isn't an exact science. Some patients respond better than others."

"Yes, but there must be an average."

"If we go with the most aggressive treatment, between eighteen months and three years."

"Do you mean more aggressive against the cancer, or against me?"

"Sadly, it amounts to the same thing. To fight the cancer, we use drugs that significantly impair the body's functions."

"And if I don't have any treatment?"

"There's no exact timescale in that case either. I'd say between six months and a year. Without treatment, the last weeks can be extremely hard."

"Perhaps I wouldn't have to reach those weeks."

"As a doctor I can't tell you that's an option."

"You don't have to tell me. And don't worry, I won't ask you to do anything that goes against your Hippocratic oath."

The oncologist's expression was impassive. He would make a great poker player, Aarón thought. He didn't need him, though. Aarón had friends who were doctors and he knew he could count on one of them, perhaps on Raimundi himself, to ease his way out when the time came.

"I'm not going to have any treatment, Doctor."

"You should talk this through with your loved ones."

"It's precisely because of my loved ones that I would like to say goodbye while I'm still well enough. I have grandchildren, three daughters, close friends I would prefer to remember me as I am now, rather than prolong the agony for another year."

"All the same, I'd recommend you think about it."

After leaving the clinic, Aarón decided to walk through Belgrano. The time had come to die. That didn't seem so terrible to him. He had started coming to terms with the idea when Raimundi did the first tests. This was simply confirmation of the fact. He thought about how lucky he was. The cancer would give him enough time to leave everything in order. He should start preparing his own farewell. As someone who had always been self-sufficient, who had never liked to rely on anyone else's help, what lay ahead did not seem so onerous. Life was a succession of irritating admin tasks, punctuated by the odd moment of happiness or disquiet.

II

She was in that half-waking state where dreams begin to mingle with the sounds and sensations of the real world. In the dream, Federico was touching her between the legs. They were in a bar, she was wearing a miniskirt and he had put his hand up under it without caring about the people around them. The most vivid aspect of the dream was not Federico's touch, though, but his smell, that mix of perfume

178

and post-fuck sweat. She could feel that the dream was fading, that his hand was no longer between her legs, but she clung like a dog to that smell; the smell of Federico's body was still there, on the pillow, on the sheets.

Ángeles woke up drenched in sweat. And alone, as women who have married lovers do. Federico wasn't technically married, but that was a small detail given the situation. She was alone, while he would be sleeping with his arms around his wife. For a second she hated them, him and his wife.

The air conditioning was off, and the lights wouldn't come on. Another power cut. Ángeles looked out of her bedroom window into the street. The traffic lights were off too, so it must be an outage in their area. She showered and put on casual clothes (jeans, flat shoes, a lilac silk shirt) so as not to look too lawyerly in front of Roxana Mayer; Soldati was her maiden name, but she was still using her ex's surname. Ángeles realized the negotiation would likely go more smoothly if she came across as a potential friend rather than a lawyer for the other side. She put on a little make-up and set off for Vicente López in a taxi paid for by the firm.

Roxana had invited her to brunch at her house, so they could continue their conversation. The fact that only Ángeles was invited had taken Diana Veglio aback. She was in charge of the negotiation, after all, and Ángeles had originally gone along in a supporting role, as bag carrier. And now suddenly the younger lawyer was the one leading the negotiation, while Veglio could only look on mutely. And all because she knew a bit about Mesopotamian culture.

Fortunately Veglio had an admirable capacity to adapt herself to less than favourable situations without making a fuss. When they had left Roxana's house, she hadn't upbraided Ángeles or scolded her for speaking out of turn. On the contrary, she had conceded that Ángeles's reference to the

179

Egyptians was inspired (Veglio hadn't retained the name of the Sumerian people). She had simply asked Ángeles to keep her briefed on whatever happened in the next meeting with Roxana.

In the end Veglio didn't wait to hear from Ángeles, though, and that morning had already sent three voicemails with advice, suggestions and red lines. Ángeles was tempted to remind Diana that she wasn't her boss, but she held back. She didn't like wasting energy on being annoyed with people when it was easier to ignore them.

A uniformed maid led her into the garden behind the house. Roxana was swimming in the pool. She looked happy to see Ángeles and waved to her. "Would you like me to lend you a bikini? The weather's perfect for a swim."

It was true that it was incredibly hot, heavy and humid, as Buenos Aires tended to be in the summer, although this was the middle of spring. But it was also true that Ángeles wasn't there to swim. And if it was one of Roxana's own bikinis she was offering, the top would probably be too small for her and the bottoms too big. She was able to confirm that hunch when Roxana got out of the water and dried herself with a big towel before putting on a robe.

"Well then, let's go to the veranda and have a delicious restorative juice while they bring us something to eat."

Roxana put a short, sleeveless cotton dress on top of the wet bikini. She looked about forty-five, with a body honed through diets and the gym, expensively maintained skin and a nose that had doubtless been fixed a long time ago. Strangely, she seemed not to have had breast implants. Perhaps she was due another trip to the operating room.

The maid brought out artisan bread, jams, cheese and scrambled eggs for each of them. Ángeles helped herself to coffee and to some slices of prosciutto, a piece of brie and eggs, while Roxana recommended some hypoallergenic lipsticks she had brought from New York but which you could get in select perfumeries in Buenos Aires. It was Roxana who brought up the subject of her divorce and the division of assets.

"How pathetic of Sergio to say no. Doesn't he realize he's only making everything more complicated?"

"Have you been able to consider any of the alternatives to the security firm? To be totally frank, I think you could probably get all of them if you wanted. I shouldn't really tell you that."

Roxana smiled. "I'm grateful to you for the generosity my ex lacks but finds himself obliged to offer. We never had children. He already had some, and I didn't want to be a mother. I was the one who pushed him to set up Tuentur. There was nothing like it in Argentina. Sergio is a genius at setting up businesses, but a disaster when it comes to developing and maintaining them. If Tuentur had failed, or become just another security firm, he would never have been able to achieve all he has in the last fifteen years. He had the contacts to set it up, I had a lot of local clients. Remember I was a corporate lawyer – that's how I met him. He was still married to the mother of his children. I was the one who said 'With your contacts and my clients, we'll be millionaires in two years.' He promised that, if we made it, he'd take me round the world. I kept my side of the bargain. He always wants to spend vacations in Miami."

"Didn't you go to the Seychelles?"

"A beach day, a business day, a beach day, a business day. The same sort of arrangement when we went to London, to Israel, to Mexico. The only place he can fully relax is Miami."

The maid poured them coffee and offered more dishes, but neither of them wanted anything else.

"And that's why the company means so much to me, darling. Because it's the child we never had. I'm not going to give him full custody. At the most, I'll offer him forty-nine per cent. Fifty-one per cent and the controlling interest are for me, as befits any good mother."

Ángeles found equating a company with a child ridiculous, but she put on a face of total agreement.

"I was very surprised you knew about the goddess Inanna," said Roxana, abruptly changing the subject.

"And the god Anu."

"The god of the sky and the constellations. Are you interested in meditation?"

"Very much so. I just don't have time for it."

"That's not true."

Ángeles briefly thought she had been found out.

Roxana continued: "One can always make time. You should come to a meeting in Uruk."

"Isn't that in Iraq?"

Roxana laughed. "Actually, Uruk hasn't existed for a long time. It was the first great city in antiquity. But I'm talking about a centre near here, in Vicente López. We practise meditation, conscious breathing, communication with our own cosmos."

"A cosmos made up of each of our stars."

"Exactly. Our lives are a small universe organized into galaxies and systems. Our emotional galaxy consists of family systems, in the present, past and future. The work or professional galaxy is made up of everything we have done or will do, thanks to our skills, and the galaxy of desires is based on our sexual system, with its fears and dreams. The goal is to link each system in its galaxy and each galaxy in our cosmos."

"It sounds fascinating."

"You'd love it. You must come. But you can only come to Uruk by invitation."

"Are you going to invite me?"

"Obviously. You're coming to the next meeting."

For a moment Ángeles felt slightly dizzy, along with a need to relieve herself. She asked where the bathroom was.

"Go back into the living room and take the first corridor on the left, first door."

Ángeles did as instructed. There was a pressure in her stomach, as though she needed to burp. As she entered the living room she saw a man coming down the stairs from the rooms on the first floor. He was thin, tall, about fifty years old, with pale blonde, almost white, hair. He seemed very agile. "Hello," he said, smiling but without paying her much attention.

It was only one word, and yet enough to give Ángeles the impression that he was foreign, perhaps English. Was he Roxana's boyfriend? She hadn't introduced him.

There wasn't much time to think about this because, as Ángeles was about to say hello back, a wave of nausea swept through her and surged into her mouth like a tsunami. Ángeles had no choice but to vomit right there on the living room floor, throwing up the scrambled eggs, the prosciutto, the cheese, the artisan breads. Maybe she was vomiting up the nervous tension of the past few days. Maybe she was vomiting up the man's greeting. Maybe she was vomiting up things and situations she hardly dared imagine.

III

Like a bride jilted at the altar who puts on her wedding dress and ponders what might have been, every so often María Magdalena Cortez tried on the nun's habit she had worn in the Order of the Daughters of St Paul. Ever since the second Vatican Council had absolved them from wearing traditional garb, the Pauline sisters used clothes that might easily be chosen by any modest woman: long, dark blue skirt, white shirt, blue sleeveless cardigan on top of that and, for some occasions, a headdress that was also blue – a small headscarf that was nevertheless enough to identify them as nuns. The fact that their headwear was less ostentatious than that of other congregations didn't always strike María Magdalena as an advantage. After all, the first time she had thought of becoming a nun was as a child watching television: she had wanted to be like Sister Bertrille, the character played by Sally Field in *The Flying Nun*, and she wore a corvette, that outlandish wimple that looks like a delta wing stuck to the head, a key element in the dress of the Sisters of Charity. María Magdalena never got to wear a religious uniform like that. Over the years, remembering the origin of her vocation, she came to the conclusion that what she had really wanted wasn't to be a nun, but to fly.

She often put on her Daughters of St Paul outfit, headscarf included, and wore it all day. If she had to go out (to the supermarket, to the bank, to a pharmacy), she would set out dressed as a Pauline Sister (admittedly removing her headscarf first).

For the umpteenth time, María Magdalena went over Viviana's papers without uncovering any links to a current case. Everything seemed to belong to past events either resolved or forgotten. She poured herself a whisky, then another, breaking a promise to herself not to drink before midday. Her phone rang: an unknown number.

"Is this Sister María Magdalena?"

For a few seconds her blood ran cold. It had been many years since she had been referred to as "Sister" by anyone, including her own flesh-and-blood sister.

"I'm sorry, I think you must have the wrong number."

"María Magdalena Cortez?"

"Yes, but I no longer wear the habit."

"That surprises me, Sister. The habit doesn't make the monk, or nun. I speak as someone who's wearing a habit right now."

The person on the other end of the line must have sensed that María Magdalena was about to end the call.

"Don't hang up, Sister. I'm sorry, dear María Magdalena. We met a few years ago in an ecclesiastical meeting in Paraná. I'm Father Anselmo."

She remembered him: a cheerful priest, borderline blasphemous at times. He had been the head of a monastery, back then at least.

"Father Anselmo, what a surprise."

"Don't be alarmed, they haven't sent me to ask you back. We forgive all sins apart from the renunciation of God. For internal purposes, that's our capital sin. I'm calling you about something else. I'd like you to visit me at the Capuchin monastery."

"If it's not to persuade me to take up the habit again, tell me what the reason is."

"I can't tell you anything in advance. Just that it's urgent. You have to come right away. And I'm going to make an odd request: have you still got your work gear?"

"You mean my nun's clothes?"

"Exactly. Please come dressed like that."

"You're pulling my leg."

"I swear I'm not, María Magdalena. And I swear by all the saints that you will not regret coming."

María Magdalena got changed into her Daughter of St Paul dress, arranged her headscarf in front of the mirror and went out. This was crazy; she felt as though she were setting off to satisfy the erotic fantasy of a priest, one who was at least interested in adult women and not children, a point in his favour. But she didn't mind: at least this mission gave her a chance to get out of the rut her investigation was currently stuck in.

She shouldn't have been so meticulous with her uniform, because now she was dying of heat. Deciding it was far too hot to take the bus to Saavedra, María Magdalena hailed a taxi. The driver eyed her in his rear-view mirror. Nuns were never invisible.

Arriving at the monastery, she asked for Father Anselmo, who appeared instantly, walking towards her with so much emotion on his face that María Magdalena feared he would embrace her – a false alarm. He simply squeezed her hand fervently.

"You're a sight for sore eyes, Sister," he said and, dropping his voice, "Did anyone follow you here?"

"Father, you didn't tell me I had to look out for stalkers."

"I couldn't say that on the phone in case the line was tapped. I trusted you would always take that precaution anyway."

"Well, I didn't take it. And I'd ask you please not to call me Sister. It makes me uncomfortable."

"As you wish, María Magdalena. I'll tell you why I asked you to come. For a few days now, a person has been living here with us who would like to see you. He asked me to arrange a meeting. Obviously, at least for the time being, nobody should know he's here. And since we aren't allowed visits from laywomen, I thought the best way to arrange this encounter would be for you to come dressed like this, like a woman of God."

As Father Anselmo spoke, they walked through the monastery's corridors. María Magdalena was briefly reminded of that other religious house, the one she and Verónica had been in a year previously. A shiver ran through her body.

They arrived at one of the rooms off the cloister. Inside were a pallet bed and a chair. Anselmo asked her to wait there, and María Magdalena weighed up whether to do as he asked or make her escape. What if the priest had gone mad, or was a friend of those baby-stealing nuns she and Verónica had exposed? Before she could make up her mind, someone else came into the room. It was the last person she would have expected to meet there: Pablo, the graphic designer who had worked with her on the magazine *Vida Cristiana* and who, days before, had guided them to Viviana.

Pablo came into the room on his own, unaccompanied by Anselmo. He said hello and struggled to articulate something else, managing only to embrace her, weeping. María Magdalena tried to soothe him. She looked for a tissue in her bag and passed it to him. Pablo blew his nose. He seemed to relax.

"Viviana knew they would go there to kill her. She was sure of it. Once you had left, she cooked up some ridiculous excuse to get me out of the house too. Then she sent me a text. She asked me not to go back and…" He faltered, then made himself go on. "And she told me she loved me. We had been together for a long time."

"They used us to get to her."

"They would have found her sooner or later. They weren't looking for the tablet, as you had thought. That's why she gave you any old one."

"How did she know they weren't looking for the tablet?"

"For two reasons: because they had already been in her apartment, where the tablet was along with many other useful documents, and because they hadn't taken anything. They wanted her."

"How wonderful that she was able to look after you and save you."

"She was always like that, generous and heroic." A smile crept over Pablo's face. "She sent me another message too. She told me to give all the material to you."

"The blessed tablet?"

"Yes. She wrote '*the tablet and any papers that are useful to them*'. I don't have any idea what she was talking about. But here's the key to her apartment. Take it and look for whatever you need."

As she left the monastery, María Magdalena checked she wasn't being followed. She walked a few blocks against the flow of traffic, then turned 180 degrees, paused by a kiosk, looked all around her, then jumped into a taxi seconds before the lights went red. She kept her headdress on, so people would see her as a nun. Nobody mistrusts a woman of the cloth. She reached Viviana's building and opened the door with no difficulty. Luckily there was no sign of the caretaker.

The key to Viviana's apartment also worked perfectly. María Magdalena switched on the lights, not wanting to open any blinds. She made her way to the bedroom, where Pablo had said the tablet was hidden under the base of the closet. She had to lift up a tile and there it should be.

She took in the tidy bedroom, the clothes, hanging in the closet, which had belonged to Viviana and now waited uselessly for their owner. Nothing made sense, but María Magdalena nursed the hope that she could at least put the tablet to some use on Viviana's behalf. She bent down and tapped the floor, located the loose tile and, with some effort, moved it out of the way to reveal the hiding place. But the tablet wasn't there. María shone her phone's light into the space: nothing. Perhaps there was another tile? She tried all the others, one by one. None could be moved. Somebody had got there before her.

María Magdalena went to the living room, where the desk was, to search for the papers Pablo had mentioned. To her surprise, there were several folders. One had a Post-it stuck on it, with a street name and number. She recognized the address of the house where Goicochea had been murdered. As she picked up the folder, she heard a noise in the corridor. She listened intently and was terrified to hear a key turning in the lock. María Magdalena raced to the bathroom, clutching the file. She didn't have time to close the door fully, because someone was already inside the apartment.

Whoever it was who had just entered seemed to have paused in the doorway. Doubtless he or she had noticed the lights were on and was advancing slowly, measuring each step. María Magdalena guessed this was the person who had killed Viviana and Goicochea. Her body started shaking and sweating copiously. She was scared her teeth would chatter and give her away to the assassin.

Finally the person, a man, reached the desk. María Magdalena could see him from her hiding place. He was young, probably not more than twenty. Skinny, a bit gawky, he was wearing a black T-shirt that said RAMONES. In his hand he carried something that could be a razor, or a small knife. The man started leafing through the papers on the desk but seemed not to find what he was looking for. It was probably the folder María Magdalena was pressing against herself.

Taking out his phone, the guy made a call. "The folder's not here." He paused. "Well, I'm telling you it isn't, it's not here. Come and have a look yourself if you don't believe me." Another silence. "If you'd taken it yourself the last time, we'd have saved ourselves the trip. Go on then, I'll wait for you. Wait, don't hang up. Did you put the lights on when you came?"

The youth looked around him. It must have occurred to him that the person who had the folder was still in the apartment. María Magdalena sized up the situation: the person the young man was talking to might be downstairs and about to come up to the apartment; once they arrived, she wouldn't be able to escape, and it would be easier to fight off one aggressor than two. There was no time to lose: picking up a hairdryer, she burst out of the bathroom and flung it at the man who, with quick reflexes, raised an arm to protect himself then came at her, holding the knife. As he lunged forward, María Magdalena couldn't get out of the way in time and the youth managed to slash her clothes and right arm. She screamed and ran towards the door, then through it and frantically down the stairs as the sleeve of her white shirt began to turn red and blood dripped onto the steps. The man seemed not to be following her, but María Magdalena didn't stop until she reached the ground floor. With unaccustomed dexterity, she opened the door to the street and ran away as quickly as she could.

Exhausted, she stopped in a square and sat down on a bench. From there she could watch out for the young man following her. She found a sanitary towel in her bag and pressed it against her arm, which was burning like hell. Though still bleeding, it didn't seem to be a serious wound. María Magdalena couldn't help thinking that she looked like a martyr in her nun's clothing. Glancing at her watch, she saw it was already time for her meeting with Vero and Rodo at Patricia's house. What with the folder and an open wound, she was going to make quite an entrance.

IV

He lit a cigarette, for the sake of something to do. Of the many jobs he did, a stake-out was the most annoying. Those dead times that movies gloss over in a five-second shot but which, in the real life of a vigilante, can last hours. At least when you were waiting to kill someone there was the excitement of anticipation, but if all you had to do was spend hours surveilling a civilian, that was the pits. Better to work in an office.

A message arrived that read: *Any news, Maluma?* and he replied *None, Little Boss.* A pointless exchange because, if there had been any news, he wouldn't put it in a text. Nobody called him Maluma, apart from the boss. And nobody apart from him called the boss Little Boss: he didn't do it out of affection but to remind him about the bigger bosses higher up the chain. It was his way of getting revenge, because he didn't like being called Maluma. He didn't think he looked anything like the Colombian singer.

He had managed to park right outside the building; that was a miracle, in Buenos Aires, finding somewhere you could pull over. From there he had a good view of the entrance. He hated these dead times, like when he'd had to look after Locatti, the chick they had kidnapped for a few hours. Although to be fair, crashing into her car had served up a bit of action. And you had to hand it to the boss, he had covered all the bases. He was always a few steps ahead of the others. When he made the call to the journalist, Rosenthal, his boss already knew everything about her. "Intelligence, Maluma," he would say.

And he'd been sent here to monitor this building for the same reason. He wasn't the only one the boss asked to do this kind of job. The boss had a powerful team around him. Subcontracted, obviously. The only one who worked directly for the boss was him. The boss trusted him. And rightly so.

Their target arrived at the building, wearing her little suit and carrying some bags from the supermarket. She was a lawyer, Ángeles Basualdo, a feisty little thing. You could tell she had good tits, plus an ass she knew how to move in that tight skirt. He had suggested putting cameras inside the lawyer's apartment, but the boss didn't want to go to the trouble, said it wasn't necessary. He was disappointed by that: he would have liked to see her naked or fucking, that is if she had someone to fuck. She looked a bit prudish, like one of those girls who never cut loose and die a virgin. He wondered if he would have to kill her. They hadn't spoken about that at all. And if it did need to happen, surely the boss would kill her. After all, he had been the one to liquidate the journalist and that other chick. He didn't delegate the skilled work. An admirable work ethic.

The girl had already gone into the building. He took a few photos. The boss was bound to have hacked into her computer or phone. He'd be enjoying the selfies she must have taken with those tits. *She's arrived, everything normal, I don't think she'll come out. Shall I go? No, wait*, the boss replied. "Fuck your sister, you shitty little boss," he said under his breath.

But once again, the boss knew what he was doing. If he was being asked to stay it was because something might be about to happen. And it happened: he saw Dr Córdova, the guy who lived with the journalist and worked with the lawyer, get out of the car parked behind his. Córdova walked towards the building and rang the entryphone. He looked furtively around, as if sensing he was being watched. Seemed like an intelligent guy. He had to make an effort not to be spotted, so he could get some nice pics. Ángeles appeared, opened the door, and scarcely were they inside it when the little minx put her arms around the lawyer's neck and planted a big, movie-style kiss on him. *Look at that little hypocrite snogging someone else's husband.* He took quite a few photos of them kissing. And he cursed his luck, knowing now what he was missing by failing to place cameras inside the apartment.

11 *The Only Question*

"Let's get out of this dump, they don't even serve good coffee," said Eitan – although Verónica couldn't get used to calling him that. For her he would always be El Chino.

They went down in the elevator, where he stood so closely that Verónica had an absurd fear that Eitan was about to kiss her. She could smell the cologne that had so scandalized Rodolfo Corso.

"I can't believe you didn't know my name."

Lucía, Martín, Hernán, Flavio, Gonzalo and El Chino. Those were the names of the Villa Crespo gang. She must at some point have known El Chino was called Eitan, but she never associated that name with him. Perhaps the other children had given him a nickname because his real name sounded strange to them. By the time Verónica joined the gang, Eitan was already El Chino for all intents and purposes. As for his surname, nobody knew that, nor any of the other children's either.

They walked along Esmeralda towards Santa Fe. Verónica couldn't believe she was walking beside El Chino, as she had done so many times along Padilla or Malabia. She even had the sensation that they were adopting the same weary gait as in those childhood days. They spent these minutes repeating their surprise and happiness at this unexpected reunion.

Reaching the corner, they went into a bar that didn't seem to have much going for it. Verónica liked the fact that El Chino hadn't sought out somewhere cooler.

Eitan was sizing her up, more amused than anything else. "Look at the woman you turned into. Who'd have thought it?"

"I'm the same though! I've got photos from back then."

"Have you got photos of us, of the gang?"

"No, not a single one. It's a shame. What about you? Are you a diplomat now?"

"I never got that far. I tried to get into the diplomatic corps but I was rejected. Did you take a degree in journalism?"

"Well actually I graduated in communication studies, but yes, I'm a journalist."

"Wasn't your dad a lawyer?"

"Still is. He's still working away. Listen, Chino. One day you were playing ball on the corner with us and the next day you weren't there any more, neither you nor your family."

"Ah yes. We left in a hurry. Without saying goodbye to anyone. If you like I can give you a quick rundown of the last twenty years."

"I'd love that."

"My old man had a broom and brush factory. When the market opened up to imports, the factory went under and my dad got into a lot of debt. Before the creditors started coming after him, he decided to move us all to Israel. There had often been talk of that possibility at home. It was like our family utopia. My mother was always saying we'd be better off in Israel. And so my dad let her have her way. He left the furniture, the television set and some of the clothes to one of his brothers, who was a trucker. In exchange, my uncle drove us to Ezeiza for free. We flew to Tel Aviv. My father had a cousin who lived there and there were a lot of Argentinians he knew. None of his creditors, luckily. I had to carry on with school there. It wasn't easy to learn Hebrew, but I did it. I grew up, did three years' military service, studied sociology. I worked for an NGO that fights discrimination against Israelis of Arab origin, which was controversial because of the Palestinians' living conditions. Things were getting heavy, so I opted for a change of scene. Someone put me in touch with a regional director of the UN Food and Agriculture Organization and I worked with them for several years, first in Paris, then in London and Athens. When the chance came up to apply for a position in the Argentine Foreign Ministry, funded by an international organization, I jumped at it. They chose me, and I've been here for two years, drinking *mate*, eating dulce de leche and empanadas. Although, truth be told, those things weren't hard to get hold of in Tel Aviv or London."

"A nomadic life."

"Tell me about it."

Verónica in turn told Eitan about her career in journalism. She tried to make it sound like dull and routine work, avoiding any details that might suggest the opposite.

"Are you married, have you had children?"

"I didn't get married, but I've been in a relationship for nearly a year, and no, I don't have children."

"What's the lucky man's name?"

"Federico. He's a lawyer and he works with my father."

"The full Oedipus."

"I hadn't thought of it like that. Could be. What about you?"

"I'm single, and feeling the pressure. I can't get any girl to take me seriously."

"Because you wear very tight shirts, and that can give a girl the wrong impression."

Eitan laughed. "You're right. Perhaps I should ease off the gym and the protein shakes." He seemed to be thinking about something. Finally he asked: "Did you know that my father and your mother went out together?"

Verónica's mouth fell open. "You're fucking kidding me."

"You didn't know?"

"I'm dying here. No, nobody told me."

Verónica searched her memory. Her mother had never spoken about this, neither had her grandparents. It was true that she didn't know a lot about the lives of her parents before they'd got together, but wouldn't somebody have mentioned that her mother had once gone out with the neighbour?

She remembered something else: "Chino, you missed Atlanta's promotion to the Nacional B. Later on we were relegated again, then went back up. But I was very sad not to see you in the stands during that first promotion."

"Ah, it wasn't a big deal. I only went to the games to be with my dad. I always liked River more, and in the last few years I've started supporting Barcelona."

"Oh, Chino. How can it be that in less than an hour I've gone from one of the happiest moments of my life to the greatest disappointment? What do you mean you don't care about Atlanta? Tell me that's a joke."

"I'm just not that interested in soccer."

"Now I feel like crying."

Eitan doubtless thought she was kidding, but Verónica was genuinely hurt. Clearly he hoped to get the conversation back on track by changing the subject. He asked her about the other members of their gang, but neither had any idea what had become of them. Verónica couldn't help harping on about the subject of their childhood club, so Eitan gave up fighting and turned the conversation to Viviana.

"Your colleague wanted to know about Viviana Smith."

"Who was murdered, like Andrés Goicochea."

"I read that it was a robbery gone wrong and that's why they were killed. But I don't think that's the reason, at least not in Viviana's case."

"Exactly. And not in Goicochea's either – the two crimes are linked."

"They had been partners, no?"

"Goicochea was investigating something, and we suspect Viviana was his source."

"I worked with her. She kept a low profile, few friends, always on the defensive. A lot of people thought she was a pain in the ass. But she was cool with me – in fact, we travelled to a conference in Istanbul together once and she was good company."

"And she was already getting mixed up with powerful people at that time?"

"It was actually in Istanbul that she exposed an irregular arrangement between Israeli and Turkish agri-tech companies. There aren't supposed to be direct links between companies accessing the programme we were working on, and she discovered that they shared a third company based in Cyprus. But that kind of annoying situation crops up all the time. There were ruffled feathers, some lost business, but nothing that would make someone come to Argentina and kill you."

"I suspect she was killed because of something she never managed to expose."

"Of course. Something that wasn't in the public domain."

"Perhaps she still didn't have enough evidence to inform on someone."

"Or possibly she wasn't sure that what she had managed to find out was enough to prove anything."

Verónica asked the waiter to bring another round of coffee and soda water, then continued with her speculations.

"What surprises me is that she had a lot of experience blowing the whistle on people and companies."

"And states. Once she picked a fight with Tanzania, which a lot of people here still remember."

"But she always confined herself to the organizations involved. In some cases, there might be repercussions in the press, but that was nothing to do with Viviana. Whereas in this case she made sure there was a press report before she went public."

Eitan nodded thoughtfully. "You know what? You're very intelligent."

Verónica eyed him suspiciously, scanning the phrase for irony.

"Seriously. As a little girl you were really clever too. I'm not surprised you're such a good journalist."

"I don't know how to respond to such praise. You're very intelligent too. It was a smart idea to let go of the bike so I would learn to ride it on my own."

"A risky strategy, but it paid off. What do you know about Malena Goicochea?"

"Nobody knows where she is. The same day Viviana was killed, she told her workplace and friends that she was going away for some time."

"She had an internship in the Foreign Ministry and worked with us."

"Did you have dealings with her?"

"Yes, perhaps a little more than advisable. She was the complete opposite of Viviana. Two days after starting work here she'd made friends with half the office."

"So she was nice."

"I don't know if 'nice' is the right word. She was quite stand-offish in groups, in fact, but really cool when you were alone with her. Seductive, for want of a better word."

"And she seduced you."

"Well, she tried, but I thought she was too young for me. We had a good bond, though. I was sorry when she left, because she was very capable."

"Very intelligent."

"Yes, she was very intelligent too. Just like us. Do you think she could be in danger?"

"She certainly seems to think so."

"Then she should be protected, shouldn't she? And it won't be any use going to the police."

"None whatsoever."

"Let me know if I can help in any way. The Foreign Ministry sometimes has resources for that kind of thing. We could put her in a friendly embassy. Something like that."

Verónica thought this was a good idea, but part of her mind was still on what Eitan had said about not wanting a fling with Malena. That was a point in his favour. It was the first thing she planned to tell Rodolfo Corso. Not all men were lechers like him.

The second round of coffees were finished. The soda too. It was either a third round or —

"Look, Vero, how about this. I have access to the files and papers Viviana left behind when she retired. I suspect there's nothing significant in them, but you can never be sure. I'm also going to try to talk to other people who knew her and are now on diplomatic postings abroad. Whatever I can get my hands on, I'll pass on to you. And if you need a hand with anything, count on me. Because you already know how to ride a bicycle."

They said goodbye in the street and she crossed over to the Metro station. She was walking on air. Two decades ago, El Chino had disappeared from her life. She had never looked for him; he seemed to belong to an era that had ended with the death of her grandmother. Now suddenly she had had a chance to meet him again, to solve some of the mysteries of the past and to be happy that here was a man whose life was plainly on the right track. He hadn't been her first love, because she would never have fallen in love with a kid from the block as Lucía had done. But perhaps the way he had vanished into thin air had allowed her to fantasize, for some time afterwards, that he had been like a first love, chaste and platonic. A fear struck her: what if he were now in danger because of wanting to help her? The killers had attacked Paula, they had used her to get to Viviana. What if they targeted him now? She needed to put him on the alert and try not to expose him. She called him before heading into the Metro.

"Sorry to be pestering you again so soon. I wanted to tell you that the guys who killed Viviana and Goicochea are professional assassins. I wouldn't want you to take any risks or put yourself in danger. Be really careful who you speak to. Don't get into trouble."

"Trouble is my second name: Eitan Trouble Boniek. I also know how to look after myself. Don't worry."

As soon as she could, she'd tell Federico that she had been reunited with a childhood friend. She would try to be as open and honest as possible. She didn't want seeing El Chino again to be part of a secret life. She would rather be truthful.

Verónica needed a cigarette. She took a packet from her bag but, when she put one in her mouth, the nausea came back. At least that would be over soon.

II

Verónica wondered if Dr Rivarola performed more than one abortion a day and if one woman had to wait while she

201

attended to another. She imagined there would be several women in the waiting room.

They arrived twenty minutes early. The consulting room was in a rather shabby building, about fifty or sixty years old, whose residents would once have hailed from the comfortable middle classes but must now come from a sector fighting to keep its head above water. The entrance hall and the corridors were very clean, but that could not conceal a great deterioration wrought by the passage of time. The doctor's rooms were on a floor accessed only by the back elevator. That provided some privacy from the rest of the building.

Both Paula and María Magdalena (and Corso too, in his way) had offered to go with her. Paula had made such a point of this that she ended up getting offended when her friend declined. Verónica knew she'd get over it. In fact, a few minutes ago she had received a WhatsApp from Paula saying *Love you loads, babe*, followed by a string of little hearts. Verónica had chosen to go with Federico. He was the person she most wanted to be with right then; besides, he couldn't bear to be apart from her, given the circumstances.

A woman, presumably a nurse, opened the door to them. There were no other patients there, and the waiting room exuded a sobriety worthy of a Franciscan monastery. Bare walls surrounded a deep leather sofa, two armchairs and a coffee table on which there were three or four magazines. They hadn't fully settled into the armchairs – she kept tapping Federico's knee, as if to calm him – when Dr Rivarola appeared. She greeted Federico and Verónica formally. The woman appeared never to soften or seem friendly. She took Verónica to a little office and here too there was nothing to suggest an interest in decor, or any desire to convey warmth. Verónica waited to be asked again if she was sure she wanted an abortion, and had prepared a robust response. But the doctor didn't ask her anything, just talked to her about timings and how she would feel afterwards, and assured her that there should be no post-operative consequences apart from, at most, a little discomfort. Dr Rivarola would in any case be reachable at all times. She asked if they had brought the money, and Verónica took out the thousand dollars Federico had withdrawn from a safe-deposit box the previous Friday. The doctor put this money into a drawer and ushered Verónica through to another small room, where she could leave her clothes. "Top on, bottoms off, bare feet," the doctor explained. The blue dressing gown was too short and the ceramic tiles were cold underfoot.

Once she had changed, Verónica went into the other room, which was no bigger than a dentist's consulting room. Waiting there were the nurse and an anaesthetist, who greeted her in a more friendly way while continuing a conversation with her colleague about trivialities, perhaps to make her feel relaxed. Verónica settled back on the examination bed that was designed to hold her legs open and high. The nurse helped her to get comfortable.

"All right, darling?" asked the anaesthetist as the doctor appeared. This time the doctor smiled at her, and for some atavistic reason that smile worked like a genuine tranquillizer. The anaesthetist, fitting a mask over her mouth, explained the best way to breathe. Verónica took deep, rhythmic breaths.

Verónica heard the doctor's voice and then Federico's. She wanted to open her eyes, but that felt difficult. Only the sensation of Federico stroking her arm finally brought her round.

"How do you feel?" the doctor asked. The nurse and anaesthetist had gone.

"Fine, though my mouth's a bit dry."

"We'll bring you a tea and some cold water. In a moment you can get dressed, then you're free to go."

Verónica noticed she was still wearing the blue gown. She inspected it for bloodstains, but it looked immaculate.

"Are you all right?" Fede asked.

"Yes, a bit tired."

The nurse appeared with tea and a glass of water. The tea was very sugary.

A few minutes later, when she was dressed and fully awake, Verónica and Federico left the building. At the front door she paused to look for something in her bag, fished out the packet of cigarettes she hadn't touched for two weeks and took one out to smoke it. But such a wave of nausea came over her that she thought she might vomit there and then. She threw the cigarette to the ground.

"I still feel sick. What if this didn't work?"

"Vero, don't be paranoid."

"Even paranoid women can get pregnant."

"Shall we go home?"

"No, let's eat. I'm hungry. I feel like a rump steak with fries."

As they walked towards the car, Verónica texted Paula: *It's all gone smoothly.*

Her friend was quick to reply: *You mean they shaved everything off?*

You're disgusting, Verónica texted back.

III

Federico had felt progressively more relaxed during the course of that morning, especially once they came out of the clinic and he could confirm that Verónica was her usual self: querulous, doubtful and hungry. For days he had been feeling so anxious he could hardly bring himself to speak to her. Instead he had tried to reassure her without words, showing steadiness and calm, two qualities that seemed inadequate to the reality of the situation. The only certainty he truly felt was a desire to support Verónica in her decision. He would never have presumed to raise the slightest doubt, the smallest "but" to whatever she decided to do. He didn't plan to talk to anyone about the abortion – there was nobody he had that kind of conversation with, apart from Verónica. Perhaps it wouldn't be a bad idea to return to therapy with Dr Cohen. He needed to be able to tell someone that he wished Verónica had made a different decision. The idea of becoming parents, sharing the project of raising a child together, seemed to him a logical consequence of the love they shared. He pictured himself as a first-time father containing the neurosis of Verónica's first-time mother. Swapping bars and restaurants for parks and ball pits. After a few years he might sneak in a PlayStation, with the excuse of playing on it with his son or daughter. As Verónica had said herself, her decision was a matter of family planning, not a rejection of motherhood. Maybe in a year – or two or three... Of course, now they wouldn't even be able to talk about having children for some time. It would sound like a veiled reproach on his part. They would have to wait.

Federico and Verónica had lunch in a grill in Palermo, surrounded by tourists eager to sample the marvels of an Argentine asado. They talked about nothing in particular, praising the quality of the meat. Verónica ate heartily, but Federico still had a knot in his stomach and made heavy work of his steak with a rocket and Parmesan salad.

They were having coffee when she said to him: "I got back in touch with El Chino, a childhood friend, through the investigation I'm doing with Rodo and María Magdalena."

"What a nice surprise."

"'Nice' is an understatement. It's twenty-four years since we last saw each other. He lived opposite my grandparents' house."

"Another Atlanta fan."

"Kind of. He was also sort of like my first love."

"Ah, tell me more."

"Well, not exactly a first love. We didn't kiss or anything. Once he was out of my life I started wondering if I had liked him more than I realized at the time."

"And now? Did you like him again?"

"The guy's built like a tank. But no, I couldn't convert platonic love into earthly love."

"I see you've given it a lot of thought."

"Is that a reproach?"

"No, no, no. Just a simple fit of pique."

"Don't be silly. I wouldn't be able to fuck you either, if I'd known you when we were children."

"Well, we did know each other as children."

"I mean at ten, not at twenty-something. When I looked at him, I couldn't help seeing the little boy I used to play with. I'm no longer that little girl whose knees were always covered in scabs, but for me he's still the boy with the messy hair who used to burp when he drank Coca-Cola."

Federico drove Verónica over to Patricia's house in Colegiales and then went to the office. On the way he sent a message to Dr Cohen: *Think I need to start therapy again. Do you have any free times next week?* Less than two minutes later, his phone started buzzing. It was Dr Cohen.

"Today the horoscope in *Clarín* said I was going to get a surprise. I never imagined it would be this."

"If you had imagined it then it wouldn't have been a surprise, Doctor."

"Don't get cocky then end up crying in the middle of the session."

"So can you fit me in?"

"Come now. I'm here waiting."

"I can't today."

"Putting up resistance already, I see. This won't work."

"I could come at the end of the day."

"Let me look at my diary. Does 16.30 suit you?"

"That's very early."

"Five?"

"No, that doesn't work either. Maybe seven."

"Let me see… Yes, I have a free slot at that time."

As soon as Federico arrived at the office, Rivadavia asked if they could have a meeting. He was feeling triumphant, having got closer to resolving Mayer's conflict with the ecologists.

"I spoke with the two caucus leaders in the legislature. They're both willing to vote for a reform to the construction code. One of them told me he's in direct contact with the number two at Fundación Cuidar. He can make sure the protests are mostly symbolic and confined to the website, without too much heat or aggression."

"How much would that cost?"

"Six hundred grand: two hundred each for the caucus leaders and two hundred for the guy from the foundation."

"What little turds. OK, I'll speak to Mayer. I don't think he'll put up a fight. But let's make it half the money before the reform is approved and the other half afterwards. As for the pretentious ecologist, we want to see and approve the texts before they publish them. That's non-negotiable."

"I'll get to it, then."

He called Mayer's secretary, who gave him an appointment at half past four in the bar of the Hotel Faena in Puerto Madero. He would have to hurry if he didn't want to be late. Federico put on his jacket again. On his way to the door he crossed paths with Ángeles, who tried to stop him for a word. Federico asked her if she had anything new to pass on to Mayer.

"Not much. And nothing you should tell him just yet."

They agreed that he would call her once the meeting was over.

"Come to the apartment," she said, quietly.

"I don't think I can, but I'll call you."

Federico didn't like going to Puerto Madero. He would have preferred to meet at Mayer's offices in the Bajo, or at a hotel bar somewhere in the city centre. All the same, he arrived two minutes early for the meeting. Mayer was already sitting at a table, drinking a whisky and consulting his tablet, for all the world like a businessman checking his shares on Wall Street. He seemed to relish Puerto Madero's snob appeal and touristy atmosphere.

Mayer greeted him with a kiss on the cheek, a gesture Federico found inappropriate to the lawyer–client relationship. He wondered if Mayer was in the habit of kissing Aarón Rosenthal. Surely not.

"Would you like a little whisky?"

Federico opted for a coffee; he remembered that he had to think up a convincing excuse for not going round to Ángeles's place that evening.

"I've got good news for you," Federico said. "The construction permits are under way."

"And the NGO ecologist?"

"She's willing to negotiate a withdrawal from the claim. Between the foundation and some municipal legislators, the expenses will come to about six hundred thousand dollars."

"You've got to be kidding me."

"Less time, more money. It's always the way."

"All right, get it tied up as quickly as possible. And my crazy ex-wife?"

"We're still talking. Roxana is a tough nut to crack. She's accepted the division of assets we presented her, but she insists on keeping Tuentur."

"Stupid crazy bitch."

"Since the courts aren't involved yet, I think we have time to continue negotiating. In this case, more time may mean less money."

"It's got nothing to do with money. That woman wants to take away the company I founded and developed. She knows it's the heart of all my other ventures. She thinks if she takes control of Tuentur away from me I'll end up going bankrupt."

"It's possible she thinks that, but the reality's different. Your real estate businesses are solid, your media group accounts are looking healthy—"

"The media group is a pain in the ass. I don't make a peso from it. If it weren't for the fact that I need the magazine, the newspapers and the radio stations for lobbying and putting the screws on certain idiots, I would already have shut it down."

Mayer seemed to remember something.

"Your wife works for me, doesn't she?"

"Technically she isn't my wife, but yes, she works at *Nuestro Tiempo*."

"Only the other day I was saying to Aarón that Verónica is a great journalist. If she weren't so… anarchic, I'd have asked her to head up a radio station, perhaps even *Nuestro Tiempo*."

"She'll be very happy when I tell her that."

A few minutes later, Mayer ended the meeting, saying he was going to rest in his suite at the hotel.

"I hope they've replaced my little bottles of whisky."

As soon as he left the Faena, Federico called Ángeles, planning to take the bull by the horns: "I can't come to yours this evening. A pipe burst in the bathroom and I have to wait for a plumber to come round and fix it."

Federico hung up with the strange sensation, once again, of cheating on his lover with his long-term partner. Just as well he had a session lined up with Dr Cohen later that day.

IV

Patricia couldn't yet walk unassisted, but she managed to manoeuvre herself into the living room, where she reclined on a chaise longue that seemed made for the situation she now found herself in and gave her the air of a nineteenth-century romantic heroine. Even from a reclining position, Patricia commanded respect, her habitual tone blending experience, acuity and a light authoritarianism, a combination that gave her journalists the reassurance they needed to carry out their work. Every so often, though, a sad and turbid look would come into her eyes. It was clear, however much she disguised it, that Goicochea's death still hurt much more than her physical injuries.

María Magdalena hadn't arrived yet, but they decided to make a start anyway. While Rodolfo prepared *mate* Verónica told the others about her adventures at the Foreign Ministry and the reunion with her childhood friend (chiding Corso for confusing brunette with blonde). She told them that Eitan was going to seek more information among the diplomats who had worked with Viviana.

As she was finishing her update, the doorbell rang. Rodolfo passed the *mate* gourd to Verónica and made some quip about María Magdalena arriving late. From the front hall they heard the voice of Patricia's husband, a man who was usually soft-spoken but now was almost shouting. "Are you all right?" he kept repeating, to general alarm. Patricia got off the chaise; Rodo and Vero stood up and made as though to go to the door, right at the moment María Magdalena came in, followed by Atilio. The white shirt she was wearing was stained red and blood had also splashed her sleeveless jumper and skirt, although, being blue, this was less visible. She was holding several folders, also bloodstained.

"Calm down, everyone, I'm fine. It's a superficial wound."

Atilio ran to get rubbing alcohol and cotton wool. Verónica made María Magdalena sit in a chair. Rodo brought a glass of water and Patricia chastised herself for not being able to do more.

"Seriously, I'm fine. It could have been worse."

While Atilio tended to her wound, and to the astonishment of the others, María Magdalena told them about everything that had happened since receiving the priest's call.

"You shouldn't have gone alone to Viviana's apartment," Verónica scolded.

"Look who's talking."

"You should get a tetanus jab," Atilio advised.

"I had one a year ago, just after visiting a convent with Verónica."

Once everyone had calmed down, they set to analysing what had happened in Viviana's house.

"I can draw two conclusions from what you've told us," said Patricia. "First, the guy who attacked you is not the same person who killed Goicochea and Viviana. He arrived a little spooked, with a knife in his hand, you escaped easily, and he can't have been carrying a gun. Really different from the man I saw. Second, this guy had gone back to a place his accomplice had already been. For some reason they had forgotten the papers."

"It all sounds a bit seat-of-the-pants, no?" remarked Verónica.

"They clearly aren't professionals and, again, that's very different from the people who kidnapped Paula. But I think this guy and his accomplice are the ones who first found the blessed tablet. Why do they want it? Who are they?"

"In other words, three of us are all looking for the same thing," said Rodolfo, passing the *mate* gourd to María

Magdalena. "The professional assassins, the amateurs and us, the journalists."

"I'm clear about what the assassins want, and us too, but not what the other team is looking for," said Patricia.

They started examining the papers, complete with blood-stains, that María Magdalena had salvaged from the apartment. They were organizational charts from different companies, all big players and either Argentine or multinationals based in Argentina. There were some private contracts, agreements with other companies. Amid the profusion of papers, they began to notice a pattern.

"These all seem to be companies that like outsourcing their security. And they're all contracting the same firm."

"Tuentur, Sergio Mayer's company."

"I feel a divine light shining on us."

"Now it's easier to understand the reluctance at *Nuestro Tiempo* to acknowledge that Andrés was investigating something."

"Mayer behind bars. I didn't see that coming."

"Stop, stop, everyone," said Patricia. "Tuentur is practically a monopoly when it comes to security. It's logical that the majority of large companies who can afford their services would hire them. So far, there's been no crime. Nothing we have here points to the kind of criminal activity Andrés might have been investigating. We only have the tip of the iceberg. Now we need to submerge ourselves and see what's underneath."

They left Patricia's house feeling, for the first time, that the investigation had advanced. Instinct had led them to Mayer, and now there were signs they were on the right track. Rodo and María Magdalena proposed celebrating with a drink, but Verónica felt exhausted by the events of the day. Besides, she wanted to get home early to see Federico. She didn't say that to her friends, to avoid getting teased. But the truth was that she missed Fede and was yearning to be with him.

V

Federico had never felt so urgently in need of therapy as he did that evening. He arrived at Dr Cohen's consulting room in a state of agitation. Cohen also seemed anxious to be reunited.

"I don't know where to begin," said Federico.

"You see? That's one advantage with Christian confession. Catholics always know where to begin. They start with 'Hail Mary' and respond 'full of grace'. Then they continue with 'I confess before the Lord Almighty that I have sinned through thought, word, deed and omission' – and off they go."

"Verónica got pregnant, and we had an abortion."

"An interesting use of the royal 'we'."

"I mean she had an abortion. Obviously I wanted to accept her decision, whatever it was, but now I've been asking myself if, deep down, I didn't want to be a father."

"And what did you answer yourself?"

"That I should come to therapy and talk about it."

"What a nice superego you have."

"Plus I have a lover."

"Ooh la la."

"I've been seeing Ángeles, a lawyer from work."

"What one might call living the dream."

"Don't mock me, Doctor."

"I'm not mocking you. A fertile man who has two young women running behind – or in front of – his private parts. Drop the sob story. You're pleased as punch."

"You couldn't be more mistaken."

"I can mistakenly put bicarbonate of soda on a cake thinking it's icing sugar, but I assure you that when it comes to feelings I don't make a mistake even when I'm drunk. And I'm not even slightly drunk today."

"But I'm not happy about this."

"People feel ashamed about happiness and the possibility of being happy. Who forced you to take a lover?"

"Nobody."

"Do you love her?"

"You mean, am I in love?"

"Don't come at me with idiotic word games. Do you love her or not? If this Ángeles died the day after tomorrow, would you weep over her and feel that you had lost something?"

"Yes, of course I would. But that would also happen to me with…"

"With whom?"

"I don't know, with my friends."

"Of course, because you love your friends. And this girl too."

"But I'm not in love with her."

"Don't be a turkey. Love is the sublimation of desire and affection, two feelings that provoke shame. Desire because it smacks of an erotic novel, like *Fifty Shades of Grey*. And affection because people think that's a lesser emotion reserved for pets. And I'm going to tell you something: there is no more intense feeling than the one you feel for a puppy or a pussycat. I have one of each, so I know what I'm talking about. If you feel even half the affection for Ángeles that I feel for my pets, and you really want to fornicate with her, it's because you love her. That's all that matters."

"And Verónica?"

"You love her too. And you were happy she got pregnant. You felt powerful, ready to experience the power of fatherhood, the chance to stand before society as a father, someone who is respected by everyone. And you like respect the way

I like French fries. In other words, a lot, in case you were wondering."

"Suppose what you say is true. Then it's also true that I have lost my chance to exercise fatherhood."

"That's bothered you a little, it's made you annoyed with Verónica – not that you're going to tell her. And you're right not to. Don't even think about it. Forget that I have revealed your annoyance to you. It will pass. Everything passes, but everything leaves its mark. We have to learn to live with the things that are bothersome to us and contradictory. Look, Federico, you have a past, a present and a future. However complicated the present feels, nothing that's happening takes away the perspective of the future. Perspective, Federico, is everything. Anguish is not being able to see in perspective. The past seems blurred, the future is not yet assembled, and the present is a superimposition of setbacks. None of that is happening to you."

"I don't feel good."

"Surprise, surprise."

"So what should I do?"

"No idea."

"You're a fraud."

"If you want to know what you should do, read a self-help book. I'm not here to tell you what to do, but to talk about what you do. And what you're doing is neither good nor bad, so long as you don't slip up and end up on the guilty side. If I answer 'kill yourself', are you going to leave here, take the number 45 to Constitución and throw yourself under a train on the Roca line? No, you're not going to do that. Because you don't want me to tell you what to do, you want to avoid the responsibility of taking decisions by hiding behind me."

"I feel as if I'm making a terrible mistake with everything. Including coming here."

"Don't think it's a mistake. Wait. There's someone who can put this to you better than I can."

Dr Cohen stood up and seemed to be walking towards the door. Federico feared that he was going to get someone, that Verónica had been listening on the other side, but instead Dr Cohen went towards an old music system, flicked through some CDs stacked beside it and put one on. A song began to play.

"Isn't that Paulina Rubio?" asked Federico in a tone combining surprise and irritation.

"Listen and learn," said Dr Cohen, accompanying the song with gentle movements of his head and hands.

> *I don't want you to forgive me*
> *And don't tell me you're sorry*
> *Don't deny that you sought me out*
> *And none, none of this*
> *None of this was a mistake.*
> *Mistakes are not chosen*
> *For better or worse*
> *I didn't falter when you came*
> *And you, and you*
> *Didn't want to fail.*

"You didn't want to fail. Do you understand, Federico?"

"No."

"OK, did you like the song at least?" Dr Cohen turned off the CD player and returned to his armchair.

"Sometimes I feel as though I'm being unfaithful to Ángeles with Verónica."

"That's very sweet of you. An affectionate gesture towards Ángeles. I'm sure the girl deserves it."

"She doesn't deserve to settle for being someone's lover, and Verónica doesn't deserve to be cheated on."

"How you enjoy being reasonable, eh. Drop the virtuous act. Don't let the tree of false virtues blind you to the forest of responsibilities. You moved some pieces, important pieces. The consequence will be commensurate with the actions that have been triggered. You need to know that, to prepare and to try not to hurt anyone through your actions."

"I think I'm going to talk to Verónica."

"Confession is good for the soul, but bad for the reputation. And given your girlfriend's record, I'd say that it can also be dangerous for the body. She's going to fuck you up, if you'll permit the foul but accurate language. Let's wrap up or I'll miss the shops. When you're with your two beauties, face to face, ask yourself one simple question. It's the only one that counts: still yes, or not any more?"

VI

For the first time in his life, Federico entered a bar with the sole intention of drinking alcohol. He couldn't go back to the apartment in this state of tension. He felt overwhelmed by what Dr Cohen had said. Perhaps he should leave him and find one of those psychoanalysts who keep quiet for the whole session, like the one his friend Gonzalo had. He ordered a gin and tonic and knocked it back as though it were plain tonic water. He asked for another and his body began to relax. Dr Cohen must be right about something, but for the life of him, Federico couldn't think what. For now, he decided not to make any hasty decisions. Since the subject of parenthood was off the table indefinitely, he would let his relationship with Ángeles run its course and continue his usual routine with Verónica.

Federico paid for the drinks and set off home, already feeling better. He would arrive early, whip up something delicious for dinner and wait for Verónica. But when he arrived, he found Verónica already at home. She had put on some music and was looking for something in the fridge.

"I feel like drinking champagne."

"Are we celebrating something?"

"There doesn't have to be a particular reason. Plus something really cold would make this heat more bearable."

"Here, let me open it."

Verónica got out the flutes and Federico filled them.

"Now I remember: we do actually have something to celebrate. I've given up smoking."

"Congratulations. Big news."

"And I've ordered sushi. It should be coming soon."

From the living room came the sound of a woman's voice sweetly singing ballads he hadn't heard before.

"Who's this?" he asked.

"A Canadian singer, Amelia Curran. Do you like it? I bought her CD on the way home."

"Nobody buys CDs any more."

"I do. It's called *They Promised You Mercy*."

They sat down together on the sofa in the living room. He rubbed her shoulders and she purred with gratitude. A few messages came through on Verónica's phone which she planned to ignore, then, as they mounted up, decided to look at.

"They're from El Chino, my childhood friend," she said cheerfully and began to answer him. "He's saying we should get together. He's got some information that could be useful to our investigation. What an idiot. Now he's mocking me because he's remembered I used to be frightened of a parrot someone had on our block. It was a nasty parrot, though! Bit one of the neighbours once."

"Parrots don't bite."

218

"In Villa Crespo the parrots bite and don't let go. They're the Rottweilers of the bird world."

"Perhaps it was a crow."

"Crows don't bite, they peck your eyes out. One of the nice things about being reconnected with El Chino is that he remembers a whole load of things I'd forgotten. And vice versa. There are some glorious episodes from those days that I bet he doesn't remember."

Their sushi arrived. Federico went down to get it and left Verónica texting with her friend. As he was coming back up in the elevator, his phone buzzed. It was a WhatsApp from Ángeles.

I feel bad.

What's up?

I'm vomiting, my whole body hurts. I think I've got a temperature.

Sounds like a virus.

Federico entered the apartment. Verónica was laying the table. Another message arrived from Ángeles.

I don't know what it is, but I'm scared. Can you come?

Not right now.

Is the plumber still there?

No, he's gone.

Can you come later?

I don't think so.

I feel terrible.

You should call the emergency number on your insurance policy.

Thanks for the advice.

They sat down to eat and Verónica started telling him about her text conversation with El Chino. Some anecdotes from the past. Wanting to see each other again. Finally, an arrangement to meet for dinner the next day. Verónica relayed every single message to Federico while he kept texting Ángeles.

Don't be angry.

I'm not angry. I feel ill. I'm scared and sad.

What's your temperature?

I haven't taken it. It must be about 38.

"Who's writing to you so much that you can't stop to eat?" asked Verónica, dipping a California roll in some soy sauce mixed with wasabi.

"It's work: we're busy with your boss's divorce."

"He's not my boss. He owns the magazine."

"Semantics."

38 isn't that high. Have you vomited a lot?

Twice.

That's not too bad.

So you're a doctor now?

Call the emergency number.

Thanks. Bye.

Don't be silly.

I can't rely on you when I need you.

I can't leave at the moment.

Verónica refilled their empty glasses. She asked him what he thought about Mayer's security firm.

"Tuentur? Solid profits, plus a lot of marital fighting over who gets control."

"Any illegality?"

"Ha ha, you're trying to catch me off guard. If there were any illegality I couldn't tell you because he's our client, but actually in this case I think it's one of the few companies that has no legal claims against it. Everything's above board, clean and documented."

They finished eating and cleared away the plates, which Federico washed while Verónica made coffee and looked for the Lindt chocolates somebody had given her. Federico kept one eye on the phone, which was now mercifully quiet.

Lying together on the sofa, they watched an episode of *Billions*. Verónica snuggled against him.

"I have an erotic fantasy about sleeping in your arms while you stay awake, looking after me."

"That doesn't sound very erotic."

"I want to go to sleep in your arms."

After the programme finished, they went to bed and Federico fulfilled her desire: Verónica fell asleep with her arms around him. It had been a long day, especially for her. He kept checking the phone. There were no new messages.

12   *The Wounded Lioness*

I

You don't fully grasp the uselessness of a lover until you get ill and the guy can't (not that he doesn't want to, he can't!) leave his family life to come and make you a tea, take your temperature or bring ibuprofen to your sickbed. That was the conclusion reached by Ángeles after a night in which she feared she might be rushed to hospital suffering from dengue fever, hantavirus or some such. The Peruvian doctor who came to her home (note to self: if you're looking for a lover, choose a doctor who makes house calls) told her that it was likely food poisoning, especially when she listed everything she had eaten that morning at Roxana Mayer's house.

The doctor gave her an injection, and after that she slept through the night, but the next morning she was nauseous again. While she was trying to vomit – without success, since there was nothing in her stomach – an idea, a fantasy, popped into her mind: she could be pregnant. That would be hilarious. Her life might be ruined, but it would be worth it to see Federico's face when she told him, minutes before he ran off to hide in the Bitch's skirts.

Ángeles felt better after a shower, and even a little hungry. She made herself a tea (that tea he should have made for her the night before), ate some plain rice cakes and set off for Rosenthal and Associates.

When she saw Federico, she treated him with indifference. This was the way they always treated one another, so as not to arouse suspicion. On this occasion, however, Federico was more demonstrative than usual. In the kitchen he came over and asked how she was feeling. She, preparing her second tea of the morning, answered tartly: "Never better."

Diana Veglio, who they had a meeting with later on, came into the kitchen. "Who does one have to fuck around here to get a decent coffee?"

"Doctor, mind your language," said Federico with a smile. "May I remind you that your specialism is family law."

"I know how you lot look down on family law. You and your flunkeys in criminal law would gladly write off my specialism as merely another career in social sciences."

"May God and the law never entertain such madness."

"Just make me a coffee. Ángeles and I will wait for you in your office."

Ángeles was beginning to think Federico and Diana must have slept together not once but a few times. That familiarity hadn't been born in the courtrooms of Comodoro Py (not in the public sessions, at any rate). Could they still be lovers now? No, it didn't seem likely. Diana was an older woman, a lot older than the Bitch, even.

When the three of them were gathered in Federico's office, without Rivadavia, who wasn't concerned with the Mayers' divorce, Ángeles told them about her brunch with Roxana, leaving out the part where she had vomited spectacularly on the Carrara marble.

"I agreed to go with her today to a meditation and mindful breathing session at Uruk."

"Where?" asked Diana, doubtless picturing some place in India.

"Uruk is a meditation centre in Vicente López."

"I understand you want to gain her confidence, but that doesn't seem like a good use of time," said Federico. "I doubt she'll change her mind because you visited her sect."

"You're wrong, Federico," said Diana, springing to the defence. "Women, or rather women and men, sometimes need to be persuaded by a person they trust. It's obvious Roxana's attachment to the security firm is a whim, however much she goes on about it being her child and all that nonsense she told Ángeles. The way she's turned down so much money, so many properties and all the thriving businesses we're offering makes you think this woman would never give in, even if Sergio Mayer offered to keep nothing more than the china his auntie gave them as a wedding present."

"If that's the case," continued Ángeles, emboldened by Diana's support, "what I have to do is show her that she can buy thousands of china sets with the money she'll have if she just signs, once and for all."

"Touché. You two know more than I do about human motivation. You both studied family law with Eduardo Zannoni, after all."

"There's something else," Ángeles interrupted. "A man was at the house. He seemed foreign. From the way he was acting, he was either a brother or a partner. And he didn't look like a brother."

"It's not out of the question that she might have a boyfriend," said Diana.

"No, but it wouldn't be a bad idea to find out what he does. It's strange, considering how sociable Roxana is, that she didn't even introduce him to me."

Ángeles found an image on her phone and showed it to them. "Something happened that distracted everyone, and I took my chance to get a photo of him."

"It's a bit blurry and out of focus."

"It was the best I could do, but now I don't know how to find out who it is."

"Send it to La Sombra," Federico told her. "He can definitely help."

"La Sombra still works for you? He's still alive?" Diana asked.

"Who is La Sombra?"

"Our man in the underworld of hackers and cyberfrauds. I'll send you his number so you can contact him."

Ángeles left the meeting with a strange sensation in her body. Not nausea exactly, but a feeling that something inside wanted to come out. She locked herself in the toilet and burst into tears. She had no idea what was making her cry until, with a burst of clarity, she understood everything. Her heart started racing and she had to breathe deeply to calm down. Perhaps those breathing classes could be useful after all. Now that Ángeles saw everything clearly, she no longer felt like crying. She washed her face and stepped out of the bathroom with all the dignity she could muster.

She found the telephone number Federico had given her and called it.

"Hello, good morning, Señor Sombra?"

At the other end of the line, someone laughed. "Yes, that's me, who's speaking?"

"I'm Dr Ángeles Basualdo. I work at Rosenthal and Associates."

"Tell me what you need."

"I have a not very good photo of a man and I need to know if it's possible to do facial recognition and get some information on him."

"Do you have any background info?"

"Well, he could be the current partner of Roxana Mayer, the ex-wife of —"

"Yes, I know who she is. Copy the image on to a USB and send someone over with it."

"Wouldn't you prefer me to send it by WhatsApp?"

"I don't use WhatsApp. Send a gofer. And tell Federico I'll invoice him afterwards."

"Thanks, Señor Sombra."

"Plain Sombra will do."

I I

Ángeles left the office without saying goodbye to Federico then spent most of the afternoon with Roxana, who took her to the meditation centre, a big house in Vicente López. While presenting itself as a place open to the community, the centre seemed to have a small clientele and no interest in expansion. There were fourteen people, including Ángeles and Roxana, at this afternoon session. The place was decorated with Sumerian, Assyrian and Babylonian artworks. These weren't simple photographic reproductions or postcards bought at the Pergamon Museum or British Museum, but high-quality replicas. So at different times Ángeles felt as though she were in the Ashurbanipal palace, looking at a perfect copy of the relief *The Wounded Lioness*; or opposite the Ishtar door; or, when they went up to the terrace for meditation, at the top of a ziggurat.

If the Mesopotamic names were exchanged for other, more Asian ones, this group could have been gathered for a yoga class, or an introduction to Hinduism. It was conceptually similar to those schools of meditation. The only real difference was in the quest for a primitive religion, the attempt to arrive at a first religion – because all other religions were merely dull echoes of the First and Only Religion. If they wanted to become a sect, Ángeles thought, they were going to have to seek out some elements that were more attractive and more differentiated from the sects that already existed.

Roxana seemed completely engaged in the commentary of the woman teaching meditation techniques, and her erudite overview of the religions of ancient Iraqi Mesopotamia. Ángeles had to admit that she enjoyed the meeting, and even felt more relaxed at the end of the day. Perhaps these people were on to something and she should take their ideas more seriously.

"I always need a drink after meditating," said Roxana. "Shall we find a bar?"

"Let's – but I don't drink," Ángeles lied.

"Not even a little?"

"Not even chocolate liqueurs."

Roxana seemed surprised, but took this in good humour. "Right, let's find a bar that also has a good selection of juices and smoothies."

"I'd also be fine with one of those sad zero-calorie jobs."

They went to a bar that had tables on the sidewalk and sat outside so Roxana could smoke. They ordered a Negroni and an orange juice.

"You don't smoke, you don't drink. Tell me you screw at least."

"When I get the chance."

"Have you got a boyfriend?"

"Not exactly."

"A lover. A married man."

"Something like that."

"When you need advice, come to me, because I know all those guys' tricks. Listen to me, Ángeles: they're all the same."

They drank, Roxana smoked. Ángeles saw she had a clutch of messages and, what a surprise, they were all from Federico. The first exerted a gentle pressure on her to speed up the negotiation with Roxana. The later ones were more personal. Clearly Federico felt guilty about having left her alone to die the previous night. And suppose she had died from some terrible virus? Could he live with the guilt? Apparently so. Ángeles had to accept that these men were only interested in their own satisfaction. They had so much guilt invested in their stable partners that they couldn't spare even a little compassion for their unstable ones. The final messages asked if they could see each other today. She was tempted to reply *I don't know, ask the Bitch if she'll let you out.*

"When all this is over," said Roxana, interrupting her thoughts, "and I can start remaking my life, I'm going back to work. I want to open a law practice. And I'd like you to come and work with me."

"Thanks for the offer."

"Would you come? Would you leave Rosenthal?"

"Why not?"

"If you came with me, you'd be my partner."

Roxana glanced over at a car parking in front of the bar. "Here comes David. I didn't introduce you the other day, did I?"

"You didn't, and again, I'm so sorry about my disastrous behaviour."

"Don't you worry. I shudder to think how many times I've thrown up after mixing vodka and wine."

The man getting out of the car was the one whose photo Ángeles had taken. He had an athletic, confident bearing, like an actor in an action movie. Liam Neeson in *Taken*. He kissed Roxana on the lips, and Ángeles ruled out her siblings theory.

"I haven't introduced you to my favourite lawyer. David, this is Ángeles. Ángeles, this is David, the man who changed my life."

"Nice to meet you, Ángeles. Is your stomach a little more settled now?"

He had a strange way of speaking. Clearly Spanish was not his first language, even though he spoke it perfectly. Ángeles was going to ask where he was from, but David didn't give her the chance, plunging into the bar. When he came back, he told them he had already paid for their drinks. Roxana asked if they could drop her off somewhere, but Ángeles said no, she'd be fine taking a taxi.

They said goodbye, with promises to get together soon. Ángeles's phone pinged again and she expected to see another message from Federico, but it was La Sombra.

I'll be at La Academia at 20.00 hours, can you come?

She replied: *I can. In which Academia?*

Bar Academia, Callao, close to Corrientes.

OK. I'm quite far away. I'll be there at 20.15.

She called a cab from the company they used at work and, a minute before the appointed time, got out at the corner of Corrientes and Callao. The contrast in temperatures between the air-conditioned cab and the warm humidity of the street unsteadied her. She should check her blood pressure; more than once she had fainted because her arterial pressure was too low. She needed to eat something. Still feeling dizzy, she arrived at the bar and saw that a man sitting at one of the tables at the back was gesturing to her. It was La Sombra. How he had recognized her so quickly was a mystery.

"Do you know how to play dominoes?"

The question disconcerted Ángeles. "Yes, I had a set as a child."

"People still play dominoes in this bar. When I was a teen-ager I used to come to La Academia and there would be old people playing. And now there are still old people here with their dominoes. I don't know if old age confers an irresistible desire to play dominoes, or if they're the same old people from twenty years ago, who've discovered a formula for not dying."

"I guess we should try playing dominoes to find out."

The waitress came over. Ángeles noticed that La Sombra was drinking a sugar-free Sprite.

"A banana smoothie, please, and a toasted ham and cheese sandwich."

As she was ordering she noticed La Sombra looking surprised, or at least intrigued.

"It's just that my blood pressure is low and I need to eat something."

La Sombra waited for their order to arrive and for Ángeles to start eating before showing her what he had found. He passed her a couple of papers inside a folder. There was a copy of the photo she had taken on one and some writing on the other. A word leaped out at her: *Tuentur.*

"I'm afraid I haven't found out much," said La Sombra. "But let's talk about what there is. It was very useful your telling me about his link with the Mayers. I didn't find anything through the usual channels, but when I compared this photo with ones of the management and partners at Sergio Mayer's companies, I discovered something interesting. This is David Kaplan, a forty-eight-year-old Israeli citizen; he has Argentine residency and has been here for eight months. As you'll see from this page I've copied, he has a managerial role at Tuentur, which is Sergio Mayer's security firm."

"Of course, I know it. In fact right now there's a conflict situation within that company."

"There isn't much else. I didn't find anything about him in Israel. Perhaps he was born there and then moved somewhere else like, I don't know, the United States. I refined the search for the thousands of David Kaplans in the world, but I didn't find this gentleman."

"How mysterious."

Ángeles finished her smoothie and the sandwich and paid their bill. She kept the receipt to take to the office, hoping there wouldn't be a problem with what she had eaten. She could always pass it off as La Sombra's.

"Federico said you should send him an invoice."

"That was a joke – I never invoice."

"Ah," said Ángeles, without understanding what the joke was. At the entrance to the bar they said goodbye and she called Federico.

"I've just been with La Sombra," she said when he answered, not caring whether he was alone or with the Bitch.

"Did he manage to find anything?"

"One detail that seems very significant to me. Roxana's boyfriend is called David Kaplan, and he's one of the senior directors at Tuentur."

"Do you think Mayer knows?"

"I don't know. You're the one who deals with him. What's clear to me is that Roxana's insistence on maintaining control has something to do with Kaplan. I don't know exactly how much or what influence he has. If we knew that, it would be easier to get Roxana to soften her position."

"I'm thinking it wouldn't be a great idea for Mayer to know that his wife's boyfriend is also one of his employees. It could torpedo the whole negotiation, and if I want anything it's to be done with this bedroom dispute."

Ángeles could think of a few colourful responses to this, but she held her tongue. She wasn't going to gift him even the benefit of her wit.

"OK, we'll see each other tomorrow."

"Wait, don't hang up," Federico said. "Would you like me to drop by?"

"Aren't you busy?" She couldn't suppress the sarcasm.

"If you want, I can head over to your place."

"I'm just outside La Academia. It'll probably take me forty minutes to get home on the Linea D. Come round if you really want to."

"See you later."

Ángeles stood staring into the street. She looked at the scene around her – cars waiting at the lights, people walking past, the illuminated shops – and pictured herself as though on-screen, like the star of a music video in which the singer stands still while the world around her spins and then breaks into splinters.

She walked along Callao towards Córdoba. Before reaching Viamonte, she found what she was looking for. A pharmacy, not one that belonged to a chain but a traditional one. Inside, she hesitated over whether to ask for the best-known brand (perhaps there was more than one?) or a generic version. Finally, when her turn came to be served, Ángeles said in a firm voice to the pharmacist:

III

"A pregnancy test, please."

She put it in her bag and walked towards the Metro.

Once at her apartment, she did the test.

When Ángeles was about ten years old, she discovered an illustrated book called *The Book of Life* on her parents' book-shelves. Even though the title sounded promising, she could never have imagined what she would find inside. A large part of the book was given over to sex, a subject she knew nothing about. Secretly, Ángeles kept returning to this troubling book. The first article she read was about "playgirls", the female ver-sion of "playboys". But she didn't know what a playboy was, so the article seemed to be about something that happened in a world distant from her own.

One of the articles she best remembered concerned the Billings and the Ogino-Knaus methods of "natural birth control". What was most eye-catching about the article were the illustrations of naked people, a man and a woman, standing separately or lying together in bed, minimally covered, precisely in that region about which the article raised so many questions. It was thanks to the book that, at the age of eleven, without ever having menstruated and without anyone from her family or school talking to her about sex, Ángeles became an expert in these contraceptive methods. In time, once she was older, she realized that they weren't ideal, that they could fail, that many Catholic couples who practised Billings had children they hadn't planned for. There were definitely better methods out there, but at least Ángeles knew when she was ovulating.

She and Federico used a condom for vaginal penetration. At the start they had been very strict about that, but in time they became less scrupulous: first when Ángeles had her period; then on the odd day when she was sure ovulation was a long way off. They didn't see each other often enough for her to think about going on the pill. And they weren't a stable couple, at least not in his eyes. For Ángeles they were, though; he was the only man she had been involved with for such a long time. Sexual-affective relationships had never been her strong suit.

Mr Billings, Ogino-san, Herr Knaus: they could and did fail. Not for the first time.

Ángeles studied the two little lines on the test, staring at them as though they were tiny exotic animals. Two lines that marked a change in her life that she hadn't expected, although she had sometimes feared it. She put down the test and had a shower. Afterwards she looked at herself naked in the mirror, seeking some physical sign that proved her pregnancy, but her body was the same as it had been last month and for the last few years. If it hadn't been for her late period and a certain physical malaise (which could easily have been caused by some virus or food poisoning), nothing would have suggested she was incubating a live being in her body. But it wouldn't be long before she started filling out and that shapeless tadpole began turning into a being with fingers and eyes, moving in her belly. It was daunting to imagine that.

She was calm, though, and felt a kind of peace, not thinking about the professional consequences, nor about Federico or her family. Ángeles was pleased with what was happening to her. She hadn't sought it, but neither had she planned to fall in love with Federico, and that had still happened.

It happened. If anyone asked her how she had got pregnant, she would say that: it happened. "I'm pregnant, I'm pregnant," she repeated to herself. She wanted to convince herself, to start feeling different, even though she still felt herself to be the same old Ángeles: demanding at work, emotionally connected, indifferent to her family. She wished she had a close friend she could tell, but her friendships weren't deep and tended not to involve personal conversations. The person she would most like to have been able to talk to was Luciano, a fellow student during most of the time she was studying. Although Ángeles liked him, they had never been anything more than good friends. He had got married a couple of years back and she was careful not to call him at night so as not to arouse silly suspicions in his wife. She thought of calling her sister in Switzerland, but it was early in the morning there. Her sister would definitely be the first person Ángeles called, though. Because she didn't plan to say anything to Federico, at least not that day. She put on the matching lingerie he liked, a tight little T-shirt that showed off her breasts and a miniskirt she had once worn to go dancing with some friends in Rio de Janeiro, an experience she would rather not remember.

The entryphone buzzed and she went down to let Federico in. It was sweet to see the way his face changed when she stepped out of the elevator and came towards the door: from wretched orphan to bad porn actor.

"You shouldn't dress like that for me."

"Why not?"

"Because you'll make it hard for me to leave."

They got into the elevator, where she devoured him with kisses, pressing her body hard against Federico's. He slid his hand under her skirt. They went into the apartment and fell onto the sofa. She unbuttoned his shirt and kissed his chest. He squeezed her breasts and tried to take off her top, but she didn't let him: instead she stood up and pulled off his trousers, observing with satisfaction the bulge in his boxer shorts. Those came off too, then Ángeles climbed on top of him without taking off her clothes. She simply pushed her underwear to one side.

"I've got condoms," said Federico, his breath coming in gasps.

"No need," she said, beginning to moan.

Federico started to move his pelvis while he caressed her over her underwear.

"No need," Ángeles said again, and her moans got a little louder. Moans that mingled with laughter, not something that usually happened when she climaxed. There was another novelty to add to the symptoms of her pregnancy.

13   *The Family*

I

Luckily Federico wasn't at home when she left the apartment. Verónica didn't want him to see her. Not because she had dressed up particularly, or because she had put on a little make-up and perfume, things she always did when she met friends at night (or when she went out with him), but because she couldn't help thinking she was going off to meet someone she loved. The reappearance of El Chino had been like an epiphany in her life. Now she was in a taxi going to have dinner with him, which Federico knew about. The two childhood friends were sure to remember their time in Villa Crespo and swap anecdotes that had lain dormant for more than twenty years. But Verónica didn't like lying to herself. Was she half-hoping there might be some story between them that went beyond shared memories? Clearly they weren't children any more, and their lives had been filled with experiences that had taken them to very different places. But perhaps at heart they were still those two kids, missing their old gang and hanging out on the streets of Villa Crespo, playing ball in the park, buying a Coke at the kiosk to share. At any rate, Verónica was aware something could happen between them. The adult version of El Chino was attractive to her. He was likeable, well built, principled, and had a job that demanded both talent and intelligence. Then, of course, there was

Federico. Things were going well with him. Did she have to go and ruin it with a fling? Ninety-nine per cent of the time, the answer was obvious: no. But she feared that this situation with El Chino might belong to the other one per cent. "Fear" wasn't the right verb. Rather, she was worried: if she ended up screwing El Chino, it would mean she wasn't totally secure in her relationship with Federico. Perhaps they should have waited a few years more before heading down the road of coupledom.

Verónica put all these thoughts to one side when she arrived at the restaurant in Palermo that El Chino had chosen and where he was already waiting. He wasn't wearing a jacket and tie, but one of his fitted shirts, a blue one this time, teamed with jeans and Nike sneakers. He was looking at his phone when she arrived, but glanced up as Verónica approached the table.

"Hello, beautiful," El Chino said.

It didn't sound like a pick-up line, but like the words of someone who knew her well enough to observe that she was pretty, as though they were friends who had not stopped seeing each other in all those years and felt a particular fondness for one another.

Verónica didn't like those modern restaurants where the chef tries to grab your attention with ever smaller dishes of unusual items cooked in a peculiar way. She liked even less the set menu of seven courses, which might have been made for the Seven Dwarfs, so minuscule were the portions. But she didn't complain. The wine was good and, more importantly, the conversation flowed happily.

"Flavio was seven years old, the youngest of all of us."

"I'll never forget that day. You and Lucía cried."

"How could we not cry? We were both convinced he had been kidnapped and was going to turn up dead."

"To this day I don't understand how that dimwit managed to get as far as Parque Chas on his own."

"He was so little. I remember he told me he wanted to buy a superhero comic and that no kiosk in our neighbourhood had it."

"The neighbours were looking everywhere for him, even under the cars. Martín and I went to Parque Centenario and asked everyone if they'd seen him. 'He's small and ugly,' was the description Martín gave."

They both burst out laughing.

"Eventually he came home in a police car. His eyes were red from crying."

The conversation moved from memories to work, to banalities like TV and movie recommendations.

"I told you I had something from Viviana that could be useful to you."

Verónica drank from her wine glass. They were waiting for the fourth course, which she expected would be slices of beetroot cooked over a flame with a dusting of cheese from Normandy and roast chestnuts in a wasabi and sake reduction. Or something else equally peculiar.

"In the cooperation programme we were working on, we had contact with companies in Turkey, Israel and Greece. It seems Viviana discovered that an Argentine company was financing itself with Israeli subsidies to bring a particular technology to Argentina, but then that technology never arrived. If that was confirmed to be the case, the company would not only lose the subsidies but would also face the seizure of its properties, in both Argentina and Israel."

"A substantial economic loss then."

"Millions. The company is Tuentur. I imagine you know its owner."

"Sergio Mayer. I knew it! He's the guy behind all this."

"In reality, Mayer created a spin-off company to supply the technology to Tuentur. In other words, he buys from himself. That Israeli–Argentine company – it has a head office in Tel Aviv – is called Eramus. Mayer and Ariel Gómez Pardo appear as partners, along with an unknown Israeli accountant. I suspect he lent his name to make it possible to set up the company there."

"Gómez Pardo has been Mayer's partner in the multimedia group for a year. How long has Eramus existed?"

"I don't remember exactly, but definitely more than three years."

"That's a long time before he joined the group. Neither Gómez Pardo nor the accountant are partners in Tuentur."

"No, the surveillance services firm is an Argentine limited liability company, whose owner is Mayer, with his ex-wife as the other partner. If you study the details, it's really only Mayer. They're going to get me some proof of fake purchases and subsidies. Not many. I imagine Viviana had much more, but it's something."

"You're a genius, Chino."

Eitan raised his glass in a toast. The waiter brought over the last course before dessert.

"I didn't get anything on Malena, though. Nobody had a clue."

"Neither I nor my two colleagues know anything," said Verónica, "but then we're not actively looking for her. We think someone's watching us and could use us to get to her."

"Quite right. Wait a minute, you mean someone could be watching us at this moment?"

"Hmm… I don't think so, to be honest."

"Those two sitting over there look like detectives."

Verónica laughed. While Eitan was talking, she had remembered an episode of *Ally McBeal*. As a teenager, Federico had been a huge fan of that series, which, he said (slightly exaggerating, perhaps), had sparked his vocation for the law. He had downloaded all the seasons and gone to the trouble of adding subtitles to every episode. Every now and then he would get the urge to watch it again and make Verónica sit down with him. Verónica thought this series about lawyers, with its pretty, ditsy protagonist, was OK, but she couldn't grasp exactly what it was Federico liked so much about it. Anyway, in one of the episodes, Ally McBeal meets a charming, handsome, seductive, likeable man. She starts falling in love with him. One night they go out for a meal, and in the middle of dinner Ally notices that the man has a strange way of chewing; a strand of food escapes from his mouth and stays hanging from his face. From then onwards she can't help seeing him in this light, and any possibility of romance is crushed. Verónica studied Eitan carefully, but she couldn't find any flaw: he ate daintily, waited for her if she was taking too long because of talking too much (Verónica always noticed this kind of gesture: the guy who was too quick to clear his plate was also too quick in bed); he was attentive when it came to serving her wine and water. It was as though he had escaped from a romantic novel. Verónica sighed to herself.

And then there was the story of his father and her mother, who had been sweethearts. How far had that relationship gone? Had they had relations – she couldn't bring herself to use a more direct expression – or simply exchanged kisses?

"I can't believe my mum and your dad went out together."

El Chino grinned: not even the slightest trace of parsley between his teeth. "For real. Your mother and my father. When they were both very young."

"My grandfather didn't get on with your dad."

"It was actually my grandfather he didn't get on with. After my grandfather died in 1985, he transferred that resentment to my father."

"Was your grandfather Polish too?"

"Yes, from Krakow."

"My grandpa got on well with everyone."

"I think they fell out in the sixties, when my grandfather was a director of Atlanta."

"My Grandfather Elías was also a director of Atlanta in those years. Why would they have fallen out?"

Eitan paused to sip his drink. "Perhaps your grandfather wanted to keep the money from the transfer of some player and my grandfather found him out."

"My grandfather would never do something like that."

Suddenly, as in a horror movie, or one of those episodes of *Ally McBeal* in which the protagonist sees imaginary scenes, El Chino turned into an abominable creature right in front of her eyes. Worse than some guy chewing with his mouth open and drooling, worse than Quasimodo wearing a Chacarita shirt, worse than all the demons in Hell. How could he have said something like that about her Grandfather Elías? Of course, he might have meant it to be funny, or droll, but Verónica couldn't allow such a stupid and aggressive comment, not even as a joke. If there had been a time earlier that day when she thought something could happen with El Chino (should she start thinking of him as Eitan, to preserve her childhood memory?), that possibility had now vanished forever.

The coffee arrived with some petits fours, which turned out to be the best part of dinner. Verónica promised herself that the next day she would go and eat *milanesa a caballo* at Don Ignacio's. She had been craving their schnitzel topped off with fried eggs.

Eitan paid the bill and, as they left the restaurant, he offered her a lift home. She hesitated and he took this opportunity to lean in, stroking her face and hair.

"Chino, no."

"I feel as if we have some unfinished business."

"There's something beautiful that will stay forever in our hearts. We're not those children any more."

"Fortunately. Now you're a beautiful woman."

"And you're a charming man, but I've got a partner and I'm happy with him. I don't want to have an affair. I'm sorry."

Eitan looked crestfallen. That image of defeat touched Verónica, and she put what he had said about her grandfather to the back of her mind.

"Chino, it's been wonderful to see you again, and I'm so glad you're back in my life."

"Then I won't give up hope. Men come and go, but I've been in your life for more than twenty years."

"That's true. I can't deny it."

Verónica told him she would prefer to take a taxi, and he waited until one stopped for her. They said goodbye, promising to meet again once he had the papers from Mayer's company.

As she travelled home, Verónica couldn't help feeling upset about what had happened. Then again, it was a great relief that she didn't have to have an affair and hide it (or not) from Federico, or take her clothes off for the first time in front of a new lover. Worse still, one who had known her as a child. Gradually relief won out over disappointment.

Arriving at her building, she was presented with the same two options as always: she could make the taxi go around the block to drop her off at the door, or she could walk fifty yards to the entrance. She opted to get out and walk. At that time of night there was no one on the street. Her feet hurt because of the new shoes she had put on that evening, and the sound of her heels striking the sidewalk sounded strange to her. Verónica didn't hear a man approaching, and by the time she saw his shadow loom over her it was too late. Someone had grabbed her from behind and put a wad of damp cotton over her mouth. She tried to scream and break away, but it was impossible. The cotton smelled like nail polish remover. In a few seconds she had lost consciousness.

II

Verónica could hear a woman's voice in the distance and tried to open her eyes, but found she couldn't. Her head hurt. Better to go back to sleep until she felt better. But she needed to wake up; she'd been attacked, her life was in danger. With the little energy remaining to her, Verónica made a great effort and managed to raise her eyelids. The light was low and seemed reddish, or perhaps an internal wound was making her see everything the colour of blood. When she could focus a little better, she realized there was a mirror on the ceiling. She could see herself splayed on a bed. It wasn't a comforting sight.

"Looks like she's waking up," said a man's voice.

Verónica tried to raise herself into a sitting position, but her head hurt as though thousands of needles had been stuck into it. "Where am I?" she managed to say, and she wanted to keep speaking but found she had no energy to do so.

Overhead, the reflection of a man appeared. Why had he brought her here? What did he want? Was he going to kill her? She managed to lift part of her body. Then the image of a woman appeared. A young woman. Against the light, Verónica couldn't recognize her until the woman spoke.

"Hello, Verónica."

It was Malena, the daughter of Andrés Goicochea.

"Water," said Verónica and the man, who looked about twenty, went to the bathroom and reappeared with a full glass.

Verónica gulped the water down, spilling some of the contents.

"Why have you brought me here? Where am I?"

"First of all, I'm so, so sorry," said Malena. "I can't risk them seeing me. The only thing Damián and I could think of was to kidnap you. We put you in the back of the car and brought you to a safe place. Well, hopefully it's safe."

"We're in a love motel," explained the boy.

Now the mirror made sense. Or mirrors, because there were more of them on the walls, Malenas and Damiáns multiplied to infinity. The effect was nightmarish.

"Are you mad? What have you given me?"

"Home-made chloroform. The effect will wear off, at least that's what it says on the internet."

"You could have killed me."

Verónica sat on the bed. Malena and Damián stood watching her, silently. The effect of the chloroform (and a home-made version at that – could she have been poisoned?) was diluted in her body. Her instinctive fear, which had grown into anger, was also slowly dissipating. Suddenly she understood something: she pointed at Damián.

"You attacked my friend."

"The crazy nun? She was the one who pistol-whipped me with a hairdryer. I was just defending myself. I thought she was going to kill me."

"We're desperate, Verónica," said Malena. "They killed my dad. I couldn't go to his funeral for fear they would be waiting for me. They killed Viviana."

Verónica was trying to get a sense of her surroundings, but it was difficult. She needed to understand what was happening, then plan the next steps.

"You think these guys might kill you because you've got something they want?"

"Yes, I've got Viviana's tablet."

"You're the ones who took it from her. Why are you asking me for help then?"

"Because when I used to go to the newsroom, I watched you working. My dad said you made his life difficult at the magazine with your stubbornness. So I have no doubt about your integrity, and I know you can help me. You only need to hide me for a few days until things settle down."

"OK, let's do this. I'll take you to a safe place. You can rest. Both of you can rest – you're together, right?" She felt a bit silly asking the question and hurriedly continued. "Tomorrow morning, you and I are going to have a long chat. Today, let's just get away from here. I'll take you both to my apartment. It's empty, nobody will bother you there, and they shouldn't find you, if we're careful."

"There's a small problem," said Damián. "We've run out of money, so we haven't got enough to pay for the room."

Verónica looked in her bag for a few notes, which she'd had the foresight to bring with her, and they prepared to leave, deciding that nobody would raise an eyebrow if three of them left rather than two.

"What about the car?" asked Verónica.

"It's stolen," said Damián, proudly.

Verónica felt as though she were in the middle of a stupid, amorphous nightmare. Drugged, locked up in a cheap motel with two twenty-somethings (and absolutely no sexual angle to any of this), paying for the room herself and leaving in a stolen car. It was a nightmare from which she very much hoped to wake up, once they had driven out of the hotel parking lot.

In the meantime, she couldn't get a wink of sleep. After making sure nobody was following them, Verónica had left the couple in her apartment. She told them not to go out for any reason; she would return early the next morning. She had taken the stolen car and left it parked on a deserted street in Almagro. When Verónica had arrived at Federico's apartment, she found him sleeping soundly. She lay down beside him, but couldn't drift off. In the morning, she got up at the same time as Federico, to his surprise. She explained to him what had happened with Malena and her boyfriend, and also told him some things about her dinner with El Chino, enough for him to see that there was nothing more than friendship between them.

Verónica left early for the apartment in Villa Crespo, filled with dread at the thought of finding the bodies of Malena and Damián there. When she arrived, she knocked gently on the door then let herself in with a spare key. The couple were sleeping soundly in her bedroom. She went into the kitchen and put a kettle on to boil, planning to make *mate*. In the cupboard she found an unopened packet of Don Satur cookies. At least they would have some kind of breakfast. Verónica called from the kitchen to wake them up. It crossed her mind that this must be what life was like for a mother of teenagers. She waited in the kitchen for them to get up, use the bathroom and get dressed. When she went to the living room with a flask of hot water, *mate* and the cookies, they were already there, politely waiting.

There was a certain tension in the room. At first Verónica thought the couple might be intimidated by her, but it wasn't that; the tension seemed connected to some argument between them. As the minutes went by, Verónica realized they had disagreed about something. She asked Malena if she had known they were looking into Viviana and her father. Malena hadn't known. Why then, Verónica persisted, had she thought she was in danger? There must have been a mistake, Malena said, because she had no idea about any of this. Verónica wasn't satisfied by these replies. She had the feeling Malena knew more but didn't feel able to say as much. Perhaps out of fear; she mustn't put pressure on her. If Verónica could win her confidence, maybe Malena would end up telling her everything.

Later she asked her about the tablet. Malena had it with her. She went to the bedroom to get it and Damián looked wryly at Verónica, subtly chiding her for the way she had interrogated Malena, who reappeared quickly before Verónica could ask him what was going on, why he had given her that look.

Malena handed over the tablet. "It's out of battery. We tried a few times to get in and look at the files, but we couldn't, even though Damián is a hacker."

"A hacker, eh?" asked Verónica, without trying to disguise her cynicism.

"I'm more like a white hat."

"I'd say you're a grey hat," said Malena, correcting him.

"I've literally no idea what you're on about, guys."

"I go into systems, sometimes using unusual methods, to expose the atrocities carried out by many companies and public bodies."

"Sounds good."

That boy wouldn't even last one round against La Sombra, thought Verónica. She put the tablet in her bag.

"Let's talk through a few safety protocols. You shouldn't leave the apartment. You're going to be safe here. Marcelo, the doorman, is a very good friend of mine. If you have any problem, no matter how serious, call him and he'll protect you."

"I can't stay locked up in here the whole time," complained Damián.

"Well, you're not leaving me here alone," said Malena.

"Damián, do the people who might be following Malena know you?"

"Where would they know me from?"

"I don't know, perhaps they saw you with her."

"Impossible."

"Well, in that case you can go out and buy whatever you both need."

"I don't want to be here on my own," said Malena.

"Plus we don't have any money for shopping," added Damián.

"He'll say he's going to the store on the corner and disappear for a week – I know him."

Verónica was getting tired of these two adolescents who seemed to complain about every trifling thing as though there weren't more serious things going on.

"It's fine. I'll leave you money. You can also eat whatever you find in the kitchen cupboard. Meanwhile, let me get organized, then I'll come and stay here with you both. That way Damián can come and go as he pleases. Obviously I can't be here all day because I have to work, but at least we can take turns to stay in so you're not on your own."

Verónica left the apartment with a sense of foreboding that these two youngsters were going to be trouble. Marcelo was at the door to the building. She could speak plainly to him.

"A boy and a girl are going to stay in my apartment for a few days. It's possible that the girl, Malena, is in danger."

"I'll keep an eye on them."

"Don't go out of your way. I doubt anyone knows they're here. I'm going to move in with them too."

"Welcome home. Are you bringing Chicha?"

"No. I've got enough on my hands with these two. Ah, one other thing. The security cameras."

"They're all working – the ones on the landing, the ones in the corridors and the ones outside."

"Which company are they from?"

"Protección Total."

At least they weren't from Tuentur. Mayer wouldn't be able to watch them. Many neighbours had thought it was over the top to put cameras in the corridors, but it wasn't hard to make the case for extra security. In fact, the cameras had been proposed by Marcelo, at the request of Verónica, who wanted her apartment monitored in case someone tried to attack her. It wouldn't be the first time an assassin had tried to enter her home.

Once outside she called La Sombra. She told him she had the tablet and needed to know what was on it.

"Bring it over and we'll have a look. Hopefully it won't be a fiasco like last time."

Verónica headed over to the apartment where La Sombra lived and worked. It was on Lambaré and Sarmiento, not far from the house where her grandparents Elías and Esther had lived. Not far from her own home, either, so she went on foot. The apartment was on the first floor, with its own front door. From outside the building looked ramshackle, but once she climbed the stairs she found herself in an impeccable property, very light, with enormous rooms, high ceilings and pine floors. The walls were covered with posters and bookshelves and there were peripheral devices everywhere. It didn't look like an untidy house, though. If not for all the tech, it could be the orderly home of a university professor.

La Sombra lived with Mara, his wife of several years, who in her early youth had been a stripper in a cabaret bar near Constitución. Verónica didn't know her well, but liked her.

It was Mara who opened the door and later brought Verónica a coffee. La Sombra was absorbed in his computer universe and took some seconds to emerge from deep concentration to greet her.

"Let's see that tablet. I want to make sure they haven't scammed you this time."

"I hope the person who gave it to me doesn't suffer the same fate as the last one."

La Sombra connected the tablet to a power supply, while inspecting its exterior.

"There's no brand name on it. It looks like some that I've seen before, used by the armed forces in the United Kingdom or Canada. Although this one could be Russian or from Singapore. You can never be sure."

He took a couple of photos on his phone and sent them to someone.

"I have a friend in Lima who can identify tablets and phones from any country in the world."

Mara arrived with coffee and asked Verónica: "Can you stay for lunch? They do amazing *milanesas* at the rotisserie on the corner."

"Oh definitely. I've been pining for a *milanesa* since yesterday evening, with mashed potatoes if they have them."

"They always have them. I'll give you a shout when everything's ready."

Mara left them together and La Sombra switched on the tablet. While he was waiting for it to fire up, he said, "I see you lot are all flat out."

"Which lot?"

"You, Federico. Well, the Rosenthal contingent."

He started working on the tablet, trying various things, muttering to himself, sighing heavily, swearing. He tossed the tablet on to a mountain of papers at one side of his desk.

"Shit. If the other one was child's play, this is an impenetrable fortress from the Middle Ages."

"Even Montségur fell."

"True, no castle can last a thousand years. The thing is, it won't be easy to open this without destroying it."

La Sombra tried again for a few minutes, chatted with someone, sent over more images.

"The problem is that there aren't many people I can risk showing this tablet to. Not even on the tightest hackers' forums. But I have a couple of friends who can help, especially the Finn, who's a total badass."

"So – what do we do?"

"Patience. I may get an answer in three hours, three days or a week. If it takes longer than a week, that will be because the castle repelled the siege."

Verónica left after a lunch of *milanesas* with Mara and La Sombra. She had a text from María Magdalena suggesting they meet that afternoon.

IV

When Verónica told him she had woken up that morning in a love motel, Rodolfo couldn't stop laughing.

"I'd expect no less from you."

Verónica filled in the others on the events of the previous night: what El Chino had told her about Mayer's companies and about Gómez Pardo's involvement, about the possible fraud perpetrated on the State of Israel and maybe Argentina. The saga of Malena and her boyfriend Damián was less complex.

"So, we have the tablet, we just don't know what's on it."

"And we have a time bomb about to go off in your apartment in Villa Crespo."

"And we have a childhood pal who's keen to do his homework."

Verónica drank from her beer bottle, wiping her mouth on the back of her hand. "That's a pretty good summary of what I'm dealing with."

María Magdalena took her turn to tell the others about what she had been doing, including analysing the make-up of the companies that worked with Tuentur.

"Tuentur's standard procedure with large clients is always the same. It puts together a security strategy and provides the necessary people and technology. Tuentur also insists that a general security manager from its own ranks be placed within the company's hierarchy."

"Please," said Rodolfo, "give Sergio Mayer the Machiavelli prize immediately. He's brilliant. The guy has his own people on the boards of directors of the largest companies in the country."

"Up to this point there's Machiavellianism or business acumen, terms that may be synonymous, but there's no crime," said Verónica. "I think what's more pertinent is the info provided by Eitan: a case of corruption and fraud that could ruin someone with political aspirations."

"Hang on, I haven't finished yet," said María Magdalena. "There's one trait shared by the various managers chosen by Tuentur, both for other companies and for itself: they are ex-members of the Israeli armed forces. Not all of them – the others are Argentine."

"How old are they?" Corso asked.

"Around fifty. They retire young and come to Buenos Aires to make good money in the security sector."

"I realize it sounds strange, unusual and somewhat suspicious that the members of one country's armed forces, now retired, should come to work in Argentina, but there's still no actual crime I can see. Apart from anything else, Mayer has an Argentine–Israeli company. Why shouldn't he bring managers over from there? Perhaps he also takes Argentinians to work in Israel."

"That's true," admitted María Magdalena. "I searched on LinkedIn and elsewhere and I found the employment history of all the managers and higher-level staff at Tuentur. But there was one person I could find nothing about: the head of Tuentur's corporate strategy department. With a role like that, he's bound to have a seat at the smallest table, the one that makes decisions. Well, there's nothing on the guy. He's called David Kaplan. There are lots of men around with that name, but none that fit with the scant information we have on the Kaplan who's in Argentina. There's no armed forces record, he didn't study at any Israeli university, didn't go to high school either, hasn't married, has no property, no medical record… He's a ghost."

"No such thing as ghosts, apart from the one at the banquet," said Verónica.

"We have to try to find out where this fellow comes from and where he wants to go," said Rodolfo.

After they had divided up tasks, Verónica headed home to Caballito. She explained to Federico that she was going to spend a few days at the Villa Crespo apartment, because she didn't want to leave Malena Goicochea on her own. Federico thought that could be dangerous for both women, that perhaps they would do better to leave the city. Verónica tried to reassure him. Nobody knew Malena was with her. Besides, they could rely on Marcelo, who had already demonstrated his heroism on previous occasions.

They went down to get a pizza. Federico wanted a beer but
Verónica was tired of beer; it was the only alcoholic drink she
could go off. She thought of ordering a moscato, thinking it
might pair well with pizza, but sweet drinks weren't her thing
either. Instead she ordered a dry house white. The pizzeria
maintained the old Argentine tradition of serving wine in a
penguin-shaped pitcher, and she found that cheering.

She thought of packing a bag, then decided that was silly:
she could come back to Caballito every day, if she wanted.
Plus some of her clothes were still at her old apartment. So
Verónica took only spare underwear and a toothbrush, not
even the one she used every day. She didn't want to give the
slightest impression (in whose eyes —Federico's or her own?)
that she was moving back into her apartment. She didn't want
even to entertain that possibility.

Federico drove her over in the car and offered to come up
and check everything was all right, but Verónica turned down
the offer. The presence of another person might spark paranoia
or fear in her two guests, and she didn't want to have to deal
with that. All the same, as Verónica walked from the car to her
apartment, she couldn't help fantasizing that she was about
to find the couple dead, gunned down by a faceless assassin.

It was nearly midnight. Verónica let herself in, not knowing whether to make a lot of noise so the couple knew it was
her and weren't alarmed, or, on the contrary, to be as quiet
as possible, in case they were sleeping. She decided on the
second option. A light was still on in the kitchen. Glancing
in, she saw a pizza box open on the counter and some banana
skins lying around. It looked like they had yet to discover the
merits of throwing garbage in the trash can, which was under
the sink. Perhaps they hadn't seen it.

The living room presented a more desolate scene. They'd
had the good sense to leave the lights off, and moonlight

entering through the window softened the appearance of a mini-Chernobyl, which was revealed in all its splendour when Verónica switched on the floor lamp: overturned glasses, empty beer bottles, two Coca-Cola cans, one thrown onto the floor and leaking its contents, ashtrays filled with butts and also ash on the floor (but at least she was no longer nauseated by the smell of cigarettes). Had the couple been competing to throw balled-up paper towels into the plant pot in the corner? Because they were all over the floor around it. The little brats had also discovered her bottle of Jim Beam and drunk half of it.

Verónica felt like screaming, and if she didn't it was because other cries could now be heard coming from the bedroom. First a moan, little howls of pleasure, the sound of a bed creaking. Verónica looked towards the wall. Even without seeing them, she could reconstruct every movement of two people fucking. The noises from the bed got louder and louder, accompanied now by Malena's shrieks of pleasure, which had an impressive sense of melody and rhythm. Verónica stood silently, lost, unable to react. Finally the cries abated. She could imagine the bodies collapsing on the bed and might have collapsed into an armchair herself if it hadn't been occupied by another pizza box, with a portion of *fainá* still in it.

The bedroom door opened and Malena emerged, then went over to Verónica to greet her with a kiss. She was wearing an old, oversized T-shirt Verónica recognized as her own, and nothing else. Malena's kiss, like everything else that had happened since she entered the apartment, disconcerted her. She smelled of man, of semen. Had the guy finished on her face and now she was pressing it against Verónica's cheek?

"Ma... Malena, I need to ask you something," Verónica managed to say, trying not to sound like her mother scolding her when in her distant youth she used to come home at dawn.

255

"I know, I know… I shout a lot, right? Your neighbours must not be used to it. I'm really sorry."

How dare she say the neighbours weren't used to it? She could also scream when she fucked. She had never worried about the neighbours. That wasn't the problem.

"That's not the problem. Look around you – the living room's a bomb site."

"I thought you were coming tomorrow. I was going to tidy up before you came. You caught me by surprise. I don't suppose you have any weed, by chance?"

"I've run out," Verónica lied.

Now Damián appeared, but at least he wasn't wearing any of her clothes (come to think of it, had Malena had sex in her T-shirt or put it on afterwards?). He hadn't worried about putting much on either, just boxers and a T-shirt. He said a quick hello then went into the bathroom. Malena, looking a little abashed by Verónica's upbraiding, had started picking bits of pizza off the armchair.

"Leave it," said Verónica. "You can clean everything tomorrow."

Malena took what she had already collected to the kitchen. Damián came out of the bathroom and followed her there. Verónica could hear laughing and Malena saying: "Stop, idiot." Then a few seconds of silence. Were they fooling around in there? Malena reappeared, Damián behind her. Verónica couldn't help noticing his erection. As calmly as she could, she asked Malena to get a quilt out for her from the top of the closet. There was no way she was going into that room to see what they had done to it. A minute later Malena returned with the quilt. "Good night," she said and kissed Verónica again, this time on the corner of her lips.

Malena and Damián returned to the bedroom. Verónica took a few minutes to emerge from her numb state. She went to the bathroom, had a piss, cleaned her teeth. She couldn't bring herself to look in the mirror. In the living room, she drew the curtains and stripped down to her underwear. She plumped up the cushions and lay down on the sofa, covered with a quilt that was too heavy for such a warm night. She tried to fall asleep, but her damned insomnia wouldn't let her. To make matters worse, minutes later Malena's moaning and the sound of bedsprings started up again. Verónica snorted angrily and squeezed her eyes shut. She couldn't tell if she was hot with anger, or hot from the heat.

V

The following days fell more easily into a routine. Verónica decided not to spend nights at her apartment, unless Damián had to leave Malena on her own. She would drop in at least once, and usually twice a day: around lunchtime and before dinner. Damián had got hold of some money (Verónica didn't ask how) and could go out for shopping. Verónica lent them a computer she didn't use and Federico's Netflix account, on which they set up a "Visitors" profile. Even so, Malena felt cooped up. One afternoon Verónica didn't find her at home and was about to panic when the girl appeared: she had gone up to the roof terrace "to get some air". Verónica told her that if it was air she wanted, she'd buy her a balloon to inflate and deflate, getting as much air as she wanted, but not to go out again. She also asked that they keep the apartment as clean as possible, something they tried to do – she could tell – yet somehow failed at. Verónica made efforts to be firmer about this, but without much luck. It would have been easier to throw both of them off the balcony than to get them not to throw their cigarette butts in the kitchen sink.

Verónica offered to buy her clothes, but Malena seemed happy wearing what she found in the closet. Since the trousers were too big for her, she borrowed skirts and T-shirts. And some underwear and bras. Everything was loose on her, apart from the bras.

When Verónica dropped by on Saturday afternoon, she explained that she wouldn't be coming round that evening because she had her sister's birthday party to go to.

"Doesn't sound like much of a plan," Malena observed while searching Netflix for something to watch.

Malena was right. The thirty-eighth birthday party her sister had organized for the family was unlikely to be a great night out. In fact, Daniela was having two celebrations. One with her friends at a club in Puerto Madero, and the other with her family. Verónica would have preferred the club, but she was stuck with the family: her other sister Leticia, her brothers-in-law, her nieces and nephews, her father, Uncle Ariel, Aunt Lisa and their two children, Daniela's mother and father-in-law, the unmarried sister-in-law and the two of them – Federico and Verónica.

As so often, they were the last to arrive because Verónica had been delayed by phone calls with Rodolfo Corso (he had a new lead, for which he needed to arrange an interview) and a long chat about this and that with Patricia (another bored, housebound woman in need of entertainment). When she came out of the bathroom, before getting dressed, she asked Federico, who was watching the goals of the day from English soccer, to make her a gin and tonic. She needed a little alcohol in her blood to face so much family all at once. On top of that, the traffic was terrible between Caballito and Núñez, the neighbourhood where Daniela and her family lived in a beautiful house with a garden.

It was always the same with family gatherings: Verónica

set out with such low expectations that whatever happened afterwards was a win; she often came away with a rare sense of happiness after seeing her father, sisters, uncles and aunts. Something of the kind happened that evening. Verónica's nephew Santino took her to his room to see the hundred-piece puzzle he had completed. Her nieces, Clara and Nuria – Leticia's daughters – went too. Then Benjamín wanted her to listen to him playing the drum kit she had given him for Christmas (perhaps what was happening to her now with Malena was a curse invoked by Daniela, who rued the day Verónica had given her son the kit), and spending that time with her nieces and nephews had lifted her spirits. She came out of the room quipping about how old her sisters and their respective husbands were getting; she admired her Aunt Lisa's clothes and heard all about her last trip to New York, and she hugged her father a couple of times. When the sisters counter-attacked, badgering Federico to set a date for their wedding, Verónica scandalized them by saying that they hoped to incorporate a third person into their relationship before that. Obviously she made the remark far enough away from her father and the extended family.

As always with parties organized by Verónica's sisters, there was abundant food and drink. Her brother-in-law liked showing off his wine cellar, so he had put out for their delectation an impressive array of fine wines, which Verónica sampled and approved with delight. Plus Daniela was an excellent cook, having inherited recipes from her mother and from Grandma Esther. She had made gefilte fish the way Verónica remembered it from her childhood, as well as *varenikes*, knishes and a delectable hummus.

She took some empty plates to the kitchen, hoping to find more exquisite offerings there. Daniela was laying out mini empanadas, not home-made this time but bought from a local rotisserie. Verónica started helping her just as Leticia came in to get some cold water. They ended up chatting about the muscle spasms Leticia was experiencing in her back. Verónica made a remark about being forty that was intended to be funny, but neither of the other two laughed. Then, perhaps because he had seen all his daughters going into the kitchen, or perhaps for some other reason, Aarón appeared.

"What, all three Rosenthal girls in the kitchen? Will wonders never cease?"

The daughters did laugh at this joke, and their father took the opportunity to give Daniela a kiss, stroking her face in a gesture that was typical of him when he was with them, as though he had forgotten to wish her happy birthday earlier.

"Since I've got the three of you together, I'd like to give you some news. I'm finally thinking of retiring."

"You, retire?" exclaimed Verónica. "I'll believe it when I see it."

"Sure you're feeling all right?" asked Daniela, a doctor.

"Of course. Or am I not allowed to stop working?"

"You giving up work is like Verónica giving up alcohol," Leticia quipped.

"I'm getting on, I've already won and lost every kind of case. When I go to Tribunales I meet judges whose parents were students of mine."

"I think it's great that you're taking some time for yourself," said Verónica.

"I'm sure the novelty will wear off and I'll end up getting involved in the odd case, but I'd like to prioritize seeing my daughters and grandchildren, and fishing, and travelling again, like I used to with your mother."

"You certainly did travel a lot. You'd leave poor Ramira looking after the three of us while you jetted off to Europe or the United States," Daniela remembered.

"You even went on a safari," Leticia added.

"I cried that time because you didn't take me," said Verónica.

"Ah well, I see the chickens are coming home to roost."

"No, Pa, we want you to travel again. In fact, if you want, we can go with you, on our own or with the children. A Rosenthal world tour. We could even record it and let Verónica make a TV show about us."

"I do have one thing to sort out, and that's the firm. I'm not going to close it down. Somebody has to take over. And I wanted to get your thoughts on it. What about Iñíguez?"

"Iñíguez is a genius, but he's nearly as old as you. If you put him in charge, a year later he'll be taking retirement too," was Leticia's analysis.

"You have to give it to Federico," declared Daniela.

"Federico, obviously," agreed Leticia.

"Yes, that was also my thinking. What do you think, Verónica?"

"Well, since I'm his partner my vote may be tendentious."

"Unlike those of his sisters-in-law," said Aarón, wryly.

"I think you have to go with your gut. You've always been good at spotting talent in other people."

Benja and Clara came in then, complaining that the fizzy drinks had run out, and everyone returned to the business of carrying trays back and forth. Before closing the Rosenthal summit, Aarón asked them not to mention the subject of his succession to anyone. Not even to Federico. The three sisters agreed that they wouldn't.

Before arriving at Daniela's house, Verónica had been wondering about having a conversation with her Uncle Ariel. Since her reunion with El Chino, she'd kept thinking that it would be useful to speak to someone who had been a witness to those years.

When Ariel and his wife Lisa went out to get some fresh air in the garden, away from the hubbub in the living room, Verónica followed them.

Her uncle asked how work was going and she answered with equivocations and bromides. Aunt Lisa wanted to know if she had any ambitions to work in television, or at least radio. Verónica said she didn't.

"Uncle, do you remember the family who used to live opposite the house on Padilla and Malabia, the ones Grandfather Elías hated?"

"I can't remember anything."

Uncle Ariel may have been an architect, but he would have made an excellent mafioso. Faced with any kind of enquiry, his response was always negative: he didn't know, he couldn't remember, he hadn't been there. But if you pressed the point, eventually enlightenment struck and he ended up remembering.

"How can you not remember? They were Atlanta supporters too. The Bonieks."

"Boniek... Boniek... Ah yes, of course. The Bonieks."

"I was friends with his son. El Chino, as we used to call him."

"Of course, you used to go around with that boy. Your grandfather wasn't best pleased."

"He didn't like it, but he didn't stop me playing with him."

"Because at heart your zayde was a sensible man and not about to cut off a friendship between two kids. Anyway, if he'd done anything like that your grandmother would have killed him."

"I can only imagine how Grandpa must have reacted when my mum started going out with El Chino's father."

"Your mother go out with Rubén? Never in a million years."

"Perhaps she kept it secret because she knew Grandpa didn't get on well with that family."

"First, your zayde's problem wasn't with Rubén junior, your friend's father, but with Rubén senior, the grandfather, who died in the mid eighties. You never knew him. Second, your mother spent her whole adolescence in love with a boy who lived in Almagro, a certain Luis, who made a big fuss of her, used to take her to the cinema, even dancing sometimes. They went out for a while, then he dumped her. Your mother was broken-hearted, and shortly afterwards a law student called Aarón Rosenthal turned up and she promptly forgot about Luis."

"I think I've heard about that boyfriend before."

"In all that time it never even crossed your mother's mind to go out with Rubén. She wasn't the type to hide relationships or love affairs. In fact she used to bore us to tears with them. If she had been interested in Rubén, she would have said so, your grandmother would have backed her and your grandfather would have put up with it the same way he put up with you playing with the Boniek kid. Those two never went out together. Don't go thinking otherwise."

Verónica was puzzled. Why had Eitan lied to her? Or could he have been mistaken? Because he obviously couldn't have witnessed his father's relationship with her mother. Perhaps his father had invented the story and Eitan had believed him.

"So why did Grandpa get on badly with the Bonieks?"

"That I don't know."

"You must know something."

"Ever since I can remember, they were at daggers drawn. They were both directors of Atlanta in the 1970s, but I think the problem started earlier than that. I know they had already fallen out by the time they were both involved in the running of the club and that León Kolbowski was always having to mediate. At one point I think Kolbowski got fed up and threw the two of them out of the club."

"I'd love to know what happened between them."

"Won't your friend know?"

"He thinks my mum and his dad went out together. I'm not sure he's a reliable source."

"I don't know who can help you then."

Aunt Lisa had been listening with great interest to their conversation. "What about that old fellow, Ariel?" she asked.

"What old fellow?"

"The one you were telling me about the other day, the one in the old folks' home."

"Ah, old Márquez. It's true. Over the last few months we've been working in the studio on the redevelopment of a nursing home in Bella Vista. And I ran into Miguel Márquez there. I thought he'd be dead by now, but no. He's eighty-nine."

"Who is he?"

"Márquez – don't you remember? They lived on the next block. You used to play with their grandson, too. He was called Fabián."

"You don't mean Flavio?"

"No, not Flavio. Now I remember: he was called Hernán. Miguel was the grandfather of Hernán Márquez. Wasn't he a friend of yours too?"

Verónica asked for the details of the nursing home. She noted them down and decided to visit Miguel Márquez on Monday.

"You'd better be quick about it," said Aunt Lisa. "We're here today, but who knows what may happen tomorrow."

14   *Grandfather Elías*

I

What had become of Hernán? Verónica's childhood memories were starting to resurface, and it was as if clues to her own life, or at least to this particular chapter, were hidden in that past. Perhaps she was now also going to be reunited with Hernán, the calm and studious member of their gang. Would he be married by now and have children? Had he ended up becoming an astronomer, or astronaut, or scientist? The idea of going to the nursing home and running into Hernán enthralled her. She imagined their meeting: what it would feel like to see him again, what they would say to one another.

About old Miguel she remembered little, almost nothing. She recalled that Hernán had had a grandfather who didn't live in the neighbourhood. She had seen him two or three times, but couldn't have described him.

It was the first time Verónica had visited a nursing home, and she wasn't predisposed to like it. She didn't have a realistic picture of such a place, and in her imagination it was either a dirty hospice, staffed by cruel nurses, or one of those retirement homes you see in Hollywood movies, where the residents have their own room, a social life and plenty of green spaces to move around in.

She took the train to Bella Vista and walked a few blocks to the home. It was an old house, with an attractive exterior that appeared to be undergoing refurbishment (her architect uncle, she remembered, was in charge of these improvements). At reception Verónica asked for Miguel Márquez, saying she was a friend of his grandson. She was shown into a small waiting room and after a few minutes ushered into the heart of the building: a living room looking on to a terrace. It was like the American movie version she had imagined, but in miniature: the garden had been paved over, leaving scant greenery. The living room barely accommodated four to six residents comfortably. Fortunately, at that time there was only one woman watching television at full blast. What particularly struck Verónica was the smell of bleach that filled all the rooms and corridors, as though all bodily odours could be covered up with disinfectant.

Finally Miguel Márquez appeared, not in a wheelchair, as she had expected, but walking slowly. He approached her smiling, but when Verónica said she was a friend of Hernán, her companion's expression darkened. He sat down in a chair, resting his arms on the table. Without looking at her, he asked: "Is it a long time since you last saw him?"

"More than twenty years," she said.

The man smiled bitterly, not looking at her, searching some memory in his mind.

"Hernán is dead. He died when he was eighteen."

Verónica's eyes filled with tears. In a broken voice she said: "I… I had no idea."

She felt unable to speak or move, to embrace Miguel or let him embrace her. Pictures came to mind of Hernán on his bike, kicking a ball, passing the Coca-Cola bottle. Verónica's instinct was to leave, not to continue this conversation, yet she stayed at the table. For at least five minutes they sat in silence. Every so often Miguel dabbed at his eyes with a cotton handkerchief, although she couldn't see any tears.

"Did you come here to talk about my grandson?"

"No, yes, well, really I wanted to talk about my grandfather. But I didn't know Hernán had died."

"Poor boy."

Verónica got to her feet. "I'm sorry, I should leave."

"Who is your grandfather?"

"Elías Kowalczyk."

"Dear Elías. So you're Ariel's daughter?"

"No, Miriam's."

"Miriam, of course. Come back another day and we'll talk about him. What do you say?"

So that was what Verónica did, returning the following afternoon and two more after that, because it took three days for Miguel to tell the story of her grandfather's life.

"I met him in 1952, when I joined the Communist Party. He was a well-educated man, a seasoned activist. I already had libertarian ideas, but he was my mentor. Over the next few years we became close friends, so much so that he told me about his life. From his native Lublin to his arrival in Argentina and how he ended up living in Villa Crespo. I knew him as a militant and also saw him leave militancy behind and continue with the daily struggle. Your grandfather was a great man."

"Why did he hate Rubén Boniek?"

"He didn't hate him. He despised him. But to understand what happened between them, you have to know your grandfather's story too. Have you got time?" And so Miguel began his story.

II

Elías was originally called Eliasz, Eliasz Kowalczyk, and he was born in an occupied country. Eliasz's family were from Lublin, a Polish city that, at the time of your grandfather's birth in 1917, was part of the Russian Empire. Paradoxes of fate: Lublin would become Polish again after the First World War, when the Russian Empire became the Soviet Union, the model country Eliasz would later dream of.

Eliasz was the son of a shoemaker, and learned that trade from his father. Lublin was no village, it was a city, and shoemakers always had work. The Kowalczyks didn't go hungry, but they had nothing to spare either. Eliasz finished basic schooling and later started visiting a public library close to the shoemaker's shop. He read adventure novels but also got hold of pamphlets and short volumes on socialist ideas, which he had to read in secret because the Communist Party was proscribed. Eliasz couldn't have been more than fifteen when he started attending meetings of the Polish Communist Party, the PKP.

Those weren't good years for the banned PKP. Lublin was too close to the Soviet Union to evade the process of doctrinal hardening that would culminate in Stalinism. At the same time, the Communists had to try to overcome the distrust of the rest of the Poles, who saw them as Soviet agents, while they were ruled by a fascist dictatorship.

If the Soviet Union was a role model, Eliasz particularly admired Rosa Luxemburg and the German Spartacists. In other words, the defeated socialist revolutionaries in Germany. He did not get along well with Marxist orthodoxy, or the idea of a centralist party that would decide everything. He didn't believe in God, nor Country, nor the Party. Many decades later he would have been able to say that the only thing he believed in was the New Man, but that expression still hadn't been formulated at that time. At heart, Eliasz was an anarcho-Communist.

He was arrested once, and was registered with the police. That wasn't good, because he could end up becoming a victim of the fascist government or of the Communists themselves, who thought police agents had infiltrated the Party.

Around that time he met a fifteen-year-old girl, someone he would fall wildly in love with, someone he could believe in. She was Esther, your grandmother, the atheist daughter of the rabbi of Lublin.

They weren't exactly Romeo and Juliet but, between the political persecution to which he was subjected for his militancy, and his religious persecution by the rabbi, who didn't want his daughter hanging around with a Jewish atheist Communist, there was enough to make them feel like romantic heroes in a world that didn't understand them. After much back and forth, separations, tears, promises, threats and reconciliations, they decided to elope.

It was a good time to get out of Lublin. Joseph Stalin had ordered all the leaders of the PKP to be killed and, even if Eliasz was a minor figure within the Party, the truth is that many militants without political clout were also killed.

Eliasz knew he couldn't stay in Poland. He could count on his skill as a shoemaker and the little money he had managed to save during their ill-starred courtship. Eliasz and Esther had two possible plans: to come to Argentina, or to go to Palestine. It was the era when Zionism was campaigning strongly for Jews to return to what had been their homeland before the Diaspora, offering money to cover the cost of their passage and ease the integration into their new lives. That was a strong point in favour of Palestine over South America. And so it was that Eliasz and Esther crossed Europe to reach Marseille, where they boarded the boat that would take them to Palestine. A few months later Hitler invaded Poland. The decision to get far away from Lublin couldn't have come at a better time.

III

It's not clear when Eliasz lost the 'z' from his name, whether it was on arrival in Palestine or in Buenos Aires. But when the couple left Lublin, he was leaving behind a family that would soon die at the hands of the Nazis. Young Eliasz gave way, once and for all, to adult Elías, although Esther would always call him "Eliasz" without breaking the diphthong between the *i* and the *a*, and putting the accent on the *E*.

When he had chosen Palestine as a destination, Elías had been careful not to let the sponsors of their trip know that he was not a Zionist, that he did not believe in a country for Jews. He regarded Palestine as a victim of British capitalism, and believed in fighting for the liberation of Palestinians, whether they were Jewish, Muslim or Christian. A single people subjugated by capitalism. But to accept the trip was, implicitly, to subscribe to the Zionist views that had been spreading in Europe for decades. Elías, who had argued vehemently about politics for years, preferred to stay silent on this trip that was allowing him to escape all kinds of persecution.

Esther and Elías were married in the Jewish rite soon after arriving in Haifa. They didn't believe in marriage – not something they would ever say to their children or grandchildren – but it was easier for them to live together and protect themselves (especially Esther) as a married couple. There were no friends, neighbours or family at the celebrations, but there were some recently arrived Jews and others who already lived in Palestine, and they prepared a beautiful, modest and unforgettable party for the couple.

In contrast to many of the Jews who arrived in those years, Elías wanted to integrate into the Palestinian community. That was very difficult, because the Christians and Muslims spoke Arabic. He spoke Polish, a little Russian and Yiddish, although once in Haifa he found it was fairly easy to communicate with the locals.

During the first months in Palestine, Elías worked building homes for settlers. That brought in a comfortable wage. Esther got pregnant soon after they arrived. Elías had promised himself he would be working in his own trade by the time his daughter or son was born.

Someone, a neighbour, mentioned to him a shoemaker who lived in Hadar, a neighbourhood of Haifa, near Mount Carmel. Elías decided to visit him. Friendship, like romantic love, can begin at first sight, and that was what happened between Elías and Ibrahim, the Shoemaker of Mount Carmel, as he liked to call himself. Ibrahim was an Arab Palestinian who had been born in a town near Haifa. At the start of the 1930s he had moved to Hadar, the nerve centre of Haifa, to try his luck as a shoemaker with Zeina, his Maronite wife of Lebanese origin. Ibrahim was not only a shoemaker but also a Communist. As Elías knew only a few words and phrases in Arabic, it's hard to imagine how the two men understood each other the first time they met, let alone at what point they told each other about their political affiliations. Elías became first Ibrahim's assistant and later his partner. Before arriving at the workshop in Mount Carmel, Elías knew the rudiments of shoemaking. With Ibrahim, who was ten years older, he learned how to make shoes, including fancy ones, which were sold to an ever larger and more demanding clientele.

Elías had kept the promise he made to himself: by the time Ismael was born, he was once again a shoemaker. And he spoke a little more Arabic. The Kowalczyk family moved to a small apartment close to the shoemaking workshop. From the building's rooftop they could see the sea.

It was also Ibrahim who introduced Elías to the Palestinian Communist Party, the only political group in which Arabs and

Jews coexisted (not without problems). The Party followed Soviet anti-Zionist directives, yet most of the important positions in the Party were held by Jewish militants, many of them with Zionist sympathies. Elías couldn't help remembering that the Soviets had killed most of the leaders and activists of the Polish Communist Party, a point raised by him at some of the meetings. Arguments – and contradictions – were common currency at the PKP.

In the Party there were two mythical figures who, for different reasons, were no longer involved in the daily struggle in Palestine. One was a Jewish Pole, like Elías himself: Leo Lev, a carpenter and founding member of the Party who had resisted the British occupation, fought against Italian fascists and in defence of the Spanish republic. However, when the PKP took a harder line against the actions of Jewish resistance groups, Lev was expelled.

No less legendary or adventurous was the life of another character Elías greatly admired. He was Najati Sidqi, a Palestinian born in Jerusalem, who had organized the Communist Party in Haifa. He had also fought for the Spanish Republicans, called for the rebellion of Maghreb countries and, even when the Soviet Union had a non-aggression pact with Hitler, was openly anti-Nazi, to the point of publishing a book that explained the incompatibility of Muslim culture and Naziism. That book got him expelled from the PKP. Even so, Ibrahim and Elías travelled to Jerusalem to offer Sidqi their personal support. They shared not only his Communist ideology but also his spirit of rebellion against the party line. When Elías met him, Sidqi said in Russian: "Elías, like the prophet of Mount Carmel who challenged the 450 false prophets of Baal."

Then he asked if Elías believed in Yahweh. Elías thought, and answered in Arabic: "I'm a henotheist. I believe in the existence of many gods, but that only one is worthy of adoration: the god of the Communist revolution."

Sidqi roared with laughter and said that must be the first time anyone had ever said "henotheist" in Arabic.

At the height of the Second World War, the Palestinian Communist Party joined the battle against British occupation, but without resorting to the violence espoused by Zionist groups fighting for a Jewish state.

While politics and struggle went on in the streets of the Palestine of the British protectorate, in the home of Elías and Esther love and happiness flowed naturally, even though Ismael's health was fragile and Esther had to spend a lot of time taking him to doctors and hospitals.

So the years passed, the Second World War ended, the arguments over a Palestinian state for all or two states – one Palestinian, the other Jewish – to divide a population reeling from the killings and mutual attacks of the last decades ended and so too, in a chaotic manner, did the British Mandate. From then onwards, and until the creation of the State of Israel, death stalked Palestine. And for Elías and his family it signalled the end of their life in Haifa.

IV

After two British army intelligence officials were killed by Irgun – together with Lehi, one of the two most violent Zionist groups operating in Palestine – and following the subsequent wave of anti-Zionism that swept England and Scotland, the United Kingdom accelerated its departure from Palestine, with no thought for those left behind: a people facing fratricidal war. Some were recent arrivals, others had lived their whole lives in the territory and had children and grandchildren born there. And while the forces that would end up becoming the Israeli army were trained, armed and ready to fight, the Muslims (and Christian minorities) put their trust in the moral force of their claim, the support of Arab countries in the region and, to a lesser degree, a small army. Disasters weren't long in coming.

The news arrived in waves, not like the waves that bathed the coast of Haifa but gigantic, violent waves that swept away everything in their path.

That was how Elías learned about the massacre of Deir Yassin, on 9 April 1948. Fighters from Irgun and Lehi murdered, raped and destroyed the livelihoods of many residents in this small village inhabited by Palestinians. The news spoke of elderly people and children murdered, of women and girls raped. Corpses thrown over balconies, grandparents massacred alongside their grandchildren, young couples murdered with their sons and daughters. One hundred and ten homicides that demonstrated the ferocity the defenders of the State of Israel were willing to unleash, although some quarters later condemned and tried to disassociate themselves from these events.

Terror engulfed the Palestinians. They had learned that neighbouring countries would do nothing to save them, that morals were nothing against tanks and machine guns, and that their own soldiers (poorly equipped and badly led) could not halt the barbarism. If they had butchered a small and unassuming village, what would they do to the inhabitants of much richer towns and cities? The people of Haifa began to flee, escaping with only the clothes on their backs. Whole towns left everything behind because the Israeli troops were coming. For them there was no difference between Irgun and the official army of what, in a few days, would be the State of Israel.

Ibrahim decided to stay. He, his wife and their three children. The shoemaking workshop at Mount Carmel. The

Mediterranean, lapping the shores of Haifa. His land. Others left, taking the keys to their houses. Dreaming of a return once peace was restored. They didn't know, didn't even imagine, that their houses would be occupied, their belongings would be destroyed or used by the occupiers.

Seven hundred and fifty thousand people displaced.

Ibrahim wasn't going to leave Haifa.

Elías had another problem that worried him: Ismael's health had worsened. Esther and he took the boy to hospital, where he was diagnosed with pneumonia, aggravated by the precarious state of his general health. While Israeli troops took Haifa, murdering Ibrahim's family (him, his wife, their three children) in their home, Esther and Elías were plunged into unbearable grief over their son's death.

Their pain was so great that the pain of the world seemed small to them. They cried so much over the death of their son that they had no tears left to shed over the death of their friends. Nor did they have any happiness with which to celebrate the fact that Esther was pregnant again.

When they returned to their home, the workshop had been destroyed. The apartment, however, hadn't been touched. Elías removed the board from a hiding place where he kept their money: there were the pounds sterling he had been saving all these years.

Their next child would not be born in this land scarred by death and discrimination.

They would not remain in a country that had murdered its own people. In a country that didn't believe Jews and Muslims were the same.

They made the same journey they had undertaken nine years ago, but in reverse: from Haifa to Marseille. There they would board the ship that took them to Buenos Aires.

V

Verónica always left her meetings with Miguel Márquez in a strange state of emotion and surprise; even if some of the stories were familiar to her (she knew about her grandfather's militant Communist past, his rage at Israel, his Poland–Palestine–Argentina odyssey, the death of his first child), Miguel made them three-dimensional. The family anecdote was turned into an eyewitness account.

In the nursing home there was a patio with a garden area where the residents could get some fresh air. On Verónica's third visit, Miguel managed to secure a corner with two armchairs where they could continue talking. She brought him what he had asked for and his family had refused to give him: two packets of cigarettes and some whisky in a hip flask.

"The same people who can't wait to see me dead are worried that tobacco or alcohol are bad for me. That's how contradictory human beings are," he mused.

Verónica wasn't sure she was doing the right thing, but she perfectly understood Miguel's reasoning: when she was old she hoped some kind person would sneak her vices into the nursing home. She offered to bring in a carton of cigarettes and a litre bottle of whisky, but Miguel told her he had nowhere to hide such large quantities. So Verónica promised to return every now and then, to replenish his stores.

"Whisky's fine, but you wouldn't believe the hoops I have to jump through to smoke," said Miguel, caressing his gifts.

"My grandfather didn't smoke, and only drank wine."

"And gin, but he gave up a lot of things in old age. Gin was one of them."

"From everything you've told me, there's one thing I haven't got straight, and that's the part my Grandmother Esther played in this story."

"Those were different times, and women went along with the decisions of the menfolk. Besides, the story I know is the one told by your grandfather, and in those days men didn't like talking about their feelings. He could be quite tight-lipped about things like that."

"My atheist grandmother, daughter of a rabbi, who runs away as a teenager to follow her heart. Looking after a sick child who dies in the middle of a massacre. Who discovers she's pregnant and sets off on a journey to a country she doesn't know. What a shame not to know more about her."

"I'm sorry, my dear, I only know what Elías told me. But I can tell you that your Grandmother Esther was a woman of great inner strength. She spoke little, but she had firm convictions. Now, get comfortable, because we're coming to the part of the story about your grandfather and the Boniek family."

Verónica would have liked to smoke a cigarette. Better still, a joint. And to get a bottle of Jim Beam out of her bag. Miguel looked as though he would have joined her. Unfortunately, they would have to make do with cups of tea.

VI

Many years later, on the terraces at Atlanta, or at a bar drinking coffee or in his shop on Avenida Corrientes, Elías would say: "It was harder for me to learn Spanish than Arabic."

But he was exaggerating. Elías had a great gift for languages, and he and Esther made a habit of always speaking the language of the place they were in: Polish first (the language of their courtship, the thrill of first love, their elopement), then Arabic or Yiddish and, much later on, Spanish. Perhaps because they were fully immersed in their new environment, neither had much difficulty in adapting to Argentine culture.

277

Social integration wasn't easy, though. They arrived in a country where they knew no one. Without knowing the language, all they had to go on were stories of other immigrants like them who had managed to make a home in this land. Just as the Zionist Jews had helped them at the start, Elías found in Buenos Aires the solidarity of the Jewish community. They weren't going to abandon him, especially not with a pregnant wife.

Elías had a rude introduction to the reality of life in Argentina: soon after arriving, he suffered acute appendicitis and needed an operation. Despite his atheism, he thanked Yahweh that this had happened in Buenos Aires and not on the boat, where he would probably have died. They operated on him in the same place where his first daughter, Miriam, would be born: the hospital in Rivadavia. A few months after his operation, they returned for the birth. The future mother of Leticia, Daniela and Verónica came into the world with all the strength, energy and vitality her daughters would inherit.

To start with, the Kowalczyk family lived in a boarding house in Once, then they rented an apartment in the same neighbourhood. Years later they moved to a small rented house in Villa Crespo, and in time they were able to buy, nearby, the house in which their children and even their grandchildren would grow up. Elías began working in a shoe workshop close to Plaza Miserere. Since he still had some of the savings he had brought from Palestine, he was able to rent a small shop on Sarmiento and Anchorena. At one point he thought of calling his business Mount Carmel, but his pain over the deaths of Ibrahim and his family was still too raw. So he called it simply Miriam Shoemakers.

He managed to obtain some old, discarded machinery that he refurbished, to begin making shoes. The business grew and moved to larger premises in a shopping centre on Corrientes and Medrano. In the early days Esther would help him, bringing the baby to work, then they took on a girl, Susana, to serve in the shop. Elías talked to Susana about surplus value and how the owners of companies held on to money that belonged to the workers. Either Jewish guilt or a Communist sense of social justice made Elías pay a very good wage to his employee, who never left him and felt a reverential love for her boss. When he retired, she did too.

It wasn't a good time to be a Communist in Argentina. He was used to being persecuted, so Peronism was hardly going to frighten him. He didn't mind going on demonstrations or handing out pamphlets that specifically denounced torture and every other kind of mistreatment by the police.

Given his militant past in Poland and Palestine, Elías was an obvious candidate for a leading role in the Argentine Communist Party. But there was a problem, the same old problem: Elías had no faith in the Party's leadership; he despised Stalin and the followers who uncritically accepted whatever the Soviet Union ordained. This led him to be called crazy (it could have been worse) and, although he wasn't expelled from the Party, he distanced himself from it even as he continued to go to events and rallies.

His final departure from the Party apparatus came with the fall of Peronism. The Peronist ghouls, covert fascists who had harassed left-wing militants, became victims of persecution and even harsher attacks than they had endured themselves. Elías could also appreciate some of the contributions of Peronism to social justice, and although he never became a Peronist, he didn't allow himself to be an anti-Peronist *gorila* either. The coup that toppled Perón in 1955 forced him to take a side (once again in his life), and he opted to side with Argentina's poor.

But for the rest of his life his heart would remain Communist. Or rather his spirit (or his soul, but his atheism wouldn't allow him one of those), because his heart, without doubt, belonged to Los Bohemios.

Elías used to say he became an Atlanta fan in Rivadavia Hospital, when he was admitted for his appendicitis; that is, not long after arriving in Argentina. He had seen a "huge photograph" of a soccer player in the newspaper and read the word *Atlanta*. "It was the first word I ever spoke in Spanish," he would say in the Bohemio stand.

The anecdote must have been apocryphal. There was never a huge photograph of an Atlanta player in a national newspaper. But he was proud of this origin story. He'd probably first heard of Atlanta at a gathering of compatriots in Once as the club started becoming a favourite of the Jewish community. Perhaps he moved to Villa Crespo to be closer to the club.

There's no doubt, on the other hand, that he was in the stadium to witness the club's return to the First Division, on 5 May 1957, the day Carlos Timoteo Griguol debuted wearing the number five shirt and Atlanta beat Ferro one–nil.

By 1959, the Kowalczyks (now including little Ariel) had moved to the house in Villa Crespo. Opposite lived Rubén Boniek with his wife and two children. The older son was also called Rubén and would continue to live at home until the early nineties.

Rubén Boniek senior had been born in Krakow and emigrated as a small child. The fact that both Rubén and Elías were Polish immigrants was an immediate bond. Elías didn't care that Rubén was a Catholic Pole, the kind who went to Mass on Sundays and remembered the Polish fascists with affection; the strange thing was that he was married to Fanny, a Jewish girl he had met in Entre Ríos. It was hard to tell if behind that marriage there was a story even more similar to *Romeo and Juliet* than the one Elías and Esther had lived. Because Rubén always presented himself as a believer, one who took confession with the priest in the parish of Santa Clara de Asís.

Elías had no misgivings, either, about the fact that Rubén had worked in the federal police in his youth and, for some reason, was no longer officially in their employ. At the end of the day, they shared something that could fill hours of conversation between them: Atlanta.

In the Bohemian stands people were starting to talk about León Kolbowski, an entrepreneur involved with the club who, at the end of the fifties, would become its president. León and Elías shared more than a love of the shirt: they were both Communists, too. And if Elías wasn't exactly an entrepreneur, he did now employ three people in his business, which had stopped mending shoes and become a popular shoe shop in Almagro. Two Communists doing nicely in a capitalist world.

Kolbowski and Elías hit it off immediately, and soon the club's president asked him to be a board member. Elías was proud to be helping to shape the club's future. Meanwhile, Rubén Boniek had also approached the Atlanta management and managed to wangle a place on the committee.

The 1960s were a very good decade for Atlanta – within its limitations, which were always on display in the soccer itself and even more so behind the scenes. Kolbowski grew the club, and there were times when its fans dreamed that Atlanta might one day give the great First Division teams a run for their money.

Then Elías heard some dark mutterings about Rubén by other directors. They said he was a police informant. He ratted on suspected Peronists and Communists. Elías had no reason to believe Rubén had reported on him, but others were more fearful. And he was amused by those who, horrified, said that

Rubén was a spy. He corrected them: "James Bond is a spy. Rubén is a paid snitch."

You could say that something about Rubén rubbed Elías up the wrong way. They weren't friends, and never would be. Elías had other friends: old Communist militants, some of his neighbours, Atlanta supporters.

One summer evening, Elías was returning from the shoe shop. He liked to walk, to stroll through the city, stopping here and there to have a coffee or a white wine, if the weather called for it. That day he hadn't stopped in any bars. He got home looking forward to a cold shower and hoping Esther was preparing one of her tastier dishes. On the sidewalk, playing on his own, was Boniek's younger son. The others, teenagers by now, must be with their friends in Parque Centenario. The little boy was riding his tricycle and it was late, Elías thought, for him to be out alone. So he took him back to his house. But before he could knock on the door, he heard Rubén and Fanny rowing. He was shouting; she was crying. Elías asked the little boy to sit and wait on the doorstep. Then he opened the door and went in. (In those days nobody locked the door if the children were out playing on the sidewalk.) When he reached the kitchen, from where the shouting was coming, Elías saw Rubén beating his wife. One smack after another. Elías lunged at Rubén, startling him, and soon both men were throwing punches, heedless of Fanny's cries. The husband had transferred his aggression to Elías. Fanny got between them, breaking up the fight. Rubén hurled insults at Elías, who threatened to report him to the police, a futile gesture. The police never did anything about a man hitting his wife, especially not if that man had once been in their ranks.

In return, Rubén threatened to report Elías for trespassing on his property. But all three of them fell silent when they saw that Boniek's youngest son was crying. His mother grabbed him and hugged him fiercely. Then she asked Elías to leave. He hesitated, then saw no option but to do as she said.

Arriving home, furious, Elías told Esther what had happened. First she asked him to calm down, adding: "You men are all brutes," which offended him, because his wife couldn't put him in the same box as Rubén. Then Esther went to the bedroom and got changed. She reappeared dressed to go out, picked up her bag and told him that she would be gone for a while, that she didn't know if she'd be home in time to make dinner.

Through the window, Elías watched her go. Esther crossed the road, knocked on the door and Rubén appeared, with a face like thunder. Just as Elías was about to go back out and continue the fight, he saw Esther going into the house. Twenty minutes later she re-emerged, accompanied by Fanny, who was also dressed up, and the two women walked off down the street. Elías remained watching, like a prisoner looking out of his cell. A couple of hours later, the women returned, seemingly happy. They went into the house opposite. Ten minutes later Esther came out and returned home, simply saying: "That brute won't ever touch a hair on Fanny's head again."

What she had said, what she had done and where she had gone with Rubén's wife, Elías never found out.

From then onwards, Elías and Rubén didn't speak again. They only ever acknowledged one another if someone else was there. Fanny survived her husband's beatings. In fact he died before her, in the eighties and still quite young, which was a blessing in a way, although it was sad that it took widowhood to get him off her back.

The problems with the Bonieks did not end with that clash.

Still waiting in the wings was Rubén Boniek, son of Rubén Boniek, father of Eitan.

In the sixties, there was an outbreak of anti-Semitism in Argentina, the worst since the Semana Trágica of 1919. Fascist groups like the Tacuara were openly anti-Semitic, violent and cowardly. They attacked young Jews in packs, daubed graffiti on synagogues, desecrated Jewish cemeteries. In 1964, militants from Tacuara murdered Raúl Alterman, a young Jewish Communist. It wasn't easy to be Jewish in those years; it wasn't unusual to feel threatened, to fear that an attack could come at any time. A taste of what was to come later, during the dictatorship.

Every action prompts a reaction. At that time there was an increase in Jewish self-defence groups. If they were going to be attacked, people reasoned, at least they would try to defend themselves, defend their friends and relations. These groups, backed by Israel, had existed in Argentina since the creation of the state, but during this time they became more powerful and could even count on training by members of Mossad, the Israeli secret service.

While Jewish institutions set about exposing and decrying all discrimination, threats and acts of violence, these groups resolved to attack their attackers, and above all to promote identification with the State of Israel. The young men who joined the Irgun (what these groups called themselves, in honour of the violent militia that had burst into Palestine to attack the British and Palestinians) not only trained in self-defence, but also learned how to use firearms and bladed weapons. Ideological indoctrination took place in camps and clubs. In some Jewish institutions there were Stars of David that could be taken apart and reassembled as nunchucks. The preparations were both ingenious and practical.

Elías knew about the existence of these violent groups. The name Irgun revived bad memories from his life in Palestine, but he also initially thought it no bad thing that young Jews should learn to protect themselves from the danger posed by far-right groups. This was a time when violence as a form of conflict resolution was winning followers in Argentina and around the world. Elías rejoiced whenever he heard that Irgun had prevented some Jewish boys from being beaten up or a community business from being attacked.

Irgun was informed, however, by the politics of Israel, which was in turn guided by the dichotomous logic of the United States. For the young Jews of the Argentine Irgun, the Communists (whether Jewish or not) also became their enemies.

The self-defence groups began to go to Communist Party gatherings to break them up, with the same zeal they brought to their battles with the anti-Semites. They didn't care that many of the protesters were themselves Jewish. Rather, they blamed the Argentine Communist Party for the barbaric acts of their Soviet partners, who were refusing to allow Russian Jews to emigrate. "Let my people leave" was the slogan they used against activists who dreamed of imposing socialism peacefully in Argentina.

Elías was at a meeting of Communist militants (to call it an assembly would be an exaggeration; there were barely thirty people there) in the neighbourhood of Chacarita when he himself suffered an attack by local Irgun thugs. Whether they were following orders from on high or were simply a fringe group with a taste for violence, he never found out.

Among their number was Rubén Boniek junior.

Elías had gone to the meeting not because he was still an active member but to accompany his friend Miguel Márquez. In any case, this wasn't a scheduled Party event but one organized by some dissidents who wanted to find a way out of the Soviet orthodoxy.

The gang burst in with sticks and bludgeons. There were no more than ten of them, but they were well armed against a group who didn't have so much as a penknife among them. Shouting their slogan, they started smashing up everything they could: banners, chairs, windows, lights. The Communists scattered and the gang seized their chance to mete out beatings, like the federal police, who were always anti-Communist. Elías wasn't surprised to see Rubén junior among the attackers; there had been rumours about him in the barrio. The twenty-year-old set upon Márquez and, when Elías moved in to protect him, Rubén recognized his neighbour as the father of Miriam, that girl who never paid him any attention. Pulled up short, his rage turned to shame. Elías dragged his injured friend away from the melee, but not before saying to Rubén Boniek: "You're a bad lot, like your father."

"Bad lot": that was the harshest insult Elías could muster.

At the end of the 1960s, the self-defence groups disarmed, but Mossad's influence continued to be felt in different ways. Among the neighbours, the gossip was that, just as Boniek senior had been a police informant, so the son had also made a career of snitching and scheming.

And that was why Elías hated them.

VIII

"I don't remember my grandfather as an activist, going to political meetings, or speaking badly of the Bonieks," said Verónica, her head spinning with all the stories she had heard about Elías.

"As I said, he gave up on activism for good during the dictatorship. Doubtless he was scared, like many of us, but

286

also disillusioned with the way the country and the rest of the world were going."

"My grandfather being a Communist was almost a family joke. My father was always bringing it up. 'Your Commie dad,' he'd say to my mother."

"There came a point, in the middle of the eighties, when your father felt old, too. He decided to retire, transfer the shoe shop to your Uncle Ariel and devote himself to the important things in life: his wife, his family and Atlanta. He didn't want anything more than that."

Verónica remembered walking with her grandfather to Avenida Corrientes to buy an ice cream; cold winter evenings on the terraces at Atlanta; the smile with which he always greeted her when she arrived at the house in Villa Crespo.

She said goodbye to Márquez with the promise, which she intended to keep, of visiting him every so often, bringing alcohol and cigarettes.

Afterwards, she couldn't stop thinking about El Chino and his family. His violent, militant father and his wife-beating grandfather. El Chino had invented a romance between his father and Verónica's mother, he had hidden details about his family from her. Perhaps the reasons he gave her about why his family had gone to live in Israel were not true. She wondered what other things her childhood friend might be hiding from her.

15   *An Innocent Girl*

I

Rodolfo Corso wasn't made for healthy living. He was built
for marathon sessions of drugs, alcohol and sex – even if the
last of these was increasingly infrequent. He could spend a
week eating McDonald's burgers, or survive on a diet of *mate*,
rice and cigarettes, or go forty-eight hours without sleeping.
It was a lifestyle that had produced his best, most acclaimed
journalism (acclaimed by his colleagues, who respected him
but sometimes feared his self-destructive tendencies). For
these reasons he didn't feel comfortable in shorts, a T-shirt
and sneakers, running through the woods of Palermo, but this
might be the best way to run into Aníbal Monteverde, one of
Sergio Mayer's partners in the multimedia group Esparta and
owner of the magazine *Nuestro Tiempo*, among other media
outlets. Rodolfo knew if he asked Monteverde's secretary for
an appointment, she wouldn't give him one, that if he tried
catching his target going in or out of the apartment building
where he lived in Núñez, or his offices in Colegiales, he would
quickly get into his car, perhaps answering one question at
most. Better to grab him when he was tired, running through
the woods of Palermo, as he did every morning.

Of the three Grupo Esparta partners (Mayer, Monteverde
and Gómez Pardo), Monteverde was the only one who had
come up through the world of mass media. While still a

communication studies student in the first cohort at the Universidad de Buenos Aires, Monteverde had started a neighbourhood magazine in Ramos Mejía. Like many community ventures, it was supported by advertising from local businesses, but in contrast to most comparable rags, Monteverde had managed to create a good journalistic product: well-written articles, interesting interviews and a team of writers, photographers and graphic designers who were all talented people taking their first steps in the media world. At the end of the eighties, Monteverde set up a community radio in Haedo, Radio Sol, which aspired to the bubbly and provocative style of bigger stations, like Rock & Pop. It was around that time that Corso and Monteverde first met. Rodolfo presented a programme on Radio Sol at midnight on Saturdays called *Sun with Drugs* (a nod to singer Charly García's quip that he preferred drugs to sunshine). To this day, Corso couldn't fathom how endorsing criminality hadn't got the station closed down and landed him in jail.

At the beginning of the nineties, Monteverde looked like an up-and-coming media entrepreneur, thanks to business dealings with the then President Menem's inner circle. But playing in the big leagues isn't for everyone, and he only landed a few small contracts while the other ass-lickers walked away with television channels, cable networks and million-dollar advertising deals. Monteverde had to make do with crumbs from the table. He didn't do badly, but he also didn't become the media tsar he might have been.

Then, when he seemed ready to settle for his portfolio – FM radio stations in Córdoba and Tucumán, a free newspaper, shares in some cable networks in the Interior (before the big mergers in the sector) and a radio and television production company – up popped impresario Sergio Mayer, a man who turned everything he touched into gold. Mayer said he admired Monteverde, and he wanted them to put together a multimedia group that would grow in the sunlight of their combined political and business contacts.

"With your knowledge of the media world, and my business know-how, we're going to triumph."

"As long as it's not the other way round."

That was the anecdote, possibly invented, that Monteverde liked to tell about the time Mayer suggested becoming partners.

It wasn't the other way round, but almost. Monteverde's knowledge turned out not to be that useful, given the rapid pace of technological change in the mid 2000s, and Mayer's business acumen was thwarted by the voracious and savage instincts of the biggest media impresarios, who were busy turning radio stations, television channels, newspapers and magazines into cartels and didn't want new players in the sector.

Monteverde had chosen Goicochea as editor of *Nuestro Tiempo*. They knew each other, but hadn't worked together before. During the six years Goicochea edited the magazine, a friendship developed that, while not deep, was built on respect and gratitude; each made decisions that favoured the other.

Once the crisis in Grupo Esparta became inevitable, Mayer made various devious moves, such as persuading Gómez Pardo, a business associate, to invest in the media group. Mayer proposed a capital investment Monteverde couldn't match, thus forcing him to cede seventy per cent of his stake to Gómez Pardo. Monteverde had no choice but to go along with this. But then Mayer went further, holding Goicochea personally responsible for the dire financial straits in which *Nuestro Tiempo* found itself, since several journalistic investigations published in the magazine had led to a loss of advertisers. He knew that firing the veteran editor was a way to deal Monteverde another blow.

Corso suspected that Monteverde had been wounded by the crushing of his fantasy of himself as a media mogul. That would make him a good source of information on Mayer.

The November sun beat down hard at that time in the morning. Corso jogged as slowly as possible, eyeing up the other runners and thinking they must be mildly deranged, or perhaps had terrible secrets and were running away from their guilt.

Close to the Rosedal, he spotted Monteverde, jogging at a good clip along a path adjacent to Corso's. Rodolfo put on a spurt to catch up, something not easy for him. With a great effort, he came alongside Monteverde and said: "You're a sight for sore eyes."

Monteverde was wearing Bluetooth headphones and likely didn't hear him, but he did notice Corso's presence. He took off the headphones while still running.

"Corso, what brings you here? Either you're on drugs, or they've taken you off the drugs."

"Neither one nor the other. I simply saw the light and went up, to quote Miguel Mateos."

"That reminds me – what did one electricity bill say to the other? 'I saw the light and went up.' That's a good one."

"Could you stop running for a moment? I think I'm about to die."

Monteverde stopped and looked him up and down, a sarcastic smile sketched on his face. "Something tells me you actually came here to find me."

It took Rodolfo a few minutes to persuade Monteverde to talk. They had known each other for a long time, and he knew which buttons to press to revive the spirit of that media impresario who used to arrive at the radio station cheerfully announcing some deal he had struck with the pizzeria down the block. Monteverde agreed to speak for the sake of old times. His only condition was that it be off the record, which Rodolfo accepted instantly. The two men walked on until they found a tree to sit under. Monteverde offered him some water and Corso accepted with relief. It was a while before his breathing returned to normal.

"Did you know Andrés was chasing a story?"

"Yes, of course. I'm the one who gave him the information he needed."

Rodolfo wished there was gin to hand. He needed something strong to help him absorb what he suspected he was about to hear.

"You surprise me. I wonder if we're talking about the same investigation."

"The allegation concerning Mayer and his Israeli firm."

"That's the one. How did you become a source?"

"It's a very long story. Or a short one, depending on how you look at it. When the group was restructured, I didn't want them to boot out Goicochea. We could have removed him as editor at the magazine and given him an honorary role, nothing too involved but something that would have allowed him to keep his salary and us to avoid the rumour mill."

"But Mayer wasn't keen."

"Exactly. He was obsessed with firing him. And he got his way. Then he brought in Tantanian, that useless idiot with pretensions to celebrity."

"Did you stay in touch with Goicochea?"

"We saw each other a few days after he was fired. He told me he wanted to write again. Financially, he was fine. He wanted to write because it was the one thing he knew how to do."

"He was a journalist to his core."

"One of the best. He wasn't going to write moronic opinion pieces in some newspaper. Even though he was no longer working for us, he and I kept up the habit of seeing each other once or twice a month for lunch. At one of those lunches I said: 'Andrés, I've got what you need to kill two birds with one stone: to return to journalism and to deal Mayer a mortal blow.' And I passed him a folder with all the details of Mayer and Gómez Pardo's business operations in Israel. When that blew up in the media, Israeli officials would have no option but to take action against them. We're talking about many millions of dollars. Plus the end of his business career."

"I imagine there were pressures on him here, no? A media mogul convicted in Israel for multiple frauds isn't a very credible person."

"It could have been the beginning of the end for Mayer."

"And how did those papers come into your hands?"

"I knew the commercial attaché at the Israeli embassy. We'd see each other at the odd event, swap the occasional favour. Anyway, the guy called me because he wanted to talk. He said he was worried about what he'd uncovered concerning Mayer's company. He showed me a folder with the details and proof of embezzlement carried out by my partner. I told him I would make sure the material reached a journalist."

"Why didn't he make it public himself?"

"I asked him the same thing. He told me he couldn't get mixed up in local matters."

"But this was about an Israeli company. He could have sent the information to some official over there."

"Again, I thought the same thing. But I was so enraged with that bastard Mayer, who'd made me sell my shares dirt cheap so that piece of shit Gómez Pardo could buy them. There was no way I was going to miss the opportunity to play a part in his downfall."

"Except that Andrés was the one who fell."

Monteverde wiped the sweat off his face with the small towel he had round his neck. He kept his face covered for a few seconds. "Not a day goes by that I don't think it was my fault they killed him."

"And what was on the tablet?"

"What tablet?"

"The tablet that had all the info on it."

"No, I passed on all the information in analogue form."

"Andrés never mentioned a tablet to you?"

"Not that I remember."

They stood up and said goodbye, promising to meet again soon. Then Monteverde jogged off and Corso walked slowly in the opposite direction, heading for Avenida Sarmiento.

I I

First thing that morning, Ángeles had a video call with her sister Carolina. It wasn't yet midday in La Chaux-de-Fonds, the Swiss city in the canton of Neuchâtel to which Carolina had moved ten years ago, soon after qualifying as an architect and in pursuit of a Swiss boyfriend. The boyfriend turned out to be a waste of space, so she left him a few months later, but stayed living in that small city which for an architect was like coming to Mecca, because Le Corbusier had been born there.

Despite the difference in age (Carolina was six years older), the sisters had always been close and tried to keep up with each other's lives through calls, email, WhatsApps, recommendations for music, TV or movies, the odd package of *yerba mate* or dulce de leche from one side of the Atlantic; Swiss chocolates and make-up from the other. At one time, Ángeles had fantasized about going to live in Switzerland. She knew that it was famously boring, but she was hardly the queen of fun herself. As Carolina liked to say, there was always something worse, and that would be living in Liechtenstein, whose inhabitants were so dull they went to Switzerland for kicks.

The sisters might ring each other at any time of day, so Carolina wasn't surprised to get this call. They chatted for a while. Carolina showed Ángeles her drafting table, talking her through the renovation of a high-spec sports centre she was working on; it was to be a smart building, like several others that had already been built in the area. She asked Ángeles how work was going.

"It's OK. I'm on a divorce case that's a bit complicated."

"But you don't do family law."

"At Rosenthal, if they ask me to make coffee, I do it."

"Did you fall out with Federico and now he's punishing you?"

"Far from it. This is a big case. I'd say it's a mark of trust."

"Let me disabuse you."

"Hey, wait, before I forget. You saved my life."

"What? How did I do that?"

"By telling me about Orígenes. The woman involved in the divorce case I'm working on is a member of Orígenes. So I came across as someone who knows loads about the subject and she totally bought it."

"That's wild. Who is this woman?"

"You won't know her."

"Do you know how many of us are in Orígenes? By the last count, a month ago, there are 238 of us, of whom twenty-one are from Argentina. We all know each other."

"Roxana Mayer."

"I don't remember any Mayer. There was a Roxana... but she was called Soldati."

"That's her. Soldati is her maiden name."

"Then of course I know her: a platinum blonde with a nose job and an ass squeezed into tight jeans. About fifty."

"The very one."

"She came to an event we had a few years ago in Milan. She was with a guy, if I remember correctly."

"David Kaplan?"

"I can't remember his name, but I'm sure it wasn't Kaplan. I had a friend at high school called Daniela Kaplan. I would have been reminded of her."

"Actually, I called to tell you something."

"Hurry then, because I'm going out to lunch in ten minutes."

"I'm pregnant."

"Oh shit. Are you sure?"

"Very."

"Oof, Ángeles. How are you feeling?"

"All right, coming round to the idea. I did the test last night."

"And what do you think you'll do?"

"Keep it."

"Are you sure?"

"Yup."

"Is it Federico's?"

"Uh-huh. I still haven't told him."

"A baby is a complication, you know, especially for a single mother. Don't expect them to go easy on you at work. They'll be all smiles, they'll say how lovely that you're going to be a mother, but they won't give you the big cases because mothers aren't reliable, they prioritize their children, they take time off if the kid's ill. You'll end up in a dark corner, like an old vacuum cleaner."

"I don't care. It will be hard, I'll have to change a few plans, but I want to have it."

"When I had an abortion, you flew over to be with me."

"Well, you'll have to come for the birth. Every baby needs a spinster aunt to spoil it."

"Fuck off."

"I'm going to wait a bit before I tell the oldsters."

"Mamá will cry, but in a month she'll be buying baby rompers. Papá will hug you, promise his support, then tell you off about it three months later."

"I'm wondering what Federico's reaction will be."

"Prepare to be a single mother, Ángeles. If you've got some fantasy of Federico leaving his wife and running into your arms to dream up boy and girl names together, forget it, go and get an abortion."

"He's not married. And I already know we're not going to be a family. I'm not doing this for him, but for me."

"You seem so sure about it that I feel like coming over there right now. I'll buy you one of those baby carriages they sell here that look like spaceships."

"You can't imagine how much I'd love you to come."

The conversation continued for a while, and the sisters signed off feeling very close to one another. Until then, Ángeles hadn't realized how much turmoil she had felt since taking the pregnancy test. That the night of sex with Federico, the peaceful sleep afterwards and the anxious need to speak to her sister that morning had been disguising an anguish that had lessened (not disappeared, but become less intense) thanks to Carolina's words.

Ángeles had never given any thought to motherhood. Since she was a girl she had always believed it could happen, but in her imagination it was something that belonged to the future, like finding the love of her life, or her own death. It was a concept that seemed not only distant but alien. If, a month ago, she had been asked when she saw herself becoming a mother, she would have replied *Perhaps in ten years* – when she was thirty-eight, or even at forty, having established a successful career as a lawyer, complete with specialist qualifications from US universities (a dream of hers ever since high school) and with a professional standing that wouldn't disappear if she took one or two years of sabbatical to enjoy her pregnancy (would it be enjoyable, though? That was something she wasn't clear about) and then her baby. The timing of this pregnancy couldn't be more inconvenient: it came at the start of her career in a big-time law firm, with her postgraduate studies postponed, with no partner to share the adventure of raising a child. All the same, she was sure she wanted to have it. She asked herself (Ángeles loved cross-examining herself, as though she were a hostile witness) if this sudden enthusiasm for motherhood didn't owe something to her convent school upbringing, when she had been bombarded with anti-abortion pamphlets. The answer was a solid no. The nuns could go to hell, the Catholic propaganda too. Her choice was personal, private and free from the influence of religion, partner, parents and work opportunities. Come to think of it, she had always made decisions in her life that way.

III

Verónica was heading for the Foreign Ministry for the second time in a matter of days. She was in a terrible mood, with conflicting emotions. The story of her Grandfather Elías was still dominating her thoughts, and she couldn't help thinking of the Bonieks as enemies. True, El Chino and she had been children back then. She absolved the childhood El Chino of any guilt or responsibility, but what was going on with the current El Chino, with Eitan Boniek, the guy who had lied to her about her mother's love life and perhaps also about the reasons for his family's flight to Israel? Did he know how Boniek senior had behaved towards his wife? What else had Eitan lied to her about?

At reception she showed her ID and, after a phone call, was given a visitor's card and allowed through. She mulled over her doubts concerning El Chino and looked distractedly at the people around her as she waited for the elevator. The doors opened and among the people getting out was a man who caught her eye. His face looked familiar to her. People began to file into the elevator. I'm being silly, he just looks like a famous singer, someone I know from TV, she thought. She was already inside the elevator, with others following in behind, when the name of that famous singer came to mind: Maluma.

Paula, describing one of the kidnappers, had said, "The guy looked like Maluma." Verónica pushed her way back out of the elevator, elbowing people aside and blocking the doors. Someone shouted "How rude", when the correct epithet would have been "stupid bitch" or "fucking idiot", but they were in the Foreign Ministry and people minded their language in places like that.

As quickly as she could, Verónica left the building and spotted the false Maluma walking along Arenales towards Avenida 9 de Julio. She followed a few yards behind, not daring to get any closer. The man turned onto Suipacha, walked past a police station, crossed the road and went towards a parking lot. He paid and went to get his car. Verónica stayed waiting at the entrance. She thought about getting a taxi and following him, but couldn't see any free cabs. She could have settled for taking down his licence plate, but that didn't feel like enough.

When the fake Maluma's car appeared at the exit, Verónica stood in a very visible spot and made eye contact with the driver through the window. The guy saw her, held her gaze, but didn't react. It should be clear that she had found him out and now the ball was in his court. The fake Maluma ought at least to have been surprised: someone was exposing him, and was bold enough to show it. Verónica knew she was exposing herself, too, that the assassins might come looking for her, but she also believed this move might hurry the men into making a false move. At least now she had the licence plate number of the car in which the fake Maluma was travelling. She sent a message to La Sombra so he could trace the vehicle's owner.

Returning to the Foreign Ministry, Verónica repeated the process for entering. The receptionist gave her a strange look but said nothing. When she called Eitan for confirmation, he must have asked if Verónica had already come into the building a few minutes earlier, because the receptionist replied: "I don't know what happened, but she's back again."

Verónica was authorized to go through. This time she paid more attention to all the people she passed en route to Eitan's office.

As she went up in the elevator, she thought about the fake Maluma and a detail that only now registered: while Verónica had had to leave her visitor's pass at reception when she left the building, the fake Maluma had used a pass to open the gate. So he must not be a visitor to the Foreign Ministry but an employee. Perhaps she should ask La Sombra to obtain a complete list, photos included, of everyone who worked here.

She could ask Eitan too, but she no longer fully trusted him.

Eitan greeted her affectionately, asked her to sit down and brought over a coffee. Another interesting detail: last time he had received her in his office. This time he took her to a small meeting room. It might mean nothing, but Verónica was looking for clues everywhere.

"I've put together a folder with all the information Viviana had on the fraud at Eramus, the company that belonged to Mayer and Gómez Pardo."

"How lucky that she left a copy out on her desk before she retired, and with such sensitive material."

"Actually, she had given me a copy. I didn't think it was particularly important at the time. I put it away with other material relating to allegations or irregularities that we pass to our lawyers so they can decide what action to take. It was only after I'd spoken to you that it crossed my mind that this folder might have something useful for you. In fact, I've dug up some new evidence in the last few days. Amazing as it sounds, Mayer and Gómez Pardo are still operating and stealing as though nothing's happened."

Verónica glanced through the folder, thinking María Magdalena would be much better than her at analysing this material.

"Did she by any chance leave you a tablet or a USB?"

"No, nothing. Only these printed pages."

"Even to a Luddite like me, it seems very strange that the material she had wasn't digitized. Did Viviana have a computer?"

"She used a laptop, which she took with her when she retired from the Foreign Ministry."

This conversation about materials was running out of steam. And Eitan seemed keen to move on to more personal matters. Verónica too, in her way.

"I hope my behaviour the other night didn't bother you," Eitan said.

"Don't be silly. Why would it bother me?"

"I wouldn't want there to be any distance between us."

"We're nice and close now."

"Federico's so lucky."

"It's true, he's a fortunate man."

"I'd love to know what he did to win your heart."

"Nothing a good man wouldn't do."

Verónica took a breath and told him what had been on her mind since visiting old Miguel.

"I've been looking into some of the links between our families."

"Wonderful."

"First of all, our parents were never romantically involved."

"Are you sure? My father told me they were."

"Then he lied to you. My grandfather couldn't stand your grandfather because mine had been a Communist and it seems that yours was quite a slippery customer and also violent, at least towards your grandmother."

"Sounds like bullshit."

"And your father was involved in a group that used to go around breaking up Communist Party meetings, among other things."

"And I stole Martín's Caniggia figurine. What a bad lot the Bonieks are."

Seeing that Eitan wasn't going to take any of this seriously, Verónica decided it wasn't the best time to be talking about their respective families. She said goodbye and, at the door, as though remembering something, said: "By the way, do you know a guy who looks a lot, I mean a lot like Maluma and works for the Foreign Ministry?"

"I've got no idea what Maluma looks like."

She found an image on Google and Eitan said that no, he didn't know anyone who looked like that.

"I've just seen him leaving the building, so he must be someone you often walk past. If you do bump into him, please pass on my good wishes and say we'll see each other soon."

"This all sounds really weird."

Verónica left the meeting room. As she walked towards the elevator, it struck her that Viviana and Malena must also have walked along these corridors. Where would their offices have been? Perhaps they worked with the fake Maluma? She wanted to see the room where Viviana had worked, check it over. But her various attempts failed. Nobody she asked even knew who Viviana was. Some sent her off to offices in different departments. After a while she gave up and left the building.

La Sombra called her on the phone. "The car belongs to an old woman of ninety-two, a pensioner who may not even know she has a car. And I won't be surprised if it soon turns up abandoned at the side of a country road."

Verónica thanked him and hung up, feeling frustrated. She had no firm lead on the fake Maluma, and nothing positive, apart from the folder, had come out of her meeting with Eitan. Her only hope now was that Maluma or one of his sidekicks would slip up.

IV

The meeting with Sergio Mayer, a few days previously, had left Federico with a bad taste in his mouth. Ever since he'd first started working with Aarón Rosenthal he had known that representing businesspeople or other powerful types meant suspending your moral or ethical judgement for significant periods of time. He wasn't there to moralize; he tried to get his clients out of their difficulties and thereby honour the tradition of a prestigious law firm, one feared by judges and by anyone on the other side of a case. There were some red lines Rosenthal wouldn't cross and people the firm declined to represent. If one businessperson swindled another out of ten million dollars, Rosenthal could pull together the evidence and arguments to get them off. But if that same

303

person wrecked the lives of people who had put their savings into a housing scheme that was advertised then never built, Rosenthal would tell them to find another lawyer. Federico was grateful for these vestiges of a social conscience, but he would also have preferred not to have been party to defending certain clients of dubious innocence.

In any case, Mayer was embroiled in various bureaucratic claims, business or political disputes and a messy divorce. Bribes had to be paid, information had to be kept that could come in useful if something were needed from Mayer; in as friendly a way as possible, pressure had to be put on judges, officers of justice and politicians. All the usual stuff. And yet he couldn't help feeling uncomfortable. Something wasn't right. Perhaps his malaise was connected to Verónica's investigation into the death of the journalist and his ex-wife and the way these deaths had led her to Mayer. Federico tended to think that if Verónica was investigating something, she was right. Therefore Mayer must somehow be involved with the deaths of those people. And if that was the case, he needed to speak to Aarón.

Verónica wanted him to pass along her information about Mayer's dirty dealings. He wasn't prepared to do that. He didn't like the idea of doing work for her, not because that would make her his boss in some way, but because the arrangement would make him feel that Verónica set the moral standard for him. If she said something was wrong, then he would have to react accordingly, when in reality he didn't need her input to know if something wasn't going down the (admittedly somewhat murky) path of justice but taking a turn towards something much darker.

When he arrived at the office, Ángeles said she wanted a word alone with him. She seemed serious and looked worried, although this was the tone she tended to strike when they were at work. She always appeared to be thinking about weighty matters. That stance was also a way to gain respect among lawyers who were all at least ten years older than her and who would, if they could have got away with it, have treated her as the office girl. Her serious manner allowed her to keep a distance and set some ground rules about how people should behave around her. Even with Federico, she maintained this attitude while at work.

Once in his office, Federico called Ángeles and she turned up in her formal clothes, her "work uniform" as she mockingly referred to it when they were alone. Quite a change from the previous night, when she had looked like someone who'd escaped from a cheerleader party at an American university. Ángeles sat down opposite him.

"Save the cheerleader," quipped Federico, and she reacted as though she didn't recognize the quote. Or perhaps she had never seen *Heroes*. In any case, Ángeles didn't seem in a mood to make any allusion to the events of the previous night.

"I'm worried about Roxana Mayer. I've met with her a few times now, and she doesn't want to negotiate the handover of Tuentur."

"Neither does Sergio Mayer. What does Diana say?"

"Diana's gone from wanting to award her twice the assets we originally offered to suggesting we block all her accounts and use every tool at our disposal to push her into penury."

"That's very Diana. From submission to discipline. What about you?"

"I'm doing stuff that's been fairly useless up until now. We've become friends, I go along with whatever she wants, I go with her to the hairdresser if necessary. Side note: what a shitty life it is to have so much money and nothing interesting to do all day long."

"She's got her breathing class."

"It's the most interesting thing she does. Anyway, I'm trying to convince her of the merits of handing over a troubled company in exchange for a shitload of money and assets. And at the same time I'm looking for her weak point. As we know, for some women men are a weakness."

"Just as well you said 'some'."

"It may be the case with Roxana. She's obviously in love with her boyfriend. From seeing them together, I'd even say that the person behind her intransigence is David Kaplan, that he's Roxana's lover but also Mayer's right hand."

"I'm with you so far."

"If we knew who Kaplan was, we could develop a seduction strategy. Aimed at him. He's interested in security? So let's find a way to get him his own security company, independent of Tuentur."

"It's not a bad idea. We persuade Roxana to gut Tuentur, so she walks off with the biggest clients and Mayer is only left with the brand."

"Roxana's always boasting about how she landed the biggest clients. I'm going to try taking that tack. But I'll be honest with you – at this point I can't promise anything."

Federico was left thinking about this strange new actor who had appeared on the scene: Mayer's number two in the security company, a foreigner about whom they knew only his name. What reason could there be, technical, professional or otherwise, for Mayer to put someone like that in his company? Did he know about the affair with Roxana? What if the battle wasn't between Roxana and Mayer, but Mayer and Kaplan? He needed to speak to Kaplan. Or to both of them. It would be good to get a handle on this situation.

It was true that they liked arranging meetings in different parts of the city, venues that were sometimes chosen by María Magdalena, sometimes by Rodolfo and occasionally by her, but Verónica could see absolutely no reason to schedule a work meeting in Alameda Sur, a bar on the Costanera Sur. Since there was no bus that would take her close to it, she ended up spending a fortune on a taxi. And it wasn't even a bar but one of those food trucks typical of the Costanera, only on a bigger plot, with tables outside and others in a closed area that served as a dining room. You had to queue up for *choripán* and beef sandwiches but the place was almost empty, perhaps because at eleven thirty lunch was still some way off. When she arrived, María Magdalena and Rodolfo were waiting in the covered area. They had some papers spread over the table and coffee in disposable cups.

"Whose brilliant idea was it to meet here?"

"I picked it," said Rodolfo. "I brought Federico here once and he left happy. You mean to say he's never brought you?"

"Thankfully not."

To Verónica's surprise, another person appeared from behind her: Patricia. She was walking slowly, but seemed steady on her feet.

"I wanted to give you two a surprise. I asked Rodo to pick somewhere with fresh air, trees and nature. When we've finished our meeting, I'm going for a walk around the Reserva Ecológica. I need to get all these days I've been stuck inside out of my system."

Verónica had already passed on to María Magdalena the Eramus papers Eitan had given her. She told the others about her experience with the fake Maluma and that the licence plate number had yielded no useful information. Everyone agreed that it had been unnecessarily reckless to show herself to the criminal.

"We're almost sure he took part in the attacks on Goicochea and Viviana. You mustn't take risks like that."

Verónica changed the subject, telling them there was no news yet on the tablet La Sombra had.

"Is Malena still staying in your apartment with her boy-friend?" Patricia asked. Veronica nodded wearily.

Then Rodolfo gave them a summary of his chat with Monteverde: "I came away from our colloquium beneath the trees in bloom with some interesting observations. First of all, that Monteverde's in excellent physical shape, despite his heart problems. Next, from what he was kind enough to confess, like a penitent during Holy Week, I'm curious about the role of the commercial attaché at the Israeli embassy who passed on information to him. A guy from an embassy doesn't give you info because he wants to expose something. What he's doing is operating. And when you operate, you do it for or against someone. Against whom, we already know. So we need to find out on whose behalf the commercial attaché is acting."

"Rodo," Patricia interrupted, "we're talking about the Israeli embassy. They've carried out more operations than Argerich Hospital."

"The question in my mind," said María Magdalena, "is what the angle is. Generally, there's an enemy, whether geopoliti-cal, commercial or religious, somewhere in the mix. Mayer doesn't appear to fit the profile of someone who would be attacked by the embassy. On the contrary, if the guy fucked up so badly – pardon my French – it would make more sense for the response to come straight from Israel, and for them to screw him over commercially and financially."

"I want to add another piece to this puzzle," said Rodolfo. "Mayer's partner in Eramus, who is also a partner in *Nuestro*

Tiempo: Gómez Pardo. You girls are very young and perhaps don't know much about Gómez Pardo."

"Was he a Montonero or with the People's Revolutionary Army?" asked Patricia.

"Gómez Pardo was a Montonero guerrilla in the seventies until he broke with the organization in 1979. The coup in 1976 caught him outside the country. He lived in Spain, in France and in Mexico. He disappeared off the radar until the start of the nineties, when he returned as a big importer during the spending spree under President Menem. He took advantage of the Convertibility Plan to bring products from Israel to Argentina. Frippery like pretty silicone utensils that looked like Morph but without the Morph price tag, some packaged foods like hummus or olives. Nothing all that special in those days. But in ten years he built the business empire we all know."

"He's not the only one who got rich in those years," said Verónica. "Look at Mayer…"

"Exactly. Let's look at Mayer. When did they really become business partners? At the end of the nineties they were both involved in an investment fund that bought up several local businesses for peanuts and sold them on to a bigger investment fund based in the US."

"Setting aside any moral qualms we may have about a seventies revolutionary popping up as a Menemist businessman in the nineties, I can't see what the problem is," said Patricia.

"Let me take you back to the tumultuous seventies. In Argentina we're in the midst of a dictatorship. Guerrilla warfare, people disappearing. Some are lucky – they manage to escape and get out of the country. You might think OK, that's good, they're going off to exile and that's the end of that. Lots of Montoneros don't do that, though, but instead prepare to return, to fight alongside those who have stayed. When the people rise up, they'll come back, arm themselves and put themselves at the head of the movement. Let's steer clear, for the moment, if you don't mind, of any value judgements about this. This group not only dreams of a return, they get military training for it. Remember that the Montoneros were an irregular army with recognition in many places, at a time when there were guerrilla groups all over the world, from Japan to Chile via Germany or the Sahara. During those years, the Montoneros got military training in Lebanon and Syria. The Middle East was a tinderbox then, well, same as always. Who is getting trained in that camp apart from the guerrillas of the pampas? The PLO, the Palestine Liberation Organization. The Montoneros live alongside them in barracks, join them at the shooting range. But they also exchange technological and scientific know-how to improve the quality of their explosives. Obviously, that attracts the attention of the secret services. Mossad and the Argentine dictatorship are listening in. In other words, they gathered intel in those Middle Eastern training camps."

"And Gómez Pardo was among the trainees?"

"No."

Patricia, María Magdalena and Verónica exchanged glances. They didn't understand where Corso was going with this.

"At this stage, Gómez Pardo is a grey and less than heroic character compared with those training on Lebanese soil. He lives in Paris and is a kind of lackey for the Montonero leadership in exile. Every now and then one of the cadre would travel to Lebanon to see how the soldiers were getting on. And Gómez Pardo went along to, I don't know, let's say to carry the bags. But he would be there for a few days, sharing the camaraderie of guerrillas from other parts of the world, perhaps Palestinians and Lebanese among them. He chatted with them, visited the camps, saw what they were doing, what they had, what they were planning. Finally the time comes when the Montoneros, believing the dictatorship is crumbling, decide to return to Argentina. It's 1979."

"The Montonero counteroffensive," said Patricia.

"When everything is ready for their return, Gómez Pardo leaves the Montoneros. He retires. He doesn't want to be in the game any more. He wasn't the only one, for sure. Many of those who decided to return died in shoot-outs or were disappeared by the dictatorship – which seemed to have been waiting for them – and a large number survived, too. Gómez Pardo, now free of the burden of making a revolution, keeps his powder dry for a few years, then starts to do business abroad."

"With Israel?"

"Bingo," said Corso. "I have a theory, but no proof. Gómez Pardo's visits to Lebanon owed nothing to his love of the revolution. By then he had already been co-opted by the Israeli secret services, the ever-efficient Mossad, and was working for them. He used the excuse of visiting his comrades-in-arms to spy in Lebanon. Like James Bond and that guy in *Mission Impossible*, but without the glamour. In exchange for his highly secret services, Gómez Pardo was rewarded with fruitful business deals. Some directly, some through partners. Some of them perhaps off the books. Because it would be too obvious if the guy was in Lebanon in the seventies and years later had a security company with Israeli suppliers in Argentina. If something like that were made public, it would be a scandal."

"But you've got no proof of any of this, Rodo," said Patricia. "Paranoid theories are fun, but we do journalism. They're not useful to us."

"Put it in a novel," Verónica suggested.

"We don't have proof, but can't you see that something is beginning to add up here? Businessmen linked to Israel, retired members of the armed forces and perhaps of the Israeli secret services, one of whom has no backstory, the commercial attaché of the embassy who's also a player."

"We're missing the facts that would tie all this together and explain why several people got themselves killed," said Patricia.

"This has made me hungry," added María Magdalena. "Who's in the market for some *choripanes* and meatball sandwiches?"

VI

She wasn't allowed to smoke in the car, because he didn't like the lingering smell. So Roxana had to smoke before or after driving anywhere, or stop mid-journey, like an addict craving a hit. In that instant, for example, she would have stopped on a corner to smoke a cigarette, but she was with him and didn't want him to look at her with that condescension he used to draw attention to her weaknesses. She checked the time on the dashboard. In twenty minutes they would be home, and she could go into the garden for a smoke. She pressed down on the accelerator. He looked at his phone, swore and dialled a number. He began speaking as though continuing a conversation that had already begun in the text message. She could only hear David's part of the exchange.

"And who is this Verónica Rosenthal?"

Roxana thought of Rosenthal and Associates, the firm that represented her ex-husband.

"What does she know? Nothing more? We need to keep on top of this. There's no room for mistakes. Did you get rid of the car? Good. Stay alert. Any problems need to be eliminated."

David hung up, with more swearing.

"Rosenthal is the firm representing Sergio. And if I'm not mistaken, Verónica Rosenthal is a journalist at *Nuestro Tiempo*."

"Does she work for your husband?"

"Ex. I don't know. Has she got the material?"

"It seems not."

David was silent, then snorted and seemed about to say something but to think better of it. Roxana decided to change the subject.

"Ángeles, the lawyer, is delightful, don't you think? She's the sister of Carolina Basualdo. Do you remember that Argentine girl we met in Milan?"

"I don't recall. She seems like a nice girl, but I don't know if I'd bring her into Orígenes. Isn't she working for your husband?"

"She doesn't seem all that convincing as a negotiator. I'm going to make her resign so she can come and work with me. And there are so few of us in Orígenes that some new blood wouldn't be a bad thing."

David nodded but still seemed absorbed by this thought. Even though they had already discussed this, he couldn't help harping on an old theme.

"It was a terrible idea."

She knew what he was referring to. "If that journalist had stuck to the line we suggested, today our problems would all be resolved," she said, sitting a little more upright in her seat, her body tensing.

"There was always a risk."

"A minimal risk."

"But what happened, happened. Everything has been complicated in the most infernal manner. We should be busy with the Tuentur merger and instead we're trying to plug holes in a sinking ship with our bare hands."

"It's not a sinking ship. And the merger will go ahead. I need a good lawyer for the paperwork. I think Ángeles is the woman for the job."

"Don't be so trusting."

"Of Ángeles? She's a sweetheart. An innocent girl who's been locked away studying to be the best lawyer ever."

They arrived at the house. Roxana parked the car and went straight to the garden, where she lit a cigarette away from David's gaze. He went upstairs to the bedrooms. Roxana thought she should have been more forceful with her ex. Or taken more extreme measures. Perhaps her only mistake up until then had been not taking the right extreme measures.

VII

Ángeles ended the day knowing she would spend the night alone: there would be no visit from Federico. She decided to take home the Tuentur papers to see if reading up on the company would help unlock some clue that might ease the negotiation with Roxana. It crossed her mind to call her and propose the two of them go to a bar to discuss the quest for primordial religion. At the end of the day, Roxana had become the person who showed most interest in her. She felt a sensation growing inside her, some sort of longing. Her first craving? Ángeles wanted to go out with Federico, to eat together in a restaurant with dim lights, exchange sweet nothings, walk through the streets hand in hand. Before they had become lovers, they had often shared idle moments, which she realized now had been full of intimacy. She missed those junk food lunches when she would tell him about her childhood or some TV series she had seen, the conversations that had had no purpose other than to communicate. They could still talk, of course, but it was always in the context of meeting for sex, and always in her apartment. She felt as though a timer had been set that sooner or later would go off and then he would disappear, like Cinderella at midnight. It was a horrible clock, invisible but ever-present.

She had to tell him she was pregnant, as soon as possible.

Her sister was doing her best to allay Ángeles's anxiety. She had written several times that day, sending her funny videos, interesting links, silly questions ("which bit of the cow, exactly, is the *tira de asado*?") She wanted to be present, and Ángeles was grateful for that. She was lucky to be able to rely on her.

Carolina sent her photos, too: skiing in the Alps, on a trip to Venice, coming out of a pub in Dublin. That night she sent her an image with an accompanying explanation: *Look at this photo I found. It was taken at an Orígenes meeting in Milan a couple of years ago. Your new friend Roxana was there. No sign of the boyfriend you mentioned to me, but she seemed very close to the guy at the top of the photo. One Nathan Neuer. Nice-looking squeeze.*

Her sister loved using words she maintained were still current in Argentina, when in fact they were already passé twenty years before she was born. Ángeles studied her sister in the photo; she looked the same as now, except her hair was a little longer, whereas Roxana definitely looked younger: sexy and alluring, even if she had lost some of her charm over the years. Then she looked at the "squeeze": if they had been together since then, Roxana had clearly been cheating on Mayer for a long time.

The guy's face looked familiar. At first she decided it couldn't be Kaplan. Then Ángeles enlarged the photo and looked again in closer detail. It wasn't Kaplan, but it did look a lot like him. The hair was darker, a nearly black brown. His features looked different, as though the image had been Photoshopped. Or as though in real life he'd had some plastic surgery. Ángeles felt her pulse quicken: the man in the photo was David Kaplan. He had changed not just his name but his appearance too. David Kaplan was Nathan Neuer.

She started searching on the internet. Few people met the search criteria. Finally she found a retired general from the Israel Defense Force. There were scarcely any images of him. She found a low-res group photo in which she thought she recognized Kaplan. But once she got past the first pages of Google results, other kinds of article began to appear. Pieces accusing Neuer of having committed crimes against humanity. The Palestinian Centre for Human Rights accusing him of being a war criminal.

He had been behind the bombing of a hospital in Gaza. *What kind of person bombs a hospital?* Ángeles asked herself, with a flash of indignation unusual in her. But there was worse to come. Neuer stood accused of having authorized a missile attack on children playing at the beach. "Ah, what a royal piece of shit," she murmured, furious.

It was becoming clear why Neuer had changed his name to Kaplan. What Ángeles didn't yet know was what she was going to do with this new information. It was much more than she had expected to find, more than she could process. Mayer's right-hand man was a war criminal and had, for years, been his ex-wife's lover.

Ángeles felt light-headed. She thought of calling Federico to tell him what she had discovered, then changed her mind. To the cocktail of feelings that had overwhelmed her over the last twenty-four hours she must now add fear. She was terrified she might have opened a Pandora's box.

16   *Two Women*

I

In his brief stint as a public prosecutor, Federico had worked alongside some strange characters from the Federal Intelligence Agency, the organization for local spies. Some were cagey and difficult to understand. Paranoia was their guiding principle, and they tried to infect everyone around them with it. Federico had avoided playing their game, but if he hadn't left the Prosecutor's Office, he would surely have ended up in their clutches.

There was only one who seemed different, perhaps because he was younger and didn't have such a compromising past as the others. He went by Aurelio, although that was likely not his true name, and looked more like a chemistry student than a spy. He wore very sixties glasses, a sweater tucked into his trousers, and moccasins. He was forever adjusting his glasses, which kept slipping down his nose, and often appeared hesitant. However, he always had good intel and knew what to do with it. They had worked together on a couple of cases and hit it off from the start. When Federico left his job as prosecutor, Aurelio called to wish him luck, and to encourage him never to return to the Prosecutor's Office.

"Prosecutors end up bitter and resentful. There's a better life out there," Aurelio told him.

Now Federico needed his help. He called Aurelio and

invited him to lunch at a grill in Palermo that looked on to Plaza Armenia.

First, Aurelio wanted to ask him about some procedural matters, which Federico explained to him in detail. Only later did they start talking about Sergio Mayer and his security company, which Federico had already mentioned to him on the phone.

"You know there's an ambivalent relationship with Mayer in the Agency? On one hand, he has links with some people, especially veterans. But eyebrows were raised when he hired foreign ex-officers specializing in security. Many of our retired agents would gladly have gone to work with him, because of the high salaries he pays, but he hasn't considered them. It's not a good look."

"An attitude like that could lead to one of the old boys taking reprisals?"

"Could do."

"As I told you, there's something about this Tuentur business and the ex-wife who wants to keep the company that doesn't quite add up for me."

"Your instinct is on the right track. One assumes that fifty per cent of the company is Mayer's and the other fifty per cent is the ex-wife's. But that's not right. The mighty Mayer, who has frontmen all over the place, is himself a frontman. For Gómez Pardo, who gave him the contacts with security companies and Israeli ex-military. First he arranged the infrastructure for him, connecting him with Israeli exporters of surveillance cameras, then he opened the door to security agents. In exchange for that, Gómez Pardo kept fifty per cent of the company."

"And so the fifty-one per cent Roxana Mayer wants…"

"Is impossible. Because that half belongs to Gómez Pardo, who is not prepared to cede control of the company. He doesn't trust Roxana. Much less the lover."

"David Kaplan. But wasn't it Gómez Pardo who supplied the Israeli ex-military to Mayer?"

"To start with. Then Mayer himself selected them. But it's not clear who put Kaplan in there. Perhaps he was foisted on them in exchange for some favour done for Tuentur, or for Eramus, the technology company in Mayer and Gómez Pardo's names."

"I didn't have Eramus on my radar."

"Put it on there, because they may be needing the services of a good lawyer. It seems they didn't act all that legally with the subsidies they got. Moreover, Gómez Pardo thinks they're trying to frame him and that David Kaplan is behind it."

"And what do you know about Kaplan?"

"Nothing you don't know. I think it's obvious that's not his name. Do you know the story of the guy who left his family, went to live a few blocks away and they never found him?"

"No."

"I guess it's an urban legend. Something similar is probably happening with Kaplan, but in the cybersphere. It shouldn't be difficult to find out who he is. What's difficult is to find someone who would want to get involved with all this. That's something we learned quickly in the Agency: don't go looking for information you don't need, however easy it is to obtain. Managing intel always gives you an advantage, but sometimes having it can be a nightmare."

Aurelio ordered cheese and membrillo for dessert and Federico a coffee.

Before they said goodbye, Aurelio seemed to remember something.

"Tell La Sombra to stop pushing his luck. If he thinks he can hack into the Foreign Ministry as though he were playing Minecraft online, he's very much mistaken. That's espionage, and he could get thirty years for it. Be grateful that I was the one who discovered him and let him play for a bit. Don't let it happen again."

I I

As he left the restaurant, Federico saw he had two missed calls from Ángeles. She had also sent him a WhatsApp that said *I need to speak to you urgently. Are you coming into work?*

Rather than answer, he went straight to the office. He needed to process the information he had been given. The dispute over the division of Mayer's assets had just got much messier; it could no longer be treated as a simple matrimonial disagreement. This wasn't a tiff but a fight between dangerous people.

He arrived at the office needing a piss, so nodded a brief hello at the receptionist and went straight to the toilet. On the way he ran into Ángeles, who seemed to have been lying in wait for him.

"Why didn't you answer my calls? I told you it was urgent."

Ángeles had never used that tone, either with him or with anyone else at the office. She seemed very angry. Federico asked her to wait in his office, but she was still there, lurking in the corridor, when he came out of the bathroom. Clearly she didn't trust him not to get sidetracked.

"What's happened?" he asked, as they walked together towards his office.

"I've got important news about Roxana Mayer and her circle."

This was shaping up to be a day of revelations about Mayer.

Once they were in Federico's office, Ángeles made sure the door was properly closed. Clearly she didn't want anyone to overhear their conversation. "This is really serious..." she began.

"I'm listening."

Ángeles explained the context: the conversations with her sister in Switzerland, the observations on Roxana and her mystery lover. She took out her phone and showed Federico the photograph of the Orígenes gathering. "The guy standing with Roxana is David Kaplan, but he looks different, as if he had some work done later and dyed his hair."

"I'd love to see him stand trial for that, but I don't think the judge would buy it."

"Another detail: this gathering was nearly two years before Kaplan arrived in Argentina to work for Mayer."

"In other words, there was already a romantic link between David and Roxana. In days gone by, we could have adduced infidelity. But not any more."

"Before he came to Argentina, Kaplan had a different name. My sister had a list of the participants: he was called Nathan Neuer. The guy stands accused by Israeli human rights organizations of having committed crimes against humanity in Gaza. I printed off some articles about it for you. It caused quite a scandal at the time, including requests for his arrest in some European countries, but they never got anywhere. He was tried by an Israeli military court which absolved him, but Neuer immediately asked to be discharged from the army."

"Is there an international arrest warrant out for him?"

"No. The case didn't get as far as the court in The Hague, but some human rights organizations won't let it go. If he had stayed in Israel, he would doubtless have continued to call himself Neuer, but he decided to change his name to come here. That way he can avoid protests or some overzealous judge popping up, demanding his arrest. Like when they arrested Pinochet in Spain."

"It was in England. There's no way they'd arrest him here. What judge would dare to?"

"He's a war criminal, Federico. Even if he's been absolved by his peers."

Federico leafed through the material Ángeles had brought him. He tried to fit this information about Kaplan with what Aurelio had told him. He couldn't get a full picture, but was conscious of one thing: they were in much more dangerous territory than he could have imagined. His priority was to get Ángeles out of harm's way.

"First of all, Ángeles, I'm speechless. This is excellent work. What we have to do now is tread very carefully and think about what to do next. I'll talk to Aarón about it."

"We have to report this right away."

"You want us to file a lawsuit? To go to court and denounce an Israeli war criminal? We're not an NGO."

"Then we have to report it to the press."

"We're not reporting anything yet. First things first, you need to break off all contact with Roxana. It no longer makes sense for the firm to handle this business of dividing assets. Let Diana take charge, since it's her specialism."

"You're taking me off this when I'm the one who's discovered the truth about Kaplan?"

"No. It's simply that the question is no longer about the division of assets."

Ángeles was annoyed. Furious. The more Federico insisted he was doing this to keep her out of danger, the more obtuse she became: the Rosenthal practice in general and Federico in particular were washing their hands of the matter. She got up to go, but when she reached the door she turned back and, without dropping the irritated tone that had characterized much of their conversation, she said: "Try to drop by the apartment tonight. There's something we need to talk about."

"I feel as if we've already talked a lot."

"This is something personal."

Ángeles walked off, leaving the office door open behind her.

III

That morning, Verónica received a call from her father, inviting her to lunch. It wasn't a good day for her as she had various things to sort out, so she asked if they could meet at a later date. Her father sounded disappointed, but Verónica didn't yield to the pressure; she knew he could come over a bit Yiddish mama when he wanted something. She told him that she was in the middle of a journalistic investigation (not mentioning that it concerned Mayer) and that it was taking up a lot of her time. She promised that once it was over – and she expected that to be soon – they would have a lunch *à deux* and bitch about the other Rosenthals. Her father said he would hold her to it. The only thing that slightly worried Verónica was that, as he was saying goodbye, Aarón added: "I love you very much, darling. Be careful, and don't get into any trouble."

Her father telling her not to get into trouble was a constant, from the time of the disastrous Zumerland episode to the present day. But a proclamation of love was more unusual, coming from Aarón Rosenthal. He's getting old, she thought, and suddenly felt a great tenderness towards him and a yearning to go and give him a big hug. But then she was distracted by messages from Rodolfo and María Magdalena, and didn't think about her father again for the rest of the day.

At around midday she got a call from Marcelo, the doorman at her building in Villa Crespo, which was concerning. If he was calling it must be that something serious had happened with Malena.

"I've got half the building complaining about your tenants. It seems that when they aren't making love they're having screaming rows. Try to sort them out, or you'll get torn to shreds at the next residents' meeting."

Verónica went immediately to the apartment where, after making a deliberately noisy entrance, she found the couple drinking beer and watching a movie. They seemed placid. This time it was Damián who had borrowed a T-shirt, one of Federico's.

"Listen, you useless fuckers. Do you think you're still in that motel you took me to? All my neighbours are complaining. Calm down or get lost. Is that clear?"

"I'm sorry, Vero. I've already told him if he's not quieter you might chuck us out. And my life's in danger out there."

"Exactly. Think, girl, think. You behave like a teenager on a school leavers' trip. As for you, take off that shirt."

Damián undid the shirt, took it off, crumpled it into a ball and threw it onto one of the chairs. "There you go. Is that better?"

"If I get another single complaint, even if it's because you've got the music up a bit too loud, you're out of here."

Malena looked suitably contrite, but Verónica sensed this was an act. Damián's gaze was roaming lasciviously all over her body. Stupid assholes, she thought. She left the apartment and, once downstairs, told Marcelo to let her know the instant he heard shouting or loud noises coming from the second floor.

Not much progress was made in Verónica's meeting with Rodolfo and María Magdalena. They had enough material for an article that would hit Mayer hard, but still no lead on the crimes against Goicochea and Viviana. It was as if they were stalled at the point where Goicochea's real investigation had begun. What did they need to do to work out the murderers' motives?

La Sombra called later on. "Good and bad news."

"Bad first."

"I've still got nothing on the tablet. I can't mess around with it too much, because it could self-destruct if it detects someone trying out variations of a password. The trick is to get it right in one go. The only information I've obtained is that this is a tablet used by the Turkish secret service."

Verónica remembered that Viviana and Eitan, and Malena, during her internship, had worked on an industrial development plan with Greece, Turkey and Israel. She thought of the Israeli officials at Tuentur.

"Sombra, what's the chance Mossad is behind all this?"

"It doesn't bear thinking about. Listen, I do have one piece of good news. I managed to get the files of some Foreign Ministry employees. Not all of them, because at one point I could no longer get in to complete the list. But you might be interested to know that among the ones I did manage to download is a boy who looks a lot like Maluma. He's called Iván Carmona, he's thirty-five and he works in admin. I'll send you the file with his details via Telegram."

Verónica, who with gritted teeth had started using WhatsApp so as not to end up totally out of the loop, installed Telegram at La Sombra's request. She did that with gritted teeth too.

At the end of the day she received a phone call from an unknown number. Verónica was chary of those, especially when in the middle of an investigation, so she picked up sounding defensive.

"Verónica? My name is Ángeles Basualdo. I'm a lawyer at Rosenthal and Associates. I need to speak to you in person. It's urgent. And I'd ask you not to breathe a word about this call to Federico."

If Ángeles was sure about anything, it was that she had to act quickly. Federico's reluctance to do anything had surprised her. She had expected much more of him, and a determination to expose Kaplan, but he had put his client before the pursuit of justice. That was what they got paid for, true enough, but their profession also came with an ethical commitment that she, at any rate, was not prepared to overlook.

The Argentine justice system couldn't do much about it, but what about Israel's? Just over a year ago, Ángeles had taken a seminar on international law at the Universidad Austral. Among her fellow students was Sebastián, a lawyer who worked at the Israeli embassy, in the legal advice division. They had been for coffee a few times and got on well, although there was never any suggestion of going on a date. Even though Sebastián was single and good-looking. Perhaps he would be more willing to help her.

She called him and, without giving more details, asked if they could meet up. Sebastián, though surprised, accepted, and they arranged to meet at the embassy in an hour's time. Ángeles quickly prepared a summary of everything she had on Kaplan.

Once in the embassy, she passed through the usual controls and was led to an office in which she waited for her former classmate. They greeted one another affectionately, then she quickly came to the point of her visit.

Ángeles didn't want to explain the context in which she had made her discovery. She didn't talk to him about the divorce or the division of assets. She cut to the chase: the general manager of Tuentur had been accused of committing war crimes in Israel. His real name was Nathan Neuer. Sebastián listened closely, while leafing through the documents she had brought with her. When Ángeles had finished her account, Sebastián took a moment to gather his thoughts.

"I remember the Neuer case well. It was covered in the Israeli media at the time. He was absolved of all charges."

"By a jury of his peers."

"Well, that's how military justice is done. I don't think they absolved him because he was a colleague. That would be like saying lawyers can't ever be found guilty in an ordinary court of law."

"There are several human rights organizations, Israeli and Palestinian, that —"

"Those groups are always out for attention. Anyway, supposing you're right about this. Without a formal request from the Israeli justice system, we can't do anything."

"At the very least he's falsified his identity documents."

"Well, that's a crime that should be judged here. But once again, it's nothing to do with us. I'm sorry, but I can't think how to help you."

Ángeles left the embassy with an enormous sense of frustration. Apparently there was no way to act through the local courts, or those of Israel. The only thing she could do with the material was denounce Kaplan publicly, in the press. She needed to get a journalist interested in this case.

But the number of contacts she had in the media was precisely zero. No journalist had, to date, considered her a useful source. Nor had she ever needed to call on any of them (why would a lawyer in the criminal or civil courts ever need the services of a journalist?), nor did she have any journalist friends, or friends who knew journalists. The closest she had to that was the Bitch.

The first thing she would have to do, if she was going to ask the Bitch for help, was to stop thinking of her in those terms; from then on she would think of her as Verónica, the journalist. Ángeles hadn't read any of her articles, nor was she interested in reading them. She knew about Verónica's prestige, her reputation as an intrepid journalist who had made powerful people tremble. Federico himself had spoken to her (before they became lovers) about his partner's professional achievements.

It wasn't difficult to get hold of her details. She simply called Aarón's secretary and asked for the number of Rosenthal's youngest daughter. The secretary supplied it without hesitation.

As Ángeles dialled the number, her body began to shake; she had to steel herself not to hang up. When she heard a voice at the other end of the line, she felt certain Verónica would immediately know she was Federico's lover; in a nervous rush she explained that she wanted to meet, urgently. Verónica's response was so calm that it calmed Ángeles in turn. A point in her favour. They arranged to meet in an hour at La Orquídea, a cafe in Almagro that Ángeles didn't know.

When she arrived, Verónica was already waiting, tapping something into her phone without bothering to monitor the entrance, confident Ángeles would recognize her. Verónica only looked up once she approached.

Verónica was pretty, perhaps not as pretty as she had imagined her all this time, but still an attractive woman.

There wasn't much time for an informal chat, not that Ángeles wanted one. She took out the folder with information on David Kaplan and began to lay out her case.

"As I told you on the phone, I'm one of the lawyers who work with your dad. At the moment we're representing a client who has all kinds of suits against him. I don't know if you've heard of Sergio Mayer?"

"Have I heard of Sergio Mayer? More than you could possibly imagine."

Only then did Ángeles remember that Mayer was the owner of *Nuestro Tiempo*, the magazine where Verónica worked. She was his employee – what if she passed on everything Ángeles was about to say? She hesitated to go on, wondering if she had been right to contact Verónica.

"Of course. He's your boss."

"My editor's my boss. He's just the president of the editorial group."

Feeling her confidence restored, Ángeles explained about the division of assets between Mayer and his ex-wife. About the problems with Tuentur and the appearance of a mysterious person who seemed to be part of the company's leadership.

"David Kaplan," said Verónica.

Ángeles was startled. "You know him?"

"I don't know much, to be honest. I'm trying, together with some colleagues, to find out more about him, but we haven't got far yet. We thought he might be connected to two murders that took place recently."

Despite herself, Ángeles blushed. Could Verónica Rosenthal be looking for the very information she had?

"Did you know Kaplan is Roxana Mayer's lover?" Ángeles said.

"I didn't know that."

"OK, that's not the important part. Or it may be, in relation to our case on the division of marital property. But I've been digging deeper and found something on this man that may interest you. David Kaplan's real name is Nathan Neuer, and he's a war criminal."

Ángeles handed over the folder with Kaplan's profile and explained the source of the articles in which Neuer was accused of having committed a number of terrorist atrocities against the Palestinian population, specifically of having ordered the bombing of a hospital and a civilian area where there were only children playing. Ángeles felt exhausted after finishing her presentation on this subject for the second time in an afternoon. What if Verónica reacted as Sebastián had done? If she told her that he wasn't a criminal since he had been absolved by the justice system in his own country? She kept an anxious eye on Verónica, who was reading the articles and looking at the prints of the photos, not saying anything.

"As you can imagine, I can't do anything with this in the practice. I mentioned it to Federico, and his take is that we have to focus on the legal cases in hand. That's why I thought of you —"

Verónica put down the folder and looked her in the eye. "Ángeles, I don't believe in God, but you're the closest thing to an angel I can imagine. You have no idea how hard we've looked for this information and not found it anywhere. What you've got here is amazing. No, you're not an angel. You're a goddess. I'm so emotional, I feel like crying."

Ángeles couldn't believe what she was hearing. She laughed. She also felt like crying and couldn't help shedding a few tears. And she was someone who didn't tend to cry from joy. Perhaps the pregnancy was to blame, but she felt happy.

V

At the end of the day, when nearly everyone had left the firm, Federico went to Aarón's office and found his boss still sitting at his desk as though it were nine o'clock in the morning. Except that now he seemed more relaxed, enjoying a cigarette as he read some documents. Aarón barely ever used the computer. His secretary had to get him hard copies of anything he needed to read.

"Have you got a minute?"

Aarón gestured to Federico to sit down. They both enjoyed these private moments. Federico was the closest to family that Aarón had in his professional life and he often deferred to the younger man's judgement. For his part, Federico admired his boss and took every opportunity to learn something new in these conversations, which usually turned on some work matter. On this occasion, however, their exchange might be more awkward than usual; Federico would need to proceed with caution.

"I wanted to talk to you about Sergio Mayer."

Aarón put out his cigarette and sighed. He settled into his seat as though preparing for a long conversation.

Federico explained that the real estate dispute was resolved. In exchange for a large sum, politicians and an NGO had been persuaded of the scheme's merits.

"Make sure those sums are reflected on our invoice."

Then he told Aarón about the ins and outs of the Roxana Mayer case and the discovery that Mayer's right-hand man was a war criminal.

"Add that to the fact that Gómez Pardo is the real owner of the company, in the shadows, and everything connected to Tuentur seems very shady."

"Well, we don't do family law. If we advised on and managed the division of assets, that was a courtesy on our part. Let Diana Veglio handle it from here."

"That's what I thought. I can also speak to Mayer and explain our reasoning. But there's something that worries me more. I suspect Mayer, Gómez Pardo and Kaplan were involved in the murders of the journalist Andrés Goicochea and his ex-wife."

"Have you got proof of that?"

"I have leads that I can keep following to see where they take me. The modus operandi was typical of professional assassins. The secret services are also in play here, the Federal Intelligence Agency or Mossad, or both together."

"As you know, getting involved with the secret services, no matter where they're from, is like swimming in shit."

"I know, but I wouldn't want to end up defending a bunch of criminals in court, whatever their allegiance. And there's something else you should know: Verónica is investigating the murders."

This time Aarón's sigh was almost a lament. "I might have known. It's not possible to get her off the case, I take it?"

"She's your daughter, Aarón."

"Was she the one who found out that this Kaplan is a war criminal?"

Federico cleared his throat before answering.

VI

After her meeting with Ángeles, Verónica immediately contacted María Magdalena and Rodo. They agreed to concentrate their efforts on finding everything they could about Neuer. María Magdalena could read Hebrew, albeit with difficulty, so she could search Israeli websites. And they would get together at noon the next day, with Patricia too.

She was about to head home when Malena called to say that Damián had gone out and didn't plan to be back that night. She was scared to be on her own. As promised, Verónica said she would go there and stay the night. Malena must have argued with her boyfriend, although she didn't say as much.

Verónica sent a WhatsApp to Federico, which he didn't answer. He must be caught up at the office. From the taxi, she called a delivery company and ordered a pizza and two beers. At least they wouldn't be hungry.

Once at her building, Verónica waited at the door for the pizza, which must be about to arrive. A few neighbours passed her, none of them looking at her with much affection. Clearly they didn't approve of her guests. The delivery boy arrived on his motorbike; Verónica paid for the pizza, added a generous tip and headed upstairs.

If she was expecting to find dirt and disarray, her worst fears were not confirmed; the living room was very tidy, each thing in its place. Since nobody seemed to be around, Verónica called out to Malena, who didn't appear. The noise of the shower confirmed that she was at least alive. Verónica set the table for two and waited for Malena to be ready. The girl emerged wrapped in a bath sheet, with another towel around her head. She went over to Verónica and gave her a big, damp hug. "Thanks for coming, for not leaving me alone."

Malena's eyes lit up like a child's when she saw the pizza and beer. She went to the bedroom to get changed while Verónica put on one of the Nouvelle Vague CDs stacked beside the stereo. "Dancing with Myself" began to play. Malena reappeared: she was wearing a black T-shirt with PARIS spelled out in rhinestones – a T-shirt that belonged to Malena, for once – and a G-string, also black, that Verónica thought she recognized as one of her own. Her hair, still wet, tumbled over her shoulders.

Verónica mentioned how clean the apartment was looking.

"I know, right? I spent all afternoon cleaning it. Damián is the one who leaves everything messy."

"Have you two been going out a long time?"

Malena laughed. "We're not going out."

"But you're together."

"We fuck. Not much else."

"In my day, if you had sex more than three times in a row over a short period of time, you assumed you were going out with someone, even if the other person didn't know it."

"Young people are different now. We don't like to be pigeonholed."

Verónica thought she might lose her temper if the little bitch persisted in treating her like an old person.

"I actually can't stand Damián," Malena confessed.

"So why don't you split up?"

"I've already told you. He's good at fucking."

Thinking any response she might make to this observation could be taken as another sign of old age, Verónica said nothing. They finished the beers and pizzas (leaving just one portion) and cleared the table. Verónica threw the boxes and napkins in the garbage and was thankful there were no dishes to wash.

"Where's your weed?"

She was reluctant to tell Malena about the stash in the cabinet in the living room, then remembered there was enough elsewhere for one joint.

"In my bag, I'll get it in a minute."

Verónica put away everything in the kitchen and sorted out the garbage. When she went into the living room a few minutes later, all the lights were off and Malena, who had already been into her bag and found the weed, was sitting in the big armchair, in the lotus position, rolling a joint. Verónica thought this girl's attitude left a lot to be desired. She didn't believe in demanding good manners, but a minimum of respect for other people wouldn't go amiss. Malena behaved like a spoiled child, like a princess. When she had finished rolling the joint, she lit it and inhaled deeply. Verónica watched her like someone observing a rare, possibly dangerous specimen.

"Come, sit down." Malena patted the cushion next to her. Verónica did as she was instructed and accepted the joint. She took a drag on it. "I love your life," Malena said to her.

"You don't know what you're saying."

"Seriously. You have this apartment to yourself, you have good music, weed. A boyfriend who's a lawyer. What's he like in bed?"

"I've got no complaints."

"What were you like at my age?"

"How old are you exactly?"

"Twenty-two."

"At your age I was studying communication science at the UBA, I lived with my parents, I had a boyfriend I'd been going out with for three years."

"The same one as now?"

"No, another one, lost in prehistory."

"Were you working by then?"

"I'd done some internships on a magazine and I freelanced for a legal journal, reviewing books."

The joint went back and forth, the only source of light in the room. Lights and noise from the dark street outside permeated the window. Verónica felt her body relax and began to sink into the squishy cushion. She lay back her head and closed her eyes. Malena said something she didn't catch. She responded all the same: "Time consumes itself. Nothing else matters."

Then she heard Malena's voice, clearly: "When we're fucking in your bed, Damián calls me Verónica. He fantasizes about you."

"That's flattering. But you probably shouldn't have told me."

"And I do too." Malena drew closer and rested her lips against Verónica's mouth. She didn't kiss her, simply brushed her lips over Verónica's. Then she moved her face away a little.

"Malena, what are you doing?"

"Did I tell you it turns me on to wear your clothes? Does it make you hot to see me in them?"

"Let's define 'hot'."

"Have you ever been with a girl? Because in my generation it's very common, but —"

"Let's have a little less about the generation gap. Yes, I've been with a girl, someone I loved a lot."

"You don't see each other any more?"

"She died. She was murdered."

"Oh, I'm sorry."

Perhaps to help banish that memory, Malena did now kiss Verónica, pressing against her body. She took one of Verónica's hands and placed it under her T-shirt, on her breast. Verónica squeezed, less to cause pleasure than pain. Malena climbed on top of her, took off her own top and was left only in the G-string which, on closer inspection, Verónica could now confirm was one of hers.

"Malena, we should think about what we're doing."

"We're just two girls having a bit of fun."

At least she hadn't said *a girl and an older woman*. Verónica ran her hands over Malena's back and the softness of her skin reminded her of Frida's. Malena was still kissing her, with a dedication that seemed different to Verónica from the kisses of any man.

"Come," Malena said and led her to the bedroom. She moved around the apartment as though she were the owner and Verónica the guest. Malena helped her take her clothes off. Verónica decided to let her. She was left naked, seeking Malena among the shadows in the room. The girl went over to the nightstand and took something out of the drawer.

Verónica didn't know what it was until Malena came back to her side. It was a sleeping mask Verónica had once brought back from a flight. Malena put the mask on her.

"This is very *Fifty Shades*. Are you going to tie me up and discipline me?"

"I'd love to do both those things, but everything in good time."

Malena made her lie down on the bed and began kissing her legs, the inside of her thighs, caressing her labia without penetrating her, kissing up to her navel and then down, along the path marked by her pubic line. She reached her clitoris, gave it a few brief kisses, then sucked hard on her while she penetrated Verónica with her fingers. Verónica lifted her hips a little, purring as she reached her first orgasm. Malena slid up to kiss her. Verónica caressed her breasts, putting her mouth around one. Malena moaned, loudly, but for once Verónica wasn't worrying about the neighbours.

It was strange not being able to use her eyes to enjoy Malena's body. It limited her senses while opening up new pathways to pleasure; their bodies seemed to have no shape, but millions of pleasure-giving nerve endings.

The CD had stopped playing in the living room. Otherwise perhaps Verónica wouldn't have heard the sound of keys opening the apartment door. Her body tensed. Malena registered the change and took her hands, kissing her neck. "Don't worry, everything's fine."

Malena was still kissing her. Verónica could hear the steps of someone coming closer. Was this some fantasy cooked up by Malena and her boyfriend? Did they want her naked, helpless, to fuck between them? Verónica felt Malena's fingers penetrating her again and couldn't suppress a moan. She heard clothes being taken off. Was that Damián getting undressed? Malena kissed her mouth again; a hand caressed her feet. They were a man's hands. Verónica wanted to move. She couldn't: Malena had her firmly by the wrists. She hadn't got her tied up, but almost. The man's hands were moving up her body.

"Come," Malena said to the other person, and Verónica could feel the guy kneeling on the mattress, close to her face. Malena moved away a little, without letting her go. She must have been sucking his dick, and he must have stopped her because the girl complained: "Isn't it only for me?"

Verónica could see nothing, but neither could the other two make out much among the shadows in the room. She lifted her head and opened her mouth. The gesture must have surprised Malena, who let go of one of her arms, giving Verónica the chance to take off her eye covers.

It took a few seconds for her eyes to adjust to the darkness in the room. She saw Malena's face, shining with desire, and in the foreground a cock, big, powerful and attached amid abundant pubic hair to a muscular body, honed by years of weightlifting. But Damián was a skinny boy with a shapeless, almost feminine physique. This wasn't Damián's body. Verónica's intuition became a certainty. That dick inches away from her face was Eitan's. Verónica looked at him: Eitan was smiling at her with an expression she had never seen on El Chino before.

17 *The Endless Night*

I

Federico stayed in the office until late, later even than Aarón, who was usually the last to leave. As he was leaving, Rosenthal repeated the instruction he had given Federico when they talked earlier: "Invoice him for all the work to date and make it clear the practice no longer wishes to defend him in any case. And that everything outside the privileged client–lawyer relationship will be turned over to the courts."

Mayer had lost the backing of Rosenthal and Associates. This wasn't a simple matter of switching lawyers. When the news reached Tribunales the next day, it would go off like a bomb. More than one judge and some potential plaintiffs would fall on Mayer as if he were a tethered sheep. The firm was also gaining a powerful enemy, given that Mayer was in the media business and would turn his heavy artillery on them. But the Rosenthal practice was well enough armoured to withstand even a concerted campaign.

Verónica would be stuck in the middle. It would be difficult for her to keep working at *Nuestro Tiempo*, although it was also unlikely she would want to continue there. Federico needed to talk to her and let her know what was going to happen, because the jobs of her colleagues were also at stake.

However, he had a more urgent matter to resolve. Ángeles had asked (*demanded* might be a more accurate word) him to meet her at home. It was already late, but he had to go. He didn't understand what was wrong with her, or rather he did: she probably felt sidelined in the Roxana Mayer case. He owed her a proper explanation. After all, it was thanks to Ángeles that the worst of Mayer's racketeering had been discovered.

He sent her a WhatsApp: *Running very late, but I'm on my way.*

She didn't reply immediately, but Federico set off anyway, towards the apartment. When he got there, Ángeles took a while to come to the door. Any longer and he would have begun to worry.

In silence, they travelled up in the elevator. There were no great displays of affection on her part. She didn't seem angry – which was what he had feared – but rather worried, a little tense.

They sat down on the sofa. She had coffee ready in a flask, although he would have preferred something more substantial, not having eaten since lunchtime. Ángeles sat at the end of the sofa, her legs pressed together.

"I have something to tell you: I'm pregnant."

Federico kept looking at her, as though expecting a clarification that would annul the phrase already spoken: something like *I'm pregnant, but not by you,* or *I think I'm pregnant, but I haven't done the test yet, so I could be wrong.* Ángeles was also watching him, monitoring his reaction. She kept speaking, but without saying any of the things Federico would have liked to hear.

"I'm late. I did a pregnancy test and it came out positive. I know this must come as a big shock – I'm shocked too. As you can imagine, it wasn't part of the plan. Motherhood was still a distant concept for me."

"Are you OK?"

"Yes, yes. I know it's crazy, but never mind. I'm going to have it, Federico."

Federico nodded, trying to absorb what Ángeles was telling him. Now he wanted to say something back to show his support, to be as honest and respectful as he could. But he feared that the honesty and the respect might be on a collision course.

"Ángeles, the first thing I want to say is that you have my complete support and I'll back you whichever decision you take."

"It's really important for me to hear you say that. I was scared you'd be angry."

"Why would I be angry? This has happened to both of us, and we're going to do whatever you think is right."

"I didn't expect to be a mother so early in life, but I do want to have it."

"Yes, of course."

"I want to clarify something quickly. I know you're in a relationship and that our thing was always like a sideshow, hidden away from everyone else, a make-believe world inhabited by the two of us. I'm not asking or expecting you to expand that world to three. My approach will go along different lines. I'm not asking you to be the father, or to change your life."

"I'm going to take responsibility."

"I plan to have it and bring it up as what I am, a single mother."

"You realize that, with or without a partner, having a child is going to throw a spanner in your career?"

"I've thought about it a lot in the last few days. Unless Rosenthal and Associates has a policy against women who decide to have children, it shouldn't complicate things too much. No more than it does for other female lawyers I know who seem to be doing very well. Of course, I'll have to forget my plan to go and study abroad, at least for a few years, but I was already resigned to that when I joined the practice.

You lot weren't going to let me have a semester at Harvard, either."

Much to the dismay of Federico, who was having a hard time holding up his end of the conversation, the atmosphere was almost that of a wake. That wasn't fair on her. Ángeles had made an important decision and he seemed to be responding with condolences. He tried to rally, making himself as explicit as possible.

"I want to do this with you. I don't think we can be a couple, because I already have a partner and, all things considered, I'm good with Verónica. But I'm going to be there for you and the baby."

"Does that include saying you're the father? Not that I want to rush you, I just want to know what to expect."

"Give me a little time to speak to the people involved. But after that, yes."

Federico left Ángeles's apartment without Mayer having been mentioned even once. Suddenly, all that seemed banal and unimportant. As he was making his way home, he thought about the strange hand life had dealt him. He had yearned for fatherhood when Verónica told him she was pregnant. He had pictured himself as the father of Vero's child. That wasn't going to happen, though. Instead, Ángeles would have his child. And he didn't see himself as a father; however much he tried, no matter how intellectually clear he was on what to do, how to behave, something inside kept him emotionally distant from fatherhood.

He didn't regret the relationship with Ángeles. On Dr Cohen's advice, he had asked himself if he was still interested in Ángeles or if this story belonged in the past. And the answer was that yes, he still was. He had to talk to Verónica, explain what had happened. But not for a few days, because he needed to work up to it. He did, on the other hand, urgently need to speak to her about the Mayer case. He called her, several times, but she didn't pick up.

II

"No."

Verónica pushed Malena, who was clinging to her and trying to regain control of the situation, but the "no" had been directed squarely at Eitan. Verónica got to her feet and went to get her clothes. If she had one superpower in life, it was always remembering where she had left her clothes before fucking.

"I don't know what you're doing here. Nobody invited you to my house."

"I invited him," said Malena, sitting on the bed in the lotus position.

Eitan, still naked, looked like a porn actor waiting for his scene.

"I don't understand what's going on between you two. Or rather, I do: I understand you've been deceiving me all this time. Put your clothes on, assholes. Explain what's going on, then fuck off," Verónica said, then left the room, trying to avoid making contact with Eitan's body.

She looked at her phone: there were several missed calls from Federico, and a WhatsApp: *I need to speak to you soon about Mayer. Call me.*

This wasn't the time to call. Fury raged through her body, but she tried to calm down. She knew what had happened in that room wasn't just a slightly clumsy invitation to take part in a threesome. There was some sinister subtext, questions that eluded her – questions she wasn't seeing but that she had no doubt were extremely serious. She had to remove the purely sexual element to see what remained in the relationship between Malena and Eitan. Perhaps Malena hadn't been hiding from everyone after all. Hadn't Eitan asked about Malena and hadn't he said he knew nothing about the tablet? Why had they cooked up this farce for her? A web of lies encompassed her, and Verónica needed to know why she was at the centre of it.

"I want you to tell me what's going on here."

"Vero, relax, nothing's going on," said Eitan, who had already squeezed back into his black trousers and tight blue shirt and was holding a jacket, also black, in his hand.

"You already knew we had worked together at the Foreign Ministry," explained Malena. "Well, we kept in touch. I found out that you two had gone out together when you were young and I thought it would be a great idea to invite Eitan round to have some fun with us."

"We never went out together. And supposedly you weren't in touch with him. And you" – directing herself to Eitan – "told me you knew nothing about her. Who are you both, and what do you want?"

"It was a mistake, Vero, I see that now. I'm really sorry. I'll leave you two alone. I promise not to bother you any more," said Eitan, chastened.

"I don't believe it," said Verónica and then, remembering something, she turned to Malena. "And the tablet you gave me, is that also part of this farce?"

Malena's expression crumbled and, without saying anything, she shook her head.

Eitan, who had been preparing to leave, seemed to change his mind. "Did you have the tablet?" he asked Malena.

Malena seemed about to cry. Eitan walked towards her.

"No, I... I swear I —"

Eitan slapped her so hard she fell to the ground. Verónica jumped to her feet and rushed at him, ready to attack, but then Eitan took out a gun and pointed it at her face.

"You'd better calm down. We'd all better calm down. Where's the tablet? Don't even think about lying to me."

Who was this guy, threatening her with a gun, treating Malena like a rag doll and apparently ready to do them both violence?

"My father sent me the tablet the day before they killed him. I kept it safe, then gave it to Verónica."

"It's not here," Verónica added. "I gave it to a hacker to see if he could get into the files, but he couldn't. He's still got it."

Eitan took out his phone. "I have a feeling we're going to be spending some time together," he said, entering a number into it. "Maluma, come to Rosenthal's apartment. We've got work to do. Oh, and bring the most recent photos." Eitan hung up.

Had he really said "Maluma"? Verónica wanted to rattle him: "So Iván Carmona is coming over?"

She succeeded. Eitan glanced up at her, both surprised and concerned.

"You're very intelligent, Verónica. You always were, always a step ahead of the rest of us."

"Never of you, though."

"And I see you haven't changed. Touché. Who is this person who's got the tablet?"

"A hacker friend."

"We're going to pay him a visit so he can give it to me."

"The last time you made me do something like that, a woman wound up dead."

Again, Eitan seemed dumbfounded by Verónica's response. "How do you know that was me?"

"Wasn't it?"

"Never mind, we have to get the tablet. Malena will stay here with my friend. If you pull any tricks, she dies. If your friend doesn't give us the tablet, she dies. If any strange thing happens, she dies."

"He's a hacker, Eitan, he wouldn't let us into his house if the future of humanity were at stake. It's going to be easier for you to shoot us both than to get him to open the front door."

"Tell him to come to the McDonald's on Corrientes and Scalabrini Ortiz."

Verónica called La Sombra and told him she urgently needed the tablet. They agreed to meet in half an hour.

Nobody spoke in Verónica's apartment as they awaited Maluma. Minutes later he arrived downstairs and Eitan threw the key down to him from the balcony. Verónica realized Malena must have made a copy of her key. But if they were accomplices, why had he not known she had the tablet? Had she betrayed him? Who was she betraying, and why?

Maluma came into the room, passed a brown envelope to Eitan and nodded to Malena. It was clear they knew each other.

"Before we go, a quick digression. This is for you, Vero, a service to the community."

Eitan passed her the envelope. She examined it before opening it and taking out the photos inside. It was a few seconds before she understood what she was seeing. They were images that had been snapped, paparazzi-style, at the entrance to a building. The sequence showed Federico arriving there, then Ángeles appearing from inside and opening the door to him, them kissing, them hugging. In one photo she had her hand on his ass. Then the sequence was repeated, but with both parties wearing different clothes. Ángeles looked much younger when casually dressed in leggings or shorts. They kissed, they hugged, they went into the building together.

"Your beloved has a lover. She's a lawyer at Rosenthal and Associates and her name is —"

"Ángeles Basualdo."

"You know her."

Verónica finished looking at the photos, put them back in the envelope and threw it on to the coffee table. "So?"

"I'm just passing on information. Do whatever you like with it. Now let's go."

Verónica picked up her bag like someone preparing to go out for a walk. Eitan seemed about to say something else, then to think better of it. They left the apartment, while Maluma stayed to watch Malena. Verónica prayed Marcelo would see her, but at that time of night there was nobody in the entrance hall.

Eitan's Nissan was parked half a block away. He treated her with all the chivalry of a date, opening her car door, asking if she was comfortable. As they drove away from the building he said: "At least admit that the photos came as a surprise."

"Far from it. I already knew about that. Federico and I have an open relationship," she lied.

They were driving along Castillo towards Scalabrini Ortiz when Verónica felt her bag vibrate. A WhatsApp. She'd had the sense to turn off the sound on her phone. She glanced around the car to see if there were any tissues. With any luck, there wouldn't be.

"Have you got any tissues?" Verónica asked, pretending to look around.

"I've run out."

"I think I've got a packet somewhere," said Verónica, opening her bag. Eitan was watching her every movement.

Surreptitiously she read the message. It was from Malena: *I've escaped. I'm fine. Don't give him the tablet.*

Verónica took stock, breathing deeply. She had to be careful. She wouldn't get more than one shot.

She waited for the car to slow down as it approached a red light, then casually draped her left arm over the back of Eitan's seat. He could take this as a desire to curry favour or a fake attempt at seduction, which he would quickly intercept by saying he didn't believe her. But what she wanted was precisely that – for him to look at her. And that's what Eitan did: he turned his head and looked into her eyes.

"Don't go thinking —"

He didn't get to finish the sentence. Verónica took a spray out of her bag and aimed it at his eyes.

"What the —"

Eitan, reacting quickly, moved to protect himself. He was probably preparing for the sensation of pepper or mustard spray in his eyes, not a L'Occitane skin moisturizer. Verónica took advantage of the momentary confusion to grab the steering wheel. Eitan tried to wrest it back. The car in front of them had stopped at a traffic light, and they glided into it with much less force than was being exerted inside the car. Verónica got out of the vehicle and began to run against the traffic, screaming: "Rapist! Rapist!"

The few people in the street at that time of night turned to look. Eitan didn't dare follow her. Once she had turned the corner, Verónica stopped shouting, but she kept running for several blocks, only stopping to catch her breath. A free taxi happened to be passing and she hailed it, throwing herself inside. She gave the driver an address in Palermo, then texted La Sombra: *Don't go to the appointment at McDonald's. Get out of your house and go to the YPF filling station on Pringles and Córdoba.*

Then she called Malena.

After Federico left her apartment, Ángeles was filled with a strange sense of peace. The hardest few minutes of the last few days were over: she had been able to be clear with him, to tell him the truth without speculation or demands. She hadn't broken down (although there had certainly been a moment when she felt like crying), she hadn't pretended to feel unconcerned. Her behaviour had been exemplary. Now, alone in her home, she could finally relax and start considering more practical questions, like arranging a gynaecologist appointment.

She had also briefly managed to forget about work. Roxana Mayer, David Kaplan: those names seemed distant, especially now that she had passed her material over to Verónica Rosenthal, who would put her discoveries to good use. And yet Ángeles believed she could still find out more.

As if by an act of telepathy, her phone rang. It was Roxana Mayer. Ángeles answered, trying to sound calm. She had to be careful not to be caught out.

"Ángeles, sweetheart, I'd love you to come over. I want to show you some plans for my new law firm, the one in which you're going to occupy a central role."

"That sounds great, Roxana, why don't I come over tomorrow morning?"

"You'll accuse me of being over the top, but I'm desperate for you to see everything. Also, I'm so happy about this that I don't care any more about handing over control of Tuentur to my idiot ex. I've got something much bigger than that measly security company to think about now. I need you to see the plans and give me your opinion."

Ángeles ended up promising to be there in half an hour. It was very late, but she felt sure she was about to make a breakthrough.

As she was preparing to go out, she thought it wouldn't be a bad idea to take pepper spray or some other weapon of self-defence in her bag. It would make her feel safer. But the only defensive tool Ángeles had was a Swiss army knife, a present from her sister. She tucked it into her bag as though it were a revolver, then, still not feeling safe, took it out again and put it in a small pocket of her trousers. She checked her reflection to make sure it couldn't be seen. Now Ángeles did feel protected. She headed out to Roxana Mayer's house.

IV

Everything had got insanely complicated, and there seemed to be no end to the nightmare. David was annoyed with her, avoiding her, giving abrupt answers and apparently making a physical effort not to attack her. And even Gómez Pardo apparently had it in for her, when in reality he and her ex were to blame for the biggest disasters. It was easy to wash your hands when things got complicated. Talk about being wise after the fact.

From the moment Sergio first proposed setting up Tuentur and using Roxana's contacts to land clients, it had been clear to her that only the idea was his, if that. The power behind the throne was Gómez Pardo. The partnership at the beginning, the true partnership, was really between Gómez Pardo and herself. But once Roxana had started making her own contacts in Israel, Gómez Pardo no longer had anything to offer her: she didn't need him; the company had found its own way. For that same reason Gómez Pardo decided to create Eramus and stop hiding behind Sergio's skirts. Now they were partners on an equal footing. Gómez Pardo's main objective was for Eramus gradually to supplant Tuentur. Wasn't Eramus already in Ecuador and Chile, while Tuentur sold its services only in Argentina? But Sergio and Gómez Pardo had gone too far. Some men lose everything over a woman; others, like these idiots, for a million-dollar payout under the table. They were taking in so much money from so many different places that they thought they could make up the rules as they went along. They were wrong.

When Roxana first met David, he wasn't called David but Nathan. Nathan Neuer. She and Sergio had travelled to Tel Aviv to strengthen their ties with that city. David was still serving in the military and he was presented to them as a national hero, a soldier fighting fundamentalist terrorism. Sergio told David that if he ever felt like rejoining civilian life, he could count on a privileged position in his company. At the time, the chances of that happening seemed remote.

David had another great virtue: he was a follower of Orígenes, a passionate seeker after primitive religion. They were instantly attracted to one another. David and she had much in common; they shared a vision of the cosmos. The pretext of an Orígenes meeting in Stockholm – a sparsely attended gathering, there were only fourteen "seekers", as they called themselves – united them for ever. They became lovers; he left his wife while she decided to wait, but only for business reasons. She wasn't yet in a position to negotiate with Sergio for half their shared assets.

Events seemed to speed up when David was targeted by some Israeli human rights organizations (she despised those do-gooders). Even though David had the support of his peers, it was obviously convenient for everyone for him to leave the military. The offer from Tuentur began to look more attractive than ever. But there was a worry: what if one of those NGOs managed to take their case to some international court and David was arrested? It was unlikely, but better not to run the risk. There was another danger: that some extremist Muslim group would decide to take justice into their own hands and make an attempt on his life. There was no precedent for that, but he wouldn't want to be the first. Better to change his name, keep a low profile.

She was the one who chose his name. She'd always liked "David". As a little girl she'd given a doll that name. Now she could have an immensely attractive and virile adult version.

They kept their relationship secret, even though Sergio had no interest in Roxana's sex life. If anything, he might be more worried that his right-hand man, his most notable acquisition from the Israeli armed forces, would lose focus if he was fucking his wife.

When she finally decided to separate, Roxana discovered that it would be difficult to get control of Tuentur. David wasn't prepared to take orders from a frontman like Mayer. Besides, he had other plans. David had created a tech services company similar to Eramus. Once Roxana had control of Tuentur, they could merge both companies and Eramus would be greatly weakened.

Roxana thought of herself as cleverer than both her ex and Gómez Pardo, and she decided to put together a plan that would destroy them, or at least warn them off getting in the way of her ambitions.

The idea came to her when Sergio and Gómez Pardo decided to partner up in the multimedia group. Roxana knew this wasn't simply a business move, because Gómez Pardo had plans to go into politics. But it was also true that life as a politician would leave him much more exposed. It was one thing to operate in the shadows and something entirely different to have your face all over the news channels.

It was David who discovered that Eramus had serious problems in Israel and that, if nothing had yet come out, it was because Mayer and Gómez Pardo's contacts, their commercial and political interests, had put a lid on the scandal. But if the press got wind of it, their support would fall away and they'd be standing alone in front of commercial court judges, here and in Israel. And Gómez Pardo would lose what little credibility he had.

The information had come via Eitan Boniek, an employee in the Foreign Ministry who did various jobs for the Israeli embassy. David had known his father in the nineties and the son had become his protégé. Eitan, like his father two decades earlier, had done good work for David and his colleagues in different parts of the world. There was something about this young guy that set off alarm bells for Roxana, though; he seemed just as capable of murder as he was of finding information and running political operations. She believed that a person who could kill couldn't also think. It struck her as promiscuous. You're either a fixer or a killer. Yet Eitan appeared to be both things. It was he who had obtained the information on Eramus's embezzlement of public funds.

Roxana wanted to keep David out of her dispute with Sergio. So she made sure to sit down with Boniek and plan how that information would reach the media: a respected official from the embassy would contact Aníbal Monteverde, the partner who had been usurped by Gómez Pardo in the multimedia group, who would pass the information on to a prestigious journalist, one-time editor of *Nuestro Tiempo*. Nothing should go wrong. But that's not how things turned out.

Andrés Goicochea wasn't satisfied with the information that had been passed to him and continued digging on his own. By an unhappy coincidence, his ex-wife also worked at the Foreign Ministry and was a troublemaker. She was the person who could connect Neuer to David. If David were unmasked, that would be a problem all round: for them, for Mayer, for Gómez Pardo. They had to take drastic steps, urgently. And Roxana took them.

Then, in the middle of all this, another complication arose. An unidentified group had got hold of a tablet containing confidential information on David. They couldn't be serious players – perhaps they were simply after money – but Roxana and David couldn't rest easy until that tablet was in their hands.

And as if they didn't have enough problems, Ángeles had turned up. Little Ángeles, the brilliant lawyer, the sweet girl Roxana could picture working alongside in the law firm, because behind the sweetness was a rigorous professional. What Roxana did not foresee was that that same strength of spirit would lead Ángeles to discover David's true identity. Perhaps she would never have found out about the lawyer's enquiries if the alarm hadn't been raised at the embassy.

They couldn't afford so many missteps. Roxana needed to know how Ángeles had discovered David's identity. The lawyer needed to be quarantined, before she spread this virus of information any further.

"You realize you won't be able to kill her here?" said David, furious, clenching his fist. She resisted the temptation to hit him.

Roxana called Eitan, to put him in charge of liquidating Ángeles. He should take her somewhere far away, after getting what they needed from her. But Eitan made an unexpected suggestion. That boy was full of surprises. He said that before doing away with her, they could use her to get the tablet. Roxana didn't know what Boniek was planning. But sooner rather than later she wanted him to take Ángeles from her house and neutralize her.

V

Verónica felt more at ease after speaking to Malena. The taxi driver was silent, something for which she always felt grateful. Federico called again and she didn't pick up. The photographs of him and Ángeles were still playing in her head. She was furious, disillusioned, shocked, anguished – but not necessarily in that order. She tried to focus on the here and now, the crimes being committed, Mayer, Kaplan, Eitan. If Federico was in the apartment, it was possible his life was at risk. She made a great mental effort, and called him.

"Are you at home?"

"Yes."

"I don't have time to explain this, but leave right away. Pick some bar in Palermo Hollywood, let me know the address and wait for me there."

"Where are you?"

Verónica hung up before she could unleash a string of insults. She also called Marcelo, to ask him to call the police and say the apartment had been burgled. But not to go in on his own – to let the cops go in first and check everything. Marcelo told her not to worry, he was on it.

The taxi stopped at the YPF filling station. Everything seemed normal. Verónica went into the shop and, to her surprise, Malena was there, waiting for her. "Are you all right?" Verónica asked her.

Malena played down the bruise spreading across her arm. "I had a scuffle with that bastard. I think we may have broken a couple of lamps."

"Let me see that arm."

"I've had worse blows" – and she recited – "'Some blows in life are so hard.'"

"'Blows like the hatred of God.'"

355

"Wow. That I did not expect."

"I wouldn't have had you down as a César Vallejo fan either. You're a little bitch, by the way, Malena."

"I know, I know. I owe you a lot of explanations. The worst thing is that I can't give you most of them."

"What was that shit Eitan doing in my house?"

"He asked me to take him there and to have you ready for a little party. That was the word the asshole used. And since Eitan believed I was working for him, I had to do it. I needed to keep up my front most of the time."

"Did you get to me through Eitan?"

"He sent me."

"Are you working for him then?"

"It's much more complicated than that."

"Try explaining. Perhaps I'll understand."

"Eitan plays for Mossad. He's a free agent, not directly connected."

"In journalism we'd say a freelancer."

"Something like that. During my internship he offered to bring me in on some little jobs."

"Why?"

"I can't tell you. Neither why, nor what I did. The only thing I can tell you – and this is already too much – is that I wanted him to contact me and recruit me."

Malena seemed to be going round in circles.

"I really do trust you, Verónica, and so I'm going to tell you more than I should, and I hope I won't regret it: I'm playing for another team. And Mossad isn't amused when someone like me messes them around. Do you understand?"

"Who are you playing for?"

"There's no point in me telling you. And I lied when I told Eitan my dad gave me the tablet. It was the other way round. It came to him through me."

"Who gave it to you?"

"Clearly not Mossad. Other people with interests in the Middle East passed me the information about the genocidal Neuer through an intermediary, a Turkish diplomat. The aim was to expose Neuer, to make the world take notice. I passed the information on to Viviana. I made her believe I had accidentally found it. My intention was that she would give it to some journalist. I never thought it would end up in the hands of my old man, who was supposedly retired. Just my fucking luck."

La Sombra came into the shop then, and walked past Verónica as if he hadn't seen her. He picked up a juice from the fridge and went towards the till. Verónica made a sign to him.

"I didn't know if —" La Sombra explained.

"It's all good. She's the one who gave me the tablet." Verónica gave him a brief summary of what had happened with Eitan. "It's safer for me to have the tablet," she said.

"Unfortunately I never worked out the password to get in."

"I have it," said Malena. "I couldn't give it to you before, but now I can. It's twenty-four characters that I've memorized. Put a capital J, a small p, a pesos sign…"

La Sombra typed, and the screen lit up. A blue background on which only the word *files* stood out. So many days wrestling with the tablet and there it was, open and ready to yield its archive. They looked at what was there: photos of Neuer in his military uniform, others where he was accompanied by what were probably senior leaders and also images of the massacres in Gaza, visual corroboration of what had until then been only words.

There were the destroyed hospital, the murdered doctors, the shattered bodies of patients, children's sneakers. Children who, minutes before, had been playing ball, as Verónica had for so many years, children who would not grow up to be journalists like her, who would never fall in love, pursue a career, gaze at the sea in front of them. There they were, in full colour and in black and white, the images of a massacre that seemed so distant, so alien to Verónica Rosenthal. And yet she and that catastrophe were joined by the invisible threads that connected different parts of one civilization: her childhood in the nineties, the goals celebrated in Parque Centenario as they would also have been celebrated on the Gazan beach by that boy who would, minutes later, be reduced to disembowelled remains. And there were people who were guilty, people who pulled the triggers, an officer who gave the order, a high command that decided it was permissible to bomb civilian communities, a state policy that endorsed it, a public opinion that dressed up its support for massacre as self-protection, the systematic attack on a people who had been in that territory long before Verónica's grandfather arrived in Palestine and who remained there despite the deaths, the torture and the humiliations. Those images served to remind her, or show her, that that world existed.

In addition, there were images of Kaplan coming out of a clinic with his nose covered in bandages after the operation, as well as files written in Hebrew and Arabic characters, and in other languages Verónica didn't recognize.

"There are reports from NGOs like Adalah, Yesh Din and Shovrim Shtika, among others. There are documents that prove Neuer is responsible for and guilty of the massacres at Al-Shifa Hospital and on the beach by the jetty near to the Al Deira hotel," said Malena. "And most important, something nobody has had up until now: there are videos of Neuer's statements in the military court. He admits he gave the order to launch the missiles, knowing there were innocent people in the hospital, and that the attack on the children could have been avoided, but that he wanted to teach the Palestinians a lesson. There's also evidence that at least two members of the military tribunal found him guilty, and yet this position was not reflected in the final verdict, nor was it made public. It wasn't a unanimous verdict, as was claimed at the time."

"I'd better make a backup right away," said La Sombra, and he started transferring the material to his laptop and then on to a USB. "If you like I can save a copy securely in the cloud – not on Google Drive, obviously. Take the USB and the tablet," he said to Verónica.

"What about you?" Verónica asked Malena.

"I've done my bit by delivering the material. I don't collect mission souvenirs."

"Where are you going to go?"

"Don't worry. It's easy to hide in this city. I've been in worse places."

They left the filling station separately. Verónica had now received Federico's text with the address of a bar specializing in craft beers. She didn't like that kind of bar, and didn't even particularly like beer, but she thought a place like that, full of young people smeared with cheddar cheese, was safer than an intimate drinking hole. And now, more than ever, she had to keep her wits about her. Eitan, alone or with Maluma, or with who knew how many other people, must be combing the city, looking for her.

VI

Ángeles rang Roxana's bell, and the latter opened the door in her usual expansive style, although she seemed a little out of sorts. She showed Ángeles into the living room, the site of their first conversation, when Ángeles had noticed the Sumerian artworks, which were still there, like mute witnesses to the bond that had formed that day and which now would reach its apogee.

"We have to speak, dear heart," said Roxana and Ángeles was amused by the tone, because it reminded her of the way she had spoken when she told Federico she was pregnant.

"We can talk about whatever you like," Ángeles told her. Was there anyone else in the house? David, one of the maids? The silence was total.

"Who are you working for, Ángeles?"

She smiled nervously. "For Rosenthal and Associates, Roxana, as you know. At least until you start your own law firm."

"Did Aarón Rosenthal send you to investigate David?"

Ángeles decided there and then that she would answer all the questions truthfully. It was going to be the best way to combat the fear starting to grow inside her.

"Rosenthal didn't send me to investigate anyone."

"Who sent you?"

"As I said, nobody has given any instruction to that effect."

"You reported us to the embassy."

"While I was searching for information about the companies you share with your ex-husband, I stumbled across the details of David's true identity."

Roxana stiffened and began shouting at her. "Don't fuck around with me, girl. How the hell did you find out about David, and who for?"

"It was by chance, I swear. I saw some photos of Orígenes meetings in Europe" – Ángeles was no longer sure if it was safe to name her sister in all this – "and I thought I recognized the man next to you. I got his name, and the internet is full of articles about him."

"Who did you take this information to?"

"To the Israeli embassy. I know a lawyer who works there."

"And where else?"

"Nowhere else. It seemed to me that by passing the details to the embassy I had already fulfilled my obligations as a citizen, and I went back to focussing on the division of assets."

"Your obligations as a citizen?" Roxana repeated sarcastically and, apparently talking to people who were not visible, she asked: "What do you think?"

David appeared from one side, accompanied by a young man. Ángeles tried to control the tremors running through her body.

"I think she's telling the truth," said the youth.

David turned to Roxana, furious. "You created this problem. You've really landed us in the shit."

Just as Roxana seemed ready to turn on her partner, the young man stepped forward to speak. "We can turn this to our advantage. We need to get hold of the tablet. Let's swap the lawyer for the tablet."

Roxana was too angry to show much interest in this plan. "I've already told you what I want."

She wants to see me dead, thought Ángeles, and was certain they had planned a horrifying end for her, as they had for the journalist and his ex-wife. They were going to kill her. Roxana or one of these two. She couldn't hold back her tears.

David came towards her and gently told her to stand up. Ángeles looked at him pleadingly. "Please, don't kill me."

David smiled at her. "Nobody is going to kill you, Ángeles."

"We're only going to lock you up until Verónica Rosenthal, your lover's wife, gets here," said the young man. "When she hands over the material, you can leave through the same door you came in by."

Ángeles didn't even register the man's sarcasm. Meekly, she let David take her to a small, empty room, which seemed to have been prepared with a prisoner in mind, and lock her in it. David had made her leave her bag and phone on the coffee table. But Ángeles still had the Swiss army knife on her. Not that it made her feel any safer.

VII

There are moments when reality loses meaning, becomes blurred or distorted as though by one of those fairground mirrors. That was how Verónica felt in the taxi taking her to meet Federico. Reality seemed to wield an unusual power; it felt very concrete. There was a guy who might be looking for her, to kill or harm her; there was another guy who was a war criminal, and now she had all the evidence to expose him; there were people who had been murdered by Eitan, her childhood friend – at least everything suggested he had killed them. In her bag she carried a tablet and a USB with sensitive information, compromising not only people but also military hierarchies. However, at this intense point in her life her mind was entirely occupied with the photos of Federico and Ángeles. How could he have done something like that to her? Verónica didn't believe in fidelity as a precept, but she did believe in it as a concept. If she had gone along with the threesome offered by Malena and Eitan, she would have felt compelled to tell Federico about it; at the end of the day, she had never promised to be faithful to him. She simply was faithful in the same way she didn't add sugar to coffee: not because she thought sugar was bad, but because she didn't like sugar in infusions. Federico, on the other hand (and she could no longer think of the name "Federico" without the suffix "that bastard"), had constructed a parallel world, an emotional relationship, with periodic visits to Ángeles's apartment, a routine assembled with chunks of time when they were supposed to be together, even if each one was doing their own thing. She felt destroyed. Her heart was broken.

He was already there in the bar, drinking a chopp and surrounded by young people talking loudly, straining to make themselves heard above the music. Verónica hesitated before giving him a kiss on the lips, then went ahead and greeted him as usual.

"Vero, I've got some important information about the Mayers. Sergio Mayer's deputy in Tuentur, David Kaplan, is a war criminal."

"He's called Nathan Neuer, same surname as the goalkeeper in the German national team."

"How do you know that?"

"I watched the final too. Or perhaps you'd already forgotten."

"How do you know about Kaplan/Neuer?"

"I believe we have the same source: your colleague Ángeles Basualdo."

Federico's eyes opened wider than usual. "Ángeles has been to see you?"

"Federico, you're a fucking bastard. Why in God's name did you cheat on me with that piece of trash?"

Federico seemed to hesitate. He must have been wondering whether to run away or start crying, coward that he was.

"Wait, Vero, we have some really important things to talk about."

"More important than the fact you're a first-class shit? More important than the fact you've been fucking a two-faced bitch dressed up as a lawyer? What's more important than that? Explain it to me."

"Ángeles went to speak to you?"

"Yes, about Kaplan and his crimes. The little cow didn't say anything about you."

"How did you find out then?"

"You're being watched, you and Little Red Riding Hood. They took some lovely pictures of her groping you at the door to her building."

Verónica took Federico's chopp. There wasn't time to get her own drink and she needed something right away. And to smoke, to calm herself down. She didn't have any cigarettes with her. How could she have neglected to bring cigarettes?

"What an idiot I am." She felt like crying. Federico took her hand and she pulled it away, as though bitten by a tarantula. "Don't touch me, you creep."

The waitress appeared and Verónica ordered a whisky. They only had Johnnie Walker Red Label. She wasn't about to pick a fight with the waitress over the dire quality of the drinks menu, so she accepted what was on offer.

"I don't know if it helps to say I'm sorry. I've been a jerk, and I'm ashamed you have to go through all of this because of me."

"What a sweet soul you are. What a little angel. And the other one's even called Ángeles. Now the penny drops. The little whore."

"I was meaning to talk to you about it."

"How very generous. Because you were eaten up by guilt or because you wanted to boast about your most recent conquest?"

"Vero, you know me better than that."

"I don't know if I do know you. I thought I did, but now I'm not so sure."

"I was going to talk to you because Ángeles is pregnant. And I plan to take responsibility."

Verónica froze. The world spun around them both while they seemed to have been rendered immobile. They were still, the world spun, she was like a statue. And so was the other asshole.

"That might be more than I can bear."

"I know there's no point my saying it, but me too. Ángeles is a nice girl, she —"

"Stop. I don't want you to talk to me about her."

"I just want to tell you that, no matter what happens, or happened between her and me, I love you. I love you the same way I have always loved you. I don't want to lose you. Especially not through my own idiocy."

Verónica knocked back her double whisky. The alcohol rushed through her body. At least the music in this place wasn't bad. She heard the voice of Federico Moura singing: "*I'm looking for a body to love / the distance is losing its density*". The music and wine together were soothing. She needed to think more, and better. Federico had been a bastard, but since when had she measured love by the fidelity of another, or indeed herself? When the rage passed, when the humiliation of feeling cheated on gave way to the old affection, she would realize she still loved Federico, even if she couldn't stand to see him now.

Her phone rang, but Verónica didn't look to see who it was. First she needed to tell Federico what was going round her head.

"Listen, I realize there was always a risk of something like this happening in our relationship. Of course I understand you. But I want you to know something: you've broken me. And I'm not going to make things easy for you."

The phone was still ringing; it must be the third or fourth call. She looked at it and saw Eitan's name. She could switch the phone off until tomorrow, but instinct made her answer.

"Hello, Vero. Don't hang up. I have Ángeles here and I want to make you an offer. How about you give me the tablet and I give you the girl? Come to Roxana Mayer's house. I imagine you have the address. If not, take it down."

Verónica wrote the address on a paper napkin. Eitan was still speaking.

"Hang on, I've had a better idea. Give me the tablet, and I'll do whatever you say with Ángeles. I'll give you two options: I can keep her safe and sound, or I can get her out of the way for you. Think of this as a free service, for old times' sake."

Verónica was breathing hard. She looked at Federico, who was wearing the expression of a penguin caught in an oil slick. She thought of Ángeles. Ángeles in the hands of Eitan.

"Listen to me, Eitan. If you so much as touch a hair on her head, if you push her over and she sprains her wrist, if you shout too loud and give her a headache, I swear on the memory of my Grandfather Elías that I will find you wherever you are and I will destroy you in the most painful way possible. And you'll wish you'd never been born."

Verónica cut off the call. She took out a few notes to pay for the drinks.

"Let's go. They've got Ángeles."

VIII

It was a luxury if you thought about it, but there was no harm in doing this kind of thing every now and then. Like a reward for staying alive. Besides, she liked imagining her life was part of a movie someone was filming without her knowledge (although she did know, hence the odd gesture designed to burnish her heroic image). Malena had arrived with the few things she had with her (just a backpack bought in a shop on Lavalle still open at that time of night) and asked for a room. The receptionist at the Panamericano must have been used to eccentric travellers, because his expression betrayed not the faintest surprise at this dishevelled girl asking for a room.

Despite this being a four-star hotel, the room was fairly average, not all that big and at the back of the building, but it had a bathtub, a minibar, cable television and a springy mattress. She didn't need much else to spend the night. Perhaps she would stay two days. Then she would buy a ticket to Rio de Janeiro and sunbathe in Ipanema for a week. Who at the Foreign Ministry had told her about a good club for dancing samba in Rio?

Later she would come back to Buenos Aires, if things calmed down. Which they would, whatever happened that night.

She had to think about what she was going to do with her life. She was torn between returning to her studies in political science at the UBA or going to study at the Sorbonne. She had always wanted to live in Paris. Surely she could get some little job there. How could they turn down a girl like her?

In her rucksack was a toothbrush, toothpaste and a book she had bought in a shop on Avenida Corrientes: *Our Kind of Traitor*, by John le Carré. She loved spy novels, especially le Carré's. If things went badly and she had to abandon her career, she hoped to write spy novels, like le Carré, who had worked for the British secret service. She would be the first Argentine writer to dedicate herself to the genre. That wouldn't be a bad gig. She had plenty of stories.

She felt two different sensations in her body. First, grief for not having properly mourned her father. He hadn't been very present in her life, but she had been devoted to him. If she had known the intel was going to end up with him, she would never have passed it on. She wasn't willing to lose loved ones for this job or anything else. And then there was Verónica Rosenthal. When Boniek had told her to infiltrate the journalist's life, Malena had studied her and found her insufferably arrogant. She had never imagined hooking up with her. Damn Boniek for wrecking everything with his erotic show. The bitch had even been able to quote the next line from that Vallejo poem. It was enough to make you fall in love, or something disgustingly similar.

Malena answered the phone. It was Damián. Obviously he wasn't called Damián. She had dubbed him Demian after Demian Maia, and he had misunderstood and started saying he was Damián. Malena dreaded to think the world might ever depend on something that skinny ass might do.

"She left the bar with a guy, and they've parked a few yards from Roxana Mayer's house."

"Boniek must be there."

"Do I wait?"

"No. Go in. Get in, however you can. If Verónica is going there it's to give him the tablet. I don't know what he must have said to persuade her."

"And I'll clean up the scene a bit."

"Yes, before the guy comes in to do the paperwork tomorrow." Malena couldn't help smiling at her own observation. Then she added: "Only Boniek, mind you."

"Of course, beautiful. I'd like to do the others, but we can't."

"No, we can't. We're not here for that," she said, disappointed. She sighed deeply and added: "At least for now."

There was a long silence. This would have been the time to end their conversation, but Damián was drawing things out. Malena decided not to be hard on him, and to let him say something else.

"Can I see you again? Not now, I mean. But later on, in a few days."

"Hmm. No, I don't think so."

"OK, goodbye."

And Damián, who could have been known as Demian, hung up.

IX

On the way to Roxana's house, Verónica called La Sombra. She told him that he should send copies of the tablet's contents to María Magdalena and Rodolfo if she didn't get back in touch in the next two hours. She put her own copy into the car's glove compartment. Meanwhile, a WhatsApp came through from Marcelo: *All good. The police came and saw the damage (broken TV). Nobody was there. Tomorrow you have to go to the police station to make a formal complaint.*

They argued on the way: Federico wanted to go into the house with her, but Verónica wouldn't hear of it. First she scoffed at him and was even cruel, accusing him of wanting to be a hero saving his lover. But before the conversation ran into a brick wall, Verónica hit on a better argument: if they were going to ring the bell and enter the house in the normal way, it didn't make sense for them to go together. It would be better if he stayed outside. Then, if she hadn't come out after ten minutes, he should call the police. Reluctantly, Federico agreed.

There was nowhere to park on the block, and the first empty space they found was round the corner. That didn't seem a good place to Federico, but Verónica reassured him, saying it wasn't her movements in and out of the front door he had to monitor, but the length of time she spent inside. "The bad guys are already waiting for me," she said.

Verónica got out of the car without saying anything more or waiting for him to wish her luck. She strode back along the block and rang the doorbell. A dog could be heard barking.

They must be watching her through a security camera, because nobody asked her name yet the door opened all the same. Verónica entered a lawned, treeless garden and saw the dog, a black bruiser with a mean expression, barking at her. She didn't dare walk any further. From the entrance to the house a woman shushed the dog and gestured to her to come forward.

"He looks fierce, but he's as sweet as a chihuahua," Roxana Mayer said to her, when Verónica was within a few steps.

"Chihuahuas aren't sweet, just small."

In the living room were Eitan, Maluma and David Kaplan. On a coffee table were glasses with different drinks; this could have been an informal gathering of friends. Maluma didn't look at her as she entered. Perhaps he was embarrassed by his black eye. Malena had obviously done a number on him.

"Hello, Vero, how lovely to see you again," said Eitan, with his usual charm.

Verónica pulled out the tablet and passed it to Eitan, who looked at it dismissively, as if he were so familiar with such gadgets that a glance was enough for him to assure Kaplan, as he passed it over:

"This is the one."

Kaplan looked at the tablet as if he had no idea what it was and passed it on to Maluma, who connected it to a laptop and started typing something.

"Where's Ángeles?"

"Ángeles is fine. Locked in a room."

"Let her go."

"First things first. We need proof you haven't made copies of the material. We can only establish that once we've opened the tablet and gone into the black box. That might take a few minutes. How long do you think, Maluma?"

"Ten, fifteen."

If they discovered copies had been made, she and Ángeles were in trouble. The only way to avoid something bad happening to them would be for the police to arrive, but that kind of thing only happened in the movies.

"We made a deal. You give me Ángeles, we leave, you keep the tablet and we never see each other again."

"I think it might be better to lock her up with the lawyer," said Kaplan.

"Come with me, please," said Eitan and led her down a corridor. "In ten minutes all this will be over, for better or worse."

"For better or worse," Verónica repeated, following him.

They stopped in front of a door. Eitan took out a key and opened it. "Your boyfriend's lover is in here," he said.

Verónica went in but didn't see anyone. Eitan, following her in, also seemed surprised that there was no sign of Ángeles.

X

He had found it impossible to wait calmly in the car. After only two minutes he could no longer stand it – he had to get out. Federico walked towards the block where Roxana Mayer's house was and looked towards the front door. A guy was walking in front of him. Instinctively, Federico ducked behind a 4 x 4. His instincts were right because, as soon as the guy arrived at the entrance, he looked around to check who might be watching. Not seeing anyone, he quickly unrolled something he'd been carrying in his hand. It was a length of rope with some hooks at one end. The man threw the rope over the wall and in a few seconds he was hanging off it like Batman and Robin on the Batrope. In an instant the guy was on the other side.

Federico rushed towards the door. The rope was still there; the man hadn't pulled it over, but Federico wouldn't have been able to climb up it even if the wall had been six feet lower. Who was the stranger? Evidently he wasn't a friend of the household, so what was he looking for?

He decided not to wait the ten minutes he had promised Verónica. He must act straight away. If he called the police, two patrol officers would arrive in twenty minutes, stroll towards the door, ring the entryphone and ask the owners of the house if all was well. If the answer was yes, they would go away again.

They were in Villa Urquiza. At that time of night, a SWAT team coming via Avenida Córdoba could reach them in fifteen minutes. He didn't hesitate, and called a federal judge who was very friendly to Rosenthal and Associates.

"Forgive the late call, Doctor, but the daughter of Aarón Rosenthal is in grave danger. How quickly can a Grupo Albatros team get to Villa Urquiza?"

XI

The most humiliating point of that night was when she'd had to tell them she needed a piss and Roxana accompanied her to the bathroom and went in with her. They didn't want to leave her alone anywhere she might find something she could use to defend herself. With much embarrassment, Ángeles lowered her trousers and underwear so she could relieve herself. Roxana stared distractedly at the soaps on the vanity unit. Ángeles was careful not to let the Swiss army knife fall out. Then she was taken back to the room and locked up again without so much as a glass of water.

She could hear her captors talking, but couldn't catch what they were saying. She did, however, notice when another voice joined them. Time stretched out unbearably. Ángeles passed through different stages, from resignation, to the idea of her own death, to a determination to fight for her life.

Taking out her Swiss army knife – the simplest model, with only six functions – she unfolded the longest and sharpest blade and kept it in her hand.

Her plan was simple: to hide behind the door so they didn't see her, taking captive whoever opened it (hopefully it would be Roxana and not one of the men). By threatening to stab her hostage, she could reach the front door and, once outside, start running and shouting for help.

When she heard footsteps approaching she thought she recognized Verónica Rosenthal's voice, but wasn't sure. She hid behind the door. A key turned in the lock. That was when she heard a man say: "Your boyfriend's lover is in here."

Then she felt a fire inside her, a supreme hatred of this man who was revealing the secrets of her life, who disparagingly described her as a "lover". So she changed her plan: she would take no prisoners.

Verónica Rosenthal came into the room followed by the man, looking for her. Before he could react, Ángeles lunged at him and tried to plunge the penknife into his neck. She succeeded in cutting him, and blood instantly spurted out. The man screamed and swore but, when she tried to cut him a second time, he grabbed her wrist and took the knife off her. The man was furious. Not content with getting hold of the knife, he then plunged it into Ángeles's stomach. Unlike her attack, which had been wild and frenzied, the man stabbed her with cool focus. Ángeles felt the knife tear into her belly; she saw it sticking out of her body, her blood gushing out. *I'm dying*, was all she could think.

XII

Even though Damián had decided to leave through the front door once everything was over, he had left the rope on the wall, because he was amused by the idea of Verónica Rosenthal's partner trying to climb up. He didn't look like someone who could do that.

Within seconds of getting over the wall, Damián shot the dog. It barely had a chance to bark, certainly not enough to alert the people inside the house.

He circled the perimeter of the property, looking through the windows. Rosenthal was standing up and Boniek seemed to want to take her somewhere. Damián decided it would be best to enter the house through the kitchen. He didn't have to break anything, because the back door had been left unlocked and unlatched. Trusting types.

Now on to the living room. He narrowly avoided Boniek and Rosenthal, who passed two yards in front of him. In the living room Carmona was at work on the tablet. With any luck he had not yet found the password.

This close up he couldn't – and didn't – miss: the shot went straight in the middle of Carmona's forehead. One of those clean bullseyes that rarely come off outside a shooting range. The second shot was from less than two yards away.

Kaplan and Roxana Mayer had no time to react, and may not even have noticed their companion was dead. Damián told them quietly that if they did as he said nothing would happen to them. "At least not yet," he added, more out of malice than anything else. He took the tablet and put it away. Kaplan looked like he wanted to fight back, so to relieve him of the urge, Damián gave him a pistol-whipping that sent him to sleep. Now the woman did scream, but her cries were lost among others coming from the room he had seen Rosenthal and Boniek going towards. There was no time to tell the woman of the house that it was in her interests to behave, so he had no option but to fire a preventive shot at her lower leg, far from the femoral artery so she wouldn't bleed to death. At worst she might be left with a limp, but that wouldn't be counted as "unnecessary damage" when it came to the evaluation of his performance during the operation.

He ran towards the bedroom and found the journalist trying to stop Boniek from attacking another woman, who was lying on the floor, bleeding. Boniek had a knife in his hand. Damián never thought that killing Boniek, a man famous for his lethal talent for taking out enemies, would be so easy. He simply pointed the gun at his face. Boniek had half a second to recognize him and understand what was about to happen. That half second wouldn't be enough for his whole life to flash before his eyes, but doubtless Boniek had time to see that he'd been careless. It would have been more useful to have a firearm to hand and not a knife, as if this were the fifteenth century or something.

Damián fired a second time, even though he knew Boniek was dead. It was one of his tics: the postmortem shot.

Rosenthal was screaming and trying to stop the other woman, who was about to faint, from haemorrhaging. It was clear neither of them had much experience of this kind of scenario.

XIII

Everything happened so quickly, she had no chance to do anything. Only when Ángeles's white shirt started turning red did Verónica react. And just in time, because Eitan was in a frenzy and kept trying to stab Ángeles with the penknife.

Verónica threw herself onto Eitan with her full weight, but her childhood friend was much stronger than she was. "Leave her alone," she shouted.

Ángeles, sprawled on the floor, was moaning with pain.

"You were always as thick as shit," Eitan said, shaking Verónica off.

That was the last thing he said, because then Damián appeared and shot him. Verónica didn't immediately recognize this new arrival. And no wonder. The puny Damián, the slow adolescent with a libidinous gaze and the attitude of a spoiled brat, turned out to be an efficient assassin. What if she were next up? Right then she didn't care. Rather than protect herself, she went to Ángeles and pressed her hand against the wound. Ángeles was losing consciousness, and Verónica had seen in many movies that this was the prelude to death. "Ángeles, don't go to sleep," she shouted at her.

"I'm going to die... my baby..." Ángeles managed to say.

"You're going to be fine, you and your baby will be fine. Wake up."

Damián squatted and moved Verónica's hands away. He looked at the wound, then he took Ángeles under the arms and pulled her to her feet. Verónica didn't dare say anything to this armed man whom days earlier she had been treating like a boy with hormone issues.

"She's losing blood, but it isn't a deep wound. Take her to hospital." He motioned for her to take Ángeles.

Verónica passed the lawyer's arm over her shoulder and it felt as though this slip of a woman weighed half a ton.

"Come on, let's go," Damián urged.

Ángeles was able to take one step, then another, and another. They left the room and walked down the corridor, catching sight of Maluma, who was dead, Kaplan, coming to after some blow, and Roxana Mayer, holding her bleeding leg and wailing. The journey towards the street was long and slow. Outside in the courtyard, they saw the dead dog. Not so threatening now. Verónica opened the door to the street. On the other side was Federico.

"She's injured, but she's all right. We need to get her to hospital."

Federico took Ángeles in his arms as though she were Whitney Houston and he Kevin Costner in *The Bodyguard*. They ran the block and a half to the car and laid Ángeles in the back seat.

Federico sped off through the desolate streets. As he drove he called the judge, telling him that he had already left the house and that Verónica Rosenthal had never been there.

On arrival at Fernández Hospital, Federico carried Ángeles, who had lost a lot of blood and was now unconscious, to the entrance, where some nurses got her straight onto a trolley. Federico and Verónica were left alone, both of them in clothes stained with Ángeles's blood. There was a long silence. Strangely, they had nothing to say to one another. And that was horrible for both of them.

Finally a doctor appeared and told them Ángeles was fine, but that they should make a police report because she had arrived with a stab wound. Federico promised they would. The doctor left them and Federico took out his phone, perhaps planning to call the same judge he had bothered before. Or some police chief.

"I'm going, Fede," said Verónica. "You don't need me here any more."

He seemed about to say something, then simply nodded and thanked her for everything she had done for Ángeles.

"I couldn't let them kill a brave woman like that," Verónica said, smiling, and walked away without kissing him goodbye.

Outside, she saw that dawn was breaking. She didn't want to go to Federico's apartment and hers was off limits. She called her friend Paula, who answered in a bad mood after being woken up. Verónica asked if she could come to her place. Obviously, Paula said she could.

18   *My Dearest Enemy*

I

Paula was up and waiting for her, with a pot of coffee and buttered toast. She didn't ask anything. Verónica had thought she didn't feel like talking, that she only wanted to climb into bed and sleep, but before she knew it she was telling Paula everything that had happened that night, no detail spared.

"Oh Vero, what I'd pay to find out you were a mythomaniac and making all this up."

"If I were a mythomaniac I'd tell you I met Joaquin Phoenix and he took me to a suite at the Four Seasons."

What Verónica needed more than anything was to talk about Federico's infidelity. His (love?) story with Ángeles, the lawyer who worked in her father's firm. The little cow's pregnancy. Paula listened, with growing amazement.

"Barbara Cartland dropped by to say she wants her melodrama back."

"I'm so tired."

"I can imagine. I'm surprised by how calmly you're taking this, though. You haven't once suggested getting your father to fire her."

"What do you take me for?"

"I've seen you do some horrible things, Vero."

"If that shit Federico had fucked the little cow once or

twice, I'd kill them both. But they love each other, and there's a baby on the way."

"Do you regret it?"

"What, the abortion?"

Paula nodded.

"Not even for a moment."

They ate the toast and had a second round of coffees.

"Are you going to forgive him?"

"God forgives, not me."

Paula snorted. Her friend was making this difficult.

"Are you going to get back with Federico?"

"Perhaps. Not now, but maybe in ten years. Or twenty. Or tomorrow. What do I know?"

It was morning by the time Verónica fell asleep, and past midday when she woke up with a start. Paula had left her a note saying that she had to go to the publishing house, and that she loved her. She also left her a set of keys to the apartment. Verónica had a shower and arranged to meet up with María Magdalena, Rodolfo and Patricia. They had a lot of work to do.

II

Rodo and María Magdalena already had a copy of the tablet's contents, sent to them by La Sombra. After leaving Paula's apartment, Verónica called the hacker to let him know she was fine. Next she called Marcelo, who told her the neighbourhood locksmith had been round to change the lock on her door. "Since I had some free time," he lied, "I took the opportunity to tidy up some of the mess your friends had left."

The doorman also told her that a telegram had arrived for her, but she wasn't interested in knowing what this was about. There was time for that later. She no longer owed

Marcelo a case of good wine; by now she owed him an entire cellar.

When she arrived at Patricia's house for the meeting, her friends were taken up with a development that had nothing to do with the investigation in hand. Or perhaps it did, from a certain angle. Patricia – and now, it appeared, Verónica too – had received a telegram firing her. They were no longer journalists for *Nuestro Tiempo*. The company hadn't even bothered to inform Rodolfo and María Magdalena, who were only contributors, that they would no longer write for the magazine; that was a given.

"Nil desperandum, friends," said Patricia with a smile. "I've got news."

Aníbal Monteverde had been in touch with her a couple of days previously. He wanted to invest the money he had been paid for the purchase of his *Nuestro Tiempo* shares in a new online news portal.

"Nothing on paper. A website, with a presence on social media and all that crap people go in for these days."

Monteverde had offered Patricia the position of editor-in-chief.

"At first I thought about rejecting the offer and telling him I wanted to be a section editor, but then I realized that would mean putting up with some jerk as a boss, boasting about his hundred thousand followers on Twitter, so I decided to accept. He's asked me to put together the editorial team."

They didn't have a large budget, but there was enough to pay a small staff. Patricia offered the role of Society editor to María Magdalena, who happily accepted. It would be the first time since *Vida Cristiana* that she was working in a newsroom as a member of staff. Verónica and Rodolfo would be special correspondents. The four of them began throwing out names to fill the remaining staff jobs: some who worked at *Nuestro*

Tiempo, other colleagues who had irregular work or none at all, the odd big name to write major political pieces.

"And please can we have someone to cover Sports and another for Theatre. Both those sections bore me to death," said Patricia in her new role as editor.

"And someone to write *crónicas*."

"What for?"

"I don't know, every paper has a *cronista*, to bring a literary flavour to the news."

"In my day, a *cronista* was someone who aspired to be a journalist. If I'm not mistaken, the Journalist's Statute still says this. The first person to offer me a *crónica* will get sent to the congressional newspaper library to read some examples of good journalism."

"And does our outlet have a name?" Verónica asked.

"Yes, Monteverde's chosen one. It's going to be called *Malas Noticias*."

"'Bad News'? You're kidding me."

"It's a terrible name. We'll scare off all the readers."

"The slogan will be 'All news is bad news'."

"I resign."

"Guys, you sound old. It's a brilliant name. End of story."

After a couple of hours discussing the new website, they turned to the articles about Sergio Mayer and David Kaplan. María Magdalena would write a background piece on Mayer, the management of Tuentur, the Eramus fraud. Rodolfo would get to work on a profile of Gómez Pardo, his dark past and darker present. Verónica would tackle David Kaplan and his war crimes. Patricia didn't usually write but would make an exception this time: she wanted to devote an article to the career of Andrés Goicochea and how his work as a journalist had led to his death. She also wanted to devote substantial space to a profile of Viviana Smith.

Since they didn't yet have a website, much less a newsroom, Patricia arranged with Monteverde to create a proto-site bearing the name *Malas Noticias*, where they could upload these articles with the photos Corso had obtained through his contacts, plus the images from the tablet.

"In a week's time we have to have everything ready. Any longer and I don't know what we might be exposing ourselves to with the embassy breathing down our necks. While you guys finish the investigation and get writing, I'm going to work with a designer to start putting together the provisional website."

The four friends parted, with the strange feeling of happiness that comes from doing serious journalism.

III

Verónica went to the apartment in Villa Crespo. Marcelo gave her two copies of the new key and the telegram dismissing her. She looked at it, read it, and her days at *Nuestro Tiempo* already seemed distant. She wasn't going to miss that job, and especially not sinister characters like Álex Vilna. She was happy to think she would soon be working with a team she liked.

Marcelo had done an amazing job cleaning up the mess left behind by Malena and Maluma (only now did she notice the similarity of their names). It must have been an epic fight, judging by the number of broken things: the television, a lamp, the glass in the coffee table, a few CDs. She planned to replace everything, so long as *Nuestro Tiempo* paid her redundancy money promptly. Apart from the CDs. On that front, it was time to join the modern world.

Everything in the apartment looked in order, but on closer inspection, it was still dirty. Luckily Verónica had left behind cleaning liquids for the bathroom and floor, and bleach. She got changed into some joggers and started scrubbing the bathroom, then the kitchen, the bedroom and living room floors. Into the washing machine went a load of sheets, towels and some clothing (underwear used by Malena!). Afterwards she had a half-hour shower, then made coffee and drank it on the balcony as the sun went down. It was Jim Beam hour, but she had absolutely no desire to drink. She didn't feel like smoking either. Full marks for clean living.

She didn't want to drink because she had decided to go over to Federico's apartment. But when she arrived there, an hour later, nobody was home. Could he be at work? Was he still at the hospital, with Ángeles? Only Chicha was waiting for her, tail wagging. Verónica scooped her pet up in her arms.

"Beautiful doggy, did you miss me? I've been neglecting you, my love. Give your mamá a kiss. We're moving back home today."

Verónica packed some of her things into a gym bag and others into a suitcase of Federico's she planned to borrow. She was ready to leave when a key turned in the lock. Like a fool, she felt her heart start pounding.

"I just came to get my things. And Chicha," she added redundantly.

Federico looked exhausted, clothes rumpled, hair dishevelled. Verónica preferred this version to his immaculate morning appearance, when he was heading off to work.

"You don't have to go."

"I want to go, Fede."

He nodded and looked away.

"How's Ángeles?"

"She's OK. The injury didn't affect any major organs. I think they'll discharge her tomorrow."

"Bring her here, then you can really devote yourself to looking after her." Verónica corrected herself before he could answer. "I'm sorry, I shouldn't have said that."

"She told me she wants to call you, to thank you for what you did for her."

"Tell her not to call. I don't need her to thank me for anything."

"OK, whatever you say."

Verónica tried to find a way to carry the gym bag and suitcase in one hand, to leave the other free for Chicha and her little bag.

"Let me help. I'll drive you over there."

"I can manage on my own."

"Don't be silly, I'll take you in the car. There's something I'd like to tell you on the way."

They went down to the garage, put the bags in the trunk and Chicha in the back seat. The little dog settled down daintily, as usual.

"Your father and I have decided to stop representing Mayer. Obviously we can't use what we know as his legal representatives to turn him in to the authorities, nor would it be ethical to pass the information on to you or Corso. But I am going to try to channel the information on David Kaplan. I have contacts at The Hague who would definitely be interested. Although I don't think they can do anything, apart from condemning him morally."

Verónica listened quietly.

"Another thing. Your father told me he was thinking of retiring. He told me that, although he hadn't made a final decision, he was considering the possibility of my running Rosenthal and Associates."

"Congratulations."

"Thanks."

It was dark by the time they arrived at the apartment block in Villa Crespo. Federico helped Verónica get her luggage out of the back and offered to go up with her.

"I can manage. If not, I'll ask Marcelo to give me a hand. Thanks anyway."

She didn't kiss him goodbye, and Federico went off without a word.

Afterwards, Verónica cursed herself for refusing the help, because it was a nightmare taking everything up on her own. She had to make two trips, first to leave Chicha and then to drag the bag and the suitcase up to the apartment. But it was worth the effort to preserve her dignity.

Lying on her bed, she called her father to rearrange their postponed lunch. He had various commitments over the coming days so they agreed to meet the following week. Then she WhatsApped her group of friends: *Supper tomorrow in my apartment? I'm back at home sweet home.*

All of them agreed, replying *OK* or using the thumbs-up emoji, happy GIFs and Paris Hilton stickers (Paula).

Verónica fed Chicha, then opened a tin of tuna and a bottle of wine that had somehow survived Malena and her boyfriend. She went to bed hoping to sleep for twelve hours uninterrupted.

When Federico had told her Ángeles wanted to speak to her, for an instant she was touched. She felt the girl was a good sort, worthy of Federico even. And perhaps she was. But she was also a first-class bitch. Not only had she taken up with a married man – well, a man with a partner – but she had jumped into the middle of Verónica's journalistic investigation, found information before her and run a far greater risk to her life. If this were a competition, Ángeles would have thrashed her. Yet she didn't hate her; in some ways she admired the little cow. And that, without doubt, was confirmation of Verónica's absolute defeat.

IV

Over the next few days all her energy went on writing the article about Nathan Neuer, alias David Kaplan, the Israeli war criminal, and also visiting the future newsroom of *Malas Noticias*. Patricia already had a desk in one of the rooms and met daily with potential members of the editorial team and contributors who were brave enough to take a chance on the new venture. What had been the living room in this apartment would be the newsroom, as such. They had already brought in a table that occupied much of the space, with room for six comfortable workstations, or eight uncomfortable ones. But neither the computers nor the chairs had arrived yet. The third room, which would be for graphic design and photography, was empty. There was still no internet connection.

Notwithstanding, a week later they put the final touches to a special report on Sergio Mayer, Gómez Pardo and David Kaplan. The launch of the website (which wouldn't be fully operational until a month later) was a success, not so much in terms of clicks but among colleagues, and they were confident it would garner more visits as people came to know of its existence. The article on Mayer was picked up by several of Grupo Esparta's media competitors; the profile on Gómez Pardo sent shock waves through websites on the intellectual right that relished the opportunity to take swipes at an entrepreneur with a Montonero past, while the revelations on David Kaplan occupied a smaller space, like a colour piece. Who would be interested in a war criminal these days? A British website and a Belgian blog did ask permission to translate the Neuer profile, but they weren't mainstream outlets. If Verónica hadn't exactly expected her article to end up on the front page of the *New York Times*, she had at least hoped it would make life uncomfortable for Kaplan. It seemed that wouldn't be the case.

The new website didn't yet have a platform for uploading videos, so they published Neuer's self-incriminating testimonies on YouTube. Within minutes they were removed, but the hope was that they had been copied by people keen to disseminate the facts that would soon reappear on other platforms.

Neither they, in their articles, nor anyone else made any reference to what had happened at Roxana Mayer's house. Nobody spoke about the deaths of Eitan Boniek and the fake Maluma. They had died as they lived and as they had killed: in absolute anonymity. A friend of Corso's in embassy circles told him Kaplan was thinking of leaving Argentina. It wasn't clear if that was because his false identity had been discovered, or because he had been offered a better job in another part of the world.

Roxana Mayer wasn't arrested for the two crimes she had ordered, nor for attempting to kill Ángeles. The only trace of her criminal activity was a limp, the result of the bullet she had taken in her leg. Nor did she manage to wrest Tuentur from her husband. After all the bad publicity, a lot of clients left the company. They had no option but to sell it to a multinational security firm based in Liechtenstein.

If Roxana Mayer had signed the divorce papers a few months earlier, doubtless she would have walked away with more properties than she finally obtained. Mayer had to file for bankruptcy in several of his business ventures. Neither Roxana nor her ex-husband was ruined, and they would soon be back on their feet. But, as with rain at an open-air wedding, the party was over for them. The multimedia group Esparta was at its lowest ebb, and the hope was that it too would be absorbed by some bigger player in the media landscape.

María Magdalena, Patricia, Rodolfo and Verónica decided to go and celebrate the launch of *Malas Noticias* at Los Amigos. They shared the chicken with lemon sauce (speciality of the house) and two plates of pork belly with spring onions. They drank three bottles of wine and three sodas, and ate crème caramel with dulce de leche and banana pancakes for dessert. There was no coffee, to Verónica's annoyance.

A storm was brewing as they left the restaurant.

"Apparently there's a cold front coming up from the south and tomorrow we're going to have polar conditions."

"Antarctic cold in November? I don't believe it."

They all said goodbye at the door, and Verónica decided to walk home – it wasn't that far, and she felt like the exercise. She was returning to her apartment, where Chicha would be waiting for her. Her only experience of cohabitation, with a man she loved and to whom she couldn't return, was over. Not because of some petty nonsense about infidelity, but because something had broken, like a tibia or a fibula, that would be hard to mend. In the meantime, it was important to look after oneself, not to move too much, to wait for the bone to heal. Meanwhile Ángeles's belly would keep growing until it expelled the little bastard who was going to be Federico's child. Verónica had imagined Federico in many guises, but never as a father. Or rather she had, but as the father of her own future children, if she ever had them. Now he was going to have them with someone else. He would hold that baby (did they already know what they were having?), he would watch it grow into a little boy or girl; he would worry when the child had a fever and celebrate every new milestone. Perhaps one day they could be together again, but a part of Federico was lost to her, and lost for ever.

19   *The Man of my Life*

The warmest November of the decade gave way to a cold and rainy December. Buenos Aires was greyer than ever, and far from the Christmas climate the shops hoped to purvey through their windows. No resident of Buenos Aires was going to be wearing a sweater to put up the Christmas tree.

Verónica left the apartment, but not before advising Chicha to behave herself and look after the home. At the door to the building, Marcelo was sorting through the neighbours' post. For her, there was a big envelope containing a copy of the magazine to which she had subscribed for two years. Verónica asked Marcelo to leave it in her apartment and, while he was there, to check a leaky tap in the kitchen. He said he would see what the problem was that afternoon.

"Are you off to work? You haven't put on your uniform."

"I don't know what you mean by that, nor do I want to. No, I'm not going to work. I'm going to run some errands, then have lunch with my dear father."

"My respects to Señor Rosenthal."

"They'll be passed on."

What strange and dark erotic fantasy must Marcelo nurture about the clothes a female journalist wore to work? It was true she didn't tend to go to the office looking like this: in sneakers, slightly baggy, worn-out jeans and a hoodie over a loose Uniqlo T-shirt. Looking at herself in the mirror, she had thought the combination made her look younger. Reason enough to go out like this.

It had rained that morning, but now it was merely cloudy. Verónica decided to walk to her old workplace, the newsroom at *Nuestro Tiempo*. She needed to pick up her pay cheque and a few things. It would be her last ever visit to the place where she had worked for seven years.

Verónica liked Buenos Aires on cloudy days or when the weather was changeable. At times like these she felt as though the city belonged to her, unlike on sunny, temperate or pleasantly warm days when people flocked to the streets, bars and squares and she felt alienated and uncomfortable, like an exile. By contrast, on those changeable days, with rain showers and surprisingly low temperatures, Buenos Aires belonged to her and to a select few.

She strolled along, looking in the shop windows on Calle Aguirre, and then Gurruchaga. She thought that she ought to buy herself a new handbag, maybe shoes. Another day, perhaps. She didn't feel like trying on clothes, and if she was lingering it was because she didn't want to return to *Nuestro Tiempo*. The only thing that urged her onwards was the thought that afterwards she would be having lunch with her father.

Verónica reached the office building and greeted Jimena, the security guard who always worked this shift. As she headed for the elevator, Jimena stopped her. Almost apologetically, she said: "I'm sorry, but we've been told not to let you in."

"But I need to collect my things."

"I've got them here."

Jimena handed her a small envelope with her wage slip, which Verónica put in her backpack, and a larger Manila envelope with some printouts of articles downloaded from the internet, an old issue of the *El País* Sunday magazine, a used notebook that wasn't hers (from the handwriting, she guessed it belonged to the new editor of Society) and a very old postcard with a reproduction of the poster for *Les Amants du Pont-Neuf.* Verónica kept the postcard and handed everything else back to Jimena. "Do me a favour and bin this lot."

Verónica thanked the security guard and left the building for the last time. Zero nostalgia and a strange feeling of having been liberated, even though she had never felt tethered to the work here.

Walking along Álvarez Thomas, Verónica spotted a small business that restored furniture. She remembered she needed a floor lamp to replace the one Malena and the fake Maluma had broken. She wanted to buy something old, imposing, heavy, beautiful and awkward. A lamp like me, she told herself, something that oscillates between outright narcissism and an absolute lack of self-esteem. She glanced at her phone: time to meet her father. She quickened her pace towards the Cantina Rondinella, fantasizing about the possibility of running into one of the magazine's directors and insulting them, something she planned to do every time she saw one of them.

But there was nobody there from *Nuestro Tiempo,* just her father, sitting in front of a glass of still mineral water. They smiled at each other from afar, and Verónica walked towards him feeling the same happiness she always felt, a reaction so spontaneous, so natural that she would most likely exclude it from any description of meeting her father even though it was always there: that rush of joy on finding him in a public place, knowing that he, among all those people, was her father. The confirmation that she was a lucky girl.

Aarón was wearing his classic tailored suit and was clean-shaven, smelling of Acqua di Parma, the same cologne Verónica remembered from her childhood. "You're dressed like someone who's about to infiltrate a gang of drug traffickers," he said.

"Is every single person I meet today going to comment on my wardrobe? If it's little Chanel suits you want, look to the lawyers who work for you."

They scanned the menu and decided to share a starter of *boquerones* and then rice with chicken bocconcini. To Verónica's surprise, her father ordered a bottle of Zuccardi.

"Don't you have to work later?"

"If I can't lead my team of lawyers on half a bottle of wine, I may as well go to work in a Rapipollo chicken joint."

"They've all closed down. The Rapipollos, I mean."

Her father tried and approved the Malbec brought by their waiter, as she had watched him do so many times before. They raised their glasses without having anything in particular to toast.

"So you've gone back to your single woman's apartment."

"If I say yes, that means accepting there was ever a married woman's apartment."

"What a good lawyer Rosenthal and Associates lost in you."

"You always say that."

He took a packet of cigarettes out of his pocket and placed them to one side, as though he needed to keep them in view so as not to forget to smoke them later.

"Federico is the ideal man for you."

"You're the man of my life, Pa."

Aarón shook his head but smiled, flattered by his daughter's remark. Verónica returned to the subject of the apartment.

"I need to take a bit of time for myself."

"I also needed to do that, once upon a time."

Verónica, not knowing this story, looked at him with curiosity. "You and Mamá were separated?"

"You were very little. Not even a year old, I think. We had a crisis, and I went away for a few months."

"Another woman?"

"Nothing serious. I probably felt overwhelmed by the responsibility of having three daughters, a family routine, all that nonsense young people think."

"Let me get this straight: it took having three children to make you realize married life made you uncomfortable, and then you left Mamá with the three of us when we were all still really little." Verónica paused to drink some wine. "I hope she found some young guy to have fun with during that time."

"I think she did. And I kept on seeing the three of you. And, to be honest, I recognize that I was never very present as a father. Neither when I was a hundred per cent married nor during those months of separation. In any case, later on your mother and I were reconciled, without bitterness, and ready to spend the rest of our lives together."

"Mamá never said anything about this."

"Leticia knows about it, at least. She was five or six, so she must have some memory of those days."

"I can't believe Leticia never told me."

They wolfed down the *boquerones*. Verónica was hungry and ate the bread and butter her father hadn't touched. Luckily, the rice dish arrived quickly and they served themselves. Aarón asked about work and Verónica told him that she had begun a new project. Regarding the Sergio Mayer debacle, she said only: "I'm grateful for the way you dealt with Mayer."

"I did what was right. No more than that." Aarón poured out the rest of the wine. "Would you like a dessert?"

Verónica had a quick think, then said: "I'd rather have an ice cream at Scannapieco, if you're not in a rush."

"Not at all. Let's order a coffee then, and go to the gelateria afterwards."

They drank their coffee along with little glasses of limoncello. Verónica thought her father seemed distracted, as though preoccupied by some worry.

"Darling, I've got something to tell you."

A tremor ran through Verónica's body. Her father's tone couldn't portend anything good. She said nothing, not wanting to delay even for a second whatever he had to tell her.

"I've had some medical tests. I've got a brain tumour. I'm going to have an operation, but the prognosis isn't good."

Even if she had swallowed a piece of glass Verónica wouldn't have felt so acutely that her insides were being torn apart.

"What do you mean it isn't good? Could the tumour be malignant?"

"It is a malignant tumour. I have a very aggressive cancer, hard to treat and virtually impossible to survive in my current state of health."

"How long did the doctor give you?"

"Six months to a year, perhaps less. I almost feel it would be better if it's less, if that means avoiding the final stages of the cancer."

Verónica's eyes filled with tears. "I can't believe it."

Her father held her arm on the tabletop. "Hey, don't cry. I'm telling you before your sisters because you're the strongest."

"I'm not strong, Pa, I'm not."

Aarón squeezed her arm. "Yes, you are, and I want you to help me tell the girls."

"You can't die, Papá."

"Yes I can, and I will, and that's all right. When I found out there was no cure, what upset me most was not seeing my grandchildren grow up. But I thought, if this had happened to me, say, fifteen years ago – which was entirely possible, because this cancer has nothing to do with age – if it had happened to me fifteen years ago, I wouldn't have seen my daughters finish university or get married, or the birth of my grandchildren, or you becoming a top journalist. I couldn't have supported your mother through the hardest parts of her illness. If I had fallen ill back then, I would have asked, no, begged for fifteen more years to spend time with you all and to be able to experience everything that has happened to us. So I am very lucky to have had that time, and to have a few more months to keep enjoying my children, my grand-children, even my sons-in-law, if that's not going too far."

Verónica laughed. Aarón passed her a tissue, and then the whole packet. Verónica blew her nose and wiped her eyes.

"Promise me you won't cry any more."

"I can't promise you that."

"Then at least that you won't cry any more this afternoon."

"Not even that."

"If you don't cry any more, I'll buy you an ice cream."

Verónica laughed again, then she asked him: "Is it painful?"

"Not very. Nothing I can't put up with. The operation is simply to allow me to live out these final months as well as possible."

Now it was her turn to squeeze his arm. "Papá, Papá, Papá."

"Verónica, Verónica. I chose your name. I can't remember why I chose it. But I still like it."

"You need to see other specialists. We should go to the US, or Germany, Israel. Wherever the best doctors are."

"I've already looked into it, and I assure you there's no need. In fact, we sent all the studies to a clinic in Boston and a hospital in London. The two institutions that know the most about this type of cancer. There really is nothing else to be done."

"This is horrible."

"Yes, it is. I'm not going to lie to you. It's not easy to make sense of it. I always thought that, when you got a diagnosis like this, you'd decide to spend every last moment doing the extraordinary things you had never found time to do before.

Go up Aconcagua, learn to surf, take tango lessons. I don't know if it's just my personality, but finding out you're going to die is shit. It's impossible to enjoy anything. Every single thing I do is measured by that inescapable timer, and so the only thing I can think of is to continue with my usual routines. But, on the other hand, every day I wake up is a gift. Just like this beautiful meal with my youngest daughter, and just like the dinner on Saturday in Daniela's house will be, I'm sure, and each and every time I meet the little ones. Besides, this time has allowed me to organize a few things better, including the firm. I'm going to put Federico in charge."

Verónica considered this for a few seconds. "I don't think that's a good idea. He isn't cut out for it."

"Federico not cut out to run the firm?"

"He's a great lawyer, you know that better than I do, but he doesn't have the right character to run a company like yours."

"He's doing very well so far."

"Because *you're* there. Fede is a good number two. He needs someone to manage him. You have Iñíguez, who's an excellent professional and was your first partner."

"Iñíguez is getting on in years."

"OK, but you're no spring chicken and you run Rosenthal and Associates like a dream. If you don't want your legacy to collapse within a year, don't put Federico at the helm. He's emotionally unstable."

"You only say that because the two of you have fallen out."

"No, I'm being objective. What would you think if a lawyer from your firm had a fling with a colleague and got her pregnant?"

"Is this hypothetical, or did it actually happen?"

"It is happening."

"Ángeles?"

"The very one."

"What a fool."

"What a total jerk, more like."

"Now I understand the split. And how are you feeling about all this?"

"Men come and go. Federico is a man and will therefore also come and go, like a yo-yo. We love each other, despite everything."

Aarón asked for the bill, paid with a credit card and left the waiter a generous tip in cash.

"Listen, Vero, I'm going to give serious thought to everything you've just told me regarding the firm."

They left the restaurant and, at the door, Verónica embraced her father tightly, clinging to him as though she wanted to stop the wind from blowing him away. She felt Aarón's body yield, resigned, needing his daughters' love, Verónica's love. She didn't want to cry any more in front of him, although she would cry much more in the following days, the following months.

Aarón put his hand on her shoulder and steered her towards the gelateria, like he used to when she was six or seven.

"When we took you out of that summer camp, I remember driving you to an ice-cream parlour because I thought you needed ice cream as a sign of affection. Your mother was very annoyed. She said I was spoiling you."

"She was right."

Verónica ordered a dulce de leche granita with chocolate hazelnut ice cream. Her father paid for it and went outside to smoke a cigarette.

Minutes later Verónica appeared with her ice cream. As she ate it she said: "I've got an idea. Or rather, I've made a decision and I'm not going to let you oppose it. I'm moving in with you."

Aarón looked surprised, obviously unsure how to respond to this unexpected proposal. "I can't think why I would oppose it. In fact I thank you for it. There's room for you at home, and for the children if they ever want to stay at the weekend."

"And for Chicha too."

"And for Chicha, of course. I'll cook some chunks of beef for her myself."

"She only eats complete and balanced dog food."

"We'll see about that."

Verónica concentrated on her ice cream while her father smoked.

"Pa, do you have time to come and look at lamps with me in the flea market?"

"I have all the time in the world."

Verónica wiped her hands on a paper napkin and her father tossed away the stub of his second cigarette. They crossed the road to the market, which was opposite, and had to run when the lights changed and cars came bearing down on them. They arrived, flustered, on the sidewalk.

"I'm going to die. How sad that is," said Aarón in a tone of helplessness Verónica had never heard him use.

"Yes, Pa. But not today. Today you're alive."

Buenos Aires, January 2017–April 2020